# Sabrina Vourvoulias

Crossed
Genres
Publications

SOMERVILLE, MA

INK

Copyright © 2012 by Sabrina Vourvoulias

ISBN-13: 978-0615657813
ISBN-10: 0615657818

Edited by Bart R. Leib

FIRST EDITION: October 2012

Cover design by Bart R. Leib

Visit Crossed Genres Publications online at http://crossedgenres.com

# TABLE OF CONTENTS

In memory of my mother, who gave me Guatemala,
and my father, who gave me the United States;
and for Bryan and Morgan, who have given me the rest.
*Mi manda, Morenita.*

# Prologue

The source texts me.

All my sources text me these days. Or send me pictures and videos they've taken with their cell phones. The rich ones have smartphones; those with just a little money use pay-as-you-go phones. Doesn't matter to me, as long as the message gets through and the image is clear.

Most journalists have a sixth sense. So even though the message I'm looking at is bare of story, it makes the hair on the back of my neck stand up. It's going to change everything.

"Tats. Color-coded."

My source is an ex-girlfriend. Long legs, even longer memory – which works to my advantage in this case. Political dreams as bright as her copper hair.

Not that our dreams have gotten us very far yet. I'm at a small daily in a market that hardly registers a blip in the national news cycle; she's on the communications team of a first term congressman who's greener than mint chocolate chip.

But luck is better than dreams any day. And both she and I have always been lucky. Lucky to fall in with each other at college, lucky to fall out in a way that kept our friendship intact. Lucky that Rep. Anspach ended up part of the subcommittee reviewing the identity bill.

She doesn't text me from her official phone but from an untraceable throwaway.

"When?" I text back.

"Vote is Thursday."

"And?"

"It sails. Only 3 nays. Prez is :D."

I wend my way to Melinda's desk after I get the specifics. The Hastings Gazette newsroom is huge – proof of days when even regional newspapers were flush with advertising dollars – and the managing editor's desk is smack in the middle.

She tears her gaze from the twitterfall she monitors for stories.

Melinda's eyes are the same shade as her steel wool hair, and about as soft. "I'm busy, Finn."

I sit on the edge of her desk. "Anything interesting?"

She snorts. "Like you haven't been trolling all morning."

"Actually, I haven't."

"Are we going to break a story?" It comes out growly. Which means she's already feeling the bite of adrenaline. See? Sixth sense.

"I don't know. You see anything there about the identity law?"

1

Her eyes flit back to twitterfall.

"The usual. Rehash. Opinion. Speculation. How long before you can post?"

"Half an hour?"

"Which means you've got less than fifteen minutes before the rumors hit the fall. Sources?"

"One. Unnamed, but inside."

She expels a breath. "Shit. Every time we run a single-source story I die a little."

"Confirmation or jump on the competition. You can't have both."

It's hard to believe Melinda's eyes can get steelier, but they do. "So what's your fat butt still doing on my desk?"

I'm grinning all the way back to my desk. She knows I'll file the story in less than ten minutes – in plenty of time for our web dweebs to work their sleight of hand so not even the most aggressive aggregators can steal it without driving our web traffic into the stratosphere.

And by the way, my ass isn't fat.

I should have played football. People expect six-foot-eight, 280-pound men to do that. Nobody expects them to spend all their time tackling stories.

I majored in creative writing at college. Cassie says it's our mother's fault: if you're named after mythological characters you're bound to live in fantasyland. But I graduated into a world of facts. There's no mythic journalism, at least not in the hinterlands where word counts hover around 500 and city council is the top beat. Still, it's steady work with words and a regular paycheck, no matter how laughable.

We're all living in fantasyland anyway. My sister thinking she'll keep her small town library open. Melinda believing newspapers are still vital. Me imagining there's always a story or two lurking behind the facts. And then there's the inks, hoping the identity bill will never come up for a vote. Magical thinking, all of it.

I can't remember when we started calling them inks. After all, it isn't until now it's certain they'll be tattooed when they enter the country. Actually, unless I'm misreading the soon-to-be-law even the permanent resident and citizen inks will end up with tattoos, with a color scheme to indicate terminal status.

I lean back a moment and stare across the newsroom while I consider how to best shape the lede. There isn't a single ink in the Gazette's newsroom, never was. Even at the big papers there hadn't been a glut of them. Melinda catches me looking around and glares at me. They must teach that look in journalism school because all my cohorts go silent and lean into their monitors as if to convince her they haven't been goofing off.

Me, well, I keep smiling. I'm her favorite reporter even though I haven't seen a day of j-school. I file the story a full five minutes before she expects it. She edits it in two. A minute after the new media dude gives us the thumbs up, we watch as my lede floods the fall.

# PART ONE

"We are tied together by opaque, indelible pigments and something more. Even those of us without tattoos know that the ink has seeped through so many layers of skin it'll never wash away."

Quoted in Melinda Horowitz, *Pages from a Reporter's Notebooks: The Last Hurrah of the Hastings Gazette* (Marshallton, N.Y.: Blandon University Press), 128.

# Finn: Lead, lede, led

Ledes are opening words, leading is the space between lines, and leads are the embryonic matter of stories. Newspaper jargon is gleefully perverse. That line of text on the front page that serves as a teaser for a story inside is a refer – which would seem straight enough if it weren't pronounced reefer. Double trucks have nothing whatever to do with vehicles and a slug isn't a bullet. Maybe it's this habit that gets us into trouble outside the newsroom.

I'm at church.

I don't go, but I know every inch of Holy Innocents. I used to be an altar boy here. When the neighborhood was Irish. When my mother had hope we'd end up in some glorious Catholic heaven together.

The same priest's still here. Father Tom has become a friend, even if we more often meet at pubs than in any hallowed structure. Though, come to think of it, some pubs should be considered hallowed.

The pews around me are full of inks. It's been a year since my story about the national identity tattoos gave me a brief but honeyed taste of journalistic notoriety, and by now pre-ink days seem as remote and fantastic as a fairy tale.

There aren't many churches where inks can go to hear Mass celebrated in their languages since the English-only ordinances passed. Father Tom is fortunate enough to have a congregant with one of the rare authorized exemptions, so he taps her to do the readings in Spanish at the seven p.m. daily and the noon Sundays when most of the Latino inks make a point of attending. I wonder if she's the iron-haired older woman sitting close to the altar or the tiny, younger one sitting closer to the door to the sacristy.

After Mass Father Tom stands on the front steps greeting the inks trailing out of his church. Next to him stands his translator – the younger of the two women that had lectored – as well as another twenty-something woman.

The priest's translator may be full ink or part ink, but she's assimilated ink. The other woman likes aping our stereotype of fresher ink. Her hair is peeled back tight and high, her shirt is unrepentantly snug, and she's wearing the biggest hoop earrings I've ever seen.

As I walk by her to go talk to Father Tom, I hear her whispering to the translator in Spanish. I glance down at her wrist. Black tattoo: temporary worker. They never get language exemptions. Between the illicit talk and her not-quite-church-wear, I like her already.

I try to listen in on the whispered alternate conversation. I don't get to practice speaking but I've never lost my ear for the language.

"Let's go find Peña Morena," says the flashy one.

"I don't do illegal," the translator says.

The other snorts. "Not illegal. Say unauthorized instead."

They both start laughing

Pre-ink – in fairy tale days – peñas had been coffeehouses that served up unrefined but decent food and music. Since then the peñas have become something else altogether. Reputedly run by gangs and rife with illegal activity. They move from one unused space to another week to week. No one knows how many there are. No one I know has ever been to one.

"It's good to see you here," Father Tom says to me.

I grin at him. "I'll go anywhere for a story. There is a story, right? This better not be some lame evangelization ploy because, you know, I'm beyond redemption."

The priest gives me a rueful smile, then turns to interrupt the women. "Mari, Nely, I want you to meet Finn."

The translator, Mari, gives me a cautious smile; Nely, something altogether bolder.

"Finn's a reporter with the Hastings Gazette," Father Tom says. "I told him you'd tell him about the rumors you've been hearing at work. And about your theory that people are being dumped across the border."

Mari's inhale is audible.

"I'm one of the last inks left at Hipco, Father," she says, dropping her eyes. "I have to be careful about disclosing anything."

HPCO. Hastings Population Control Office. She'd be a local inside source. Nice.

I glance down at her wrist. Peeking out from under the long-sleeved shirt is the tip of a periwinkle blue tattoo. A citizen. Good. More credible.

Her features are as petite as the rest of her. Her skin is a warm brown and her hair is a darker version of the same. It makes her a study in graded shades, easy for the eye to slide over. But when she picks her eyes off the floor and finally looks directly at me, I'm struck and pinned.

Her eyes are dark amber but turn blacker the longer you look into them. Like looking into a well and seeing, so deep you disbelieve it, the movement of water. They are the eyes of a creature from myth, eons old and here on loan only.

"I'm extremely careful with my sources," I say after a moment. "Nobody would ever be able to trace a word back to you."

She looks from me to Father Tom and back again.

Nely's laugh catches us off guard. "Well, by all means, let's talk about this on the church steps, where anyone can hear us," she says in completely unaccented English. "I propose we remove this ve-e-e-ry interesting conversation somewhere more appropriate. A peña, say?"

Father Tom winces. He's lost many of the community's young men to the so-called subterranean inks – the maras, brotherhoods and mafias – gangs big and small and in between. No way he's going where he'll pad their coffers.

"Shame," Nely says, grabbing Mari's arm with both her own. "'Cause that's where we're headed. See ya."

"I'll come with you," I say.

She studies me. I don't see a shred of respect in her very pretty, but perfectly ordinary, eyes. "¿De veras, güero? ¿Y cómo nos vas a entender cuando hablemos, eh? Porque allí nadie, pero nadie, habla inglés."

Mari stifles a laugh.

Güero – blond – I'm not, but I am a white boy, which is what Nely means when she calls me that.

"I'll understand you just fine," I answer in Spanish.

A mix of expressions race across Nely's face. Mostly surprise, but a bit of guilt too.

I love it.

After an hour of wandering the streets surrounding Holy Innocents, the three of us find an image of the Virgin of Guadalupe chalked on a sidewalk near the subway entrance. Nely gives a whoop, then sprints ahead of us down the steps.

I'd forgotten that Morena is what the Mexicans call Guadalupe and so a peña under her guardianship, even a temporary one, would be signed by her visage. As soon as we see it, Mari slows down to a crawl.

"I've never been to a peña," she says.

Father Tom has warned me about how controlled she is. How you can see her physically rein in any impulse that might lead to an infraction, or a regular mistake for that matter. He says it is undoubtedly why she has risen as high as she has in the Hipco hierarchy. It's probably also why she's still a Catholic in good standing. Though, of course, Father Tom would never agree with that particular assessment.

"Me neither," I say to assure her I'm a good guy.

But then, because I'm mostly a truthful sort of guy, I add. "I'm looking forward to it."

She gives me a look I find completely puzzling. It's those damn eyes that confuse me. And usually I'm so good at reading people. Women especially.

"I'm not going to give you any insider stuff, you know," she says, very matter-of-fact.

"So, I'll just drink, then. Soak up the atmosphere."

Another look.

Nely is far down the right-hand corridor that, if followed to its end, would open to the subway station. Suddenly, she disappears, seemingly into the tiled wall, then pokes her head back out and motions us to follow.

"We don't have to go in there," I say to Mari after our pace slows to within a hair of a standstill.

It nearly kills me to say it. I'm curious about the peña and don't think I'll get another chance to experience one. But news trumps feature, as Melinda says. And Mari, as a source, would be a pipeline to news.

"You don't know Nely. If I don't go in, she'll hunt me down and shave my head." Even though she's joking, mid-sentence her voice quavers.

I'm going to tell you something: I have absolutely no fear. Never have. Cassie likes to tell people about my first skydive from 10,000 feet. I was ten. We were at the resort in the Dominican Republic where my father walked out on us and where we rode out the next two years of uncertainty with our mother. I harangued the skydiving instructor so frequently he finally strapped on the double harness and let me step off the plane. I jumped every weekend after that and never knew a second's hesitation.

But, I recognize fear in my sources.

"What, you think I'm not going to look out for you?"

It's a risky tack. She might think I mean it personally, not professionally, and take all kinds of offense. But as I look down at her – I've got to have at least a foot and a half on her – I wonder whether I can make such a clear distinction. I pretty much feel protective of all people, not just my sources. Maybe it has to do with towering, or being solid among the wispy, I don't know.

"I'm not as you imagine me," she says.

The response draws me up short. But she doesn't appear to be offended and starts walking down the corridor again.

The shallow alcove where Nely stands ends in a fire door with a yellow light flashing above.

"You sure this is it?" Mari asks.

"No. But that's the point of the shifting locations, isn't it? Seems like what Toño described to me, though," Nely says, distracted. "We just have to figure how to get in." She tries the door, but it doesn't budge. Then she looks around for some overlooked catch, lever, or keypad. Finally, she knocks on it.

When nothing happens she turns to Mari.

It's interesting. I've been thinking of Nely as the leader of this duo. But she defers to the smaller woman in a way that makes me think I've misread the dynamic.

Mari frowns at Nely, then closes her eyes.

"Try it now," she says after a minute. "The porter's looking back this way and where the eye goes, the ear follows."

Nely pounds on the door with the flat of her hand and soon enough the yellow light stops flashing. The door lists open as if it was never closed.

When I turn to look at Mari, she shrugs. "Trick from childhood."

There is another metal door ahead with a massive hasp and what looks to be an expensive combination padlock hanging on it. I see a shadow loose itself from the wall and begin to walk toward us. It's a big shadow. Built like a bouncer.

"Non fecit taliter," the man says. There's an interrogatory lilt at the end of the phrase, making it a question.

"What the hell?" Nely's voice is barely a whisper, but in this place it carries.

"Password," I hear Mari whisper back. "Toño didn't tell you anything about this?"

It's a tidy system, I think. If we had gotten here by mistake rather than intention there'd be nothing illegal to report. The phrase is in Latin, a dead language that doesn't violate the language bans, and there's almost no way anyone would chance on the right combination of words to say in response.

Witness Mari and Nely.

"Omni nationi," I finally say to the bouncer.

He sweeps past us and blocks our view while he fiddles with the lock. I hear the click of tumblers falling in place. When the door opens, it is to light, the smell of charcoal and a babble of Spanish.

As soon as we're through Nely turns to me, hands on her hips. "What the fuck?"

I can't help grinning at her. "Last line of Psalm 147. 'God has not done this for other nations.' Allegedly what one of the popes said about the apparition of Our Lady of Guadalupe in Mexico."

She doesn't say anything, just turns and stalks toward a makeshift bar set up in one corner of the dingy grey utility room that houses the peña this week. I like watching her go. And not because she's leaving.

"How did you know?" Mari asks.

"I used to be a good Catholic boy. Used to be Catholic. Used to be good." I'm grinning again. Moreso after I see her roll her eyes.

"Father Tom warned me you like to pretend to be wicked."

"He lies a lot, for a priest."

Her laugh is young. It reminds me that, despite her eyes, she's only a twenty-something Catholic girl. And an ink, to boot. Which makes her very unlike the women I'm used to keeping company with.

Except I'm not keeping company with her, I remind myself. I'm cultivating her as a source.

"I'm hungry," I say, looking around. "Let's go find some food."

There's a tin washtub on legs being used as a makeshift grill at one end of the room, filling the air with smoke and the smell of shrimp searing in a brick red sauce. Next to that is a garbage can filled with tamales and several industrial-size jars with juice.

Despite the drab space that contains it, the peña is a riot of color: party dresses, oilcloth, cowboy boots in shades nature never intended. In the corner opposite the bar a really old man is inking a child's wrist. He's working manually, with a small mallet and needles stuck to the end of a wooden measure. He dips a needle into an ink bottle – he's got black and green, ancient and crusted like hepatitis in a jar – then taps it under the skin. The child squawks.

"My turn to ask how you did it," I say as we make our way over to the food tables.

"What?" she yells. I know there's a guitarist playing – I can see him – but I can't hear him over the din of kids with their parents and grandparents, young singles and couples at the bar and folding tables, all eating, drinking and chattering.

"The thing with the bouncer or porter or whatever. Like you saw him, even though he was behind the door. How'd you do it?" I ask, bending close to her so I don't have to shout.

"Oh. That," she says. "I told you already."

She gives me a half-mysterious, half-shy smile. It's endearing. Pretty too.

"So you're like psychic, or something?"

"Something."

"Okay, see if I care. Keep your secrets."

She raises her eyebrows.

"Except the ones about Hipco."

She matches my grin.

We end up at a recently vacated table near the tattooist, and although she swears she doesn't want anything to drink, I come back from the bar with six shots of tequila.

Her eyes go round when I slide three shots her way.

"You're kidding, right? You have noticed I'm a tad smaller than you?"

"Yes, you're wee," I say, then laugh when she wrinkles her nose at the word.

"So … besides the rampant language violations, the price gouging and the tattoo forging, there are at least a dozen drug and gun deals going down. Any other illegal activity I'm missing?" I ask.

"Well, if the city council has its way we'll all be in violation of the 10 p.m. curfew they're voting in. All of us with tattoos, that is."

I'm not sure when I get it out, but suddenly my reporter's notebook is in my hand. Melinda derides reporters who take digital notes the same way she does people who can't drive standard, so I'm badass at both scrawl and clutch.

"When?"

"Tomorrow morning in open session. It's a formality, though. The enforcement wing of pop control has been on alert since this morning. And there's more stuff rumored to be coming down soon: public transit restrictions, gated neighborhoods."

"Jesus."

"I overheard my boss saying Morrow is the only councilperson who still has some misgivings."

I drum my fingers while I think. "Maybe I can ambush her before they go into session. That way I can file before anyone else. I think I have her home address somewhere."

"There you go," she says.

"How can you stand working there?"

"I'm tougher than I look?"

I laugh, but I know it isn't funny.

In the silence that follows we look anywhere but at each other. My eyes end up at the bar, on Nely. She's flirting with the tender, whose shirt has just enough open collar to show some figural ink and what appears to be the end of a hellacious scar.

He glances over at me. His eyes are intelligent, appraising. He runs his fingers over a perfectly dark and sharp-edged goatee before he rests his chin on his hand and turns back to Nely. I wonder why it's always a soul patch, chin strap or goatee with the gangs, never a full beard.

"What's the deal with them?" It's an excuse to get Mari talking to me again.

"That's Toño. His gang runs this peña. She likes him and, I think, kind of toys with the idea of joining his gang."

"Really?" I look at him more closely. He's probably a foot shorter than me but I wouldn't want to mess with him. "He's ... intimidating."

"Kettle. Pot."

"Hardly. I've been told I look like a teddy bear."

"From where, Land of the Giants?"

I lean in to her. "Okay, so that's Nely and Toño's story. What's yours?"

"I believe I already gave you a story. At least I thought I saw you taking notes."

"The other one."

"About the border dumps? It's still speculation on my part. A pattern I've noticed as I track the GPS readouts from the pop control implants in temporary workers. That's all."

"You'll tell me that one next time."

Because I've just decided this. Even if she never again gives me a lead for a story, there's going to be a next time.

"But that's not the story I meant. The other, other one."

She toys with the last shot of tequila before her. When she drains the glass, I push one of mine her way.

She laughs. "I've had plenty already. And there's nothing left to tell."

"Sure there is." I reach for her hand, turn it over and pull her sleeve up.

I can hear her intake of breath.

It is a breach, I know. Something along the lines of undressing her without her permission. But I can't regret doing it.

The skin of her wrist is a soft plush and the lines of the tattoo cut it sharp and precise. All those fine blue lines filled with the story of her life – the way the government sees it. They don't look remotely like blood, but they make me wonder if this is the kind of wound that never stops bleeding.

"Did it hurt?" I ask, raising my eyes back to hers.

She looks stricken.

The hairs on the nape of my neck stand on end. Sixth sense, remember? She understands something about me I'm not sure I want her to know. Something maybe even I don't want to know.

She tries to disengage, to reclaim her wrist and her privacy, but I won't let go.

So she tells me a fairy tale. As if I were a child. Or maybe, as if she were.

*** 

A long time ago, but not so long ago that it couldn't have been yesterday, a little girl lived in a far away land with her grandmother and grandfather, and her mother and brother. He was really her half-brother, but she was little and didn't know what that meant. He looked like a whole brother to her, and very big. He was four. Which was three years and eleven months older than she was.

They lived in a house up in the mountains. A house with dogs and chickens running through the rooms because the doors were always open to the winds. All around them stood the houses of the little girl's aunts and uncles, and they too had open doors and cousins who ran in and out after the animals. Even though the girl's brother was the youngest and smallest of the cousins he was the fastest runner, and the girl followed him with her eyes.

Because she was so little, people thought she was sweet. Wherever her mother took her, people stopped to touch the girl's cheeks as if a trace of sugar would come off on their fingers when they did. Her brother knew she wasn't sweet. He had licked her cheek to be sure.

The girl's family garbed themselves daily in fine things. Necklaces with strands of red bead and coin to wrap around their necks. Headpieces with symbols running their length. Clothes woven with threads the color of bird feathers. All of them wore these things, except the girl, who didn't wear anything.

One day, though, the girl's mother put her in a dress twice as long as her baby legs. Her brother's hair was combed down with lots of water and he looked cross when their mother made him put on stiff, new shoes. Soon the whole family started to walk down to the village, and it seemed that with them the very stuff of the mountain – winds, birds, clouds – descended to the valley also. Midway, the girl and her brother noticed things floating above the trees. She didn't know what they were. He knew more and thought, "They've gotten kites to celebrate her special day." It made him want to cry. He pinched his sister instead.

When they got to the village, the girl's brother sat with his uncles and aunts and cousins on wooden benches in the church. The girl went with her mother and grandparents up to where a man stood. He was an inside-out man, the blue veins and their little red feeders were visible through his skin.

Everyone paid attention to the man, except the girl. She reached for what she understood was there but couldn't yet see with her own eyes.

Spectral beings accompanied her family.

Maybe the girl was trying to touch the small feline that twitched its tail at her mother's side. Perhaps she reached for the weasel that scuttled three steps behind her grandfather, or the monkey clinging to her grandmother's shoulder.

But wherever she turned, the girl's hands closed on air. She wouldn't be able to see the animal counterparts until her seventh month, when her own magical twin would be called from deep within her and coaxed to step outside her body. That day her grandmother would weave a garment for her in a design that told the story of twinned beings who walk a layer of world like and unlike our own. The girl would be married in that garment, and buried in it.

The inside-out man — who had no animal twin next to him because he wasn't born on the mountain or in its shadow — poured water on the girl. She cried.

Outside, people screamed.

The girl's mother placed her hand over the baby's mouth to muffle her crying and turned to see the children running out of the church, driven by their curious natures. Uncles and aunts scrambled to follow.

The children were fast, and the girl's brother the fastest of them all. The girl's mother made the sound a cat makes when you step on its paw, then handed the girl to the person on her right and chased after the boy.

The girl was passed from hand to hand until there was no one else to pass her to. Finally she was placed on the floor and left alone at the foot of the sanctuary. The adults ran after the children who ran after the strange beings that drove other children and villagers before them, like goats to be corralled and milked.

It was hard to pin down exactly what the beings were. Viewed sidelong they seemed dwarven and formed from granite; head-on, they had human faces twisted by something harsh and unyielding. No matter what they were, the adults gave chase and the girl was left alone in the church.

Alone, but not completely helpless.

She had an infantile magic, something she'd lose as soon as her real magic rose to take its place. She could see the world through other eyes.

She had looked out of her mother's eyes and seen her father's face on a piece of paper creased with folds. She had looked out of her grandmother's eyes as the threads shuttled on the loom. She had looked out of her grandfather's eyes and seen the lush estates where he sometimes traveled to work.

This time, it was her brother's vision she shared.

He had tucked himself behind one of the water troughs in the plaza and watched as the strangers in boots and clothes the color of clay and mud drove the villagers out of the square, past the buildings. He saw uncles, aunts — even his mother — scurry past his hiding place without noticing him. After they passed, he inched out behind, keeping close to the shadowy hideouts too small for any but him.

The strangers drove the children to the edge of the village where others of their kind waited. They caught them up — first the ones from the village but soon the cousins as well — and swung them by their ankles, slamming them against the huge tree that marked the entrance to the community. The children's heads went out of round, the tree's trunk ran wet, and the children's spirits wafted away from them like smoke abandons a fire.

It wasn't until the shooting started that the girl's brother turned and ran. On the ground, the abandoned parachutes he had thought were kites blurred from his speed. At his side – the girl saw it only because she looked through his eyes – a button buck matched his stride.

The girl raised her arms to her brother when he burst through the doors of the church. He looked down at her. Doubled vision or single, there was a brother's heart broken open in that look.

"Psst."

The inside-out man motioned from the altar. He unlocked the gold-colored cupboard underneath the cross. The girl squirmed when he picked her up and carried her over. He put her inside, even though there was already a covered cup there and she hardly fit. He kept catching her feet as she kicked them, then held them as he slipped a piece of paper between the folds of her diaper.

"What's that?" her brother asked.

"Birth certificate. I hold the ones of all the children I've baptised," the man answered. "Yours too. Here."

The inside-out man shoved a folded paper into her brother's hand. "Tuck it somewhere safe. In case none make it back."

The girl started to cry as the priest closed the cupboard door. The last thing she saw before the shadows stole her sight was the lid knocked off the top of the cup and a multitude of white discs showering out. Full moons of the instant, brilliant in the dark.

Back to seeing out of her brother's eyes, the girl saw the key the man handed him. He pushed the boy toward a full-size statue of Our Lady and slid open a door hidden in the statue's pedestal.

"In there," he said, then nudged him to climb inside the cobwebbed space. "Wait until I come get you. If I don't come back, wait until you don't hear any more shooting and take your sister from the tabernacle. Run, as fast as you can, until you get to the next village. And if the soldiers are in the next village, then run to the next and don't stop until you are far from them. Understand?"

Her brother nodded, even though some of the words were big and others were garbled. He waited. He heard distant screams and heavy thunking noises far, and then near. There was the sound like belts of firecrackers set off on the village feast day, and the boom of bigger loads of gunpowder. Obedient, the boy spent a long time hidden, long enough to fall asleep. When he woke and couldn't stand the dark and the hot air any longer, he put his grubby, sticky hands flat on the sliding door and dragged it until a small gap appeared. He wormed a finger through the gap, then pushed it open.

The church was quiet.

Her brother saw a chair knocked on its side, close to the side door and not too far from the altar. Sticking out from behind it was a pair of shoes so shiny they glinted across the room. He inched forward until he could see around it. The inside-out man was there, eyes and mouth open. There was something metal and jagged wedged inside him.

The girl's brother dragged the chair, then stopped when he heard the loud squeal of wood on stone. When nobody came to the sound, he started dragging it again – stop, start, squeal, stop, start, squeal. He stood on the chair to reach the cupboard. He stuck the key in the lock and turned it first one way then the other until he heard a click, then opened the door and reached inside.

The girl grabbed her brother's finger, held it tight. He gathered her in both arms and jumped to get off the chair.

Nobody knows how her brother got to the neighboring village, but he did. There weren't any soldiers there, but the villagers had heard the shooting. They peered out from behind closed doors, then seeing he was a child with even a smaller child in arms, stepped out to take his burden. Later they'd tell him that he and the girl were the only two survivors, but not that day. And not the next. Not until another inside-out priest appeared and took the children with him.

And those papers, damp from her diaper and his sweaty hands? Weeks later, when the girl's father came from another country to get her, one of the papers went with him as he carried her away.

Before she left, the girl reached out to her brother and the little deer invisible at his side.

The boy rubbed his soft and snotty face all over hers in send-off.

*\*\*\**

She ends the tale there.

It is not a completely unfamiliar story. I recognize its Central American motifs and know of other narratives from the genocide that are similar in detail, if not in the manner of telling. Given time for research I'm sure I'd even be able to pinpoint the date of the massacre and the name of her village.

"I'm glad you survived," I say after she falls silent.

It's like nothing I've said to any of my sources before. And what follows isn't part of the playbook either. I draw her hand up to my lips and kiss the wrist where the lines mark it.

When she pulls away this time, I let her go.

She doesn't say goodbye, not even to Nely, and after she's gone there's no reason for me to stay.

# Finn: Lead, lede, led

## 2

Finn Riordan's rule #1: Never chase after a woman who runs away from you.

Rule #2: Even if you can't stop thinking about her, don't think about her.

Rule #3: Don't engage in behavior that could in any way be construed as stalkerish.

Rule #4: If you are going to ignore rules one through three, for God's sake, don't get caught.

Three of the things Mari mentions during our conversation turn into front-page, beneath-the-fold stories: curfew, housing and transit. The border dump story looks like it might have legs too. I'm keeping my ears open. Melinda's hard eyes turn avid around me and she's started asking for my spent reporter's notebooks. For safekeeping, she tells me.

I'd worry about this – newsrooms are cutthroat places, and editors are even more ambitious than reporters since they think collective instead of individual – but she's constantly harping about the future redaction of news and her paranoia is so sincere that I stop doubting her motives.

The media group's investors are cozy with certain politicos, Melinda says, eyebrows raised in the physical equivalent of exclamation points. They're not supposed to meddle with editorial content, but she's not so sure.

I've taken to calling her Stormcrow. But not to her face. I value my life.

The other writers are leaving all the enterprise – whatever requires digging and finding rather than being assigned – to me. Which is not such a great plan. For one thing, I'm distracted.

I don't have Mari's number. I don't dare call for her at Hipco because even besotted I retain enough sense not to out a source. But I know where she is every weekday at 7 p.m. and, without consciously setting out to do so, I end up at Holy Innocents too.

Since I'm ignoring the first three of my rules, I try very hard not to break number four. I pick the pew nearest the forgotten shrine of St. Roch. I know from my server days that the spot is nearly impossible to see from the sanctuary.

Every time I go, I relearn the planes of her face, the way she moves, the cadence of her Spanish. It is rekindling on a 24-hour cycle. Weekends I do without, but it's a conscious effort.

Nely is always there, somewhere in the crowded middle section of pews. I wait an extra half-hour to leave after she does, and a whole hour after Father Tom and Mari have stopped greeting congregants on the church's steps.

So at least rule four stands, right?

Not.

One evening Nely slides into the pew beside me instead of departing at her usual clip.

"¿Q'hubo, güero?"

Despite my dark hair I'm fair enough that when I blush it's semaphoric. I think even the farthest corners of the place turn red from this one.

"You considering the benefits of becoming a daily communicant?" Nely's remembered to switch into English in case we're overheard by informants. "Or are you hanging around waiting for another story to fall into your lap?"

Rule # 5: Admit nothing.

When I don't answer, she snickers.

"Who would have guessed a big guy like you would be put off balance by such a tiny woman."

"Who says I'm off balance?"

Nely studies me for a few moments, then turns her gaze to the sanctuary as if the Mass were still going on. "It's the part of her that isn't exactly human that does it, you know."

"Funny way to talk about a friend."

"Love doesn't have to be blind," she says, turning back to me.

"I'm not in love with her."

"She's my best friend – *I* love her. And if you screw with her head or her heart, I'll mess you up. Okay?"

It's a novel thing, this, and maybe I blink a couple dozen times while I adjust to the idea of being threatened in church, because she's gone before I have time to respond.

Maybe I'm still thinking about everything that's happened or raced through my head recently when I end up at Con's.

Maybe I'm not surprised when I look up from my whiskey and see Father Tom sit down on the stool next to mine at the pub.

Maybe nothing in my life surprises me while all of it does.

Joe – the co-owner of Con's who knows us both rather better than either of us would like to admit – plunks a glass of Jamesons in front of the priest without being asked.

"Your mother would be happy," Father Tom says after he takes a pull and smacks his lips.

"My mother's never happy, as you well know."

He grins. "And yet …."

"What? Spit it out, padre."

"You seem to have found your way back."

"50<sup>th</sup> and Callowhill has always been my backyard, so no finding involved. And just because I've been seen in your church doesn't mean I'm *in* the Church."

"You think?"

"God, you're irritating."

His whole face – liver spots, creases, saggy jowls – turns beatific. "I find enjoyment in witnessing how the same hormones that fueled your exodus from the Church are going to be what brings you back."

When he gets tired of following the permutations of scowl the comment prompts from me, he sighs. "That wasn't what I was referring to anyway, son."

The Jamesons is almost gone but he keeps his hand on the glass to roll it, every so often, along the thick bottom edge. I notice with a pang that the hand shakes with a discreet palsy. He doesn't have to call me son to remind me that he's as close to a real father as I've had and, like all sons, I'm losing him to old age before I'm ready.

"All right, I'll bite. What would make my mother happy?"

"Your writing's full of passion again."

I snort.

He has the grace to blush, then plows on. "No, I mean, it matters to you what happens to the inks, and it shows in what you write. I think your mother would see that as a good thing."

"I doubt my mother would deign to read anything published on newsprint. It can't be the Grail if it's lining the bird cage, right?"

"You underestimate her," the priest says.

"Spare me. She's smart and interesting and a lot of other things I'm sure you appreciate when she comes to Holy Innocents for her confessions. But it's no fluke she concentrates on writing about mythology. The ways of mere mortals – especially her children or some woebegotten inks – aren't especially interesting to her."

He stays quiet for a very long time after that.

"So change her mind," he says finally. "Make it bigger and more universal than newsprint. Your grail quest."

"I'm not named after a grail knight, Father. Finn McCool's greatest test required nothing more of him than to keep his eyes open and stay awake. "

"So there you are," he says.

He holds at three Jamesons, I down five. When we get up to leave he teeters a little, I don't. It may be the only way I ever best the old man.

***

She's got a story, she says.

It's a message on my landline at work, and I wish it wasn't there.

In the old days, I would have admired it. The tease of significance, the promise of discussing it at a bar neither set of our colleagues frequents. In the old days I would have thrilled to the way she trusts me with her unlisted number. Actually, I still thrill to that.

But I'm not happy. I feel the creep of something tight and heavy in my stomach. The Gazette's landlines are being monitored. Melinda's convinced of it and while I know she's completely paranoid it doesn't mean she's not right.

Mari's sitting in a booth at the Lebanon, exactly where her message said she'd be.

I slide in the booth seat beside her without saying hello. It doesn't take any magical power on her part to know I'm furious.

Her hand shakes as she reaches for the beer she was drinking before I came in. I shove the glass away, reach up and pull her head close to mine. My mouth

17

buries itself in her hair, next to her ear.

"Don't ever leave me a message like that again."

"Fine. Let go, I'm leaving." She's furious now, too.

But I don't let go. I kiss her.

Furious can turn into amazing kisses. Like honey when it warms.

I pull away first, but not too far.

"Don't you *ever* ask permission?" she asks.

I don't think she realizes she licks her lips. Or maybe she does. Either way, it has an effect. I have to hold myself from drawing her to me again.

"The old saying. I'd rather ask forgiveness than permission," I say. "Give me your phone."

She looks at me, puzzled, then digs it out of her backpack.

I program my cell phone number into it, then hand it back to her. "Text me. Or call this. Not the Gazette's landline. Ever. It's not safe."

She waits until the barmaid who's come over to take my order leaves. "Aren't you being a little, you know, over the top?"

"I'm serious, Mari. If it's like my editor thinks, after tonight they'll have proof you're the Hipco leak."

The barmaid brings my drink. Waits for her tip. It's that kind of bar.

"Nice digs," I say to her when I hand her the bills.

She smiles at me. "Better since you got here." She casts an appraising glance at Mari, then leaves.

"Guess I'm not getting another drink," Mari says.

I laugh, take a slug. When I turn back to her, she's studying me. I can't hold her gaze for very long.

"You have a story," I say.

"Always."

"Am I going to like it?"

"You'll like getting it before anyone else."

"Give."

"You've heard all those reports about ink-related leprosy and plague outbreaks."

"Yeah. Unsubstantiated trash. Unless you're telling me otherwise."

She shakes her head. "But I hear there are plans circulating for state sanitariums. Well, more like internment centers, I say."

"Anything on paper?"

"One of my colleagues told me she's seen the blueprints for one upstate. Near Lake Algonquin. I think I can get my hands on them. At least for a couple hours."

"Jesus. All right. If you've got a pipeline to the Big Guy you better pray the Gazette's phones aren't tapped and that nobody finds out you're the leak until after we break this."

"Okay," she says, a smile playing at the edge of her lips.

Lips. Damn.

# Finn: Lead, lede, led

I pull her to me, kiss her again. Turns out her non-furious kisses are even better.

"Was that for the story, or for me?" she says after she opens her eyes.

I toy with a strand of her hair. "If we pull this off, and you still have a job, you can't give me any more leads. Not for a while."

"Either way I won't be able to give you any more," she says. "Because if this goes through I'll probably be living upstate."

"Now who's being over the top? You're an ink, but you're also a citizen. None of this stuff can touch you."

"Right." She looks away. The crowd is changing at the bar. It's getting younger, noisier. The jukebox — one of the old ones, a real collector's item — kicks on.

"It's almost curfew," she says, still not looking at me. "And the ink buses stopped running from this part of town 15 minutes ago. But, I'm a citizen so I guess it doesn't touch me."

I'm an asshole, but an asshole who knows how to apologize. So I do.

She nods but just keeps staring out at the people milling around the juke, the bar, each other. They're about her age, I think. Probably have more in common with her than me.

"I'm not like them," she says as if she's heard my thought. "When I look out of their eyes I don't recognize the world they see."

I get up, reach for her hand. "Dance? I like this song. At least I like the Chris Isaak original."

She shakes her head.

"Mari. I'm asking."

Maybe she looks out of my eyes and sees herself as I see her. Because she stands up and moves into my arms. Three Days Grace keeps singing. We keep dancing. She misses curfew.

\*\*\*

She seems surprised by how her body matches mine, but for me this is our most human magic — the way our bodies understand that we'll fit together without seam.

There's magic of another kind in Mari.

I see different features ghost over her face as we're having sex. An animal's countenance: heavy bone under velvet fur, a match for the eyes. It is a creature of earth, of a land where the greens are stitched together by lianas and the phosphorescence of moth orchids. I know at that moment that I'm caught like I hadn't thought to be.

"It's true then. That part of the story," I say after we've exhausted ourselves.

She turns her back.

Eventually I realize it's a movement not of refusal but of defense.

19

"My mother's people go through the twinning. But early, before they build the habits that pass for adulthood," she says. "My father always believed it was because of his blood that I didn't change."

"He was non-ink?" I realize as I ask it that, even though I've been thinking about her a lot, I know little outside of the fairy tale she offered up.

"American. Mostly Anglo, though given the surname, he had to have at least some Italian in his blood." Her laugh is short. "His blood. It guarantees my citizenship, but in that just as in this, it turns out his blood isn't strong enough to undo the taint of my mother's."

I hesitate a moment, then wrap my arms around her waist and draw her back against me. "Don't. There's no taint."

"Isn't there?" She turns to me, eyes blazing. "Why else do you write what you do? Why else do I leak the information I've sworn to keep confidential? Why else are we here together, two people with nothing in common but the stories we tell about inks?"

I don't have words to counter, I just keep holding her.

In time her head grows heavy on my shoulder and her body relaxes into sleep. I stay immobile in this posture until dawn, when she stirs out of it.

"Stories are all any two people ever have in common," I say to her as if our conversation hadn't been punctuated by hours of sleep.

The face she turns up to me is the purely human one, the one I could draw from memory if I had the skill.

"Why care which stories brought us here, so long as they did?" I say. If she knew me better she'd know the comment is as close as I've ever gotten to a declaration.

"You haven't gotten any sleep, have you?" she asks.

I shake my head.

She disentangles herself, then pushes my shoulders flat to the bed. My back muscles shrill in complaint, then release.

"Sleep," she says. "You probably have two or three hours before you have to get up for work."

As she climbs over me to get out of bed, I catch her wrist. "Will you be here when I wake up?"

"No."

I keep my hold on her. "Ever?"

She looks down at me. An odd reversal, this.

"Do you want it to be happily ever after and the end?" she says.

"One of the two."

"Well, then." She drops a kiss, feather light, on my forehead before she leaves.

3.

Nothing comes of the sanitarium-internment center story. The blueprints cannot be located. No public figure or credible source verifies or confirms or acknowledges. Forget on the record, this story's not even on the planet.

I'm relegated to B-section stories, hack pieces, little better than glorified wire. Even so, some mornings when I come in I notice my desk's been rifled and my computer's turned itself on and past the password screen.

One day I find an expensive flash drive – enough gigs to store four or five years worth of notes on pdf – and a fifth of Jamesons in my top drawer. I think it means Melinda's got my back, but then, maybe not. It could be a taunt. It's a drawer I keep locked; the only key hanging, along with my badge and press pass, on a lanyard perpetually around my neck.

I carry two phones: one for sources, the other only my family and friends know about. That's the one that rings. Mari.

"Where are you?" I ask as I duck out of the newsroom.

"Stuck at work. Margie has me digitally transcribing slave ship manifests. Who knew Hastings was such a hub?"

"I knew."

"Because you know everything."

"That. And my sister has a friend whose parents bought up all of Robert Math's buildings. He designed a lot of them with access to interconnected underground tunnels so the ship owners could unload and secure their human cargo sight unseen. There are miles of tunnel under the asphalt of Hastings, all the way from Old City to the pier. Sarai – that's Cassie's friend – used to pull together raves down there."

"Does Father Tom know about them?"

"The raves?"

"No, the tunnels. Anyway, listen, there's no ink bus for another half-hour so I'm not going to make it to Mass."

She doesn't lector anymore. Or receive Communion. Not since us. But she still goes to Mass. Every day.

"I'll swing by and get you." I check my pockets to make sure I haven't left anything important in the newsroom, then punch the elevator button.

She's waiting outside the Hipco archives, a ramshackle building a good 20 blocks from the rest of the population control offices. She's been working here for a couple of months, demoted by recent ordinances stripping inks of security clearances.

I'm thinking I'm going to get her to Holy Innocents on time when we hit one of the semi-monthly roadblocks. Most of the cars get through pretty fast, a quick glance through the windshield is all the cops need to wave people through. Of course, we end up in the inspection line.

Mari rolls down the window on her side of the car. An agent dressed in a Hipco field coat leans in.

"Sorry 'bout this Mari," he says. "It's only the fake tats we're checking for but I still have to do it."

She pulls her sleeve up, sticks her wrist out the window. "It's okay, George."

He scans her tattoo.

After he waves us on I turn to look at her. "You know him?"

"I trained him," she says, looking out the window. After a few moments I see her pull out her cell phone and punch in a number.

"Nely? Let Father Tom know there's an identity roadblock on Callowhill and 39th. He's going to want to announce it before Mass, or after, or whatever. Just in case anyone's headed in this direction, okay?"

After she ends the call she goes back to staring out the window.

The hair on the back of my neck stands on end. "Which Holy Innocents congregants have fake tattoos?"

"I don't know. I don't want to know."

"You think Father Tom knows?"

She turns to look at me. "You never stop digging for stories, do you? Ask him, he'll tell you."

"Things have gotten, umm, chilly between us since I corrupted you."

She starts laughing. "Go to confession. Absolution can be yours. Just promise you'll never sin again."

"I'd rather have a sharp stick driven into my eye."

She smiles, but it's wistful. She wonders if I love her enough to marry her and make us legitimate in Father Tom's eyes. And God's. And hers.

I know this. And though I'm in love with her, I won't ask her to marry me. I can't.

\*\*\*

I'd like to say it's my mother's fault. I've told her about Mari. All of it. Or really, as much as I know. Suddenly she's developed this overriding interest in Central American legends and folklore. Particularly the tales about half-human, half-animal beings.

"They're terrible stories," she says during one of her weekly conference calls to Cassie and me. "Fundamentally uglier than others I've studied."

"Oh for crying out loud, Mom," I hear Cassie's voice fading in and out. Cell phone towers upstate are spread out and the coverage spotty. "They're allegories and morality tales and make-believe, not reality."

There's a moment of silence. "He described her as a creature out of myth."

"Metaphor, Mom." I can hear exasperation in my older sister's voice. "New girlfriend-itis."

"No, really, listen to this," my mother's enthused, the way she always gets when she talks about her work. "There's this one from Guatemala, La Siguanaba. She seems to exist only to entice men sexually. Then, after she's led them to abandon everything and follow her into the dark – but before anything's actually consummated – she reveals that under the curtain of her hair is the face of a horse. The sight alone kills them. Hmmm. Really more of a fable, then. Where lust leads."

"Well, that's not it," I finally get a word in then, to test if either of them is listening. "Not if it's unconsummated."

"Lovely," Cassie mutters.

My mother, clearly not paying attention, continues, "or maybe it's more about women's genitalia, and the primitive masculine fear of sighting something so beastly and animal amid otherwise human features."

"I'm hanging up if we continue along these lines," Cassie warns.

"How did I raise such a prude?"

"Prudishness has nothing to do with it. And Finn and I raised ourselves. Look, can we get real here? I'm more worried about what it means for Finn to be involved with an ink in this political climate."

"Hey, I'm on the line, remember? Can we do away with third person?"

"Fine. How do you know she's not with you only for the advantage you provide? You know, like getting around the restrictions?"

"Jesus, Cassie. I can't do anything like that for her. I had to move to a different part of town just so we can live in the same apartment."

"Well, then, what happens if you get married, have kids? Have you thought what it'd be like to see your children tattooed and monitored like all the other inks? Because at a quarter ink, they'd still be subject to it, Finn."

"No marriage," my mother interrupts. "No unbreakable bond until we know the nature of the creature she hosts, or changes into, or whatever."

"Is twinned with," I say.

"Oh. My. God. I give up. Talk to you guys next week." Cassie hangs up.

"Two days ago she was in church when I was waiting to go to confession. Tom pointed her out to me," my mother says. "She's not your type."

"Priests are worse than old women. And, she's redefined my type."

She does her snorting laugh thing that has, in my lifetime, gone from endearing to annoying and back to endearing.

"Finn?"

"Yeah?"

"Did you read my last monograph?"

"The Tibet one? Bits of the intro and first chapter."

"So much for filial devotion. You should dig it out and read it. Chapter ten for sure."

"One of these days."

"It's just ... there are places in the world where the mythic doesn't stay buried in the past. And within those places, pockets of people who are swimming in the fantastical. And within those pockets, individuals who've inherited magic."

When I don't say anything she adds, "Tell me it wasn't metaphor."

"I sort of wish it had been."

"What I wouldn't give to interview her. But you're not going to introduce us, are you?"

"No. Not until I exact a vow that she won't be part of some study you later publish. And that's never going to happen, is it?"

Silence. Then she says, "Protective. Must be love."

After it's clear I'm not going to respond, she sighs.

"Just don't slip up and have a kid, okay? This sort of magic seems to be passed along in the mother's blood. Like baldness."

"First Cassie, now you. Who said anything about kids?"

That snort laugh again. "You really should pay more attention to my work. Everything, and I do mean everything, comes round eventually to legacy, children and blood."

# Finn: Lead, lede, led

## 4

The day distinguishes itself by being the first time we have a fight.

I make the mistake of telling Mari I interviewed Toño for a piece I'm writing about the subterranean inks who run the peñas and hold the freetrade zones right under the authorities' noses.

"You just make it worse for the rest of us by writing about them," she says while she pours our morning coffees. "The gangs provide all the excuse anyone needs for the imposition of ink restrictions."

"There's a difference between the cartel gangs and indie gangs like Toño's," I say.

"Yeah? You think you can tell which is which when the bullet rips through you?" She hands me the cup with enough violence that some of the coffee spills over and scalds my hand. "You're such a white boy sometimes."

Her reverse disdain pisses me off.

"So tell me why Nely agrees with me."

"Oh, she flirts with it – with Toño – but she's a moral person. She'd never fall in with a gang."

"She's in."

"What?"

"Who do you think convinced him to do the interview?"

She slams her cup in the sink. "You knew and you weren't going to tell me, were you?"

I could lie, I suppose, but I don't. "No."

She closes her eyes for a moment, then brushes past me to pick her Hipco badge out of the basket where we keep our keys and lanyards.

I glance up at the clock. "We've got ten minutes before we have to leave."

"I'm going to take the bus."

"There isn't an ink bus for another 20 minutes."

"It doesn't even bother you to say it, does it? Ink bus. Like it's the most normal thing in the world that I can't ride the same bus as you."

"Of course it bothers me. But it *is* normal now."

For the first time in daylight I see her face unsharpen and the features of the great speckled cat overlay themselves. But in a moment the animal visage is gone and it's only the face of the woman I love. Her eyes are round and glazed with water.

She runs out the door.

Her cell phone goes to voice mail, every time. I call the Hipco landline, but I get hung up in the switch from one extension to the next and end up in interdepartmental limbo. Texts and emails go unanswered. Finally, when she doesn't come home in the evening, I go looking for her at Holy Innocents.

"She hasn't been here," Father Tom says as he guides me to sit in one of the empty pews after Mass. "I thought perhaps you had finally convinced her to stay away altogether."

I drop my face into my hands. I've already disappointed the old man in dozens of ways, but I don't want him to see me fall apart.

"Nely wasn't here either. I wonder if they went off somewhere together? That must be it." He pats me on the shoulder

"Toño would know where Nely is, wouldn't he? Now that she's one of his?" I say, looking up.

He looks like he's been fed something sour. "That's the way it seems to work."

"Can you get in touch with him, somehow?"

He hesitates, then, "Yes. Come. Let's go to the rectory."

He ensconces me in the kitchen, a fresh pot of coffee at hand. I hear him making two calls from the hallway before he comes back in.

"Did you talk to him?"

"To someone who can reach him," he says. He pours himself a cup and sits across the kitchen table from me.

"I'm so fucked, Father. I feel like I did when my dad left. Like my heart is leaking blood."

"I don't think she left you, son."

"We had a fight."

He waves it away. "Everyone fights. Listen, I've got someone checking to see if they're unconscious in some hospital somewhere, but I fear worse."

"Worse than a hospital?"

He nods. "There's a very active set of Cleanse America groups working the area. My people have traced three border dumps in as many weeks."

"Your people? You mean like nuns and priests?"

"Well, there are some of those too, but mostly just an assortment of lay people who help me whenever an ink from my congregation comes up missing. Mari traces GPS chips for us. She knows some sort of back door that gets her into the tracking program even though she's only supposed to have access to the computerized archives. Of course, we've never had to trace a citizen. They don't usually get dumped."

"And don't have GPS chips embedded in their necks."

"But Nely's a temporary worker, so she does. And I have photocopies of all my congregants' tattoos. So long as we can figure out the corresponding numeric code – and I've been assured we can – we'll be able to go online and get Hipco to flag them so they can't be taken through a border checkpoint without setting off all sorts of figurative bells and whistles."

Around 9 p.m. the rectory's doorbell rings and when Father Tom comes back into the kitchen a tall blond follows him. She's stunning, all honeyed shades: hair, skin, eyes, clothes.

"Finn, this is Meche. She owns Peña Caridad, among other things."

Caridad – Our Lady of Charity. Cuban, then.

"You're the journalist," she sticks her hand out to shake. As soon as the pleasantries are done she sits down and pulls out a tablet so new I don't think it's officially hit the market yet.

"All right, so according to Toño, Nely was slated to run some stuff up to a freetrade zone this afternoon and never showed. Now, since we've lost the only one of us who could trace GPS chips, we're going to have to rely on eyes to monitor dump routes. Mexican mafia's got the Rooseveltown corridor, Toño's group has Route 17, and the maras the thruway. I don't have as much contact with the non-Latino gangs but there are reciprocal agreements in place when it comes to dumping, so western corridor's covered as well."

"You don't look like a gang member," I say.

She gives a short bark of a laugh. "And what would that look like? But you're right, I'm not. I'm a businesswoman. And a chemist. Which makes me someone the gangs like knowing. And since Father Tom doesn't like dealing with them, I run interference. Any other questions?"

I shake my head.

"Hand over the copies of the tattoos, Father. I'll get them flagged."

I don't recognize the app she uses. "Proprietary," she says when she notices my look. "Reads the tat and converts it into its numeric code, just like the proper scanners. Though sometimes it hits a snag. Like now. It can't seem to convert Nely's tat."

She slides the papers back to Father Tom. "But with Mari's tat flagged it'll be near impossible for the group to get her through an official crossing. Just pray they don't split them up."

She leans back in her chair. "Damn, I hope we get your girlfriend back soon, or that she walks in tonight from some spa day she didn't tell you about. And not just for your sake or hers. This is all so much more hit-or-miss without the information she pulls for us from Hipco's database."

"Do you know her?"

She shakes her head. "Just Father Tom. He's the hub of our little group."

I turn to the priest. "Why didn't you bring me in on it?"

He looks away guiltily.

"Well, now that you're in," the blond says, leaning forward, "are you all in? Because there's more."

"Like what?"

"Like we've got to recruit more people with undeniable rights and not a hint of ink. Preferably ones with homes adjoining or within hailing distance of the proposed inkatoriums."

I clench my hands so hard I'm scared if I look down I'll see blood seeping out of the folds. "The rumors about sanitarium-internment centers are completely unfounded. I know. I dug around."

She gives me a sidelong look. "They've finished almost all of the facilities on the southern border already. They're called Fair Hills hyphen Maricopa – or whatever the locale is – appended on the end."

"You mean the ritzy rehab chain?"

"Yeah. Funny front, huh? But people don't question top-flight tech and huge structures when they imagine it protecting the privacy of detoxing celebrities."

I feel sick to my stomach. I think the Gazette even ran a wire story about the Fair Hills phenomenon.

"Things are taking a little longer up here. Only one has opened instate so far, and it's nowhere near the attention hog its southern kin are. We're calling them health centers, and from what I can gather there's a state board forming to refine detention criteria and start hiring staff. It cost me almost as much as my brownstone to secure, but I've got locations and timetables for the remaining 12 sites, so we know exactly where, and how fast, we need to get to work."

She keeps talking but I stop listening.

If I help them, I can't write the story; if I write the story, I can't help them. And each means losing what I love.

I know I said I've never felt fear.

I lied.

# Mari: Once upon a time

## 1

When I try to open my eyes they are glued shut. Also, my shoes are gone. I feel air curling under bare toes. For a second I imagine they stuck me in a coffin thinking me dead. But they don't kill, only maim and intimidate and count on the shackles of fear and isolation to do the rest for them.

I understand the scal on my eyes isn't embalmer's glue, even so, it takes all my faith to rip lid from lid. It's not my skin I hear tearing, I tell myself, it's gunk from my wounded sleep. A sleep that might have been hours. Or days.

The space I'm in is much bigger than the coffin of my imagination. I know this because somewhere behind me – somewhere I cannot turn because the first attempt to do so has left me swamped with pain – light leaks in. Not much but enough to see the curve of a shoulder on the floor beside me.

I reach out, touch. Nely doesn't move. But under my fingertips I feel pulsing warmth. My hand comes away smelling of flaked iron and blood. I call to her, but if the word finds its way in her ear and through the byways of the brain it loses itself before it arrives. She doesn't respond. Not a twitch.

I turn my face away from her.

They struck her harder than they did me. The tire iron splintered something. I heard it.

I had caught up with her a few blocks from Holy Innocents. We were yelling at each other so loud we had to duck into the narrow alley next to the Golden Cup coffeeshop to avoid the notice of people walking down Callowhill. No good comes from drawing attention to yourself when you're an ink.

I don't think I've ever been angrier. Mostly at the way she extolled Toño's gang and rationalized their actions as protective. But probably there was some of it that came from feeling that her turn to Toño was a turn away from me and the life I wanted for her.

I remember being thankful she was too new to be packing heat, and spent most of my words on trying to describe what would happen to her soul the first time she let a bullet tear through human flesh.

Then, when we were jumped, I wanted to take it all back. Even though she fought like a polecat, and I felt a roaring leap of fury fueling my movements, we went down fast. A gun would have given us a chance.

Something grazes my shoulder, the one closest to Nely. When I turn to the touch, I realize the contact is not hers.

Three small shadows, darker than the dark surrounding us, have moved between me and my friend. For a moment I wonder if these are the malignant dwarves that attended the bloodshed in my mother's story. In my story.

I push myself to sitting with the arm that still works. "Nely," I whisper again.

Why do we call to the familiar even when we know it cannot answer?

"She's asleep," says one of the shadows. In Spanish. A child's voice.

"Not asleep," I say. My throat feels scraped down to its last layer; a tissue set to tear. "Hurt."

"They hurt all of us."

"The men?" I ask, but it's not really a question. Of course the men.

"We're bleeding." That one's a boy, and not much older than a toddler from the sound of his voice.

"Here." He grabs my hand and guides it to the back of his neck.

It's my injured arm and the movement plunges keen blades into my flesh from elbow to shoulder. When I catch my breath, I feel a wet, fleshy divot the size of a quarter under my fingers. The men must have cut a GPS chip out of the boy's neck. I know if I lifted his wrist to a light I'd see a black tattoo – in this case an i.d. to identify not the child but the temporary worker under whose guardianship he's here.

"Does it hurt bad?" I ask him.

My eyes have finally adjusted to my waking and I can see more detail. The boy's small shoulders move up and back in a shrug. It makes me want to hug him.

"Are the rest of you cut too?" I ask instead.

"Yes." It's the girl – about the size of an 8-year-old with messy, long hair and arms wrapped around a smaller, silent girl – who answers. "But it's scabbing up already."

The space we're in jerks into motion, and with the movement the shadowy details make sense. We're in the back of a delivery van. An old one by the ride of the shocks.

After my ears adjust to the road noise I ask the children their names and where they were snatched. Predictably, they don't know street names, and describe landmarks that would fit any number of Hastings' neighborhoods. Nely and I were already heaped unconscious in the van when the men cut the children's trackers out and tossed them inside.

I go quiet, wishing uselessly that I had roused earlier to raise a commotion and give the kids a chance to get away.

"Are we going to be okay?" the tiniest, Lalo, asks.

"I'm going to think of some way to get us out of here," I say, though my mind is blank and I can't seem to make it work the way it normally does.

"You're little." Julieta, the eldest, says after I fall silent again. "Can you beat them up?"

Julieta's Spanish is different than Lalo's. Despite the way it sings, there is something hard and sharp in it. A Mexican accent like Nely's. Lalo swallows the ends of his words, which locates his heritage somewhere more Caribbean. They are bonded by circumstantial, not familial, blood.

# Mari: Once upon a time

"I can't do that, but I can reason with them. Or try to trick them so you can get away," I say. "How about you help me think of some ways to do that?"

They make a couple of half-hearted attempts, but it becomes clear to me that thinking about the men just makes them panicky.

"You should try to nap a bit while I figure this out," I say, aiming for calm. And time. I need time.

"If you want us to sleep, you have to tell us a fairy tale," Julieta says.

"I don't know any," I answer.

I've often said I am formed by tales; that if you cut me, that's what seeps out instead of blood. Except now I know it is not so. The stories? I can't think of one.

Julieta moves to my side, between my good arm and the wall of the van. "Please," she says. Her voice is wobbly and small, closer to Lalo's than what I've heard from her up to now. As if my refusal to tell her a story is the final breach in her defenses.

My good hand finds her hair, smoothes it in short pats. "Shhh."

As she settles against me her breathing sounds more like whimpering to my ears. I hook my good arm under Nely's armpit and pull her closer. Something rises in me, fiercely protective and strong, but mute. I fight my way to the words that usually come as easy as breath.

"A lot of the fairy tales I remember have scary parts," I warn after a while.

"But they all end happy, right?" Alicia finally breaks her silence.

"Yes," I lie.

The children snuggle close; my best friend doesn't budge.

"Érase una vez." Once upon a time.

Every story should start with the promise and disclaimer of those words.

2.

The vehicle stops short, slamming the children against me, and me to the floor. I suck air to quell the nauseating wave of pain that follows. Then the cargo doors open and the sunlight flooding in precipitates a different sort of nausea.

"Would you look at this," says a voice I last heard in a Hastings alley, punctuated by the thuds of a tire iron on my body and my best friend's. "If it isn't the fucking Pieta."

"Shut your mouth," I say. "Don't you dare compare this to anything meaningful or good."

I hear another laugh.

The younger one, the one who had actually swung the weapon, reaches in and pulls me out. He's got a beaky nose, pallid skin and a watchman's cap pulled down over longish blond hair.

The older one is bald, all his hair's migrated to a full, dark beard that reaches his collarbone. His teeth are stark against the hair when he smiles. "Way you talk, you'd almost think you weren't an ink," he says to me.

I think he believes he's paying me a compliment.

"Way you talk, you'd almost think I wasn't a citizen," I spit out. I glance over his shoulder, quick so he doesn't notice. We're behind an interstate rest stop, hidden from any patrons.

"Tattoos can be faked," the man says as he leans over the van's sill to prod Nely. She doesn't move.

"Not even the best forgers can produce credible blue ones. My dad was born in Ohio. I moved to the States when I was a few months old. I'm as American as you."

He shrugs as he straightens back up. "You don't see me having to wear a tattoo, do you? So not quite as American." His smile grows wider. "Now, go take a piss so we can get moving again. And make sure the ankle biters do their business while we're stopped. If any of them makes my van smell like a latrine it won't go well for you."

He turns to the younger guy before he walks away, "Keep an eye on them."

"C'mon," the young guy motions to a stretch of trimmed grass.

I head for the spot he's indicated, the kids trailing behind me. We stop about fifteen feet into the grass. I can tell the guy's embarrassed by having to watch us because he's half turned away.

"What's your name?" I ask while the kids relieve themselves.

"Steve."

"Don't you want to know mine?"

"Nope."

"Might make me human, huh?"

"You done yet?"

"Kids are. I can't pull my pants down with just one hand. I think you broke

32

my shoulder."

I see him flush all the way to the roots of his hair.

He trudges over. The pants I'm wearing are snug enough around my hips that he has to grip the waistband with both hands and lean in to pull them down for me. I don't wait long – just until I'm sure I'll clear his skull – to drive the elbow of my good arm into the back of his neck. At the same time my knee rises to slam his chin.

I yell at the children, motion for them to run.

But they don't. They stand and gape.

I've taken a step away from Steve toward them – I know I have – but then my cheek is flat to the grass and dog poop, and my ears are ringing. A new pain chimes in with the chorus of the old.

The toe of a heavy boot plows into my side, flips me over as easy as if it were a spatula and I a pancake. It's not Steve – he's still down – nor the unpleasant older man I've seen before but a woman not much older than me.

There isn't a shred of mercy in the brown eyes trained on me. She lifts her foot, poises the chunky tread of her boot a centimeter or so from my nose. "Give me a reason to make you scream."

I'd like to say it is a snarl that comes out of her mouth, but it is not. The words are calm and not born of any great passion. Ordinary. Worse.

She must see fear in my face because she moves her foot back to the ground. "Get those kids in the truck or I'll carve them up in front of you."

It isn't until then that I notice the hunting knife in her hands. I'm guessing I'm on the ground because she clocked me on the head with its knobby handle.

"Believe me. The only soft one among us was Steve, and I think you've taken care of that," she says when she notices where my eyes have landed.

Shortly after the van starts up, Nely rouses.

I don't notice at first, because I've scooted back to the van's wall and I'm staring at a black-painted window webbed with cracks, the provenance of light in this benighted place. While I stare I pretend I'm at home, held safely in Finn's arms and saying what I've kept from him for who knows what reason.

Nely tries to speak. But it comes out hisses and unstrung consonants. When I drop a kiss on her brow, the light catches on the water in her eyes. She curls into a ball beside me, eyes open but unfocused. Julieta, on my left side and echoing my posture against the van wall, pats Nely's foot. "Would you like to hear a fairy tale?" she asks.

The old Nely, the uninjured one, would have laughed and said the only tales worth hearing can't be told in the company of children. But this Nely twitches in what Julieta assures me is yes.

The children turn their eyes on me. Julieta keeps patting Nely's foot as if she were a restive pet, and I … well, I've got to figure how to swallow my heart before I can go on.

## 3.

When we stop again the older man hauls us out of the van.

It's twilight, and we're nowhere near an interstate rest stop now. We're on a narrow packed dirt road that cuts through towering conifers.

"Are we in Canada?" I know that's where we're headed.

"Not yet," the man answers.

"What's your name?"

He glares at me but eventually answers. "Ted."

"That's my dad's name." A lie.

"He was from Toledo." It's good to pepper the lies with some truth. "Have you ever been there?"

Ted shifts his weight from one foot to the other, scratches his head. "No. You got to piss?" he asks, "because if not, I've got to get you to the campsite."

I nod.

He motions for me to squat beside the van.

I walk a few feet away from him, turn my back and try to undo my pants. I've regained a little mobility in my shoulder, but not much, and the process is painful. I keep talking.

"Listen, you seem like a decent guy." Lie.

"I guess I can understand why you want to dump Nely and me across the border." Lie.

I glance at Nely who's swaying a little as she stands by the door of the van. Her eyes are on the pine needle carpet underfoot. Julieta's hanging on to her, and the others hang on to Julieta. All of them are so hunched into themselves and miserable I feel a pang in my gut. Again I picture Finn, and try to imagine his gigantic, protective presence next to them. But then I realize what his being here would mean. And if my heart feels splintered now I can't imagine what it'd be if I had to see him cowed and beaten, or worse.

I meet Ted's eyes for a second, then turn back to the business of peeing on command. "The children are innocents, and they're scared out of their minds." Truth. "It wouldn't be any big deal, even now, to drop them off somewhere that an adult would find them quickly. Like a mall, maybe. "

"No malls around here," he says.

When I'm done, he ducks into the front of the van and emerges with a rifle. He herds us together for the trek to the campsite.

"You," he pokes me with the muzzle while we walk.

"Mariana," I say. "Mari." The movies I've seen suggest that hostages are safer when their kidnappers know their names.

"Maryanna," he says. "I wouldn't yak so much when we get around Carl. It gives him an excuse to be mean."

"Meaner than the rest of you?"

"Major league, girl. You understand?"

Red and blue dome tents are pitched near a chinked log lean-to full of cut firewood. A section in front of the tents is open – it looks like the pine and spruce needles have been swept clear – and a fire crackles in a fire pit dug in the center.

Steve hauls a large piece of firewood from the lean-to to the fire. He sits on it, then shifts, repositions it closer to the warmth. The woman who knocked me down rummages in a cooler. A man seated near her glances up from cleaning the rifle held upright between his knees. Carl, I guess.

"Took you long enough," he says to Ted. "What did you do, take one of them out into the bushes? I hear you aren't too picky about what kind of pussy you get these days."

"Shut up," Ted says amiably. He pushes the children closer to fire. "Sit."

Nely, still unstable, flops right where she stands. But it's getting colder and we're too far from the fire so I coax her to crawl to the edge of the ring of warmth. She leans against me when I sit. The kids come swarming back to huddle around us.

"The new meaning of black and blue," Carl says. The woman laughs.

"Are you a Cleanse America group?" I ask.

Carl turns to the woman. "That one's so sharp she could cut herself." Again the woman laughs. A simpery sort of giggle. It sets my teeth on edge.

"If you get caught dumping us across the border you'll be prosecuted. And pay a fine," I say.

"Assuming your tat is legit," Carl concedes. "But, we'll get around to verifying that unlikely scenario tomorrow. The Statics and Feds don't bother their heads about dumping anyway."

"City population control offices do," I say. "At least the one I work for does."

He raises an eyebrow. "An ink in pop control. A bit like putting the fox in charge of the henhouse, wouldn't you say?"

"A *citizen* in pop control. And so long as I can keep people like you from having any real power ...."

He laughs this time. "I've got plenty of power, spink."

I hate the ethno-specific variants – spink, vink, mink, hink – even more than the generic. But I don't twitch when he says it and my expression doesn't change.

I study him as he studies me. He's handsome: well built, perfectly cut dark brown hair, eyes a blue color you only see in Pacific northwestern skies. His smile might be described as charming if it weren't for the context.

"You're a pretty little thing," he says after a moment. Silky. Soft. Some horrible parody of seductive. "Tits just the right size for my hand."

He stands up, stretches his back. "But I don't fuck ink."

He glances at the woman by the cooler. At his look her fair skin pinks up, and I can't figure whether she's upset or gratified by his attention.

"I'm off to bed," he says after a long moment. "You coming?"

The woman nods, scrambles to her feet.

Then Carl turns back to me. "You all sleep out here." He motions with the arm that holds the rifle. "We're miles from any town. You might be tempted to make a run for it, but you know none of the others would make it. And you're not going to leave them here alone with me, are you?"

As he ducks into the tent he calls out, "Ted, watch. Wake me or Jan when you're tired."

A half-hour later, after we've all fidgeted through the sounds coming from the blue tent, Steve gets up and shambles over to the other one. The children and Nely manage to fall asleep, but I can't. I watch Ted watching us across the firelight.

"Thing is," he says after what seems hours of silence, "I don't think it's fair."

"What?"

"There are just so many of you. My kid can't even fall in love without making certain first whether the girl's got ink under her skin. No grandfather wants to see one of his own grow up with a tat."

"That almost sounds like you feel some compassion for us, Ted."

He makes a rude noise. "The blues are uppity, greens ungrateful, and the black tats are every other country's waste. I've got no compassion for you, just questions about why you can't go away and leave us be."

I blow a loud breath. "I'm one of you, Ted. There's no place for me to go away to." Then, without intending to, I swear. It comes out in Spanish.

He gives me a strange look. "That's why we decided to follow you two, you know. You aren't supposed to be speaking anything but English."

"I've got an exemption."

"Does your friend?"

He's right about the language ban. Whenever Nely could get away with speaking Spanish she would. And I never stopped her.

"Look at me, Ted," I say and lay my hand softly on Nely while waiting for him to meet my eyes. "This is my best friend. She's smart and funny and has won nursing association awards two years in a row. If your mother or father needed geriatric care and she were their nurse, it'd be like having a doctor looking out for them 24/7. She's that good."

"And them," I motion to the sleeping children. "I don't really know them, but I know this: they're just like your kids were. Or are. Sweet, trusting, good in ways we adults hardly even remember. We have to look out for them. Not because of the tattoos, or in spite of them, but because they're kids and we're supposed to look out for kids."

"They just need one good, lucky break, Ted. Just one," I say.

He doesn't say anything, but he doesn't look away from me either.

I see us out of his eyes.

We're darker and smaller but no less human than those he loves. I hadn't seen that when I looked out of Jan's or Carl's eyes. Not even Steve's. Ted is the only one who sees us as made of the same flesh and blood as he is.

# Mari: Once upon a time

"I don't think this border dump was your idea," I say, keeping my voice low. "I don't think you really want to be here. I think it makes you uneasy hurting women and children. You didn't swing the tire iron, and you didn't cut the chips out of the kids' necks. I can see it in your eyes – you still own your soul. But you won't if you go through with this."

"You and I aren't any different, Ted," I say after a pause. "We're both looking for a way to get out of an awful situation we never thought to be in."

He stays silent so long I start dozing off.

"Thing is, you're wrong," he says quietly. He comes to stand beside me, then squats to look me in the eye. "We *are* different."

He reaches out and touches the side of my face. Tender.

He keeps his fingers soft as he trails them down my cheek, and what comes to mind is the image of grown-ups doing something similar in my father's fairy-tale retelling of my early days. Like I'm reminding Ted of something sweet and almost forgotten.

I can't control the shudder that rips through my body.

Ted's shoulders draw in and his pupils get tiny as if they're reacting to a strong light following the dark. He clamps his hand over my mouth.

I've been scared of Carl, but it's Ted who rapes me.

There's a dusting of snow on the ground in the morning. The tents are packed in their bags. The fire is out, not even smoldering since Steve dumped a bucketful of dirt in the pit. Someone's driven the van and a pick-up I haven't seen before down to the campsite.

I flinch when I feel Ted's touch on my shoulder.

"Thank me later," he says. I choke back the gorge rising in my throat.

He guides me to the pick up truck where Carl is half in, half out of the passenger seat.

"Ted reminds me I haven't verified your ink," Carl says, looking up. "And, for some reason, he's suddenly believes it might be real."

Carl grabs my wrist and turns it over to look at my tattoo. He rubs his thumb hard through the lines, then reaches under the seat to retrieve something. It's a portable scanner, but not one of the cheapo knockoffs they've started hawking on infomercials. This is a sturdy, government-issued one like I used in my work at the Hastings Pop Control office before they demoted me to the archives. It has a border patrol insignia.

I meet his eyes.

He smiles. Not a nice smile. "Told you, no official gives a shit about border dumps."

He scans my tattoo and peers into the machine's small monitor for the readout.

"Mariana Girardi." He pronounces the name properly, then starts laughing. "Well shit, girl, you *are* a citizen." He looks up, "We'll leave you here then. No damage done."

I swallow back the hysteria that rises to his words.

When I finally find my voice I say, "I'll report you. I've got your first names and faces, and I memorized the plate number on the van."

"You could report us, but you won't," he answers. "Funny thing about inks, you don't trust cops or authority figures even when you're on the right side of the law."

"Want to bet? I'm carrying evidence of rape and the attacker's DNA around in me. All I need to do is find my way to a hospital, or even a phone, and your friend here will be wearing cuffs."

He looks over me, to where Ted stands, and narrows his eyes. He seems angry, but when he speaks again his voice is even and expressionless.

"That's unfortunate. On the other hand, this is a very isolated section of the country's largest national park. It's going to take you a long time to stumble back onto civilization."

"Then why bother dumping the others across the border? Leave them here with me. We'll probably die anyway. Make you happy."

His eyes crinkle as from mirth. It makes him look even more handsome. "Oh, I don't need you to die."

"Well then?"

"Your tat is legit, theirs aren't. That's what you inks never get. The legitimacy makes a difference to me."

"Go swap the plates on the van," his voice is harsh as he addresses Ted. I feel the man beside me hesitate, then trundle away. When he does, Carl turns back to me, "I don't have to prove anything to you, but I will."

When he motions, Jan drags the children to him.

"We didn't find GPS trackers when we cut their necks," he says. "If you really work in pop control you know what that means." He flashes the scanner at each child's wrist in turn. None brings up a valid Hipco record.

"Not even anchor-babies," he says as he pushes them away. "Just border jumpers."

I feel a moment of relief when it's Nely who's led up to be scanned, but when Carl motions for me to look at the scanner's read-out, it, too, is gibberish. The tattoo's a fake. I never knew. I hadn't ever thought to scan her myself.

And if I had? Would I have turned her in?

"You can't trust," Carl says, but his voice isn't as hard as it has been. More like he's trying share his wisdom with an especially dense colleague. "You may be an ink who plays it straight but, the sad fact is, the majority don't."

He turns to Steve. "Get them in the back of the van and pack the rest of the stuff. We've got to get out of here pretty quick to get them through where I've mapped to cross."

I understand as soon as he says it where he's thinking of heading.

"You can't dump them in a wilderness area. They won't survive. If you need me to beg, I'll beg."

I drop to my knees heedless of what the percussive jolt wakes in my shoulder. "I'm not saying don't dump them, but do it near an attended border crossing. Somewhere they'll get medical attention."

The look he gives me has a trace of sympathy in it. "Go home, ink. Someone cares that you're gone, your tat's been flagged."

He pauses before climbing in the driver side of the pickup. Jan's already in the passenger side, boot up against the dash. "This park is pocked with old corduroy roads," he says. "Maybe, if you try real hard, you'll find one."

I'm still on my knees when the pickup and van disappear from sight.

Sunlight filters through the woods in patches. The early dusting of snow has melted off, leaving glittering droplets of moisture hidden like jewels among the evergreen needles.

At first I believe I'm surrounded by a great silence, but the longer I listen, the more I hear. Wood creaking as sunlight warms it. A cone tumbling from the heights to land on the needle-softened floor. The rhythmic thunking of a woodpecker, five rapid taps then a pause, and over again.

Everything – noise or silence, breath or pulse, love or loss – has a pattern. You can try to alter it but, in the end, the pattern wins through. This is mine: through no merit of my own I luck through terrible and into survival. Most of the people I love do not.

Not mother. Not best friend. Not the children who trusted me to get them out of our situation. Most likely not my half-brother left behind in Guatemala.

It is a bitter fairy tale. No colorín colorado, no happily ever after.

So, with my knees pierced by needles and my shoulder sewn together by the slender thread of endorphins, I keep to my genuflection and end my story the only way that really fits. As a prayer that seals surrender.

World without end.

Amen.

## 4.

*Nothing is as it should be.*

*I was supposed to be woken from my slumber through ceremony: a grandmother or mother pouring song in the child's ear. The strains would have reached down through muscle and bone to that place so hidden no science can track it.*

*Where I was waiting, like all of my kind, just one breath from waking.*

*Had it been as it should, Mari would have known my company on the edge of every moment and of every memory.*

*But I slumbered undisturbed, and around me her being settled dense and stratified with the accretion of years.*

*Still, there is ceremony resident in the act of love, and a kind of song that streams in with it. I heard it. I stirred. And woke to the hard work of surfacing in an adult rather than infant.*

*I learned the ways of increment. So she would come to know me as a companion, not a possessor. So she would understand I'm a part of the whole, not a break from it.*

*But when instead of love the sounds that filtered down to me became those of fear and pain, I faced a dread choice: to jump free of Mari's body and shift the fight onto the layer of world where I can protect her, or not.*

*I could have shredded her aggressors. Especially the last one. After I was done with him, he wouldn't have inhabited their common layer of world in the same way. Not all that hobbles the body comes from a physical source, and in my fury I would have left him little more than a skin envelope around a dead zone.*

*But instead, I chose to wrap myself around the little grain of heart Mari has been harboring. With claw and tooth I made sure it would not be dislodged. Love must triumph over violence or there is no reason for my kind.*

*Or Mari's.*

*So I emerge, twinned, but late.*

*I step fully outside of her in that northern woodland, under trees welling with resin and stars rushing to their winter habitats, She's curled tight on the forest floor, knotted with hurt and despair. She will not move. Not for the child she carries, not for herself.*

*But I am not so easily dismissed.*

*I nip and prod. I drive her safely through the forest and, days later, when we win through to where her kind gather, I harry her until she seeks out the ear that should hear her story.*

*I am her protection, and these things I do from nature, and in service.*

*Still, during the recounting we are caught by the sickness that isn't sickness but simply a sign of life growing and, because of that, instead of justice we find a cage.*

*I will not see her suffer again, I vow as we're locked behind walls.*

# Mari: Once upon a time

*But even I am sometimes wrong.*

*Time passes unmarked, except for Mari's growing belly.*

*When they take the baby from her, I have to hold her heart in my teeth so it doesn't go to pieces.*

*When they move us to yet another enclosure, another place to lose track of time, I jump and soar so she won't forget what joy feels like. Remember, I tell her. A child. A love. A life. A hope.*

*But she believes the walls more than she believes me, and keeps to her silence.*

*So I do it.*

*Even though she is the storyteller, I am the one who moves her lips in the telling.*

# Del: Words written on wind

## 1

We talk about loss while we're laying carpet. Ray, the owner of the business and my father's friend for years, speaks about his son who died in the Persian Gulf War and about my dad; the way he went and the emptiness we've both felt since.

Ray is in his 70s but he still manages to take the lead in the carpeting process, though he doesn't carry the rolls anymore.

"That's what the temporary help is for, Boss," Chato says to me. Every so often Chato calls me Del, but mostly Boss, though I'm not.

Chato and I are foremen of the carpeting crews, but it's clear to both of us that Ray prefers to give me the important jobs. Chato believes this is as it should be, that as Ray's best friend's son, I am entitled to the preferential treatment. Inks believe in obligation to family, and to friends who might as well be family.

Truth is, Chato is a better crew manager. By all rights he should be Ray's right-hand guy. But Chato's Mexican and, despite the green tattoo, Ray doesn't count on permanent residence from any ink.

When the tattoos were first instituted, the black tats – temporaries – rotated in six months at a time but now, a couple of years in, we face an entirely different crew every three months. We don't even bother to learn their real names, we mostly call them by the name of their country of origin. Since Chato likes to hire as many Mexicans as possible – and they all can't be called Mexico – we call them by Mexican regional names. Right now, we're on our third Puebla and second Michoacán – both on Chato's crew, along with Liberia and Haiti; Honduras, the third Jalisco, and Salvador are all working on Ray's crew, and I've only got Oaxaca – the fifth worker we've called that – on mine because the residential job we're working is relatively quick business.

I don't know how much English Oaxaca knows, but most of the time he nods in time to my conversation as we lay carpet. It isn't until I tell him one of my father's stories, though, that he breaks his silence.

It happened during the Great Depression. My father was young, and though my grandparents didn't have much, they were farmers and perhaps a little less affected than city dwellers. That's the thing about farming – it's hardscrabble in good times as in bad.

One day my father walked into the barn where the tractor was parked and found two strangers sleeping in the heifers' hay. They were shabby and unshaven, and my father said he had never before, or since, smelled anything as bad as the body odor emanating from the two of them. Around their sleeping

42

bodies were the scattered remains of a meal: chicken bones, apple cores, the feathery greens of carrots pulled clean from the ground.

As my father stood there, wondering whether to go get his BB gun, one of the strangers stirred into wakefulness. When he saw my father he poked the other one.

"Your family let us stay the night," one of them said, quick, as if he was scared my father wouldn't believe him. "And fed us."

"Are you hoboes?" my father had finally asked.

"No, just looking for a way to make enough to feed our families back home."

It's here that Oaxaca interrupts the story.

"Like me," he says. "And Chema and Rogelio."

"Who?" I say.

"Salvador and Jalisco. We also slept in a barn here until we got our tattoos."

Except there's no official tattooing station in Smithville.

I suddenly understand that there is a good possibility that all Chato's recruits have a falsely black tattoo. And that leaves me, good-as-a-son to Ray, with an awkward choice to make.

***

The snow's deep enough when I get to the top of the field that I consider donning snowshoes. I pull on a pair of pac boots I keep in the truck instead, and by the time I'm on the path I'm glad of my choice because the snow tapers and is only deep enough to tickle the roots of the old oak that somehow seeded itself in a multitude of hemlocks.

When I knock the snow off my boots on the porch, the cabin door flies open. Light from the propane fixtures pours out of the door along with the smell of venison stew.

"Oh, it's only you," Cassie says.

"Whoa. Should I be worried by that greeting?"

"You've forgotten," she says. "Haven't you?"

She's right, I have forgotten whatever *it* is.

"You invited someone over for dinner," I cast about hopefully.

She makes a face at me, then walks to kitchen to stir the stew. It's an open floor plan so it's not like she's putting a room between us. Still, it reads like dismissal. She's irritated more than angry, though, and that's good, or I'd be sleeping in one of the guest rooms.

The sleeping arrangements make it click.

"When are the houseguests scheduled to arrive?"

She snickers. "You are so lucky, buster." Then, "They were supposed to be here already."

"If they don't hurry," I say, "they'll lose the light and it'll be a bitch driving down." After a moment, I add, "I hope they rented a car with four-wheel drive."

"Sarai's in charge of transportation so they'll probably arrive by pontoon. Or maybe Venetian gondola," Cassie says with affectionate irritation.

I help her set the table because that's what husbands do when they're trying to ingratiate themselves. Midway through the napkin rings and linen, she remembers the wine. Which I forgot. So I bundle back up, and walk to the truck.

The night is going to settle clear and cold even though it's misty now and still a couple hours from twilight. The snowy trees on the far hill are barely visible in the vaporous light that halos them. White on white on white. It's an afternoon out of a storybook and, as if on cue, I hear a chorus of coy-dogs start howling across the creek.

The last thing I want to do is go back into town although it's only fifteen minutes away. Moments like this are why I moved onto this property. All I really want to do now is wander about the woods, in this strange light, and hope for a glimpse of the spirit-creatures my maternal grandmother swore hid in the gorges when she and my grandfather lived here. I never could figure out if the beings she described in such vivid detail to me were born of Seminole or African or French tales – she claimed all three bloodlines – or from her unique imagination, but I don't disbelieve their coexistence with us.

The prospect of a weekend full of houseguests and no alcohol, however, doesn't thrill me. The trip to town is quick. Walking back from the liquor store, I look into the window of the pizzeria where the college kids from the next town usually hang out after a night of drinking. It's early yet, so the place is empty except for the corner booths where the whole ink crew sits wolfing down slices. I wave to them as I pass, then I double back and go inside.

It's unusual to see them eating out. The quarters Ray provides for his temporary workers are spare but include a fully functional communal kitchen. From what I hear, Puebla can really cook.

The booths around the guys are empty, so I slide in a bench behind them. "Night out on the town?" I ask.

"Rogelio found out his wife gave birth today. He's got a new baby boy back home," Chato says.

"Congratulations, man!" I slap Honduras on the back, and when they all start laughing, realize my mistake and do the same to Jalisco.

This double name crap is the pits.

"You guys going out to have a drink after dinner?" I ask, motioning across the street to the bar. "That news is worth at least one beer."

They look uncomfortable. Finally Chato says, "Well, Boss ... they don't really like us to go in there and drink."

"They serve you, don't they?"

"Yeah," Chato says, "But as soon as we're done with the glass they smash it on the floor so no one has to drink from the same one."

"You'd think they'd use paper cups, then. Less expensive," I say, a little stunned. I'll have to ask my friend Kurt who bartends there if he does it too. And thump him if he does.

Chato grins. "Paper doesn't sound nearly as good when it breaks."

The others all look embarrassed that Chato's told me, and I scramble for anything to shift the mood. "Plans for the weekend?"

They get really animated. Seems Chato's taking them to a hockey game, and though none of them knows a thing about hockey, he's told them it's a bit like soccer on ice. I wonder if he's also told them that the noise of skates cutting ice, bodies slamming into glass and pucks winging off hard surfaces takes some getting used to.

"Except Oaxaca isn't going," Salvador (Chema) says, rubbing his thumb against his index and middle fingers to indicate money.

A couple of the inks give him the kill sign, but I pretend not to see and reach for my wallet.

"No, Boss," Oaxaca says. "I don't want to go. Honest."

"Tell you what," I say when I realize insistence would further strip his pride, "why don't you come up to the cabin for dinner tomorrow instead? My brother-in-law will be up for the weekend so my wife'll cook enough for a giant. Which he is, by the way."

He smiles, but I'm not entirely surprised when he declines. Inks seem to be keenly aware of class and social status. Even though I'm no higher in the carpeting hierarchy than Chato, the fact I have no tattoo and claim friendship with Ray makes all the difference. They'll be unfailingly amiable, but they won't socialize with me.

When I get home with the wine, our guests are still M.I.A. I go to the easel that's set up near the cabin's large south window and fiddle with paint tubes while I stare outside. The light is still extraordinary. It plays on the surface of the snow, muting the glitter of icy particles to the softer sheen of talc. There's also a pattern on the surface.

I rummage in a pack basket for binoculars and return to the window.

"Tracks out there," I say.

"What kind?" Cassie asks.

"Human."

I hear her chair scrape against the floor, and feel her come to stand at my shoulder. I hand her the binoculars. She looks for a while, then passes them back.

"Fucked up," I say. "People trespassing."

She laughs and kisses me on the forehead. "It's just land. Don't be so possessive."

As she walks back to the table I turn to my canvas.

It's an odd landscape I've been painting. In the upper right quadrant are a couple of black morel mushrooms – depicted as realistically as I'm able – but the bulk of the painting focuses on the mass of interwoven hollow threads that feed the mushrooms underground.

I lose track of everything when I start mixing pigments. It always happens this way. The color is like a portal to the rest of the painting, and once I've stepped through, I won't emerge again until I hear an inarticulate call, the *now, step back, look at what you've done* of the paint itself.

This time I step away just as the sound of a vehicle chugging through snow fills the cabin. I drape a cover over the wet paint I've mixed, wipe my brush and set it down with a pang. Like the land, painting is one of the reasons I live where I do. Art feeds off this particular solitude and quiet, which is really neither since it teems with energy and the clamor of millions of unseen lives. It always takes me a while to adjust back to the simpler and louder ways of human interaction.

As Cassie and I step out on the porch, I can see Sarai hanging half out the car window, squealing, and waving at us while Finn tries navigating the hulking car around a sizable but partially snow-obscured woodpile. As soon as the SUV slides into the spot we've left clear for it, I head out to help unload the car.

I shake hands with Finn as soon as he comes around to the cargo door. The big guy doesn't look out of place here and at least he's dressed for the weather, which is more than I can say for the terminally hip but already shivering Sarai. Allison climbs out of the back seat a moment later and nods in my direction. She and Sarai haven't been a couple for very long so I hardly know her, but she makes me feel scruffy in the way Finn makes me feel short. I'm neither really, except by comparison.

"Nice place," she says. "Cassie says you built it?"

"I added rooms onto the cabin my maternal grandparents lived in," I answer, grunting while I try to hoist a large cooler out of the car. "What did you guys pack in this thing, stones?"

"I'm paying for our weekend with bourbon," Sarai pipes up from the porch.

"God help us," I mumble.

Finn hears me. "Yeah, you'd think at least she'd have the decency to make it Jamesons."

He smiles at me but his eyes stay sad. As they've been for the past six months, ever since a woman none of us had met disappeared from his life.

He's the reason for the invite that's mucking up all my favorite weekend routines but, suddenly, I don't have the heart to hold it against him.

\*\*\*

I'm at the easel while the others linger over dinner. Between the daylong slow cooking of the stew and the woodstove cranking out BTUs, we're all basking in warmth and even have one of the windows cracked open.

"Ah," Finn stretches his long legs, pushing his chair away from the table. "Why do any of us choose to live in Hastings when this is just three hours away?"

"Bekamian's Pastry Shop," Allison says.

"The oyster bar at Genessee Station." Sarai.

"East Street Market's cheesecake. I actually have dreams about it still." Cassie says.

Finn raises an eyebrow, "Do women always think with their stomachs?"

"And what organ is it, exactly, that men think with?" counters Sarai.

Finn points at his heart, which makes Sarai and Cassie razz him in concert. "Help me out here, Del, I don't think they believe me."

"You're on your own, man," I say, waving a brush at him. "My favorite organ's the eye."

He laughs. "Now that's just fucked up."

"Speaking of fucked up," Cassie says, "Mom sent me a beautiful little christening gown last week. Antique, I think. No note, no explanation."

"Grandkids," Finn says. "She wants them. Tick tock."

Cassie smacks him. "Hey, we're doing our best. Hurry up and get married and give her some yourself."

I confess as an only child I don't really understand the thrust and parry of sibling interaction but I wince at her comment.

Finn reaches for the open bottle of Maker's Mark then thinks better about it. "I'm going out for a walk."

The cabin's quiet after he leaves.

"O-o-o-kay, then," Allison says. "I'm following him out. As far as the porch, anyway. I'll give him a smoke trail to follow back to the cabin."

"Well, shit," Cassie says after Allison's left. "He can't still be harboring any thought that Mari's going to return, can he? It's so unrealistic."

"I think it's sort of romantic, actually," Sarai says.

"Because it's impossible, you mean? For all he knows she's dead. Or with somebody else."

"I think maybe he just knows, somehow, she's not," I say.

Cassie rolls her eyes.

Sarai gets up and stretches. "I can't imagine having someone I love disappear practically out of my arms."

"Yeah, like you haven't ditched any of your lovers," Cassie says.

"Finn didn't ditch her," Sarai says. She walks over to the iPod dock, scrolls through the menu of songs. "It's different."

"Not if it ends the same way."

Sarai turns to her. "Cynical, much?"

Cassie laughs. "Am not. It's just that I know my brother, and I'm telling you, he's feeling endebted to memory. And that's no way to live."

As soon as Allison comes back in and the smell of cigarette wafts in with her, my own craving for a hit of nicotine kicks in. I head outside. But I don't stop to smoke on the porch. I cross behind the cabin, down to where the stream has nearly iced over. Up the steep bank roughly parallel to the cabin's south window I start scanning the ground looking for the tracks I spotted earlier.

Moonlight pools in the glade as I squat down to them. I put one hand on the footprint, digging into it until my fingers hit ground, and close my eyes.

It is a slide I take, down to the chambers of my heart. I can count the seeds slumbering in this piece of land, and the fiddleheads curled under snow waiting for a distant wake-up call. My blood can course along the sappy viaducts of birch and oak, the resinous gullies of hemlocks. And deeper still, I can hear the molten buzz of a mantle perpetually in motion.

And the footstep? The land lets me know where its owner headed from here, and how long ago.

It is my secret, this dialogue with my land. It started when I was ten. Until then, land had been land; any patch of it fulfilled my temporary desires: a place to play ball, run around with my dog, dig for nightcrawlers. But the summer after my mother died it all changed.

I camped out at the cabin with my father for weeks, his way of avoiding the need to go through her things and admit she had truly died. He sat inside, I wandered. I turned my dungarees clay-brown from scrambling up the gorge walls to reach cave openings that looked like sad, downturned eyes. My father's eyes.

But up close, the caves were more sinister, like open mouths.

I elected to explore the largest which narrowed quickly to a tunnel. On my belly in the dark, I pulled myself forward on scabby elbows. The journey ended with sharp rock protrusions – I always picture them as the incisors of a colossal carnivore – clamping down around my shoulders. I couldn't go forward, I couldn't go back.

For the first ten minutes I was okay. Then, I began to hear things. The scratch of claw on stone. Skittery movement. Something inhuman vocalizing in human tones. I thought I felt the touch of something and my ankles prickled as if tiny sharp teeth were grazing them in advance of clamping on.

I'd dislocated a shoulder to get out, my father told me later, but I don't remember that. Only the shocking Prussian-blue sky I emerged to, and the phthalo-green sea of clubmosses that were there to cradle my body. That's the day I started to believe my grandmother's stories. And picked up a paintbrush.

A strong north wind kicks up, swirling snow up to my knees as I make my way back to the cabin. Cassie stands by the door, arms wrapped around her body.

"You've been gone forever. You okay?"

"Of course," I say. "Don't waste worry on me, Finn's the one who doesn't know his way around this joint."

"He's been back for a while. I don't think he went very far. Just far enough to get past his desire to beat the crap out of me."

We stand for a while together outside until I can't hug away her shivers. Inside, the great room of the cabin is empty and quiet.

"Everyone's gone to bed, thank God," Cassie says. "I'm beat."

"I'll be up in a while," I tell her after kissing her.

I move the dock near the easel, set the music to shuffle, then loosen my

48

shoulders. I start with fresh colors, mixing powdered pigments with oil on the old enamel palette. When I'm happy with the color – always the most time-consuming part of my process – I pick out a broad, flat brush and slash across the painting's surface, covering it with long strokes of thin, oily paint. After a moment I put the brush aside and work the surface to translucence with my fingers. Then I switch to a thin brush, with three or four squirrel hairs, and move in to add detail.

Los Lobos are playing when I step back from the work, pausing to dig a cigarette from a smushed and tatty pack.

"Cassie's going to kill you when she smells that inside," Finn says as I light up. He gestures to the Morris chair. "Do you mind?"

I shake my head as I watch him try to fit himself comfortably in it, which might be impossible.

"Painting always makes me want to smoke," I say. "Like somehow whatever I'm tapping into needs fire to focus it."

"Vices. Can't live with them, can't live without them. Want some of mine?" Finn waves a half-empty bottle of bourbon. When I shake my head again, he adds, "Good, because I don't want to have to get up again to get you a glass."

I grin as I move around the easel. We maintain a friendly silence until I wipe my brushes with a filthy mop-up cloth, upend them in an empty jar, and go sit on the floor by the woodstove.

"You okay?" I ask.

Finn tips his head to rest on the back of the chair, closes his eyes. "Does pissed off at my sibling, my mom, my life count as okay?"

"Sometimes I think that's the definition of okay in your family."

He laughs. "You're part of my family."

"Yeah, I'm doing okay too."

He grins at me, but soon enough his face reverts to its new melancholy set.

"I'm just going through the motions. I haven't written a single story worth spit since... well, since. And words were always what moored me. Now, I'm flotsam."

"Hey, as long as you're floating you're one up on most folks."

"Ha."

"So, I know why you're pissed off at Cassie, and your life, but why your mom?"

"She's more or less okay that Mari's gone. Penelope and Odysseus is what she calls us. Epic is how she describes what's happened. Two people kept apart by the vicissitudes of gods and tides and political machination. As if it were a heroic journey."

"So maybe it is."

"Yeah. Except I'm Penelope in this recasting. Holding on to what I can't touch or see, only remember."

"Thing is, sometimes I don't want Mari to come back. I'm terrified of her story. I'm terrified of all the inks' stories. Which is why I can't write about them anymore. Just mall openings. And new fees for trash pickup. And plans for highway bypasses." He falls silent for a moment. "And then I feel guilty for feeling that way, because nobody else is writing about them either." He looks at me, then away again.

I stare at the toes of my workboots. "You know, we're never going to get it anyway."

"What?"

"What it's like to have to wear the tat."

Finn fiddles with the cap of the bourbon bottle, but doesn't take another drink. "Hey, did you finish your painting?"

"No. I'm stalled."

"Can I take a look?"

"I guess."

He looks at the whole composition first, then ducks down to look at the mycelium more closely. "Freaky," he says, straightening back up. "All those little beings tied to each other."

He makes me look at my work again. He's right. Somehow, the interwoven web beneath the mushrooms has gone from fungal to human without my noticing.

***

When I wake up and make it out to the great room, Cassie is seated alone at the table, sorting through bills.

"Where is everyone?" I ask after I get my coffee.

"Out snowshoeing," she says. She pushes the stack of bills away. "I need to talk to you anyway."

I get a second, maybe two, before she plunges. And, it's not like I don't know what's coming. Even with her job at the library, we're hardly making ends meet. That's the price of living where pay and pittance are synonymous.

"This is no way to live," she says.

"I love our life," I answer.

As I say it, I see the very nature of who my wife is reflected in the intelligent and beautiful face in front of me. There's something missing from her face, I don't know what to name it, imagination perhaps. Or daring. But I think it's a quality that skipped her to reside more fully in her brother.

"Look," she reaches for my hand, which telegraphs that the worst part of this conversation is about to come out of her mouth. "If we move to Hastings and sell this place we'll have enough to travel, to put money away and feel the kind of security we can't even imagine right now."

"I don't know who I'd become without this place," I say.

"So, okay, maybe we wouldn't have to get rid of it. We could come up here for vacations. But we'd be making enough money in Hastings to actually take some."

"There is no guarantee I'd get anything better paying in the city."

"I would," she says. "Allison's made me an offer already. The law firm is looking for good researchers. Librarians are at the top of their list."

I extricate my hand from hers, push my chair away from the table. "So you're not really asking, are you?"

I'm already by the door, half into my coat, when she sets her trump card.

"I'm pregnant."

It should be a happy moment. For a second I want to turn around and take her in my arms. Instead, I slam the door on my way out.

*** 

I stumble upon a new set of footprints.

They aren't pac boot prints but something with a heel, like a cowboy boot, and lead through a cluster of hemlocks to a stately yellow birch I tried my hand at painting last spring. Its luminous bronze and shreddy bark proved impossible for me to capture in pigment.

Someone's nailed boards into it, making a rudimentary ladder up its trunk. I look up. There's a teenager sitting on a treestand wedged in the crotch of the first really big branches. He's got a rifle    a .22 it looks like from down here – cradled in his arms.

"Hey," I call to him. "What're you doing?"

"Saw a nice buck over there," He motions northwest. "Eight-pointer, I think."

"You're not going to get anything bigger than a woodchuck with that gun," I say.

He shrugs. "My dad gave it to me."

"Did your dad also tell you to come up here to hunt?"

"Owner of the property did," he says.

"Well, that's interesting since I'm the owner and I don't know who the hell you are."

He scrambles to gather his stuff into a camouflage backpack before he climbs down. On the ground, he turns to face me. Some courage at least.

"What's your name?" I ask, hoping he's the son of someone I know who might have assumed I'd be okay with this.

But he's not. It's not a surname I recognize at all.

"Did you nail those up?" I nod at the footholds and the stand.

"Yeah."

"Didn't think twice about what you were damaging, huh?"

"It's just a tree. People do it all the time."

"Not here. So, now listen, if you walk through the woods there," I point past a grouping of aspens, "in less than a quarter mile you'll hit the tractor road. It shouldn't take you more than fifteen minutes to get off my property. In about half an hour I'm going to drive down that tractor road and if you're still here it isn't a puny .22 I'm going be pointing at you. Got it?"

He nods.

"You know," I say as he slings the pack over his shoulder, "the posted signs have my phone number on them. You could have called and asked for permission."

"Nobody ever gives permission," he says.

I watch him tromping through the snow to disappear into the trees. He's right. Even if he had called I wouldn't have okayed it, because I don't know him or his family and friends, and because I don't trust what I don't know.

I'm not sure what's guiding me as I resume my walk away from Cassie and toward the heart of my property, but I allow myself to be led without making any conscious choices.

Whatever it is takes me to the enormous boulder that stands as solitary evidence of a glacier that moved through here ages ago to find its terminal moraine somewhere south of Hastings. I sit at its snowy base, leaning back against the flattest of its stone faces and try to imagine the journey of this erratic – that's what boulders like this are called – dragged so many miles from its bedrock origin. It must be the loneliest inanimate object around.

I pat it. Me in Hastings. And then I'm crying, stupidly bawling like a kid. Like when I found out my mom was dead.

Of course I'll leave. She's asking me to pick between loves, and who would pick any but the human one? I'll pack up and go with her and live the kind of life she envisions us living. I'll just have to learn to do it without this. My heart.

# Del: Words written on wind

Working as a jobber contractor in the city is as different from working for Ray as living in a 700-square-foot apartment is from living in a cabin on 200 acres. Nobody knows me here so I have to prove myself over and over again.

Cassie is happy, as she knew she would be. She hangs with Allison and Sarai. And Finn, whenever he's around. And she's made a bunch of new friends at the law firm. She hardly notices that we don't do much together anymore. At least nothing other than what falls at the intersection of our routines. She fills her spare hours following leads on a larger apartment for when the baby comes.

"There's time," I say, but she wants to cement things.

Cement. That's mostly what the city is and, predictably enough, I don't understand it. There is one little park I like to go to, though. No yellow birches or hemlocks here but a rangy white oak that reminds me of the one by the cabin. Every day after work I go and sit there for an hour before going home.

I'm there when I get the call.

When I dig out my cell phone and answer, it's a voice I don't recognize.

"Hello. Del? This is Father Tom," the man says. "A friend of Finn's. He suggested I call you. I was wondering if I can borrow your truck?"

"Look, Father Tim," I start.

"Tom."

"Right. Well, I'm sure you're a great guy and all, but I'm not in the habit of letting total strangers drive my truck."

"Oh, I can't drive," he says.

I laugh. "Moreso then."

"What I need is to borrow your truck and you."

"Do you need some furniture moved or something?"

"Yes, something like that. Tomorrow if possible."

"Well, I guess if you're Finn's friend it's all right," I say. "After work, around five-thirty sound okay?"

"Yes, yes, that's great." He rattles off the address of the church where he needs to be picked up, then pauses, "Finn says you have a firearm ... perhaps you'd be kind enough to bring it with you?"

In the time it takes me to recover from my surprise, he's hung up.

My father gave me a 20-gauge shotgun for my first hunt, when I was 15, and I never wanted to trade up to the 12-gauge most Smithville hunters favor. It's no automatic rifle, but it's not a small weapon either. I'm betting the priest imagines I own something more discreet.

When I pull up in front of the church the next day, Finn's standing there, waiting for me. He leans in as soon as I roll down the window.

"Park it and come inside," he says. "I'll explain."

"Explain it here and now. I've got the shotgun behind the seat and I'm not leaving it in a parked car."

He looks around. "We're going to retrieve an ink that made her way to

Bedford after being border dumped."

"Your girl?" I ask.

He shakes his head.

"Why doesn't the ink just stay put?"

"Bedford's a 'safe community.' A nice but nervous Methodist minister found her at an interstate stop on the way back from some sort of ecumenical gathering where Father Tom was the speaker. Anyway, she took the ink home with her, but wants us to get her out of there before she gets caught. Bedford's got some pretty punitive measures in place for renting to inks. And the difference between renting and sheltering is awfully vague in their book. To complicate things, there are a number of blockades on the main access routes. Voluntary civic patrols, which means no one's got any training but they've all got firearms."

"Hence, the shotgun request."

"Yeah."

"But I'm not shooting anybody, Finn. Got it?"

"Of course not," he waves the suggestion away. "If Meche does her job, you won't have to do anything but sail straight through. It's just, well you know, I want to be sure you can at least threaten your way out of any ugliness."

"That her?" I ask, glancing at the door of the rectory from which an old priest and a blond woman have just emerged.

"Yeah," he turns his head to glance at her. "Cuban. A former chemist. Well, I guess she's still a chemist, just no longer employed by the pharmaceutical company that holds her patents," He turns back to meet my eyes. "On her own she's developed this absolutely dead-on synthetic skin. All you need is a small jar of the compound, one of the powdered catalyst, and water to activate it. Sets up quickly. Can be dyed to match different skin tones, so it's perfect to cover tattoos. And it's undetectable. For a few weeks at least, until it starts degrading. Some of the Cuban inks have been paying through the nose to get it at her peña. As long as you have money and don't have an accent it's the way to go."

"We're not all going to fit in the truck."

"Just you and Meche."

"So you're using me for my shotgun and truck, is that how it is?"

"It's so not like that."

"It's okay," I say, amused by his earnest tone.

"But," I add, "you better explain to Cassie, because she's expecting me home in an hour."

He nods as the others join us. After a round of introductions, and some discussion about a number of possible routes in and out of Bedford, Meche tucks a large handbag behind the seat, and climbs in the cab of the truck. We're 20 minutes into the journey, turning onto the Breen Parkway, when I get tired of the silence.

"So, what's your story?" I say. "Beside the chemist end of things."

She smiles a little. "My grandparents came over when Castro made his triumphal entry into Havana, bringing with them family and a tidy sum of money. My parents turned tidy to tremendous. I'm turning tremendous to my advantage. I own the Cuban peña – *all* of it. Not a single enterprise there belongs to the gangs. My tattoo is blue, without a language exemption, and I've developed three variants of instaskin; we'll be testing the field version of the latest one on this run."

"Finn said inks pay a lot for the instaskin they get at your peña."

"I'm not adverse to a little luxury," she says. "You ever wonder why all the other peñas have been busted but not the Cuban one?"

"Better patron saint?" I joke. When she looks startled, I add, "Finn told me they're all named and identified with those."

"Well, La Caridad is a top-tier patroness, but no," she answers. "It's because the peña's at my house, and nobody can prove it is a peña as opposed to a series of parties full of people who don't look or sound like what you all think of as inks."

"A gated peña."

She nods. "If you can't pass, you won't pass."

"Morally dubious."

She laughs. "I prefer morally ambiguous, thanks. And still, here I am, on the other side of the gate. Giving away the product my clients pay for. What about you, nothing morally ambiguous about your life?"

"Not at the moment."

"Lucky," she says, then closes her eyes, and leans her head back against the headrest.

I wake her fifteen minutes before we get to Bedford.

"Roadblock ahead."

She shakes off sleep immediately.

"Don't call me Meche in mixed company. My driver's license says Mercedes O'Gorman, which is old-fashioned but still acceptable as an Anglo name."

"So who came up with that doozy?"

"It's my real name."

"Oh."

"It's okay. I like Meche better, too."

She pulls down the visor and smoothes her hair in the mirror. When she's done she turns again to me. "Do I pass?" she says.

"Of course you pass. Aren't you a real blond?"

She's still laughing when we come to a stop at the pylons. A man in a Bedford Lions cap motions for us to roll down the windows. He comes over to the driver side. At the same time the woman standing beside him heads for the passenger side.

"Wrists," the man says. He's got the butt of a .35 Remington handgun sticking out of the waistband of his pants.

55

I turn the truck off and have an instant when I want to refuse, because this little snot has no real authority, other than the one earned by his vigilante bent, to make me do anything. And because I know if I did refuse, there wouldn't be any real repercussions.

For me.

But there probably would be for the woman at my side, so as soon as the car is in park, I shove both wrists out the window. The guy grabs one, then pulls out a scanner gun and flashes it at my blank wrists. They say the scanners can read tattoos even through make up and greasepaint, and I feel my stomach go jumpy at the thought it might be able to read through the instaskin covering Meche's tattoo right now.

"I need the gun," I hear the woman on Meche's side call. For a moment I don't know which of the two she's referring to.

The man walks around the front of the truck and hands her the scanner.

Meche is absolutely still as the woman scans both her blank wrists.

"Get out," the man says.

When I see Meche reach for her handbag I remember the gun.

"I've got a shotgun behind the seat, slugs and shells in the glove box," I say.

"And why's that?" The guy moves fast to my side again, and reaches behind the seat for the stock after I get out.

"I'm going up to my cabin in Smithville," I say. Loud enough for Meche to hear, I hope. "I might do some hunting while I'm there."

"Roundabout way to go up there," he says. "I would have taken 17 instead. And it's not hunting season."

"It's always hunting season if you own property."

The guy laughs, as I thought he might. Plenty of folks in Smithville say the same – everyone upstate is pretty much Libertarian when it comes to hunting rights.

"I just wanted to show my girlfriend some great places on the way," I look over at Meche while I extemporize. "She's a Hastings girl, and you know how narrow-minded they can be about upstate."

I see the woman rooting through Meche's handbag. She opens the wallet, aspirin bottle, a lipstick. When she pulls out a couple of small screw-top jars I see Meche's shoulders tense.

*Hold it together, kid,* I think at her. *Just come up with a story.*

The man beside me is going on about how much he hates the city and how the city folks he's known don't know their asses from their elbows. All of which I've heard before. Only in Smithville we consider Bedforders city folk and include them in our disdain. I nod where appropriate but keep watching the women.

Meche says something I can't hear, then dips her finger in the powder of one of the open jars and strokes it onto the woman's eyelids. The woman barely glances at the hand mirror Meche holds up to her, but she gives Meche her bag back moments later. Then she ducks into the truck to retrieve my registration and insurance cards.

"So, where is it you and your boyfriend are going?" the woman asks.

"Smithville. He's got a place there."

The woman shuffles to the registration. "What's his address in Hastings?"

*We're cooked,* I think. And the guy's still holding my shotgun.

But Meche recites it perfectly. When she turns to look at me and I lift my brows in question, she gives me a small smile.

"We're clear," the woman calls over.

The guy hands the shotgun back and I wave at him as I drive around the pylons.

"Oh my God," Meche says. "She's wearing about $500 worth of compound as eyeshadow."

"And very fetching it is," I say, grinning and buoyant now that we've gotten through. "That was brilliant. How did you know my address by the way?"

"Finn made me memorize his sister's address and phone number. In case something happened to you."

"He didn't give me yours."

She gives me an odd look. "That's because nobody's waiting for my return. If I died doing this it would all just end with me."

"Jesus. We're not really talking death, are we?"

"You think if the instaskin failed and we had to make a run for it that guy would have hesitated to shoot?"

"He's a self-important dick, but he wouldn't shoot us."

She's quiet for a moment. "Sometimes I wonder if people like you and I live in different universes."

"Ouch."

"Sorry. But you're doing this as a favor to Finn, and I'm doing it because if I don't I might as well be dead. Different planets at least."

I go silent until we get to Bedford proper.

The pastor ushers us into her kitchen, disappears and returns with a frail woman in her 70s she introduces as Nadia.

"How did she survive being dumped?" It's out of my mouth before my internal censor kicks in.

"They didn't drop me far in," Nadia answers, even though I've referred to her in third person. "A trucker hauling logs to a sawmill across the border saw me when I found my way to the road, and picked me up. He hid me under a pile of blankets to bring me back over. I guess the border folk see him so often they don't bother to check the cab. He dropped me at the rest stop where Judith found me."

Meche clears her throat. "I have to see the skin on your wrist to match it."

The old woman lays her wrist flat on the table. The green of her tattoo overlays a blue tattoo of veins visible through the skin.

Meche pulls out the two screw-top jars I've seen before, and what looks like a more traditional eyeshadow case, with plugs of pigment in a range of skin tones and a few jewel shades. The compound itself, when she pours some out on a white saucer, is a pearlescent powder with a pale shell-pink tint. She picks through the eyeshadow case, goes for a yellow and a toffee and uses tweezers to mix pigment grains with some compound partitioned on the plate. She smears a trace of the color she's created on Nadia's wrist. It's really off.

She reaches for the apricot. I stop her, then spin the case so the mauve is under her tweezer. "You're going to need it to cut all that yellow. Her skin's got an ashy undertone."

"I think this'll correct it," she contradicts.

Watching her mix the pigments – not the right hue at all – makes me crave a cigarette. I pat down my pockets, find a pack with two left.

"Okay if I smoke in here?" I ask the pastor. She nods, scoots a dirty saucer my way to use for an ashtray.

"No," Meche says. "I'm not letting any ash or particulate mix in and screw up the color."

"Any more than you've screwed it up already?" It earns me a scowl, and I put the grit back in its pack.

After another fifteen minutes of adding different shades from bronze to butterscotch, Meche finally unbends and adds the mauve I suggested. And even though she's mucked it up with all the other pigments, the color does its job and moves it closer to Nadia's skin tone.

"Two grains of the lightest blue, and half a grain of white should do it," I say after I study what's on the plate.

After they're added in, Meche pours the catalyst and a measure of water into the now-fully-pigmented compound. She mixes it gently, with a light, flexible palette knife. It bubbles up then turns thick and glossy.

"So keep completely still now," Meche says, grabbing the old woman's wrist firmly, palette knife poised just above it. "It may sting a little. Like an astringent you might use on your face. You tell me right away if it's any worse than that, okay?"

The old woman nods.

Meche may not be the most accomplished colorist but I'd put her impasto skills up there with the best. She spreads the paste evenly on the skin, then scrapes it down within a hair of translucence. But it's not translucent, it's opaque, and the tattoo's gone.

"Now we just have to wait for the skin to set up, so the texture's right," she says, pushing her hair behind her ears. "Should take about 20 minutes. You've got to just sit until then, Nadia. No jarring movements and don't touch anything, okay? After that we'll test it, and hopefully you can get dressed and we'll be on our way."

Meche gives me a look when she passes me on her way to the front door. I follow her out of the house.

# Del: Words written on wind

"You some kind of artist?" she asks, resting her forearms on the railing of the porch.

"A painter. Color's my thing."

She nods. "No wonder Finn insisted on bringing you in."

"So, is this going to work?"

"Well, old skin is very thin," she says. "It might look a little off. And pray she doesn't have an allergic reaction."

I light the delayed cigarette and lean on the railing next to her.

"Worse than bad for you," Meche says after a moment, waving away the smoke. "Terrible for you. I've never understood why people feel the need."

"It's relaxing. And you make me nervous."

"Wow. Honest."

"No reason for me to lie. I'm sure you already know you have that effect on men."

"It's artificial you know."

"What? It's all instaskin, and beneath it you're really ugly, stupid, and incompetent?"

She laughs. "It's just adrenaline you're feeling. The rush of being on an adventure with someone you think is a bit dicey and amoral. It'll wear off soon, and unless your adrenals are completely shot from the smoking, you'll be right back to normal."

"Good God, do you reduce everything to its chemical impulse?"

"Hazard of the vocation. More or less like people who can't keep their hands off other people's pigments."

"And here I thought I was going to get a thank-you for my effort."

She grins at me. "Yeah, me too."

The instaskin doesn't look as perfect on Nadia's wrist as it does on Meche's, but it passes muster at the roadblock we hit on our way out of town. It helps that it's late and that the patrol is shorthanded. We don't even have to get out of the truck. Nadia falls asleep resting her head on Meche's shoulder. The Cuban woman looks down at her every so often, and each time she does, her face goes soft.

When we get to Holy Innocents, I pull the truck up behind the church. The rectory is dark, but as soon as I knock, Father Tom opens the door and ushers us in. He points Meche and me to the kitchen, where he has a freshly brewed pot of coffee, then shows Nadia to the room he's set aside for her until one of her daughters can come to get her.

"What a trip," Meche says between sips of her coffee. She's standing against the counter, cup held between both hands.

"I'm disappointed it was so much more exciting on the way in than the way out," I say, dropping into one of the chairs facing her.

"I'm not. Most people try to avoid chasing disaster, you know."

"Says the woman who runs a completely illegal peña."

"Yeah, but everything there is under my control."

59

"Until it isn't. Anyway, we did good. Nadia seems happy to be back."

"She's got family and friends here," Meche says.

I stare into my coffee cup. "You didn't really mean what you said out there, about nobody waiting for your return?"

"Father Tom and Finn, because of the work we do together, but nobody else."

"I find that hard to believe."

"Do you? You think you know me well enough to say that?" She smiles a little.

There's a quality about her I'd love to try to capture in paint. She's golden and hard, like a knight's armor or an archangel's splendor. But beneath it is something else. Something darkly complicated, carrying the trace of many living things at once.

"You aren't really what you seem, are you?" I say.

"I suppose that depends on what I seem."

"You seem perfect. Remote. Like a goddess."

She laughs, but I don't think she's amused. "That must explain it then. The way mortals run when I show up."

"I didn't run."

She sips her coffee, looks away.

"1521 Lombard in the Bardstown section of the city," she says after a few minutes.

"Huh?"

"The Cuban peña." She sets the mug on the counter and picks up her handbag.

"Are you offering me a job blending pigments?"

"No, not exactly," she says, then ducks down and kisses me quickly on the lips.

"Tell Father Tom I'll talk to him tomorrow," she tosses the words over her shoulder on her way out.

She leaves a flurry of tiny golden bees in her wake.

"Mercy. What a night," Father Tom says, coming into the kitchen and straight through the golden cloud.

Okay then. I'm seeing things.

He heads for the coffeemaker. "Caffeine. My downfall."

He sits opposite me, looks at me over the rim of his cup. "Tired?"

"Perplexed."

He nods. "Most of us are these days. And I think it's going to get worse before it gets better again. You just have to hang on to your faith."

"I don't have any."

"Sure you do," he says. "You believe in something or you wouldn't be here. In this particular place, at this particular time, on this particular journey."

I shake my head. "I was brought to Hastings kicking and screaming and against my will."

He laughs. "But that's almost always the way, son."

I wonder if he knows that, like Finn, I'm a son who's lost his father. And like my brother-in-law, I'm always waiting to hear my father's voice again. Or an echo of it.

I stay longer than planned. When I get home the apartment is empty, but there's a note from Cassie about deciding to spend the night at her mother's place. I crawl into bed and fall asleep immediately. My cell phone wakes me at 2 a.m. It's Francine, my mother-in-law, and moments later I'm peeling out of my parking spot and leaving rubber trails down the street.

I get to the hospital moments before the aide wheels Cassie back to the ER cubicle from wherever a technician has been performing the ultrasound.

"Hey," I kiss her forehead. "You had me worried."

"I'm fine," she says. Her eyes are all water. "They couldn't find the fetal sac."

"I know. The nurse told me."

"It's probably on Mom's car seat, among the blood. Along with my cell phone and who knows what other things I managed to lose on the way." The tears drip from the slope of her nose, down the channel above her mouth, all the way into her ears.

My eyes well up too. "We can try again. We'll end up with a beautiful mini Cassandra or a spoiled little Delevan. Hell, maybe even both at once, and wouldn't that make your mother happy?"

She tries laughing – a messy, mucousy effort – then half-sits on the examining table to fit herself in my arms. She's so exhausted she falls asleep there, and after a while I shift to lay her back down.

The hair around her face is limp and dark with sweat. I brush it away and notice her face now has the wintry precision of an Andrew Wyeth painting: all sharp angles, dark hollows and frozen lines. A glacier's beauty.

It is a landscape carved by an uncaring universe that thinks nothing of severing the piece from the source; of sending its erratics out, without care for where they'll end up.

No matter what the priest says, there is no faith to be found in any of this.

3.

The brownstone looks like any other, except for a discreet representation of Our Lady of Charity on the doorjamb. I wouldn't actually know who the little plaque depicted if Meche hadn't told me that the Cuban version of Mary is always shown hovering over the ocean where she appeared to three fishermen storm-tossed in their boat.

I don't think about religion much, but it strikes me, as I stand in front of the door wavering about whether to knock, that turning to Mary is all about unexpected rescue. About getting on your knees and asking a woman to take pity and intercede.

I almost turn around then. But a young couple – she an attractive brunette in a bright cocktail dress, he light-haired and tall – join me on the stoop.

"Have you knocked yet?" he asks.

I shake my head.

The woman does the honors.

I expect Meche when the door opens, but it is an older man with scant hair and aquiline features. He glances at our wrists. None of us has a tattoo.

"Cuba libre?" he asks.

"Mentiritas," the couple next to me say in unison.

The doorman waves the couple in, then turns to appraise me.

"Can I help you with something?" he asks in perfect English.

"Meche gave me the address."

He cocks an eyebrow. For an instant I'm struck by the unfairness of whatever would give him scant head hair but such profuse eyebrows.

"I see. Wait here," he says, then closes the door in my face.

I sit on the steps, back to the door, staring out at the quiet street. It's not late, but there's no one around. It's clearly a high-end neighborhood – the houses are restored down to the last dentil. And even the trees, enclosed in mesh cages to keep the dogs off them, look groomed.

I hear the door open behind me, and the doorman motions for me to follow him.

"She said she'll find you as soon as she's freed up," he says when I'm in the foyer. Through the glass of the second door, I see a group of people, dressed up, drinks in hand. It looks like a cocktail party.

"Second floor's off limits unless she tells me otherwise," the man says, opening the inner door I've been gazing through. "Bar's in the living room, all the way through to the end. Meche asked me to give you the employee password – oriente – so you don't have to pay for your drinks."

"That password never changes. The ones to get in change every hour. Most everyone here is registered to get them via RSS feed," he says.

"Efficient," I say.

He smiles.

The front room I enter has sideboards and buffet servers shoved against the walls, laden with chafing dishes. Twenty or thirty people congregate in the center of the room, chatting with each other in Spanish. Every so often one peels off and goes to get food. An attendant fills a plate with whichever dish the guest indicates, and then quickly – so quickly it takes me several times to be certain it's happening – the guest pays the attendant.

After the front room, I pass a room closed off by pocket doors; to judge from the clanking emanating from within it is almost certainly the kitchen. The living room on the end has four sofas in the center and they're full, even the sofa arms and the low table in the center serve as seating. The far wall is so crowded with people standing I immediately know the bar is there, though I can't see it through the press of bodies. On the same wall but opposite corner is a door with an iron grate, leading outside.

The wall on the right is lined with bookshelves. An old man sits in a hard side chair there, looking at the tips of his buffed shoes while a young woman stands behind waving a thick wad of money. She's talking to a pleasant looking man, roughly her age. After a few minutes he pulls out a wallet and retrieves what looks like a condom packet. After he counts the bills, he hands the packet to her and walks away. Her hand drops on the old man's shoulder.

Without my having noticed, Meche's at my elbow.

"You're here," she says. "But, you have nothing to drink."

"Hadn't gotten that far."

She links her arm through mine, parts the crowd around the bar and directs a rapid stream of Spanish at the bartender. Then she guides me to the grated door.

"Let's sit outside."

"What drink did you order for me?" I ask her as we sit at a table at the edge of the deck that overlooks the backyard.

"If you think you're getting anything but rum at a Cuban peña, you're sadly deluded," she says. "We don't sell anything else."

"Well, food. And something else that comes in little packets that look like condoms."

"Instaskin. The pricey version," she says. "And we do actually sell a couple of other items, but none you need to know about."

"Illegal stuff."

"Every last thing at the peña is illegal, remember?"

"It's not exactly what I expected," I say, looking inside through the window. "The peña Finn described to me was, well, rowdier. More street festival than cocktail party."

Meche nods. The light coming through the windows falls on her in such a way that she's turned molten.

"The peñas that move from week to week are that way. Hectic and abuzz with the energy of what will never be the same twice," she says. "It's an intoxicating mix. Still, people like that it's much safer here. No gang members running things, just my own staff. And we don't allow guns. Except the ones we sell, of course, and those you don't get until you're already out the door."

The man with the eyebrows comes through the door with our drinks.

"Silvio manages the peña for me," she introduces him as he places the drinks on the table. "And, Silvio, Del doesn't need a password to get in."

The eyebrows shoot up again, but he nods and returns inside.

"What am I drinking?" I stare down at a fizzy, clear drink with a green leaf floating in it.

"Mojito," she says. "Rum, lime juice, club soda, sugar and mint." She laughs when I make a face.

"Want mine? Rum and coke. Cuba Libre," she pushes it toward me. "Free Cuba. Or as some of us call them, mentiritas. Little lies."

"Don't you drink anything without sugar in it?"

"No." She looks amused. "My grandparents made their fortune in cane and its derivatives."

I take a sip of hers, keep the mojito.

"So now we won't have any secrets from each other," she says, reclaiming her drink.

"What?"

"If you drink from the same glass, you share each other's secrets," she says. Then, "maybe it's an ink thing."

"Don't you ever just think of yourself as American?"

"Hello? How was it we met?" she says. "I'll think of myself American again when I don't have to wear an i.d. bracelet printed on my skin."

I stare into the window. "I thought there were lots of black Cubans."

"Sure," she says. "Just not so many in the first wave of the exile community or their kids. The upper crust in pre-revolutionary Cuba was mostly white. And the upper crust always has a better chance of escaping and getting their families to the new homeland. That's my clientele. But you didn't come to the peña to talk about Cuban politics, did you?"

I stay silent for a while. "Would you do it?"

"What?"

"Leave everything you know and go somewhere foreign for the rest of your life?"

"Sure. If I was as scared as my grandparents were. Or if I thought I couldn't take care of my loved ones otherwise."

"But that's not exactly what you're asking, is it?" she adds after a moment.

I look down at her garden. The scrawny arborvitaes are strung with white Christmas lights that make them look frosty even on this warm night.

"I don't know what I'm asking," I say after I return my eyes to her.

"You're asking if you should stop being a stranger in a strange land and go back home," she says.

I don't know if it's the mojito or the hour, but my eyes are damp, and I have to bite the inside of my cheek to keep the icy lump in my chest from cracking into sharp little pieces.

# Del: Words written on wind

"Cassie is here and shouldn't the people we love define home for us?" I say once I know my voice won't give me away.

She leans in to study me. "That's one view. The other is that home defines who we love."

After a few seconds she leans back in her chair again. "Of course, since the second view is the excuse for why I'm marked with an identity tattoo, I'm not partial to it. But, it's also why my peña is such a comfort to the people who frequent it, so who can say it's wholly wrong?"

She picks up her drink, but doesn't put it to her lips. "Exile is a strange and cruel state, Del. But the sense of being in exile isn't precipitated by the land you inhabit."

"There's no land in Hastings."

She exhales loudly. "How is it you can draw on magic and still be so literal?"

I give a short, startled laugh. "What I do with the colors of my paintings – or your instaskin – isn't magic."

"No?"

I drain my mojito in the silence that ensues.

"I should go," I say when I put the empty glass down.

She nods, stands up.

"It's okay," I say, "I can find my way out."

She moves toward the door with me anyway. "You know what I really think? I think you're feeling guilty."

"Yeah, well, it's not like Cassie would exactly groove on finding out I spent the evening with a woman like you."

She shakes her head and an irritated expression crosses her face. Then it softens a little. "No, you feel guilty because your struggle is real, and fundamental to who you are, but also incredibly privileged. You're the only person at my peña tonight who's considering self-deporting – and it's because you don't *have* to."

When I groan, she laughs. "Just drawing your attention to the irony of it."

"I'm an idiot. Sorry."

She waves the apology away. "I get it, you know. I'm operating on privilege too. It may be a number of notches down from yours but it's every bit as unearned. I think the trick is to never forget it."

"Anyway, I think I must have a soft spot for idiots. Come back anytime," she says as we get to the space between inner and outer entry doors. She's my same height, so when she tips her chin up I know she intends to kiss my forehead in goodbye.

But I don't let her. It's my mouth I pull her to.

Kissing her is like adding orange to a painting: a reckless move that can ruin the most careful composition. And there's nothing careful about what passes between us. It's similar to what I feel on my land, an exchange so elemental I am able to sense the flow of blood in the veins deep beneath her skin.

When we draw apart I can see the tiny golden bees again.

"You see them," she says, following my eyes.

"I thought I was imagining them."

"Only if you're imagining me."

"Am I?"

The next kiss is hers.

I can smell fox grapes and bur cucumber and honeysuckle – plants that separate sunny waste places from woodlands – and I envision the bees dancing between the vines before they home back to their hive.

This time when we part, she moves her hands from my shoulders to my chest and edges me away. She doesn't give me time to wonder whether there will be more between us, just clicks the door shut when I clear it.

I walk to the park and sit there for hours.

Later, I make so much noise I wake Cassie. Every window is flung open and I pretend to be on the pitcher's mound. I was a fair baseball player in high school so my body remembers the movements. Each jar of paint sails through the open window in a beautiful, flattened curve and slowballs to the street below. The plastic jars break apart with a sucking splat, but there is real satisfaction to be had in the shattering of the glass ones.

Cassie is standing just outside of the bedroom when I finally notice her. Her eyes follow the trails of cadmium orange, yellow ochre, and burnt sienna on the walls and floor leading to the window. Our largest soup pot is on the coffee table, overflowing with the ashy crumbs of burnt paper from my sketchbooks and strips of shredded canvas. Empty frames hang on the walls – not a single painting of mine remains.

"What are you doing?"

I run both hands through my hair, smearing it with bone black. I can't do more than stand, still and mute. I have no answer.

She busies herself closing windows and scooping up debris. A scrap of paint-stiffened canvas flutters on a leftover draft into her hand. When she turns it over we both see it is a piece of that mushroom painting from what seems so long ago. One of the little root people caught in the mycelium's net.

She tosses everything into the kitchen trashcan, except that scrap. I see her tuck that into the pocket of her bathrobe. Later, we turn to each other for comfort, one of the few times since the miscarriage. I think she knows even then.

The next morning before she wakes, I leave for Smithville.

***

Chato is the first to find me.

He shows up in the middle of the night, when no rational person would be awake. But I'm not rational when I'm painting. And I've always known he's not quite normal either.

# Del: Words written on wind

I see pity in his eyes when I open the door and he sees the cabin packed full of canvases, mostly blank, but a few so freshly painted the space reeks of linseed oil and mineral spirits. He thinks I've dropped off the deep end.

"Hey, Boss," he says. Old habits.

He doesn't say much. "Yes," to my offer of coffee, then sits on the couch, holding his steaming mug.

"What you doing up here by yourself, Boss?"

"Call me Del. I'm no one's boss any more."

"Ray would like it if you went back to work for him."

"He's got you."

"I'm not like his son. Just a good worker."

"Even better. Less complicated."

He puts his coffee down, gets up to look at each of the paintings hanging on the walls. "What happened to you in the city?" he asks finally.

"I don't know. But this is the only place I can be," I say.

He looks back at the paintings. "I don't think I'll tell Ray how you're living," he says slowly. "He'll worry, Boss."

I go back to mixing pigments.

He comes to visit every week, always late at night. I look forward to it, even though we don't talk much, just drink coffee and look at my growing stack of canvases.

"Why do you come so late?" I ask him one night. "Not that I mind, but it must be weird for you to walk through the woods in the dark. Especially on nights when the coy-dog pack is out and howling."

"Nothing up here is going to hurt me, Boss." Then, "I don't get done with work until late."

I stop painting. "You're not saying that to make me feel guilty, are you?"

"No, Boss. You asked, I answered."

The next time he shows up, he brings Chema from the old crew with him, and a six-pack of beer. All three of us stand in front of a row of paintings.

"Are all of these new?" Chema asks me.

"Yes," I say.

"Ah," Chema says, nodding. He glances at Chato. Out of the corner of my eye I see Chato nodding back. I wonder if it's confirmation of the insanity verdict.

"You want to get a pizza, Boss?" Chato asks. "The students are back so the pizza place is open late."

"Sure. My cell phone's on the table, order whatever you want. And stop calling me boss."

"Nobody's going to deliver a pizza here, Boss," Chato says.

So we go to the pizzeria in town.

It continues like that.

Bit by bit.

The inks bringing me back to life.

# Abbie: If u cn rd ths

I feel the tires spin, grab for a second, fail. The car slides down a quarter-mile broadside, gaining momentum. I don't touch the wheel. If I weren't a kickass driver, or used to Smithville winters, I would make the critical mistake just about now as the steering wheel dances by itself.

I force my hands to be still. Soon enough I'll be at the end of the secondary road where the municipal plows will have piled an edge of snow, salt and cinder to absorb the impact of out-of-control vehicles on the real road. As long as the highway guys haven't banked the snow too high, this pile-of-shit SUV my mother gave me should be able to handle it.

My love of this rough back way out of the trailer park isn't the only thing that makes my mother cringe these days. But if you choose to work multiple shifts – including graveyard – you don't get to complain about the route your kid takes to school in the morning.

I hit the embankment with a soft whoosh and wait for the wheels to stop spinning before shifting the vehicle into low-four. When I clear the pile of grey-crusted snow I pat the dashboard. Not such a piece of shit after all.

I get to school fifteen minutes late. Mrs. Walker at the registration desk waves me through. In Ms. Addison's trigonometry class, I slide into the seat behind John. He turns around to grin at me. Addison doesn't even notice.

"Nice that you finally joined us, Abs," he says loudly.

I hear a couple of snickers from Rose and her posse. I wallop John high on the arm. Addison keeps droning.

John laughs a couple of times as I open the textbook, leafing through until I find the chapter Addison is pretending to cover.

"What are we doing this weekend?" he asks as I settle on page 147.

"Nothing. I'm grounded. My mom just got the insurance renewal on the car and she's not letting me drive anywhere."

"You're here."

"School, computer club, the inkatorium for community service, that's it."

"Sucks."

"Sure does, doesn't she?" Rose says from the seat beside John. Rose has liked him since the seventh grade and hated me for the same span of time.

I pretend to crank up my middle finger.

"Original." Rose says. "I don't know why you hang with trailer trash, John."

But Addison's finally made her move. She's standing in front of Rose before any of us notices and taps the book open on Rose's desk.

"How about you show us how this problem is done, Miss Cantinelli," she says. "Whiteboard. Up front."

I know better than to think Addison's protecting me. She wouldn't care if Rose decided to pull my nails out in class. It's the trailer trash comment that prompted a reaction. What kind of neighbor would she be if she let that one stand?

Gotta love the reasons adults choose to act.

"Saturday?" John whispers now.

"If you want to do the inkatorium."

He smiles at me.

I wish he weren't so cute. Rose and her ilk wouldn't hate me half as much if he looked like dog meat.

"Chagas and leprosy and Hansen's. Sounds like my kind of date, Abs. Pick me up when you go."

"Hansen's *is* leprosy, you moron."

But I'm pleased. I haven't lost him to the princesses yet.

***

The inkatorium is in a huge new brick building surrounded by really spectacular landscaping. The quality of the landscaping is what started the rumors that there would be celebrities housed here. And who knows, maybe there are some among the inks.

"Money is so weird," I say to John as I pull into the parking lot.

John shrugs off his seat belt. "What do you mean?"

"Well just that, remember when people thought Charlie Sheen would be coming here? Everyone was really excited. Even though he's an ink."

"Famous ink," he says.

"Still...."

"Still nothing. It's fame that buys you a pass. Money's just a useful convenience."

I click the remote to lock the car, and hurry after him. Near the door we slow to count the number of vans lined in front of the entry.

"They must have gotten a shipment," he says. "Your mom's going to be swamped."

"Good. That way she won't have time to worry about you being here."

He grins at me.

"She thinks you're a really bad influence," I say.

"Yeah, right. Like it isn't you who's always the instigator."

*But nothing happens to you when we get caught.* I don't say it.

It's no use complaining that John's family has enough money to buy him out of trouble and my mom doesn't. That's just the way the world is. Maybe John's right about the fame being better than money bit, but having loads of the green stuff isn't bad either.

John swings the heavy glass entry door open, holds it for me. Valerie, behind a reception desk that's like an air-traffic controller console only with video monitors, looks up and waves us forward.

"Hey, Abs," she says. "Glad you're here. We're overwhelmed this morning. Your mom could use another pair of hands."

I can't help it, I make a face. "You're not going to make us work with her, are you?"

Valerie's friendly expression disappears. "No. I'm going to make *you* work with her." She scribbles out a pass, places it in a plastic sleeve with an alligator clip, and hands it to me. "She's at check-ins."

I clip it on my shirt. The plastic sleeve has a bright purple "CS" of community service stamped onto it, visible from a hallway away.

"Him I can't use," Valerie says, nodding at John without looking at him.

"Come on, Val. You just said you need hands."

Valerie's gaze dances between us. John puts on his best smile. Nobody can resist him when he wants to be charming. The aura of entitlement, my mother calls it. Hotness, I say.

"Oh, all right," Valerie huffs, scribbling a pass for him. It goes into a plastic sleeve with the baby blue "CC" – college credit – stamp. She hands it to him. "You can help Thaddeus on draws."

"And I better not hear that the two of you were socializing before your lunch break," she yells as we head down the same hallway.

Check-ins take place in the building's largest room. It's also the nicest. Like it's not bad enough they're locking up the inks in here, but they go ahead and deceive them into thinking the rest of the place is as sunny and open.

The room is full of inks today, hands bound with polymer handcuffs. Great. So not even a shipment of voluntaries. The involuntaries are always much more problematic.

My mom's at the desk at the end, with two of her assistants. They're all dressed in blue and green scrubs and paper surgical masks. When she looks up at me I see first relief, then anger chase through her eyes.

"I've told you before. I don't want you walking through this room without scrubs and a mask."

"You've also told me they're almost never sick."

My mother's eyes turn hard. "Just go get ready and then go to the tracking room. That's where we'll be working this morning." She turns to one of the CNAs, "Bennett, I want you to work on registration and paperwork." She shoves a scanner across the desk. "And let Renfro do the walk-throughs. I have a feeling we're going to have a rough day."

I walk to scrubs storage and open one of the cupboards. I hate pink, but the volunteers all have to wear scrubs that color. The first time I saw John dressed in them I died laughing. Not that I didn't still love him while I was laughing.

He's my best friend, the one who really hung with me during my parents' divorce. He was even held back the same year I was – after I missed all that school from the family upheaval – so we're both a year older than our classmates. Nobody quite gets us as we get us, and that's a strong bond.

Suited and gloved, I cross to the tracking room. The room is just big enough to hold two scary surgical chairs – one for adults, a smaller one for children – an autoclave, trays of instruments, and storage cabinets.

"Abs, you can't say stuff like that in front of the staff," my mom says when she comes into the room. "Officially, everybody here is sick."

"Yeah, I know. Sorry."

"This morning's batch is huge. I'm glad you're here to help out."

I hate the gratitude I hear in her voice. Like I hate it when she tries to hug me. *Let's not pretend,* is what I wish I could say to her. *Let's not pretend I'm here for any reason other than I'm a fuck-up.*

I turn around when I hear Renfro entering the room with the first ink. It's a kid, dwarfed by Renfro's blue-clad bulk.

"After this, I think we should do the adults first," my mom says to him. "The children aren't going to give us any problems, and if it takes us until the afternoon to get them settled in, it won't matter if we're exhausted."

"Sure thing, Kim," Renfro says as he prods the kid toward the smaller chair.

The first thing my mom does is uncuff the boy. "Do you speak English?"

The kid, maybe seven or eight, nods, sticks his wrist out. It has a blue tat.

Which figures, since most involuntaries are blues. They never remember that the minute an inkatorium van is called in, their rights plummet from citizen to non-alien.

"Are your parents here?" my mother asks.

"I don't know," the kid says. "I threw up at school, so they reported it and that's where the van picked me up."

My mom nods, snaps on her latex gloves. "Okay. This is my daughter, Abbie. She'll walk you through when we're done here. Renfro's a nice guy but he's so big you can't help being a little scared of him."

The surgical chair pitches the kid forward against padded chin and shoulder restraints that leave the neck clear. I squat down in front of the boy and hold both his hands. "My mom's going to spray some stuff on your neck, which is going to feel really cold, but it doesn't hurt at all."

"Then she'll give you a shot, but it won't hurt since she's already sprayed your neck. Then, after a bit, when she cuts it, you'll feel a little bit of pressure, like someone is poking you. But that won't hurt either."

By the time I've finished saying it my mother's done with the incision. I get up and grab a tracker pack from one of the cabinets, open it and hand the GPS unit to my mom without looking. The chip should slide easily into the incision.

I go back to the boy as my mom inserts the chip, then puts a quick staple stitch in the numbed skin. The kid's eyes are wide, but I don't see any pain in them.

"Hey, what's your name?" I ask as my mom removes her gloves and pulls the mega-scanner-on-wheels toward him.

"Pete Nguyen," the boy says.

I turn the boy's wrist over so my mom can scan the tat. The floor scanners are the most reliable models but it still takes her several tries to get something onscreen and then to punch in the new GPS tracking number. Everyone with a tat gets a tracker here.

"We're done. Abs, walk him all the way through, would you? Even the draw."

"John's there today, he'll make sure Pete's fine."

She looks at me, then turns away. "I wish I had as much confidence in John as you do. But okay, if you want to drop him before the puncture, that's fine. I know how you hate blood."

Hate is too mild a word. Phobia might fit.

"You all right?" I ask as I take Pete's hand in my gloved one and lead him out of the room.

He nods.

I take him to Nate, who seats him in the barber chair. In five passes he's shaved off all of the kid's hair. The shavings are incinerated at the end of the day to ensure the site remains louse and nit free.

"Here you go, young man," Nate says, handing him a lollipop he buys himself so he can give them to the kids. "Don't eat it until after your shower or it'll be a hairy pop."

I take Pete to the mandatory shower, and wait for him outside. One of the attendants throws his clothing into the "incinerate" bin, and after the final disinfecting spray, Pete emerges dressed in a black jumpsuit. He looks smaller than he did and I wonder if it is just that the jumpsuit is oversized and pools around him, or if the walk-through has diminished him as it does the adults.

Before I open the door to the puncture room – where his blood will be drawn to be tested for Chagas, Hansen's, tuberculosis and the New Delhi superbug – I squat down and give him a quick hug.

When I get back to the tracking room, there's an ink seated in the surgical chair, but my mom's just leaning back on the counter playing with a new pair of gloves instead of putting them on.

"You know, of course," the ink is saying, "that Hansen's isn't even particularly contagious. And of the 100 or so cases reported in the U.S. every year, about a third of them can be traced to contact with armadillos – not inks."

The speaker has long blond hair, long legs and the look of a model. I hate her immediately.

"You a doctor?" my mom asks.

I wish I didn't hear the want in her words. Want to have had the money and opportunity to become a doctor. Want for the second chance life never gave her. She's certified as an inkatorium practitioner – so she can prescribe – but it's not the same as a regular nurse-practitioner, and nothing like a doctor.

"Chemist," the woman answers, then swivels in the surgical chair to give my mother a challenging look. "Before. When I wasn't marked."

I think it's instinct that drives me to step in front of my mom to shield her.

"This must be your daughter," the ink says. "She looks like you."

The comment cements the hatred. My mother carries an extra twenty-five pounds, dyes her hair an ugly shade of red and has a face seamed with worry lines. There's nothing resembling a resemblance between us.

"Thanks," I hear my mother say.

Shit, what a betrayal that agreement is.

"Darker, though," the ink says.

"Her father is mostly Mohawk." I hear my mother finally snap on the gloves.

"I didn't mean looks," the ink says.

It startles me into really looking at her.

She's got bruises up and down her arms and neck. That fact doesn't awaken any pity in me. Beauty isn't power. Or protection. So there.

"Abbie, braid the lady's hair so it's off her neck."

"Meche," the ink says. "My name is Meche."

My mother studies the ink in the chair before her. "You know why you're here?"

Meche nods. "But, the vast majority of us aren't public health risks or carrying the diseases people are panicked about. It's really a way to make it more palatable to see so many people locked up."

"My mom knows. She's always saying that. Well, something like that."

"Get me the betadine swabs, Abs." I hear warning in my mom's voice.

"If you know how can you be part of it?" There's no outrage in the ink's voice, just a tired sort of curiosity.

My mom doesn't answer.

When I hand her the swab, she's taking a closer look at the bruising on Meche's neck. "Any of these hurt?"

"No."

"Boyfriend hit you?"

Her laugh is short, humorless. "A guy riding a bike ran me down in front of the grocery store. Everyone's so scared by the damned health alerts that when they saw me on the ground and noticed the tattoo they thought I was having a seizure. Kicking appears to be the preferred remedy."

"Hmmm."

I'm familiar with that response. It's my mother's way of saying "I'll reserve judgment until I hear the policeman/guidance counselor/principal's version of the story."

My mom swabs the area she's determined would be a good GPS insertion spot then injects the topical anaesthetic.

"You know why I don't wear a wedding ring?" she asks as she grabs a sterile scalpel from the autoclave. 180s in the conversation are my mother's specialty.

"Two winters ago I had to sell all the gold I had to be able to pay our heating bill. What's sentiment when your kid's freezing in a cold house?" My mom puts pressure on the incision while she reaches for the suture gun. "You do what you have to do."

"That's why I'm here even knowing that most of you aren't sick," my mom adds as the stitch punches through skin. She inspects her handiwork, swipes the area with more betadine.

"You're done," she says.

"I know," Meche says, and this time I understand exactly what she means.

*** 

You can learn a lot lunching at the inkatorium. Like, people inside are pretty much the same as people outside. We've got somewhere around 1,000 inks of all kinds here now and if you walk into the lunchroom you'll see them sitting clustered into ethnic groupings. And within each group, they sit pretty much by color of tat. Unspoken hierarchy, a lot like high school. The only ones who seem to cross the boundaries are kids too little to recognize distinctions other than size.

John and I are watching the new batch of inks. Meche is an oddball. She sits the first place she notices a spot, and then, doesn't eat. She just stares out the small, high windows at the steely patches of sky visible through them. Later I see her pick up her tray, still full of food, and carry it over to the table where all the little kids band to eat together. She sets her tray down and lets them claim her roll, juice box and jello cup. None of them will touch the tuna casserole. Smart kids.

I have to admit, I have sort of a sick fascination with her. I swear it has nothing to do with wanting to look like her. When it starts growing back in, her hair is almost as mousy as mine and that does a number on her golden aura. No, it has more to do with how she carries herself. She's arrogant. And in this world of subdued humans, it makes her seem like an immortal down from Olympus on a day pass.

I keep track of other inks too. Pete, for example. He and a bunch of other boys his age improvise baseball games in the cafeteria, using crushed pint milk cartons for balls and their arms held out stiff for bats. We're not supposed to bring anything in for the inks but the very next week stuff appears: scuffed aluminum bats; balls roughly the size of real baseballs but made of soft rubber so they won't break windows; battered leather gloves with old names scrawled on the thumbs. My mother, who administers the place by an exhaustive set of regulations for the adults, turns a blind eye when it comes to the kids. So long as a ball doesn't land smack in her lap she won't confiscate the contraband.

I don't see Meche interact much with the other inks, though to my annoyance, she likes talking with John whenever his volunteer work puts him in contact with her.

"She says the phone cards they sell to residents at the inkatorium are only good for a week after they're activated, no matter how much talk time you pay for," John says some three weeks after Meche's arrival at the inkatorium.

"Did she buy one?" I ask.

"No. She only had about $15 dollars on her when the van brought her in. But she's really smart about this stuff."

"Hmph."

"She says the same company that issues the cards pays big time to be the phone carrier for inkatorium, and then sets it up so you can't make collect calls and so each call you *can* make costs three times as much as it would on the outside. That's why the inkatorium has that rule about no cell phones for the residents. So both parties continue to make a shitload of money off the phone arrangement."

"Sounds far-fetched. And how would she know?"

"I think she'd actually done some research on inkatoriums before being hauled in, not sure why. But, anyway, she has nothing to gain from lying about it."

*Except your sympathy,* I think.

"It'd be easy enough for you to find out if she's telling the truth," he says. "Just ask your mom."

As if. My mother might be a bitch-on-wheels, but she's mostly a fair bitch-on-wheels and she'd never institute a system that nefarious. But I do ask her. And she confirms it.

"I don't do it to fleece the inks," she says when she notices my expression. "Most of them aren't picked up with a lot of money on them and, since we're required to keep the resident list private, they mostly don't get visitors to buy the cards for them either. But the carrier-contract income really counts come review time. As for the cell phones, they're just too easy to jigger so they'll explode."

I smuggle a throwaway cell phone into the inkatorium the next weekend. At lunch I find my way to the end of the table where Meche's doing her pining for sunlight thing and sit on the bench next to her. Her eyes come down from the rafters and settle on my face.

"Abbie, the administrator's daughter."

"Abigail to you. Abigail Adams."

"Patriotic," she says.

I'm pretty sure she's making fun of me, but I can't say I blame her. "My mother's idea of cute."

"So what can I do for you, Abigail Adams?"

"Here," I say, then drop the cell phone in her lap. "Now, stop filling John's ear with garbage."

She moves one of her hands to the phone to cover it.

"I don't know what you think you'll gain from it, but don't play him. Got it? Otherwise I'll inform my mother you're in possession of contraband."

The honey eyes stay on my face for a while. "I will do whatever I have to do to get out of here. Even if it means playing your young man. As I believe you will do whatever you need to do to protect him. Even if it means running to your mother. We are two of a kind, Abigail, and the good in that is that we understand one another perfectly."

She gets up, empty-handed.

I have no idea where the cell phone's gone.

"Thank you," she says. Then she walks away.

Of course I don't tell my mother.

Next weekend there's a shipment from the first inkatorium built instate. It's already at double its capacity, so 300 of its residents are being transferred to Smithville. It is a mix of black and green tats, with just a few blues. There is one particularly sad group of inks among them: mothers who gave birth while at the inkatorium. None of them have their children with them. My mom won't tell me what happened to the babies, no matter how hard I press her for an answer.

The group sits together heedless of ethnicity or tat color, and everyone else steers clear of them, as if their especially horrible luck might rub off on contact. Most of the group has mental health issues, my mother tells me, though mainly they just seem depressed. One of them is visibly crazy, though. She doesn't sit. She paces the stretch of the wall under the windows. Back and forth. Every so often she'll stop and raise her eyes to those same patches of sky that Meche stares at, then starts pacing again.

She doesn't break this routine until Pete and the boys get up to play. One of them cracks a ball that sails far above the woman's head. She jumps, sinuous and higher than would seem possible, and catches the ball. Then, a little tentative, throws it back to the boys. After that they hit ball after ball in her direction, and she catches each as effortlessly as the first.

By now the whole lunchroom – staff included – is focused on the display.

"That's so freaky," I hear John's voice at my ear. He's come to stand beside me to watch. "You'd never guess she'd be that good."

"It's desperation," I say.

He gives me a strange look.

"Check out her face. It's like if she doesn't move to jump and catch she's going to die," I say.

After a few moments, he says "What does that to a person?"

"This," I say. "Us."

I'm surprised when I feel John's hand wrap itself around mine.

Next week, the crazy woman and Meche start sitting together. Well, really, they sit alone side-by-side. When they do, the crazy one grows less antsy. Sometimes, from where I sit, I see her lips moving and I wonder if she is praying.

"She recounts fairy tales," John tells me one day when he slides his tray next to mine at the table. We're in the staff area of the lunchroom which is like the upper tier at an amphitheater looking down on the level where the inks eat. "At least that's what Meche figures they are."

76

# Abbie: If u cn rd ths

We look down at the pair of them, openly spying. The crazy one's lips are moving and Meche sits next to her, as aloof as usual. Then I see Meche's shoulders hitch as if she's clenched them against a blow. She reaches over and lays her hand on top of the crazy woman's. Now it's Meche's lips we see moving.

Moments later a yowl tears out of crazy woman's throat. I've never heard anything like it. It stands all my hairs on end.

Renfro moves with a speed that belies his size. Not even a minute after the display starts, a hypodermic slips into the crazy woman's arm and she slumps over on the table. The big guy scoops her up easily, carries her out.

In the ringing silence I hear what must be Meche sobbing. Like the other, it is a raw sound, but somehow it's so much worse because it's issuing from her. My mother's got a hypodermic in her hand as well, but when she sits on the bench next to the ink and says something, Meche shakes her head. She walks out of the lunchroom on her own.

It takes a week for Meche to reappear.

She sits as she normally does, at any old table in the lunchroom. But she doesn't get a tray to fill, she just sits. I don't remember when I do it but I'm up and walking to the stairway that leads down to the amphitheater's bowl.

She looks up at me when I come to stand across the table from her.

"You have to eat," I say. "My mom will order a feeding tube put in you if you don't. She did that once when a group of inks went on hunger strike."

When she doesn't say anything, I move to the lunchline and fill a tray, then I bring it back and set it down in front of her. "At least pretend, okay?"

Slowly, as if it costs her, she lifts her arm and starts to move the food around.

I sit across from her. I want to ask her what happened, but I don't, I just watch as she plays with her unappetizing meal.

"You know the worst part of being here?" she says. "You start forgetting who you were before."

"You were a chemist, and from the look of the clothes we swapped for the jumpsuit, a frigging successful one," I say, a little freaked out by her tone.

She looks down at her food. "When I first got here I'd give people element names based on whether their proper names started with with same letters as the atomic symbol for the element. Now I'm not sure I can even remember the whole periodic table."

"Did you assign me an element? Or John?"

"I could never settle on which of the A's yours should be, and there are no atomic symbols that start with J. But I gave your mom one."

"There's a K?"

"Two, actually. Potassium and Krypton. Which do you think?"

I start laughing as I get up.

"Seriously, eat," I say before I leave. "Even Superman needs food."

"His Achilles' heel was Kryptonite, not Krypton, I believe."

"Same dif."

She shakes her head, but she's smiling and I think I see her take a bite as I walk away.

The crazy woman doesn't return to the lunchroom until another week goes by. She makes a beeline for Meche and sits on the bench with hardly any space between them. For a second I think they are holding hands but then I realize that what I'm seeing is an exchange. Meche places the cell phone I smuggled in for her in the smaller woman's hand. It disappears up the sleeve of the jumpsuit. I find myself hoping nobody but me sees it.

Renfro tells me what happens a few days later.

First, my mother confiscates the phone. Second, she has Renfro take the crazy one to the visitor's room. It doesn't get used much, only family and spouses are permitted to visit the residents but first they have to know the residents are here. The man who stands on the other side of the glass is even bigger than Renfro, dark-haired and pale-skinned. He is neither spouse nor family but he is, Renfro tells me, how my mother found out about the contraband phone.

The crazy one doesn't have any money and never bought a phone card, but she leaves him a message and he moves a mountain to come see her. Namely, the mountain that is my mother.

Renfro stands on the woman's side of the glass; my mother on the visitor's side for the full half-hour she's allotted them. Like all visitors, Renfro tells me, the first thing the man does after he sits in the hard plastic seat is put his hand flat to the glass. The crazy one matches him, then rests her cheek on her hand, as if it were his. She tells him about the baby without looking at him.

And then, just like that, their half-hour is done.

"Did Renfro and your mom hear all of their conversation?" John asks. "Because that's really sort of creepy."

"I know, right?"

We're at the top of the chute of the cement factory not far from the trailer park. It is one of the places I've promised my mother I'll never get caught in again, and I intend to keep my promise.

"You think they're still in love with each other?" He flips pebble-size chunks of cement block off the chute.

"I want to think so," I say.

I turn on my back and look up at the sky. I like watching the sky from here. You can see more stars in Smithville than the surrounding areas because there isn't much light pollution.

John turns on his back too and skootches so he's parallel to me. "So now what happens to them?"

"They wait, I guess. Until something changes and the inks go back to being like the rest of us and they can be together. My mom sure as shit isn't going to break the rules for them again. "

"That sucks butt."

"I know."

"If you ended up somewhere like the inkatorium I'd come rescue you."

I turn my face to look at him. "But the thing is, as much as that guy might want to rescue her, he won't be able to. Because he doesn't know a thing about being on the inside."

"But we do," I say after a moment.

"Oh, Christ," John says. "You already have more community time to serve than any three people, you can't be thinking about this."

"Game?"

His hand touches mine. "Shh. I hear the security dude making his rounds."

"Oh fucking hell." A whisper.

"Shut up or he's going to catch us up here again," he says. Says, not whispers.

I start to say if we get caught it'll be his fault. But then it turns out that's not true. Because he's really quiet when he kisses me.

## 3.

It's good thing that we decide to break out Meche too because without her we wouldn't know how to begin.

"Here," she says and slips a scrap of paper my way. The other inks avoid her in the lunchroom so it's a good place to consult. "Call the top number. His name is Finn. And by the way, you can stop calling his girlfriend 'the crazy one.' She isn't, you know, and her name is Mari. Anyway, he'll need to know all the details of the plan."

"We have a plan?"

"Funny. Ask him to get that list of ingredients for us, in those quantities. How good are your chemistry skills?"

"Crap. The only thing I'm good at is computers."

"John?"

"Bio Boy, but he's probably fine at chem too. So long as it doesn't involve math, 'cause he totally sucks at that."

"Got it, no math. Once we have this stuff you're going to have to borrow your school's science lab and not get caught. You think you can do that?"

"I could pick the locks at the school before I was ten."

She raises her eyebrows but just goes on. "In all likelihood Finn's going to have to tap into the gang network to get the ingredients, and maybe even to get them to us. The second number on that paper is Toño's dedicated line. I'm sure Finn doesn't have it. Also, since we're going to need something to pay Toño with ...."

"None of us has any money," I say quickly.

"I know. And I can't free up any of mine from here, so the easiest way is to have Finn negotiate with Toño. Tell him to offer up to half of our product in trade for the raw materials and transport."

"What are we making?"

"Skin."

I call.

"Speak," says the voice that answers.

I read Meche's entire spiel as I've written it down because my memory is for shit. There's a crackly silence on the other end when I'm done.

"Hello?"

"Patience, chola, I'm thinking. Tell Havana Barbie I'll do it for 90 percent of the output. You take delivery of raw materials this Monday at four p.m. at the Route 17 rest stop just south of Smithville. And chola, that's a freetrade zone, so there's going to be mara around. You stay cool and don't flake out, hear?"

I swallow hard. I can't believe I dialed the wrong number. I can't believe I'm going to have to tell "Havana Barbie" that I've already screwed the plan.

"How do I recognize you?"

"You don't. I recognize you. Have Havana Barbie tell you how." Then he hangs up.

I'm going to have to bag the last class of the day to make sure I make it in time to meet up with a gang member. Leader. Scary dude I wasn't even supposed to be talking to. John wants to go with me, but Meche won't allow it.

"Vary one bit from what Toño agreed to and we'll bollux the whole deal," she says. "Besides, it works in our favor that Abbie's pretty. Toño has an eye for it."

She tells me I must wear the colors of the Mexican flag: red, green and white. That way I'll be instantly identifiable as a supplier or client of Toño's gang. The Central American flags are mostly blue and white so people doing business with the mara will wear those colors. It's one of the ways the freetrade zones manage to stay functional, the gangs don't step on each other's business no matter how much they might be tempted to.

The red hoodie and the white sneakers are easy, but I don't own anything green. I have to go searching in my mother's closet the night before. The only green piece she has is a spangly, stretchy dress she hasn't worn since way before she packed on all those extra pounds.

There are a bunch of cars at the rest stop when I pull in. I park Blue Belle – my beloved piece-of-shit SUV – in one of the spots out front, then waste time trying to make my skimpy dress go where it won't. Finally I get out and walk into the building. It's one of those unstaffed rest stops with nothing but vending machines and publication racks in the one big room. There are at least three people dressed in blue and white inside, two by the men's room and one rifling through the visitor brochures. They all look up at me, then go back to back to their badly disguised loitering.

I sit on one of the benches just inside the entrance. About ten minutes pass before anyone else comes through the door. He's a skeevy guy who looks like he hasn't washed his hair in weeks. Since he's not dressed in flag colors he must be a civilian. I watch in fascination as a bug crawls out of the guy's hair and across his forehead. I must make a face because he leers at me and makes a grunting noise.

"Get lost," I say.

He walks into the men's room. I hope there's Lysol in there so he can deal with the bug situation. When he comes back out, he's talking on his cell phone and walks out the back door without looking around. Three or four more people come in, but since they're not in colors, I don't pay any attention to them or what they do.

After another contactless fifteen minutes I walk over to the coffee machine, feed it some quarters and punch the "regular" button. Even the minimal bending involved makes me worry the dress is going to ride up and expose some butt cheek. And maybe it does because one of the blue-and-whites comes right over to me.

"What are you, seller or buyer?"

"Tired driver," I say holding up my coffee, then walk back to reclaim the bench.

I sip the watery coffee and wait. Another uneventful twenty minutes and I've hit my forty-five minute mark. I walk back to Blue Belle, unlock the doors and bend down to rummage in my bookbag for my earbuds and Mp3 player.

"I want you to thank Havana Barbie for me."

I knock my head on the sill in my hurry to turn around. The man leaning on my hood has intensely dark eyes, a perfect little goatee, buzzed hair and a blue tat hidden among a multitude of figural ones on his arms. His muscles are cut enough to show through his clothes. Regular, unflag clothes.

"Why do I thank her?"

"I've gotten to see you bend over twice now. Third time and I'll be in love."

I blush to my knees.

"What're you doing involved in this, America?"

I shrug.

He cocks his head, studies me. "Unlock the car, I'll have some of my boys load up the stuff."

They materialize out of nowhere. None of them is wearing colors. One of them, I know, has bugs in his hair. They start piling plain cardboard boxes in the back of Blue Belle as soon as I open the rear door. The gross one rubs up against me. When I move away, he finds a way to rub up again on his next foray past me. I go to back away again, trip and am held up by something hard and unyielding. Toño. He says something in Spanish, not very loud or threatening sounding, but the gross guy blanches under his grime.

Toño's arm is around my waist. He pulls me tight to him, tight enough that I can feel the flexing of his deltoid as he reaches behind his back with the other arm. "Don't worry, America, there's no chance at all I'll be letting him get his hands on anything so fine."

The arm that isn't holding me comes forward, a gun in hand. He brushes the hair back over my ear with that hand, then his mouth is there and the breath skittering across it makes me shiver.

"I'm underage," I say.

"I know," he says, but doesn't move his mouth. "Havana Barbie would never have sent you otherwise. She knows exactly which few shreds of decent still cling to me. But thank me for this, America. From this moment on you can walk through a roomful of gangsters and not one will look your way for fear I'll cut out his eye."

He keeps hold of me like that until the load up is completed and his men vanish as quickly as they appeared. Then he releases me and takes a step back. "Tell Havana Barbie I expect delivery of the finished product to the same site. She's got a week to produce. She misses deadline, I start taking it out on her folks on the outside. Oh, and, I require the same delivery person. Got all that?"

I nod, move around him into the driver seat. As I reach for the door, he prevents me from closing it.

"First time, America?"

"What?"

# Abbie: If u cn rd ths

"First time you've felt your body pinned by a man rather than a boy?"
I yank the door shut. He watches me drive away.

*** 

We're at the school's chem lab. John is setting everything up to follow the bazillion steps of the process Meche has written out for him; I'm on pigment detail and taking care of the stopwatch.

As John mixes ingredients he wants to hear again about the meeting with Toño. I've given him a heavily edited version, but I was stupid enough to let it slip within his hearing that I had expected Toño be scary, but not so hot. Now, every so often, I catch this injured look in John's eyes.

Chris, my favorite custodian-slash-security-guard, is on for overnight. He's a laid-back guy, often reeking of weed. I've figured out he does the full round every hour. We kill the lights in the lab at 50 minutes and crawl in the space between the wall and the furthest table, thinking the overhang will shield us if he actually decides to come into the room. So far he hasn't. He just shines his flashlight through the window panel of the door and rattles the handle. We wait five minutes after he's left to turn the light on and get back to work. That means we work 45 minutes out of every hour and things are going slowly.

Meche's flying by the seat of her pants with the new recipe. Since she can't afford to mix the instaskin to order she's altered the formulation and is working with a limited palette she hopes will cover most skin tones. The stuff sets up as a dough which has to be rolled out thin and cut into squares large enough to cover the tattoos. The hard part about this is that the skin is sticky, so it'll self-adhere, and it's a bitch to roll out.

As soon as the pieces are cut and squared we sandwich them between sheets of cooking parchment and roll those in cling wrap, then newspaper. The rolls go into mailing tubes. With all the extraneous material around the skin patches, only ten rolls – with ten patches in each – fit in each tube.

We've got 50 tubes to fill tonight and 50 to fill on each of the next three nights. At the end of the night we'll gather up the tubes and sneak them into Blue Belle. I'll be storing the tubes in the chest freezer in our basement. I just hope that my mother doesn't get the idea to cook a roast until after delivery is made.

While we're in the dark waiting for Chris to do his sweep, John can't keep his hands off me, which freaks me right out. I like making out, but I know this can only end one way: we have sex. And I won't.

The test patches adhere fine. I put one on, leave it for a day until I remember it's there and swab it with acetone. It's a strange experience to see what looks like skin bubble up then dissolve into foamy scum. There's just more blank skin under mine, but I imagine with the inks the tattoos reappear line by line, like a story being written.

Before the delivery is scheduled I run into the discount mart and buy a pair of cheap green yoga pants and a plain white t-shirt to wear under my red hoodie. This time when I pull into the rest area I spy Toño sitting on one of the benches outside the visitor structure.

"Hey, America," he says when I walk up to him. "Your car unlocked?"

I nod.

He motions to someone, then points in the general direction of my car.

He pats the bench beside him. "Sit. I never take blind delivery, so my guys'll check each of the packages and report back. Then you can leave."

"Mec ... Havana Barbie told me to tell you we had to store the rolls in the freezer, but we thawed them already and tested the patches. The final appearance isn't compromised."

"Got it," he says. "It's a shame, you know."

"What is?"

"That Havana Barbie was never willing to come work fulltime for me. I would have kept her out of that P.O.W. camp."

"It's not so bad. My mother is the administrator and she is a good person who tries to treat everyone well."

"Bad move, America. Didn't Havana Barbie warn you about giving me personal information?"

She had. Emphatically. I swallow hard.

"Can I ask you a question?" I say after a bit.

"Sure."

"Do you know what happens to the babies born in the inkatoriums?"

"Why do you want to know?"

"Just do."

"Private adoptions. Big money, which gets funneled back to the inkatoriums. Wish I could figure a way in on that action."

"But who would adopt an ink baby?"

"They only take the ones that'll pass."

"Yeah, but Havana Barbie passes, and so do a lot of other inks inside. And they're still inside. Why would you want to raise a kid, love him, and see this sort of stuff happen to him the first time he has a runny nose or barfs in public, and somebody calls it in to the public health line?"

"Well, it's like this, America, if you've got enough money you can pay to destroy any record of your adopted baby's ink blood. You buy him an uncontaminated history and a future. It costs the adoptive parents big time. Big time enough to fund the ongoing operations of the inkatoriums."

"Oh."

I look over to Blue Belle. A couple of Toño's men are still there by the back door. No bug guy. I wonder what happened to him.

"Once they're adopted there's no way to retrieve any information about them?" I ask when I look back.

"Not that I've found."

One of the guys walks from my car to Toño and offers his wrist. The patch isn't a good match in terms of skin tone, but otherwise looks good.

"How many shades of patch are we getting?" Toño asks me.

"Five. That's one of the two lighter shades."

He grabs my wrist and turns it over to where I'd have a tattoo if I were an ink. He motions to his minion to put his patched wrist next to mine. The patch is almost a perfect match to my skin tone. "Figures," he says.

"I'm not so white," I say, offended.

He laughs. "You're a strange one. Tell Havana Barbie I accept shipment, though I'm disappointed by the limited quantity overall and the color selection specifically. If I find this a profitable enough venture, I'll place another order, but I'll expect more and better."

He stands up and smoothes the front of his jeans. "I'm saddened not to see your legs this time. Or your other assets."

"This is more me." I meet his eyes. There's amusement in there, and something else I don't recognize but makes me shiver.

He gives me a mocking smile. "You ever get tired of your safe world, America, you know how to find me."

***

There are real advantages to being my mother's daughter.

No matter where in the inkatorium I wander, nobody stops or monitors me. With that realization comes a sharp kick of remorse. I'm coasting on a trust I didn't earn. But it doesn't stop me from going into the tracking room and swiping a pocketful of betadine wipes, anesthetic spray and a couple of disposable scalpels from the samples an equipment rep left for my mother.

We do it Sunday, when there are no other volunteers around because they, unlike teenagers or inks, have real lives. I've chosen a storage room where staff members sometimes hide out to smoke. It's a gross and unsanitary space filled with rolling bins used for collecting clothing, hair and soiled linens. A couple of chairs have been hidden in the far corner so smokers can chat or fit a page of reading in with the hit of nicotine.

Of course, there's not supposed to be smoking in the building at all, but the smokers have disabled the security cameras. Their restoral is pretty low on my mom's list of concerns given that the room doesn't lead anywhere or house anything of significance. Outside of her office, it's the only place inside the inkatorium that isn't on camera 24/7.

Everyone's decided I should remove the GPS trackers since I've watched the reverse procedure so many times. I agree to it because I have the brain of a flea.

Meche first. My incision is sure and quick. Perfect. Then the thin red line I've drawn on her neck turns to a gusher. I hit the floor in a dead faint. I don't actually hit, though. Mari anticipates the trajectory of bodies as easily as baseballs and catches me on the way down.

Except it isn't Mari. It's a something that resolves itself, after my brain clicks through a series of shapes, to the oddly-reassuring semblance of a wolf. Its eyes are alive with something other than animal intelligence.

WTF?

Translucent strands of gold mantle around us. The walls of the room run with a red, fiery substance that sizzles when it meets the floor, itself a dark glassy version of what's dripping on to it. I feel like I'm pulling in scorching liquid stuff with each breath.

Stranded in the center of this pyroclastic flow is Meche. The gold strands emanate from her, stringing out in a flurry between her outstretched fingers. John is a small and hunched figure next to her, caught also in whatever she's weaving.

*On my layer of the world, this place is built from fire that cools into blades.*

It is the wolf's voice, I sense this, though it's all in my head.

*Only those who ply its same element can hold against it without being changed. For, on all layers, it is a place meant to shred the spirit.*

I know, I think. Even my mother senses that.

*But it is only a stop on the way to a worse and more fearsome place. It will get sharper and more punishing from here.*

What can we do?

*We each have our magicks to add.*

But I don't.

I know I'm not out long, just the time it takes John to finish the job for me (pull chip out, mop up with betadine, slap an instaskin patch on the spot). Meche's banking on the instaskin's astringency to help stanch the flow of blood and for the adhesive to serve, more or less, in place of a suture. When I come to I feel like its been hours.

"Put the GPS chip in your bra and keep it on you at all times," Meche says as she finishes inspecting Mari's neck. "When we get out of here we're going to have to find a place to plant them."

"When are we leaving?" Mari asks, looking straight at me. She's the same person from before my dream/hallucination/whatever but I can't fully meet her eyes.

"Soon," I say.

But, truth is, I haven't even started on that part.

First I have to convince my mom to let me drive to Hastings. For spring break. With John.

As if.

So I lie. I tell her I'm going to see my father.

I haven't seen my dad in a year. It doesn't mean he doesn't love me, he's just strange that way. Plus, he moves around a lot. Cell phone, Harley, odd jobs – he prefers portable and impermanent to anything that pins him down. He comes through twice a year and visits me on his way up to the rez to spend time with his mom and cousins.

"He called you?" My mother's not even pretending to believe me.

"I called him and he told me he's working a swap meet on the outskirts of Hastings these days. I invited myself down."

"Doesn't sound like much of a vacation."

"And working with you at the inkatorium does? Look, I never get to see him. I miss him. I want to spend time with him too."

She gets this tired look in her eyes and turns away from me. "Fine. But you pay for gas and tolls from your savings because this isn't a pay week and we're pretty close to tapped out. And, just so you know, I'm going to call him beforehand and set him straight on some ground rules."

Alrighty, then, I'll have to call him up first and warn him that I've used him as an excuse for a getaway week with my boyfriend. When I talk to him, he's less receptive than I had hoped. I finally manage to get him to agree, but only by wielding some heavy-duty abandoned daughter guilt. It makes me feel as if I've turned into my mother, and I'm not at all sure he gets the details of the tale right.

I volunteer at the inkatorium every night in advance of the exit date. My mom tells Val she thinks I'm doing this to spend extra time with her before bailing. "She thinks it's sweet," Val says, patting my hand as she passes me the community service badge.

Like so much with my mom, it makes me mad. I'm only there to scrutinize the shift rosters and mess with the computers, and now she's loaded me down with emotional debt, the kind that's impossible to pay off.

I've picked a day I know she won't be on campus – she's heading to the state capital for her annual performance review – because I might be a bad daughter but not so bad that I want her around to get blamed for what happens. Val's off shift too.

I park Blue Belle in the back lot, close to the door. My entire savings are in the glove box; John's and my duffles are in the back seat area, and under those, the clothing in Mari's and Meche's sizes I've picked up at the thrift shop. Plus a tube with instaskin patches. The cargo cover is unfurled and hooked in. As hard as it is for me to do so with all my savings in there, I leave Blue Belle unlocked.

When I run into John he looks a little green. I think it's finally dawned on him that if we get caught we'll be in the type of trouble his parents can't buy him out of.

The staff is easy without my mother around, and at noon a bunch of them go to the mothership console to watch a show that involves people winning money if they're able to keep down whatever gross beverage the producers concoct.

In the lunchroom John and I deliberately stay away from Meche and Mari, but I can see them from where we sit. I swear to God, Havana Barbie looks as impassive as the doll Toño chose for her name. Mari plays catch with the kids, but I can tell she's preoccupied when she misses a fly ball. The kid who threw it hops around with her arms in the air as if she had accomplished the impossible.

After lunch, when I pass the mothership again, I see more staff gathered round. It seems a good omen that they're distracted and not as vigilant as normal.

The fire alarm is set to go off at 6:30 p.m., when John and I are getting off shift and the third grouping of inks are heading to the cafeteria for dinner. Mari and Meche are on third and, if all goes well, will be closer to the back exit than the front one when the alarm rings. We'll be out and together in the back parking lot, hidden in plain view with a crowd of inks and volunteers and junior staff. The senior staff will evacuate to the front lot with the inks from the infirmary and from the higher security rooms where the disruptive inks are held.

That's how it's intended to work, anyway.

I'm near the back door, where I'm supposed to be, and I can see Mari and Meche more or less where they should be when the alarm goes off. There's no John. And the staff is holding, not exiting.

I punch keys on my cell phone.

"Where r u?" I text John.

"Improvising."

"WTF?"

"Later. Pick up = frnt."

Within seconds Bennett is beside me at the door, listening to Renfro's voice rendered crackly through the 2-way radio: "There's a lot of smoke in A-wing. I don't think this has anything to do with the other, Bennett. Fire trucks should be here soon. I say it's a go."

Bennett starts calling out orders. The door opens, but I wait. Mari goes through first and stumbles into Bennett before straightening up and heading in the general direction of my car. I meet Meche's eyes in the brief moments before she too sweeps by in the crowd. I snag Bennett before he goes anywhere.

"John was working in A today."

He gives me a sympathetic look. "He'll be okay, Abs."

"Our shifts are over," I say. "Can I drive out front, pick him up and get going before the fire engines come and block me in all night?"

He nods. "I'll tell Renfro."

When I slip out the door, most of the staff and volunteers seem to be on the other side of the parking lot herding inks onto the back lawn and away from the building. I get into Blue Belle and haven't even started the car up when Bennett's at the driver side window motioning for me to roll it down.

He leans in and looks around.

"Amy and Greta are off shift, too, and have little kids to get home to. You think you can give them a ride? I think you can fit everyone if you put your bags in the cargo area."

"Sure," I say, after a second. "Are they out front?"

"Yeah. Renfro is sending them over to where John's waiting for you."

I nod a goodbye then roll the window up and watch him walk away. "You heard?"

Mari's voice comes out from under the cargo cover. "Those bags aren't going to fit in here. We hardly fit."

I maneuver Blue Belle to the front lot. About when I spot John, I hear the first fire engine racing down Manor and, from the sound of it, pretty damn close to the inkatorium's driveway.

"Shit, shit, shit. We're not getting out after all."

But John and Greta and Amy are thinking the same thing and they sprint up to Blue Belle and scramble inside.

"Punch it," John says. "We can still make it."

We do, just barely. Ed Sweeney, the cop who's blocked part of the road to give first responder vehicles clear access, honks angrily as I swing by him in flagrant violation of emergency rules of the road. He knows who Blue Belle belongs to and my mother'll hear about this from him. God, I'm going to be grounded for life.

Dropping off Amy and Greta adds 30 minutes to the trip, and because John's in the car I have to pretend I'm dropping him off next and start in the wrong direction. By the time we're in the clear, we're nearly an hour delayed. I pull over about five miles out of town, to a spot I know will be abandoned.

"What the hell happened? Why didn't they follow the established fire plan?" I ask as soon we've unhooked the cargo cover and let Meche and Mari out of the cramped space.

"Who knows?" John says. "But I overheard Renfro say he wasn't letting anyone outside unless he actually smelled smoke and located the source inside the inkatorium. So I set one in the bin with hair waiting to be hauled to the incinerator. Oh my God, it stank."

While we're talking, Mari and Meche change out of their jumpsuits, hide them in the weeds, then cover their tattoos with instaskin. In minutes we're on the interstate.

"I think we have a problem. Get off at the next exit," Meche says about 15 minutes on. When I look at her in the rearview, she's gone dead white. "I forgot to get rid of my tracker," she says, then pitches the chip out the window she's opened.

"Mari?" I ask when I've run out of names to call Meche.

"Remember how I tripped into Bennett? He's me for now. Until my tracker falls out of his clothes."

We try to find our way to Hastings on local roads. Without a map, and without GPS because cars that belong to people like me aren't equipped with options. Instead of three hours, John guesses it's going to take us five.

I fume as I drive. John watches me out of the corner of his eye but knows better than try to talk me out of it. After an hour, he leans over and turns on the radio. That's when we figure out what the staff was doing earlier glued to the television.

Across the state, cities and towns are burning.

Please, I think as we listen to the list, don't let the state capital be one. It is. And there's a ring of fires around Bedford, where my dad really is at the moment.

"Cell phone," I say to John. He digs it out of my bag, flips it open then shakes his head. Nothing.

The newscaster's up to the Fs on the list.

I pull over on the shoulder while we wait.

"What do we do if Hastings is burning?" John says.

We go from a bad place to a worse and more fearsome one. But I don't repeat the wolf's words because, hey, I don't believe in quoting figments of imagination. Still, I think it's right about one thing.

We're going to need magic.

# Part Two

"How do you elude a giant who takes out 400 with the swipe of one hand and carries the very mountains on his back?"

Francine Riordan, "Mythic Motif and Genocide in Central America," *Journal of Myth and Folklore* 57, 1: 64.

# Mari: Intercession

1.

The building where Finn and I rented our apartment is burning. So is Holy Innocents, both church and rectory. Abbie drives where we tell her to go, shock written on her features.

Meche gives me a look when we pass Hipco's headquarters – intact – and again when we go by its archives engulfed in flames. The fires aren't really random, they're in emergent neighborhoods that still rent to inks. The newspaper office, housed in one of those eccentric Robert Math buildings Finn once told me about, is untouched. Two blocks away, the city's Chinatown is char and cinder.

I look out the window onto a streetscape like I've seen in the photographs my father brought back with him when he went to Central America to retrieve me.

A war zone in everything but declaration.

I've never seen so many weapons out in the open. Vehicles full of guard and reservists rumble through flashing traffic lights. Intersections are barricaded. The night sky is orange from fire.

The flash mobs precipitate it, if you can believe the radio reports. Coordinated by twitter and cell phones, people flood transit centers and municipal buildings. The mob – all ink – tramples bystanders and overwhelms anyone who stands in its way. There is no manifesto to explain the action. What explanation needs to be written that isn't already engraved on our skin? Fifteen detention hubs and several safe communities are affected. Hastings isn't the only city responding to the havoc by firebombing its own people, only the most efficient.

We're stopped multiple times. No tattoos in this car, officer. See?

At Meche's direction, Abbie parks outside a brownstone in the toniest section of town. No slow burning shingle. No brick darkening under flame. Just the smoke from other sections of the city carried on heedless winds. Meche leads us to a house in the center of the block. I wonder who she knows here and whether they'll open the door to her ragtag cohort. Then I watch in surprise as she lifts the cover on a keypad by the door and punches in a string of numbers. The front door clicks.

"Come on," she says, "we're home."

The house is impeccably restored and appointed. Abbie walks around it in a haze, too honest to hide her envy. John plops down on the sofa as if he's been invited. And that's the hardest adjustment, we have been invited. By a woman different than the one we thought we knew from the inkatorium.

92

# Mari: Intercession

This one is an entrepreneur whose once-thriving peña is down to skeleton staff, just a line cook, Napoleón (green tat), and an older man named Silvio (blue). He removed the image of La Caridad that marked it as a peña a couple of weeks ago, he reports immediately, as if that's the most important thing he must explain to the boss who's been away for months.

Post-traumatic stress, I think.

But no, Meche gives him a significant look. "And?" she asks.

"And, nothing," Silvio says, defensive. "We're okay."

She mumbles something I don't quite catch.

"I've taken other liberties, too," he says in Spanish to Meche. Then, glancing at the teens, he switches to English. "So many people have been burned out by the fires, I've said some can stay here. At no cost." He lifts his chin and juts it just a little.

"Of course," Meche says, and suddenly she's entangled a conversation about freeing up the money it'll take to house and feed an unknown number of guests.

I wander, stroking the spines of the books lined neatly on shelves in her living room, then drift upstairs. The house has three floors, with a computer hub on each, and rooms ranging from grand to monastic.

Back on the first floor I find myself at the living room windows, looking out. My animal twin stretches. It feels like it's always been this way, *she* and me together on overlapping layers of existence. But every so often it still makes me wonder. Where does *she* end and I begin? And, can I even make that distinction?

Before I know it I've slipped the deadbolt on the backdoor, and again I don't know if it's her instinct or mine that leads me outside.

There's actually a fourth floor to the house, one level with the fenced-in garden I'm overlooking from the deck. I haven't seen any staircase leading down to it, and the front of the house has no separate entry, so its access must be hidden somewhere.

Meche finds me. She leans over the railing beside me. "I've told the children to call their parents and let them know they're alive and safe and that they won't be leaving until it's safe to transit the city."

I nod. "We owe them, you know."

She makes an irritated sound. "Of course I know."

After a while she says. "I don't recognize my city. Weird how your life can become unrecognizable and somehow you adjust, but when your city turns…. If my grandparents were here they'd feel some sense of déjà vu seeing the streets we drove through."

"I was thinking something along those lines about my parents."

"I wonder if we'll end up repeating their lives."

"Since my mother died violently, I vote no."

She turns around, leans her back on the railing. "Finn is here, by the way."

I start. "Now?"

"No, but he's staying here, so he'll be back. He's one of the people Silvio knew for certain I'd want to help. Father Tom too. They came by a few hours before us, with a West African family in tow. I've just met the mom, Laurene. She's got little kids so Silvio made her take the basement apartment where they can run around without getting underfoot." She sighs. "He really has a sadistic streak. I think she's more scared of the access stairway than what's happening outside."

"How *do* you get down there?"

"Stairway inside the closet next to the bar. A lot of the Civil War era buildings in the neighborhood have hidden stairways like it. Or had them, before remodels. They're all acute angles, narrow steps and steep pitch. Dodgy and scary, but kids never seem to have a moment of fear running up and down them."

I look out over her garden. It's not its season, but it's still pretty and just wild enough that I find myself making a noise an awful lot like purring.

"I'd give anything to remember what it's like to be fearless," I say after a moment.

"These are frightening times."

"No, I mean...."

"I know what you mean," she says when I can't finish my thought. "Sometimes the landscape of the heart becomes more foreign than any other."

Her face softens a little and she looks away from me.

I'm struck by how little I know her. And now I've cast my lot with hers, based mostly on chance and an instinct I can't even wholly call my own.

"Thanks," I say after a moment.

"For what?"

"For this."

She shrugs, then turns back to me. "I like the idea of having a bunch of people living here. It's like having family again."

"How long can you keep this going?"

"For years and years, probably." She raises an imaginary glass to the sky, "Thank you, Grandpa O'Gorman."

"I have enough money to have bought my way out of a tattoo way back when," she says. "Not that I considered it. What's the point of having principles if they aren't going to make your life difficult, right?"

She flashes me a sardonic grin, but soon goes serious again. "And now I find there are reasons to be glad for life's difficulties." After laying her hand fleetingly on my arm she goes back inside the house.

\*\*\*

Showers. Decent food. Conversation that jumps freely between Spanish and English. Every so often a person knocks at the door and gives Silvio the password he, Finn and Father Tom have agreed will identify those sent to seek

94

refuge or a meal on their way to some ill-defined elsewhere.

After eating, Silvio and John end up on separate couches, both leafing through books they've picked off Meche's bookshelves. The West African family retires to the basement apartment, and snatches of the song the mother sings to her children as she puts them to bed waft twistily up to the first floor. It isn't in any language I understand, and I've never heard it before, but the melody is sweet and I find myself repeating the words as if they were a prayer.

Later, Meche gets on the computer tucked into a corner of living room to – who knows? – manage investments or rabble rouse or galvanize her virtual network. I'm pretty much convinced she can do anything she sets her mind to do. A few times, when she's particularly intent on whatever is happening on screen, I think I see something moving just above her head. Like her thoughts take shape and swarm around her.

Abbie stands behind Meche, watching over her shoulder. The girl peppers her with technical questions about the custom software she's got installed. After a while Meche goes upstairs and comes back down with a sleek laptop.

"Here, play with this," she says to Abbie. The look that comes over Abbie's face is the visual equivalent of a squeal.

"Jeez, this is sick."

"Knock yourself out," Meche says with a smile, then goes back to whatever she was doing.

Father Tom drags in just after nine.

His eyes register his surprise at the scene. He looks from Meche to me and back again.

"Woe to him who underestimates women," he says finally.

"Or teenagers. Meet our rescuers," Meche says, introducing him to Abbie and John.

I see tears in the priest's eyes when he hugs me, but he dashes them away quick and talks to me as if we had stood together on the steps of his church just yesterday. Silvio gets up, ducks behind the bar along the far wall of the room and pulls out a couple of bottles.

"I'm in despair that among your peña stock there is nary a bottle of Jamesons," the priest says to Meche as soon as Silvio hands him a glass with dark rum.

She rolls her eyes. "Explain to me why anyone would pick a mouthful of peat over a mouthful of sugar?"

There's some back and forth about the drinks from their respective islands until they run out of jibes. Or pretense that these are normal times.

"How are things out there?" I ask.

Father Tom's eyes slide away and he takes his time answering. "Half my parishioners can't be found. And most of the ones I've located are hurt. Remember Elvira Pérez? I just barely managed to perform the anointing of the sick before she passed on. The emergency rooms are overwhelmed. And there are lines of vans waiting outside for the inks to be stable enough to take to the inkatoriums."

"Finn has been tweeting reports, filing stories, and taking photos and videos with his phone," he says. "The people at the Gazette are scared there'll be a news blackout pretty quick, so everything's going up as soon as it comes in. The state of emergency declaration has us all thinking like conspiracy theorists."

He glances at his watch. "I hope he's on his way."

"Is he going to be anywhere near a street called Callowhill?" Abbie asks without looking up from the laptop.

We all stare at the girl.

"Very likely," the priest says.

"I'm seeing tons of stuff on twitterfall about a flash mobbing there. Like, now."

Father Tom pulls out his cell phone, starts punching in numbers.

"Is there anyone left to form a flash mob?" Meche says.

I don't think it's supposed to be a question, but Abbie answers.

"From the way the call's multiplying on the fall, I'd say plenty."

"I'm not getting through to him," Father Tom says.

"Here we go," Abbie says, then moves the laptop off her lap to the coffee table where we can see the screen.

All of us cluster around jerky, pixilated footage of hundreds, maybe thousands of people running down Callowhill, past the charred skeleton of Holy Innocents. Soon the recording device ends up clipped to a belt, and the image shifts to a view of asphalt and the lower half of bodies and feet of the mob in motion. We can hear several languages being shouted out in proximity to the camera.

"Bloody hell, pick up the camera again so we can see where you are," Meche says to the anonymous auteur filling the screen with images.

"Won't happen," Silvio says. "They need to keep their hands clear."

"For what?" I say.

"For that."

Boots appear among the civilian footwear. Nightsticks hop in and out of view, and the sound is punctuated by the thud of wood on flesh. Gunfire starts peppering the audio.

"It was like that in Cuba," Silvio says. "Didn't matter which side you were on."

"Mother of God," Father Tom says.

At the corner of the screen we can see a girl, not much older than Abbie, go down under a volley of hard blows. She covers her head with her hands as she hits the pavement, but blood seeps through her fingers and she stops moving. A couple of people drop to their knees next to her, then begin to uluate their grief. The camera moves out of visual range but the audio picks up the keening for a while longer.

We peel away, one by one, each of us turning away from the reality unfolding virtually.

"I think I miss the inkatorium," I say.

*She* swats me hard enough that I stumble on my way to the sofa.

*Walls saved my life once,* I answer.

*It wasn't the walls*, she manages before I push her away.

But the thing is, *she* is right. The walls of the tabernacle had been a blind that hid my infant body, but if I had remained there I would have died. What had really saved me was the hand that opened the tabernacle's door. The one that reached in and carried me out. The one that held me as it ran.

Only, what if your brother's hand is raised against you? Or cuffed and held back? Or oblivious? What breaches the walls to save you then?

I don't know how long I sit on the sofa letting the conversations fold around me. I don't keep track of time any longer, it's a meaningless construct that runs in circles. Once upon a time? No way.

I fall asleep on the sofa as I'm changing the fairy-tale beginning. Ever upon a time? Or, never upon it? One or the other, that's the real opening.

\*\*\*

*I smell the char. She doesn't. Her nose is a poor instrument for such things.*

*Because she does not open her eyes, I spring away from her slumbering body and stand beside her. If there is danger I'll fight for her, as my kind always have, on my layer of the world. A layer her kind almost never credits with bringing about change. But it does. It does.*

*He stands at the entrance to the room, paralyzed.*

*If it were the girl standing in his stead, she'd see an enormous wolf bristled and alert beside the prone figure; if it were the old man, he'd see a creature of wing and celestial light wielding a sword.*

*This one sees me as Mari knows me. A jaguar, dappled light and dark.*

*I open my mouth and curl my long tongue. He has nothing to fear from me, her loves are mine.*

*I cannot speak to many minds other than hers, but I try him anyway.*

*Come close, I say.*

*When I don't sense a response, I draw back.*

*I understand. Fear immobilizes. It gives predators the taste of what it is to be prey; it reminds prey that they were created to feed something other than themselves.*

*But I have no fear. And I do not keep immobile. I unsheath my claws a second before I rake Mari's leg.*

*She jerks up to clutch the muscle twisted by a cramp on her layer of existence.*

*When I am sure she is awake, I jump back inside her. I find my way to what birthed this guise and splash in the ancestral river of her blood.*

"Am I dreaming?" he asks.

"No." I say.

He looks exhausted, smudged and marked by the dark, ashy disappearance of people's lives.

"Are you all right?" I ask.

He nods.

"We were worried about your getting caught in the mob." I look around. It's just two of us. Everyone else must have gone to bed. "What time is it anyway?"

"One," he says. "It took me a long time to get back here. And I was only ever on the fringe of things. But I'm thinking it's no story compared to yours."

He's as I remember him and yet he's not who he was before I left. The fact I'm not already in his arms is proof of that.

"Why care so long as both stories end in the same place?" I choose his words from long ago as a prompt.

But he doesn't meet my eyes and stays where he is.

I'm a fool. Never upon a time it is.

I pull myself up from the sofa.

"Mari...."

"I know," I say. I pat his arm on my way to the staircase. "Everything's changed."

I've picked a smallish room on the third floor. I can't remember who's in the rooms flanking mine but I hope I'm far enough away that they don't hear the sounds I make while I cry.

*She* surfaces partway. I feel her wrap her velvet around my heart, as she does at every real loss. The bed is soft and the linens smooth. They're scented with something much nicer than the antibacterial they used at the inkatorium. I drift to sleep focused on these small joys.

I wake a couple of hours later. The moonlight sneaks some silver through the blinds, and the room looks like a shell lit from within.

*Look. How beautiful it is*, I think at her.

*She* flicks me away and moves deeper into her catnap.

When I turn on my other side I see Finn stretched out beside me. His eyes are closed, his breathing even. It is the deep sleep of exhaustion. His arms are flung – one almost obscuring his eyes, the other crosswise over his torso – as if he's fending off what assails him simultaneously from without and within.

I don't think. I move into the nimbus of warmth he emanates when he sleeps and let my eyes rake over him. There isn't a centimeter of him I've forgotten. I want to touch him, but I don't. My love and desire aren't his obligation.

I hear the intake of breath and when I look up at his face, his eyes are open.

"You're in my bed. Still not one to ask for permission?" My voice is teasing, but I move away.

# Mari: Intercession

His arms go around me and pull me in tight.

"Marry me so I don't have to ask permission," he says, his voice rough.

I laugh, but it is a hurt sound. It's not me he wants, but a woman who lives now only in his memory.

He shifts onto his elbow and leans over me.

"Marry me," he says again.

"Even…" I start.

"Even," he cuts me off.

There is a smear of ash on his forehead and the smell of smoke in his pores. And something so complicated beneath I can't begin to identify its component parts, but I think love is part of it.

"Vale."

It's just a small word in Spanish – battling against the thunder of my heart, the sirens howling through the city, the sound of lives reduced by element to elemental.

It means okay. But also: it has worth.

It's barely out of my mouth when his hand tangles in my hair and he pulls me up to his mouth.

I remember it being good between us.

But not like this.

2.

*While she sleeps, I hunt.*

*I can wander hundreds of miles from her body if I believe she'll be safe during my exodus. Tonight, his arms around her promise this. So I jump.*

*The streets of this place she loves are dark, punctured by pockets of flame. I head to the fires. Her kind gather around light, even if it is the light of destruction. I nose around the smoking skeletons where embers still smolder.*

*I find a child half buried under ash and beams crossed over each other in a loose thatch. He is a sensitive. As I skirt fire to get to him, he sees me almost fully enfleshed, even though I usually appear semi-solid only when I'm seen out of the corner of their eyes or in the near dark.*

*He shrinks a little at my approach.*

*I can smell his fire-kissed skin, but no sores running foul. No clear waters leak out either, as when the body has no more blood to spare.*

*"Will you help me?" he calls out. He's scared of my staying but even more scared of my vanishing.*

*I cannot speak to his mind, but I can make myself understood. When he knows what I'm set to do, he sees me as a huge dog, shaggy brown and white, with a small keg strapped under my chin. The image of rescue from a story he heard before he was buried in his avalanche of cinder.*

*I shovel him clear, each paw tossing fast and wide in syncopation, then nose beneath the remaining grayness to reach an arm. I take it in my mouth and pull. Some of his body is freed from its bank of ash, but not all. Not enough.*

*It is his leg, pinioned under wood. that holds him down. It is not supposed to twist in that direction. The wood isn't heavy, I shove it away with the flat over my nose, and flick my ears away from his cries.*

*Even though I have hurt him by the freeing, when I drop into a crouch he throws an arm around my neck. Inch by inch I flatten and press against him. When nearly half his body leans on my back, I push fully under. He flings his other arm around my neck and buries his face in my fur.*

*I rise slowly off my haunches, testing his hold. He hangs on, I leap.*

*It is not hard to find the place where they take their wounded. It stinks of blood and burnt skin and the harsh stuff they use to clean both. I tip him off my back just outside the building under the strongest light. Where he will be seen best and I least.*

*Then I go back to my work.*

*I pass other spirits on the streets. Dreamwalkers. Scraps of being propelled by people sleeping restless in the city. The dreamwalkers are not like me. As they pass through the landscape they can change nothing. But they leave a trail. Most are luminous and their track smells of green and golden afternoon or silvered night. I notice only a few among them that leave the smell of carrion when they pass.*

*If I have learned anything since I've come fully alive it is that, in waking,*

# Mari: Intercession

*their dreamers cannot tell the one from the other.*

***

I'm in the shower the first time they come through the door. They don't need warrants during a state of emergency. At least they pound on the door instead of breaking it down. I step out and drip on the mat in my preferred bathroom on the second floor when I hear the commotion.

Finn's at the newspaper and Father Tom at the diocesan center trying to figure where he can celebrate Mass for his remaining parishioners now that the church is rubble. Silvio and Napoleón have roped Abbie into driving them to get groceries and more alcohol. The inks who still have jobs are at work.

Abbie's figured out how to get into the Hipco database, so she's sanitized Meche's and my tats back from non-alien status to citizen – as if we'd never been admitted to the inkatorium – but we're the only two inks currently in the house whose tats won't code to garbage.

I crack open the bathroom door. I can hear the civil patrol downstairs with Meche. Every ink is a suspected flash mobber these days but it can't hurt that she's gorgeous and filthy rich and just a tad supercilious. Not that it'll stop them from scanning her, but they'll be nicer about it.

I cross quietly to the stairway to the third floor. Inks come out of their rooms and follow me up. On the third floor, tucked between the smallest bedroom and the stairway is a small alcove with a folding, pull-down ladder for roof access. It is a metal contraption that looks much too corroded to support weight but in reality is solid enough. The joints unlock smoothly and the rail the ladder travels up to the roof is so well oiled it moves in complete silence.

I watch as the inks start climbing. The first one is Loreta, a middle-aged Filipino nurse. She moves up the stairs without problem and opens the trap door. A current of cool air swirls down to raise goosebumps on my damp, exposed skin. The last one through closes the trap and I climb up to slide the deadbolt. When I'm back down, I fold the ladder and push it back up the rail. I've stranded them on the roof but there's nothing that can be done about that until the house is clear.

I run, poking my head briefly in each room to check for telltales of habitation. When I hit the second floor, I nearly bowl over John.

"Where are they?" I ask.

"Basement."

According to Meche's plan for just this situation, the family living in the basement apartment was to leave out the back and through the three loose boards on the privacy fence that surrounds the garden. Supposing they had warning enough to do so, and supposing they weren't sandwiched between patrol members coming down the stairs and through the gardenside entrance at once.

"Anyone caught?"

"I don't think so. By the way, they really grilled me when I told them I was her nephew."

"Thanks." I slip back into the bathroom. I barely have time to drop the towel and put on my underwear before one of them shoulders the door open.

He checks me out.

"Wrist," he says when he's done looking.

My hand shakes as I hold my tat out to be scanned.

At least it's an official scanner he carries, not one of the knockoff fails.

He studies the readout for a while. "Maryanna?"

I try not to shudder. The last time I heard my name pronounced that way I was in the woods near the Canadian border.

"Why are you here?" he asks. "That's a Hastings address."

My old one. Before Finn, before the inkatorium, before the fires. Once upon a time.

"It was Mercedes' birthday last night. I drank too much and she wouldn't let me drive home." That's the agreed-upon story.

"Is your car is parked outside? Which one is it?"

I describe Abbie's Blue Belle, which is on script, but then belatedly remember the car's not there at the moment.

He's unconvinced, I guess, because he keeps questioning me. While I stand there in my Hello Kitty underwear, wet hair dripping down my back. After a while his cohorts jostle him to get moving. I get dressed while they search the rooms on the second floor and as I start downstairs a few of them are going up the stairway to the third.

I find Meche by the window, staring at a man poking around her garden.

She turns when I come in. "They done?"

"On three."

"Oh God."

"I know. Has he noticed the loose boards in the fence?"

"Not that I can tell. Heads up," she says after a moment.

A few seconds later a man opens the door between house and deck. Unlike the others, this guy's got brass. A fire chief who's been deputized to lead the civil patrol, I think.

"Nice place," he says. "I've always dreamed of having a garden."

He does a circuit of the living room, running his fingers over the keyboard of the computer on his way. He glances at the monitor as it wakes from the touch. When he passes the bookshelves he runs his fingers over the books. As if all the information he gleans comes through his fingertips. When he's done he sits on one of the sofas and pushes the laptop aside to put his feet up on the coffee table.

"Where do you work?" he asks. One of us, both of us, I can't tell.

"I work at Hipco," I say.

"Well, I used to," I amend. I've gone off script.

"Oh yeah? Why'd you leave?"

"I'm getting married soon and my fiancé doesn't want me to work." *This* is the script.

"A little old fashioned, if you ask me," he says, then looks up at Meche. "And you?"

He's tall and lanky, blond in almost exactly the shade she's re-dyed her hair. Even though his eyes are dark brown, they could pass for twins.

"Self-employed," she answers. "A technical writer."

"What do you write? Better living through chemistry?"

I feel my muscles tense. Where did that come from?

But Meche keeps to the script. "Programming. Computers."

"Figures," he says. "I noticed multiples. And this one." He pulls his feet off the coffee table, leans forward and reaches for the laptop.

When he lifts the lid it comes to life with swirling pixels onscreen instead of the static logo that branded the desktop last night. They coalesce into what appears to be a room. In the center is a golden globe that rotates, then begins to unravel as if it were a ball of yarn. As the animation progresses hundreds of threads uncoil and whip around and eventually fill the screen. As soon as that happens, the normal desktop reappears.

"Nice," he says as he closes the lid.

"An evening's work," Meche says without missing a beat.

Not even a couple hours, I think. The equivalent of a doodle. Which makes me wonder what Abbie can really do.

A couple of men come down the stairs and into the living room. "They're clear," reports the one who burst in on me in the bathroom.

"All right," the brass answers. "Start on the next house. I'll join you in a sec."

"The house to the left belongs to an elderly couple who can barely get around, the one on the right belongs to a woman who is part of the Daughters of the American Revolution," Meche says. "None of them fits the profile of the flash mobbers you're looking for."

The man shrugs. "On my watch everyone gets searched, no matter their age or pedigree. Otherwise, what's the point?"

"There is no point," she says.

He studies her before he gets to his feet. We trail him as he walks to the front door. As we pass the staircase I catch a glimpse of John lurking at the top.

"I think you can expect more like me to come through here in the next number of weeks," the man says as he pauses in the space between the inner and outer doors. "Not through any report of mine, you understand, just protocol during a state of emergency. If I were you I'd, ah, smooth the edges of your routine a bit."

We watch him leave.

"Coño," Meche says.

I sag against the door. "Where'd we mess up?"

"Roof," Meche calls up to John, then goes to stand in front of the living room computer. She clears the screensaver and stares at it.

"Come here," she says. "What does this read as to you?"

I look at groupings of letters and numbers I know must be chemicals. "I don't know, compounds?"

"Formulas," she corrects automatically as she scrolls down to the bottom of the screen, then zooms the view. "And this?"

I shrug. "Another one. You don't expect me to recognize these, do you?"

I hear John coming down the stairs. Meche scrolls back up to the top, then waits for him to come into the room.

"What's this look like to you?" she asks again.

He doesn't even pause. "Formulation for instaskin. A variant of the one Abbie and I made."

When I meet Meche's eyes, they look pained.

"John only recognizes them as such because he's made the stuff," I say to her. "Otherwise, he might know what the individual chemicals are, but not what they become."

She scrolls down again. "Now what do you see, John?"

"The chemical you use to dissolve instaskin."

Meche's shoulders slump as if a weight had been dropped on them.

"You're supposing the brass had time to register what he saw onscreen," I say. "And that he has enough of a science background that he might recognize the compounds. And then that he can figure out what you're making from all of them. I think that's a huge stretch."

"And even if all of that were true, the components aren't exactly commonplace, right?" I add.

"The solvent is," John says. "It's acetone. You know, nail polish remover."

"Come on. If you don't know something exists how would you know to read that as its solvent?"

"Mari's got a point," John says.

But Meche's no longer really paying attention to us. She's studying the screen and more or less talking to herself. "Given enough time I can work out an acetone-proof variant and set up a production line here. I'll have to contact Toño, and arrange for delivery of raw materials...."

And then it's clear to me that thinking this out, coming up with yet another formulation and another problem to solve is Meche's attempt to wrest control from the uncontrollable. To feel, again, wholly the woman she was before the inkatorium. Or maybe even before that, back to the days when her wrist and her future were clear.

I surprise her – and myself – when I give her a hug.

***

I'm helping Silvio and Napoleón make dinner for twenty when I feel Finn's arms wrap around my waist. His body is hard against mine.

# Mari: Intercession

"Isn't there a news story you're supposed be covering, like the after-effects of riots?" I say. I wish I didn't catch sight of Silvio's smirk as he and Napoleón move to tasks that take them to the other side of the kitchen.

Finn ducks down to kiss me behind the ear. "I don't care. You're purring by the way."

I unwrap his arms and turn to face him.

He wears the dazed look you get when you feel newly soaked in love. The one I noticed in the mirror this morning.

"Let's skip dinner," he says.

Silvio and Napoleón half turn toward us.

"Umm, you know we're not alone, right?" I say.

"Guys, you going to object if I take your helper away?" he asks without taking his eyes off me.

"Yes," they both say, snickering.

He leans forward and kisses the top of my head. "Okay, I'll wait," he says, so quiet only I hear.

At dinner we hold hands under the table. It's weird, the way something innocent becomes erotic in the right situation. I hear the plans Meche lays out for returning the teens to Smithville. I hear Father Tom's tales about people I remember from church, now in need of shelter. I hear Silvio's replay of some of the calls he's fielded from peña regulars. I hear all this, and it matters to me, but I don't pay attention.

What are words to the fact of a hand? To the skin and blood and sinew of it? To who it belongs to and what it wakes? I can't keep my mind off him for more than a few seconds at a time. It's on my face, I know it. Each time he turns to me, his eyes register a sort of shock, and get darker with desire. His hold on my hand tightens.

After dinner he gets up from the table to hunt down his cell phone which is forgotten in some corner of the cavernous house, ringing the Cranberries ringtone that indicates it's a call from his sister. Meche makes her way around to my side of the table picking up plates.

"Oh for God's sake," she whispers while she's paused at my spot. "If you get any more obvious the kids are going to use it as license and Father Tom is going to refuse to sleep under the same roof."

"I used to be such a good Catholic," I say, my face getting even hotter than it's been.

"Well, that ship's sailed," she says.

"You think it's okay?"

She starts laughing. "Are you asking for permission or forgiveness?"

"Maybe both. Or a blessing."

"Funny, I thought love was blessing enough."

I look at her. She looks back.

"Tell Finn I've gone upstairs, would you?" I say, pushing my chair back.

She rolls her eyes. "Yeah. Like I'll have to."

I probably don't wait long, but it feels like forever before I hear his tread on the stair.

*She* pricks her ears.

*Go away,* I tell her.

Do jaguars laugh? I think so as *she* sinks deep to where I cannot access her nor she me.

But maybe *she* isn't wholly distinct from me. Because when he opens the door and stands there, desire rolling off him in waves so strong they're almost visible, the distance means nothing. I spring into his arms.

# Mari: Intercession

*The night is at its darkest moment, just before it remembers to turn toward dawn. I start back homeward, then burst into a flat-out run. I love this part.*

*But several blocks from the house I notice across the street another matches my pace.*

*"Kai, kai, kai," the creature calls.*

*I know it is the first syllable of its name, because I know its name.*

*It is a kaibil. A dwarf like the ones in Mari's story.*

*It aims to reach the house before I do. And it does. But I've already gathered myself. I sail over its head and contort my body mid-air so I land on the stoop facing it. Snarling.*

*It is only a borrowed home, but it holds Mari and everything I am born to defend. Love. Community. Hope. What the dwarves seek to destroy in every iteration of our story.*

*"We meet far from home." The dwarf's mouth is a round sinkhole on the pitted ground of his face. His hair is dappled, like my fur, and his eyes flinty.*

*"This is home."*

*His laugh fractures as it comes out of his mouth. Great jagged obsidian teeth chew on the sound.*

*"What is this," he points back to the smoldering section of the city, "if not proof of the opposite? Your kind is not welcome."*

*"You are my kind," I say, though the words taste bitter in my mouth. It is gall to know we spring from the same source.*

*"I meant the ones you protect," he says.*

*While he talks his hands shuttle back and forth as if he were weaving. And he is. He gathers to him the wisps of walking dreams that fit his design.*

*The first dreamwalker he brings forth wears its skin in tatters. Beneath the shreds of blooded velvet are the gleam of bone and spike and the empty socket of something removed by force.*

*Another – many small, teeming parts moving as one – is without feature but pale and foul with rot.*

*Behind that, a third dreamwalker oozes an oily ichor as it moves. Its maw opens to row upon row of fine, long teeth, each as keen as steel.*

*"Stand aside, Jaguar-of-the-Moon." The dwarf needles me with my formal name, a name from another time and place when I was much greater than I am now. "You cannot withstand what faces you."*

*"The dreamwalkers have no power over me," I say. "And you are just a lone kaibil."*

*His hair-tipped ears twitch. "But, do you hear?"*

*The cries of "kai, kai, kai" are faint, but growing nearer.*

*"My brothers are coming," he says.*

*"And these," he motions around him with stone hands, "are not intended for you." The tapestry of human nightmare that accompanies him blows forward*

*with his words.*

*Even as I bare teeth and claw and raise a spine of fur, I know the dwarf is right. If enough other kaibiles join him and I fall, the dreamwalkers will enter the house and coat every living surface with a slime of hatred and despair.*

*What happens on this layer affects all layers.*

*I strike.*

*Where I rake the dwarf with my claws a fetid, clay-like slurry of dirt and blood pours out. A full swipe cuts him in half and he falls into two piles.*

*But behind him is another kaibil. Before I can reach to batter this one with my paws, he drives his stone fists deep into my flesh. I jump backward and flick my tail while I try to breathe.*

*The kaibil's eyes dart to the left but I've already heard his brother's approach. It is ever this way. Though I am the stronger, there are always many more of their ilk than mine. And here, it is just me.*

*I launch myself onto the kaibil's back. My mouth fills when I bite through his neck. His brother slams into me and I feel the ragged, obsidian teeth punch through my skin. I don't let go until I've shaken the first into slurry, then I rip the second off me. His teeth leave streaming gashes in my side.*

*Each time a kaibil lands a blow, my lungs have to work twice as hard to catch the next breath. My body is marked where they've bitten through my pelt. One, larger than the others, catches my face in his maw. I bite through his tongue, and when he jerks away, the tongue stays caught in my teeth.*

*I continue like this until fifteen piles of clay and blood stain the sidewalk.*

*When the street finally goes quiet, I limp up the steps to the house.*

*But one last, unseen kaibil has timed his attack perfectly. He thuds into me as my ribcage is above the edge of one of the concrete steps. I hear bone crack when I go down.*

*The dwarf hops to the door, a look of triumph on his face.*

*I drag myself to standing and sway in place, unable to take a step.*

*The dreamwalkers course around me to join the kaibil.*

*The kaibil's hands draw a rectangle. Midway up the wall, near the doorframe, the same shape limns itself and begins to glow.*

*Whatever hope I have held to wicks away.*

*The portal is etheric, bypassing safeguards against invasion put in place on the brick-and-mortar layer of existence.*

*But when the dreamwalkers try to reach it, they are bounced back. The kaibil, too, though a more solid kind of spirit, cannot get close. Time and again he approaches and is rebuffed.*

*The glow reshapes and drops away from the wall. Neither as vaporous as the dreamwalkers nor as enfleshed as the kaibil, the shape is something like each of us. And more.*

*She wears a heavily embroidered robe over a dress that spreads wide as the bottom of a triangle. Water splashes up on it in waves, but the fabric is dry when the waves recede. The dress narrows, turns blue and spangled with stars and instead of water lapping, it is the moon beneath her feet. The stars glide off her dress and swirl up to constellate for an instant above her head before they disappear. She finally resolves into a woman dressed in a long, close yellow dress, with dark golden skin and unbound hair. She drops a slender hand on the creature by her side – by turns shaped like a wolf, or a star, or a streaming fall of ones and zeroes.*

*"Sister," the woman says, meeting my eyes, amber to amber. "Did you think you stood alone? There are others here consecrated to the same service."*

*She walks toward me, dissipating the dreamwalkers with her passage. The kaibil rushes the space she's left open, but the shifting being there flares, then turns to a chain curtain that drops heavily on the kaibil, ensnaring him in its links.*

*The yellow woman bends to wrap her slender arms around me and lifts me easily. She carries me up the stoop and past the kaibil. The house's door flies open of its own accord. The golden mesh that has held the kaibil resumes a wolf shape and slips inside the opening. The yellow woman turns around at the threshold and looks down at the dwarf.*

*"Go back and tell those you serve that you are undone at the foot of my house. There is no entry here for you."*

*"It will not always be so." The words are ugly as they come out of the kaibil's mouth, but his eyes hold true sight and I feel myself start to shake with it.*

*"No," the yellow woman agrees. "But until that time, you will not pass."*

*She shuts the door.*

***

Loreta tapes me up.

When *she* is wounded, so am I.

Loreta won't look at Finn, and he's half crazed. That I'm so injured mostly. But also that anyone would think him capable of hurting me, for that's what he reads in Loreta's gaze when she finally meets his eyes.

*She* has gone so deep inside me to salve her wounds that for a while I remember what it was like when she wasn't around. I'm curiously flattened by my sudden solitude – more, even, than by the injuries – and I sleep on and off through the day. By the time Finn gets back from work, most of our community has grown noticeably cooler toward him. Which has to sting since some of them have found shelter here only through his effort.

Meche comes into the kitchen during dinner prep. Silvio pretends to faint.

"Shut up," she says to him when she notices. She corners me. "All right, be straight with me. Did Finn hit you? Father Tom keeps telling people there is no way in hell, but you haven't given us any other explanation."

There is a betrayal of our growing friendship in the question, and I know she can read the reproach on my face. "Of course he didn't," I say icily.

"Give me a reason to believe you." It is a plea like I haven't heard, nor ever imagined, coming from her.

"I'll tell everyone what really happened after dinner."

She gives me a long look and finally nods.

*You have to show yourself to them.* The thought I convey to my twin carries a note of panic. *Even if it isn't in your nature to do so.*

I don't hear an answer.

During dinner I am the small, warm buffer between Finn and the others.

"Mari has something to say to us," Meche says forcefully as soon as the clamor of the meal starts to die down.

I squeeze Finn's hand before I stand up. I don't look directly at any of them. "Forgive me, but there is no other way to tell this," I say. "Once upon a time…."

I hear someone groan. Loudly. Pointedly. I start at the beginning anyway.

I feel *her* rise to the story. When I get to last night, I stop telling and start repeating. It is my spirit twin's memory, not mine.

There is dead silence when I finish. I walk to the entrance of the dining room and flip the light switch. The room turns twilit, illuminated only by what filters in from other rooms.

*Now,* I say. *Please?*

*She* jumps. The pain in my ribs almost makes me black out.

Then there she is, standing beside me.

Perhaps predictably, the Central Americans and Mexicans at the table see her first. Myth and legend lives pretty close to the surface for many of us. The others who have sensed her before – and named that sense with shapes from their own beliefs – see her now as I see her: a jaguar both ancient and eternal, eyes alive with the stuff of dream and nightmare.

*She* limps over to where Finn sits and butts her head under his hand. He is awkward with her, trying to stroke her unsolid head as if she were a domestic cat. I sense something like amusement bubble up in her, but also a love both like and unlike what I feel for him.

*Your magic is that magic will never abandon you,* she mindspeaks him. But, of course, he doesn't hear her and just keeps trying to pet her.

When I turn the light back on, for an instant *she* fades to what might catch the edge of your eye when you're not really looking, then jumps back inside me.

The eyes trained on Finn and me are uniformly round. Nobody says anything, and the evening ends in silence.

I'm alone in the kitchen loading the dishwasher when Meche and Abbie come in.

"Mari," Meche says, contrite.

"Shut up," I cut her off. "Where's Finn?"

"In the garden. Father Tom's with him," she says. "I think I saw a bottle of Jamesons go out with them."

They keep watching me.

110

# Mari: Intercession

"Stop it," I say, tired of being the center of attention. "It's okay. I'm not really pissed off, you know, just a little freaked out. Like I stood in front of everyone in my underwear."

"The 'Hello Kitty' ones?" Abbie says, then cracks up.

"That's bad," I say.

Moments later Meche is laughing too, and I can't help it, I join in.

Somewhere deep inside me I hear an echo.

# Finn: Burying the lede

1.

"So it's done. I've filed for divorce."

Strangely, Cassie's called me on the landline of the paper instead of my cell phone.

"Congratulations, I guess. You going to be okay if I stay friends with him?"

"You mean when he surfaces from the deep end he's gone off?"

"The whole world's gone off the deep end."

"Yeah, that seems to be one of the excuses."

I sigh.

Melinda's glaring at me. As if I might take her sudden fury as anything other than editor bluff.

"What does Mom say?"

"After all the years of scorn she's suddenly acting as if I'm being precipitous. And she really doesn't cotton to my idea of holding out for half the value of the Smithville property as part of the settlement. Go figure."

"For once I agree with her."

"Nice. I kind of expected better from you."

"Sorry. Forgot the sibling solidarity at all costs rule. The comment was uncalled for. "

"I'll say." She pauses for a bit, then adds, "I'm going out for drinks with Allison and Sarai to mark the occasion."

"Ask Sarai if the tunnels under Math's buildings are filled to capacity yet, would you? Father Tom has a few more families he has to find some sort of shelter for."

She makes a rude noise. "Ask her yourself. I was calling to invite you to join us."

"I don't think so."

"Because it sounds like a buzzkill or because you're swamped by work or because you're suddenly the poster boy for in-love?"

"All of the above? And there's no sudden about it. Should I remind you about months' worth of conversation concerning wasting my life waiting for Mari?"

"I know." She goes silent for a moment. "You're lucky. Things always turn out right for you in the end."

"God, I hope so."

"I guess I'd better get off the phone. Allison's starting to shoot me mean boss-friend looks."

# Finn: Burying the lede

"Okay. Hey Cassie?"

"What?"

"You know I hope it turns out right for you in the end too, right?"

"I know."

Melinda comes over to my desk the second I hang up.

"Rumors," she says.

"Like twitter rumors?" I make a face as I say it. Lately there have been a bumper crop of bogus leads on the fall.

"No. Like boyfriend in the civil patrol rumors."

"You still seeing that guy?"

"Tall, blond and handsome? You bet. He's like a dream come true."

"Gross. I imagined better for you."

"You're kind. And mean at the same time. Anyway, you want to hear what he says? They're expecting another mob scene."

"Where?"

"The big scanner warehouses on Amsterdam."

"Jesus. Doesn't the Senate Majority leader own a piece of that business, or something?"

"Or something," she nods. "He was on the board of directors and still has a big chunk of shares."

"They're doing it to get the feds involved."

"That's what Arthur thinks."

"When?"

"He's being told to prepare for tomorrow."

"Are you putting anyone else on it?"

"Are you kidding? I'm putting everyone else on it."

"So why are you talking to me?"

"Because I expect you'll be the only one to file anything worth shit. When all the smoke clears, you know what this'll be, right?"

"A Pulitzer."

"Damn straight."

"History isn't about prizes, you know."

She looks at me with pity overflowing her eyes. "It's all about prizes, you moron. Hey," she yells at Matthews, "If you ever again put the word 'contumacious' in a piece you file I'll string you up by the balls, you hear me?"

"Melinda?" I say before her butt entirely clears my desk.

"Yeah?"

"You know how to pick a lock?"

"Duh."

"All the flash drives with my notes are in the top drawer of my desk."

Her eyes narrow. "You losing your nerve? Because I can't imagine a worse time for it."

"No. Just being a little paranoid."

"Paranoid's fine. Paranoid's smart. Hey, how 'bout I save you like 50 column inches in the A-section tomorrow so you can include all that backgrounder stuff you're so fond of?"

"Sounds good."

"It does, doesn't it?" She flashes me a smile when she goes.

*** 

I don't want to get out of bed.

There isn't anything in the world better than waking up next to the person you love. I pity Father Tom for the fact he'll never experience this. Of course, he says he knows a love much greater than what can be had on earth, but I can't imagine it. Nothing bigger than this fits in the human heart without blowing it apart.

This is what I see when I look down into the circle of my arms this morning: Dark eyes like pools of ink underlaid with pain and an equal measure of joy. I know, without an instant of doubt, I fit in the latter and if you don't think that does something to a man, you're crazy.

"Why are you awake so early?" she asks, stretching but not breaking the contact along the length of our bodies.

"Melinda thinks there's going to be a big story to break," I say, then lean in to kiss her. "Strange days make for exciting journalism."

"I could do with a little less strange and exciting."

"The state of emergency can't last forever. It's expensive. Pile that on top of the ongoing expense of running the inkatoriums and all the lost ink revenues, something's going to give. Just about the time the state budget has to pass."

"You think it'll ever go back normal again?"

"A new normal. Kids like Abbie and John and younger won't even remember what it was like."

"Speaking of Abbie and John, I wonder if Meche's decided when exactly to drive them back to Smithville," she says. "I thought Abbie was going to die when Meche made an offer on Blue Belle."

"Good die or bad die?"

"Both. Abbie knows it's a great deal. But that one forms such tight, unbreakable bonds."

"Poor John."

She smacks me.

"I'm going to miss them," she says. "They're lodged in my heart now."

"Another one who forms unbreakable bonds."

"Poor Finn."

I shut my eyes, hold her close. *Unbelievably grateful Finn*, I think. But I don't say it.

"I don't understand the point of having a chambered heart if not to let people take up residence," she says. "Meche and Abbie and John and Nely are all crammed into one chamber. Father Tom is in the same one as my dad.

You're in another."

"See that you don't make me share it, okay? "

"Like anyone would fit in there with you."

"Ha. You're funny."

She doesn't go on to list the tenant of the fourth chamber. I don't have to ask who it is.

I open my eyes to look at her. "Maybe we should name him. So we don't always think of him as the baby."

"I don't want to think of him at all."

"And that works for you?"

"No," she says. "It doesn't. But it seems to be the new normal."

We stay silent for a while, but when I start to get out of bed she pulls me down to her.

"Is there time?"

"There's always time," I lie.

Later, she watches me get dressed. "Promise me you'll be back before I even get out of bed."

I sit down on the edge of the bed. "Ask me for a real promise."

She laughs. "You're promised to me already, silly."

I kiss her and as I straighten back up, I brush the hair out of her eyes. The other one looks out of them.

*I have a bad feeling*, I cast the thought at her.

As if I had magic.

***

"I can't believe Melinda has me covering this," Belsen grumbles. "Nothing's happening. Nothing newsworthy ever happens when I'm around. And not for Sophie either." Sophie is the young photographer interning with the Gazette, and I think it may be an indication of how tremendous Melinda believes this will be that she's decided to put her on this assignment. So far, the girl hasn't been able to shoot anything in focus.

Ag, the real photographer, is tracking tweets on her mobile so she can shoot and post even before the mob turns down Amsterdam. Matthews is the lead reporter on that end.

"Just keep your eyes open," I say.

We're sitting on a fire escape one flight above Amsterdam, and across the street from the warehouses where, if Melinda is correct, the mob will be converging.

Any minute now.

About forty-five minutes later the Talking Heads ringtone sounds from my cell phone. Melinda.

"My boy must have fucked up," she says.

"No shit. This place might as well be a ghost town."

"You better start on back to the office. There's real stuff happening."

"Like what?"

"Ribbon cuttings and such."

"Nice, Melinda."

"Hey, you've got to keep a sense of humor."

And you do.

All day I've felt doom sitting on my shoulder. I've said goodbye over and over without putting it in words. And nothing happens.

That's life for you.

2.

I'm five houses down the block from Meche's, knocking on the door of the ob/gyn who lives there. Melinda's lost her edge after the great-scanner-riot-that-wasn't fiasco and I'm here to do a simple profile at her direction.

The air is finally clear of the heavy smoke smell that has clung to the city, and standing outside waiting for the doc to open the door, I can see the first signs of a late-arriving spring.

An attractive African-American woman, fortyish, dressed in jeans and an old t-shirt with a face faded to indistinct wraith, opens the door.

"Doctor Watkins?"

"You must be the reporter from the Gazette. Come in. I hope you don't mind talking while I paint my living room. I get next to no time to take care of household tasks so I'm afraid I'm not giving it up, not even for newspaper fame." She gives me a lopsided smile.

I like her immediately.

But the interview is routine. She does the requisite amount of work at a community clinic in one of the lower-income neighborhoods of Hastings and has some state-of-the-art machines at her higher-income regular practice, but there's nothing really to distinguish her from dozens of other doctors in the city.

"Can I ask you something, off the record?" I say at the end of the interview when we're drinking perfect espressos in her stainless steel kitchen.

"Sounds dangerous. Shoot."

"Why am I interviewing you?" I know I sound rude. But she reminds me a lot of Meche and I have a feeling I'll get a real answer.

She laughs. "When Melinda came in for her pap smear ...."

"Too much information," I interrupt, putting my hands up in a stop motion.

"... I might have implied I had something that would interest you all."

"Have I missed it?"

"No. Glossed over it is more accurate."

"Okay. I'm listening now."

"I told you I presented a paper at the state medical association's conference last year."

"Yeah. I got that. About," I dig my reporter's notebook out of my back pocket and flip through until I get to the right page, "the impact of economic class on patterns of fertility. Sounds thrilling."

She grins at me. "You might not think so, but it is quite a sexy bit of scholarship."

"Ha. I imagine so."

"Anyway, on the basis of the paper I was invited to be part of the state commission on public health concerns."

"Got that. Yawn."

"One of the first things new members get to do is take a look at the bigger state-run interests that dovetail with their areas of expertise. So the other two newbies got the inoculation and nutritional development programs. I got inkatoriums."

"Did I miss something in your background? Because I'm not getting how you're an ink expert."

"I'm not. But the reproduction rate of inks is much on the commission members' minds these days. Like, is there a consistently high fertility rate or is there a lot of variation between blue tats and greens? Or black tats and the other two? And if so, what does it mean in terms of population control if they close down the inkatoriums?"

"They're considering that?"

"Indeed."

"On the record now."

"No. But I promise, I'll give you something before you go."

"So what *does* it mean in terms of population control?" Every hair on the back of my neck is standing.

"It means a sterilization program at the inkatoriums before they're shut down."

"You're shitting me."

"I'm not. The inkatorium closest to the Canadian border has pioneered the program we're thinking of adopting. They've been running it for the past six months. It's pretty cost effective since it uses implanted rods to release the sterilizing agents subcutaneously. By the time the rods disintegrate and are absorbed into the body, the effects are irreversible. It's testing at about three months after implantation at the moment. And 96 percent efficacy."

"Jesus."

She finishes her espresso while she watches me digest the information.

"What are you giving me on the record?"

"This," she digs into the pocket of her jeans and pulls out a flash drive. She places it on the counter beside my reporter's notebook. "It's a visual record of a week of procedures at the originating inkatorium. The videos aren't great quality, and the sound is dreadful. Also, I don't know if they're Mp4s or what you might need to use to open and view them, but there they are."

I pocket the flash drive. "What made you decide to give this to the Gazette? Aren't they going to know you leaked it?"

"Maybe I don't care." She meets my gaze.

I go home rather than back to work and hand the flash drive over to Abbie.

"What's on this?"

"Don't know really. Media."

She pushes it into the USB port of the laptop, but soon yanks it out and goes over to the bigger computer where John's playing a game.

"Off," she says, then gives him a shove.

As soon as he vacates the spot she sits down. "Go away," she says to me. "I'll call you when I have something."

I walk out to Meche's deck.

# Finn: Burying the lede

Spring is all about the smell of damp dirt with tender green fighting its way through it. The smell of hope. When I look out past the quiet Bardstown houses to the cindered center of Hastings I think how every story worth telling has at its heart a season of sacrifice that leads to renewal. I hope our story is one of those.

When Abbie calls me back into the house nearly everyone has gathered around the computer table in the living room.

She clicks on a shortcut she's created. "I'm opening the media files in an open source video editor I downloaded so we can stop them and watch them in 1/16 of a second increments if we want. When I save them I'll save them as Quicktime movies anybody can view. Ready?"

When I nod, she opens the first of about 20 media files. There's a lot of jiggling – and the aural equivalent – until the camera ends up on a stable surface.

The establishing shots are of something like a doctor's examination room with little to distinguish it. A 50ish man with salt-and-pepper hair fills the frame temporarily. His mouth moves, but the sound is so low I can't really hear what he's saying.

"Hold on," Abbie says. She pauses the video, then cranks both the monitor and computer sound settings. It's much more audible when she hits play again, but still not good.

"Where did he say they are?" Meche asks.

Abbie rewinds, slows down playback, but the name of the inkatorium is still garbled.

"Deliman," Mari says. "Up in the Algonquin Lake area."

We all turn to look at her.

"I recognize him," she says.

A sharp lancet pricks my heart.

"Look, he's got his inkatorium badge on," Abbie says, advancing the video by fractions.

"I don't think that's going to be readable, do you?" Meche says, leaning in.

"Wait," Abbie clicks a few dozen seconds in, then pauses it. "Here. I can read it now. Langdon, chief administrator, Deliman Health Center."

"I don't know," Father Tom says. "Is it on screen long enough for any but the youngest eyes to see? It looks like a blur to me."

"I can cut in a zoomed still image," Abbie offers.

"Later," I say.

She hits play again.

Langdon stands in the middle of the frame next to a nasty-looking chair. A 30-something ink woman is led to the chair by a "handler" wearing a badge, only this one truly is unreadable. The procedure, Abbie says, is identical to the one for tracker insertion, but here the incision goes between the spine and shoulder blade and five slender tubes are inserted instead of the GPS unit.

"Well, that's completely innocuous," I say after the stitches are set. "Not even much blood."

"Shhh," Meche shushes me. As the camera dials back to wide-angle, a group of observers come into view. They raise their hands and ask questions. What do the tubes contain? How long until the tubing disintegrates completely and the time release is complete? Any side effects? More questions and more answers until it's impossible not to understand what the procedure is, and what its desired effect.

The next video is much the same, as is the one after that, though the inks in the chair and the handlers change. And the subjects get younger and younger. The last girl we see undergo the procedure is no more than six.

The penultimate video shows the procedure performed on an ink man. The ubiquitous Langdon drones on about the same process, different chemical sterilizing agent. Again he mumbles, and we have to turn to Meche for an educated guess about what it might be.

As the last video starts to run, I turn my thoughts to the possibilities. Send the raws to Melinda to post as is? Ask her to have one of the techs see if the sound quality can be improved? Or edit it into a more polished report? I'm about to punch Melinda's number into the cell when I notice everyone has gone silent.

I glance at the monitor.

On screen, a young boy – maybe eight? – is having the tubes inserted. Same as the other videos. I'm not entirely sure why a number of the faces looking at the computer monitor look so miserable.

"What?" I ask the first person who meets my eyes. Mari. Her eyes are shiny and suspiciously full and she just shakes her head.

"His name is Pete Nguyen," Abbie answers, voice flat, as she pauses the vid. "He arrived at the Smithville inkatorium in the same shipment as Meche."

"So that gives us a timetable, right?" I say. "This most likely was done to him shortly before he was shipped there."

Abbie closes her eyes for a second. When she opens them to look up at me they are filled with the kind of anguish teenagers aren't yet adept at disguising.

"I did his walk-through," she says. "He said he was picked up while he was at school and brought to Smithville directly." She hits the play button and lets the video run nearly all the way through, slowing it only when the child's handler comes on screen to retrieve the child at the end of the procedure. There is a moment, a split second really, when the handler's face turns to the camera.

Abbie hits pause. "That," she says, "is my mother."

Nobody says anything.

Reporting hinges on quick decisions, so I make one.

"Here's what I need you to do. Edit this stuff into one strong 5-minute piece. I'm going to go sit down and write a voice-over lede, nut graf and conclusion, but we'll let the rest speak for itself, especially the Q & A. Then we'll upload it from here. You're completely in charge of the visual component, you understand?"

She turns back to the computer screen. "When do you want it?" Her voice is a little wobbly.

"Two hours ago." Melinda's standard response.

"Mind if I borrow the laptop?" I ask Meche. When she shakes her head, I pick it up and walk it over to the dining room table. None of the chairs are comfortable, but that's okay. I don't need comfort when I write. Just music. I dig my iPod out of my pocket. When I look up, Meche is there.

"That was a good thing you did," she says.

"We'll see. Edited footage is much easier to discredit." After a second I grin at her. "Eh. What's journalistic integrity got to do with anything anyway?"

I put my earbuds in, hit play, and sit down to write.

For some reason everyone is still awake at midnight when Abbie and I finish producing the piece. The girl's got a future in editing for broadcast: the pace is perfect, much more riveting than the originals. Her mother's face is out, but not her back and arms as she guides the boy into the chair. I know the piece is solid when we post it.

In the morning, my cell phone rings Talking Heads until I pick it up.

"You asshat," Melinda says instead of hello. "Couldn't you have posted it on the Gazette's web site?"

"Couldn't risk the powers-that-be nixing it. Or cutting the guts out of it."

"What do you think I'm here for?" she spits out, then sighs. "It's gone viral, by the way."

When I go downstairs, Abbie's already sitting at the computer. She turns the screen to me without a word. We're the top vid on YouTube. Digg. Yahoo. There are links and embeds all over Google+ and Twitter and Facebook, and on at least a dozen of the highest-traffic aggregator sites. When I meet her eyes I see something stirring in them.

I think I'll call it destiny.

## 3.

When the room is filled to capacity, Rep. Anspach's senior communications person gives his security people a heads up. The cameras start jockeying for position, even before there's anyone at the podium.

The rest of Anspach's communications team stands at the side of the room, my college friend included. Every so often she says something into her headpiece. In the harsh lights set up for television cameras her hair shines like a new penny.

She shoots me a glance, adjusts the earphone of her headpiece and starts over.

"How's tricks, Red?" I say when she's within earshot.

"Finn." She gives me a baleful look as her hello. She's back to Beatrice these days and probably isn't fond of the reminder that at one time she preferred to be called just about anything else. "What are you doing here?"

"You call a press conference and the press shows, isn't that the way it works?"

"Thought Belsen was covering for the Gazette."

"In your dreams."

"I had Horowitz's assurance that's who she'd send."

"Never believe an editor. Especially not Melinda."

She grimaces. "Well, then, I've got some markers to call in."

"I'm not lobbing Anspach softballs, no matter our history."

"He won't call on you. Not without some assurance from me that you'll behave."

"Which means?"

"You know what it means."

"If you think I'm the only reporter here with hard questions about the scope of the sterilization program you're completely deluded."

"Don't force my hand."

"Wow. That sounded an awful lot like a threat, Red."

"No. If I wanted to threaten you I'd trot out the fact we know you've trafficked with gangs. That you've purchased some highly suspect materials and are probably the middleman in an ink enterprise that breaks all manner of state and federal law, as well as untold local ordinances. If I wanted to threaten you I'd probably tell you we have enough to get you charged with endangerment of minors, maybe even kidnapping. Shall I continue?"

"Who's feeding you this tripe?" I ask, schooling my features to immobility.

"And if I really wanted to threaten you," she continues as if she hasn't heard me, "I'd post the unedited video from which you edited your viral version."

"You'd just screw yourselves if you did."

"You think? The one that shows your ink friends setting the whole thing up as a hoax?"

# Finn: Burying the lede

"What are you talking about?"

"I've got inkatoriums full of people to put in my recasting. Who'd know? One ink looks much like the other to most of us. By the time I'm done, you wouldn't have a career left. Probably not much of a life either. So, think. Is it worth it?"

"What happened to you, Red? What turned you into this?"

She laughs. "Aw, Finn. You were a great fuck, and that earns you lifelong points in my book. But it doesn't earn you a pass. And this is, after all, what I'm great at."

She flips her hair behind her shoulder. "So, we're agreed, yes?"

When I nod, she stoops down and kisses me before returning to her place along the wall of shame. I even get some tongue.

I get up and slip out the door.

My first call is to Meche. She twigs on fast, and I don't have to stay on long.

Next, Melinda.

There's dead silence after I explain. Then I lay out my plan. Tentatively. It is Melinda we're talking about, after all.

"You got a notebook on you?" she asks finally.

"Of course. And I *am* sorry."

"Shut up," she says, then reads me a string of cell numbers and twitter addresses.

"So we're going to give the Bulletin a gift. And channels 29, 8, 5, 2, and those annoyingly earnest folks from Media Mobilizing while we're at it," she says when she's done. "If anyone had ever told me I'd be feeding them all our inside information on a story just to save your fat ass, I'd have told them they're whack."

"I'll find a way to make it up to you," I say.

"I guess I'll retweet anything they put out. Just don't get caught texting, okay? I want you around so I can take it out of your hide."

Sandra Patten gets the specifics, and Meche's best guesses, about the various chemical agents. I pass on Dr. Watson's info about implementation timetables to Regan Waterson, and my research about the pharma company connections to Justin Coleman. Larissa Lebovitz gets the number and ages of children sterilized, and because she's my favorite competing colleague, the name and contact info for my source. Risa Q, as strident and zealous as her media venue, gets the estimate of how many nonalien-slash-citizen inks have been sterilized.

At one point, Beatrice looks directly at me.

I can't resist texting her, "You said it. I'm a great fucker."

By the time I get home from the press conference some of the inks have already taken off. Meche distributes the remaining instaskin patches to the stragglers. She's as efficient as ever, but her eyes are sad.

Abbie's finishing dumping all the information from Meche's multiple computers, except the laptop, which Meche slips into the girl's duffle despite the teen's embarrassed protests.

I send Mari to stay with my mother; Silvio to Sarai and Allison's apartment; Napoleón to my sister's apartment. Father Tom makes frenzied calls to non-ink parishioners to house the other inks, and when the list dries up way before the need, has Meche call Toño to see what the gang leader can arrange.

That is the worst of it, the way we have to set aside what we believe in order to survive. It's the best of it, too. How those we imagine will laugh off our need come through instead. Mere minutes after the call, a virtual flotilla of limos with hawks painted on their driver-side doors idle in front of Meche's house. The remaining inks get in by twos and threes.

"Hawk's Flight Limo Service," Meche says as she comes to stand next to me while I watch. "Los Gavilanes."

I nod. When I had interviewed Toño I had learned the gang took its name from his surname – Gavilán. "Funny. If I hadn't seen it tattooed on his stomach, I'd assume it was just a company logo."

"That's the point," she says. "It is a legit company, by the way. A front, and a pretty good source of income."

"Speaking of income," I say. "How're we paying Toño?"

She glances back at the brownstone.

"You're kidding."

"It's just a house. And worth enough to guarantee his help for everyone we sheltered for the next number of weeks. I've programmed his direct line into most everyone's cell phone. Even Father Tom's." She snickers.

"But what are you going to do when you come back from Smithville?"

"I'm not coming back."

"Jesus. Have you told anyone other than me?"

"Mari. By the way, you'll find my wedding present for the two of you when you get your next bank statement."

"Meche...."

"Shut up, Finn."

Soon enough it's only Blue Belle parked in front of the brownstone. John and Abbie dump their bags in the back, wave at me, then climb inside.

"Time to go," Meche says, turning to me. She digs a scrap of paper out of her pocket. "This is where you need to drop the house keys. I don't guess we'll probably ever see each other again, but my number's also programmed into your cell phone."

I hug her – a sharp-edged sword of a woman, washed with gold that's no surface but a center vein that leads straight to her heart. After the SUV pulls away, I close up the house and pocket the keys, then sit on the stoop. The street is quiet, ordinary. Nothing to indicate what's broken on the asphalt today.

Father Tom's knees creak as he sits on the stoop next to me.

"How long?" I ask him.

"What?"

# Finn: Burying the lede

"Before this stops. I'm tired of saying goodbye. I'm tired of people disappearing from my life because others won't leave them even the dregs of an existence."

The priest looks down. "'How long, O Lord? I cry for help but you do not listen. I cry out to you, 'Violence!' but you do not intervene. Why do you let me see ruin; why must I look at misery? Destruction and violence are before me: there is strife, and clamorous discord.'"

When I don't say anything, he looks up. "That's from the Book of the Prophet Habakkuk. You want to hear the answer?"

"Yeah. Sure. I'm already depressed."

"'Then the Lord answered me and said: Write down the vision clearly upon the tablets, so that one can read it readily. For the vision still has its time, presses on to fulfillment, and will not disappoint; if it delays, wait for it, it will surely come, it will not be late.'"

"I wish I could believe it."

"Act as if you believe and the real thing follows."

"That easy?"

"Who said anything about easy?" he says.

"What are we going to do now that we're homeless again?"

"You're going to write about this. And, for a while, you'll do it from your mother's house. While she studies the woman-slash-supernatural-being you've brought to live under her roof. Should prove quite interesting. For all of you." He grins at me.

"I never knew you had a cruel streak." I sigh. "What about you?"

"After I marry the two of you, you mean?"

I grin. "Sure."

"I'll be around."

"Promise?"

"Yeah, son. I promise. I won't disappear on you." He slaps me on the knee, then gets up. "Think it's too early to get a Jamesons at Con's?"

I get to my feet. "It's never too early, Father."

# Abbie: OMGWTF

## 1.

Meche's got more cash on her than I've ever seen. Some of it is for me.

When we get to Smithville I'm turning Blue Belle over to her. I don't know how I'll explain it to my mother. If I ever speak to her again, that is. I can't get past the video memory of her looking straight into Pete Nguyen's eyes.

I don't know Meche's plan for after Smithville, and I find it bugs me. I think it's the fifth time I ask that she finally tells me she has no plan. Just to drive until she or Blue Belle gives out.

I think the whole thing sucks. And maybe because of something other than the affection I have for my beat-up, piece-of-shit SUV. The golden woman in my rearview is, for the first time, just a woman. Frayed with doubt, pleated with uncertainty. I don't like it. I like my goddesses seamless.

"What's that?" I ask as I zip by a truck weigh-in station sign flashing an l.e.d. message somewhere around mile marker 324.

"Checkpoint ahead," Meche says.

"But we're almost to Smithville. The craziness wouldn't have reached this far into the boonies, would it?"

She's right. Less than five miles on we come to a barrier. First we have to offer our wrists for examination, then the Staties haul us out of Blue Belle for a pat down.

I expect normalcy when we get to the Burger King sign at Smithville's town limits, but I'm wrong. Ed Sweeney's parked the cop car just a few yards behind the fast food joint's lawn. When I roll down the windows, he takes his time looking at us.

"Wrists out."

"You've got to be kidding," John says. "Do you think anyone cares enough about Smithville to flash mob it? Puhleese."

"You never know what inks will do," Ed says after a moment. "And Smithville isn't just some sleepy little town. "

"Could have fooled me," John says.

The cop's face turns stony. "No more lip, Montgomery. I assume your family doesn't have the taint to put you on the wrong side of this, but rules are rules."

We all stick our wrists out the windows. He hangs on to each a long time.

"Really, we've got to get home before my parents think that someone has been harassing us," John says as Meche yanks her arm back inside the car. "They're good friends with Judge Fisher, you know."

Of course he knows. Everyone in town knows that piece of business.

126

Ed's eyes go to Meche. "Your aunt going to be staying up at your place then?"

"Duh."

Ed seems to weigh what to do next, then smacks the side of Blue Belle so hard I jump.

"All right, then," he says as he waves us through the barricade.

"What a douchebag," I say when I'm driving again. "What do want to bet he's set up multiple roadblocks just to feel important?"

"Yeah, that way when next year's budget comes up for a vote he can argue for double the funding," John says. "My dad says you should never underestimate what people are willing to do for a buck."

A couple of minutes later I hear Meche clear her throat. "We've got a bit of a problem," she says.

Déjà vu.

"I don't know what that guy had in his hand when he inspected us, but I'm bleeding," she says.

"His class ring. He files an edge on it so when he grabs on during an arrest there's an added surprise. You're not getting blood all over Blue Belle?" I ask, suddenly queasy.

"No, but my instaskin's torn."

"Can't you stick it back down? You know, smush the edges together?" I say.

"Tried."

"Well, dig out whatever spares you kept for yourself. You need me to stop so you can get them?"

Silence.

I swallow the acid rising in my throat. "Could you be more arrogant? You didn't think you'd need any?"

"I forgot to count myself in the distribution."

Before I can pick one of the many insults I'm thinking, John says. "We probably have enough leftover stuff to pull together a tiny batch."

"And who do you suggest she stays with until spring break is over and we can get into the school lab? In case you've forgotten, my mother knows who she is. And with my mom's scruples, that'll mean we're handed over to Ed Sweeney's tender care."

"She can stay with me."

"I know your parents are laid back and all but won't they frown at their son bringing home a cougar?"

"My parents don't care who I bring home, as long as she doesn't get into the silver. They're in England anyway," he says.

"Nobody knows their way around this place better than us," I say after a moment. "If we hit another roadblock we'll figure it out."

When traffic starts slowing at Conestoga Road, John points me to Commons, then River Road. The next time it's Johnnycake to Chestnut to

Manor. We end up circling around the inkatorium. I have the irrational desire to turn up the driveway and be done with it.

"Just drop me somewhere along this road," Meche says, after the third time we detour. "I'm making it impossible for you to get home. And home is what this is all been about in the first place."

I feel a lump form in my throat. I despise crying. I have to pull Blue Belle over and put all my attention on making sure the tears don't come through.

I hear her rummaging around in one of the duffles, then feel her hand on my shoulder. "It's okay, Abbie. Really."

John mumbles something awkward but comforting to me, and somehow we miss it. The moment the door clicks shut after her.

By the time we notice it's too late. We get out of the car and shout for her, but there's no answer other than the yipping of a pack of coy-dogs in the distance. I try to call her phone. The one time it actually rings through it goes dead before she picks up.

"Do you think we'll ever see her again?" I ask as we get back in the car. I'm letting John drive back because I'm wiped out and still don't trust myself not to start crying. "Or any of the others?"

"No," he answers after a bit. "I think we were just tourists in their world."

"Their world is our world too," I say.

He drums his fingers on the steering wheel while he drives. I haven't seen him this manic ever. After a few moments he turns to look at me. "We have our own stuff to figure out, Abs, and who says that's less important?"

Then, "When does your mom think you're coming home?"

"Sunday afternoon."

"If you stay with me instead of going home we'd have two whole days alone together. And we'd be really alone. Not like in Hastings."

I give him a look. He's known about my promise since I made it.

"We don't have to do anything," he says after a moment. "It's just … you say you love me, and shouldn't that mean you want to be with me?"

I'm not an idiot. Most couples who get together in high school fall apart ugly. My parents are the perfect example. They got married when they were 18, and their life went to shit soon after. John's wanting to be with me is the sweetest thing that's happened to me. But it's not the only good thing that's ever going to happen, and I'm not selling myself for it.

Like every argument we've ever had, I win.

***

School starts again. Every day for a week John and I drive around in Blue Belle after school looking for Meche. We call her number whenever we hit a live zone. No answer, ever. But after that, it's easy to forget there's anything other than our worries in the world. SAT prep, too much homework, and what I won't allow to happen after our long makeout sessions, fill our days.

128

# Abbie: OMGWTF

A couple of months before summer vacation, Rose Cantinelli leans against the locker next to mine. "Guess what I did last night?" she says.

"Picked your extraordinarily large nose?" I say, slamming my locker door shut and moving away from her down the hall.

She trots after me, then twirls in front. "Ask me, trailer trash."

"Not on your life, hoary hag."

The next day she even manages to ruin my computer class. Somehow, she's gotten my e-mail address and though we're not supposed to be checking during class, I do.

redrose11134@gmail: You seeing John this afternoon?

geekbubblegum5@gmail: What's it to you?

redrose11134@gmail: Be sure to get him hot before you leave. It makes him so much more anxious to get to my house.

I smack the keyboard loud enough that Mr. James turns to look at me. I'm his favorite student but even I don't get away with battering the hardware.

John finds me at my locker before school ends. He pulls me into a kiss.

"What?" he says when I push him away.

"Rose claims you're sleeping with her."

"Since when do you believe anything she says?"

"I don't. That's why I'm asking you."

His eyes shift away from mine. Just a fraction.

"Dickwad."

"It doesn't mean anything."

"Then why're you doing it?"

"You know why. I'm just using her."

I push him hard enough that he slams into the locker.

School the next day is excruciating. There are only so many ways you can ignore a person. His lying, pleading eyes. His lying, stupid texts. The fucking lying notes he slips through the vents in the locker.

Then, it just stops. And he's with Rose for real.

2.

I convince my mother to put me on computer work for the duration of my community service so I don't have to grapple with what the inkatorium is, and my part in it. I particularly don't want to run into Pete.

I do some of the work I'm supposed to, but mostly I try my hand at sabotage. First I hack into the state public health consortium's system, into the human resources department server.

They've got dirt on all of the inkatorium's administrators. My father's DUI is in my mom's file, along with her terrible credit rating and the lien on property taxes she hasn't been able to pay in full yet. Also the number of inks who have escaped the inkatorium under her watch. I know I can't erase my mother's specifics totally, but I riddle them with glaring data entry mistakes to make them seem less credible.

When I open Langdon-the-sterilizer's file, I find a report about an annual financial audit that I don't really understand but looks bad. I send Finn text messages with all the information, and get a return message composed entirely of exclamation marks.

I make sure to cover my digital tracks so nothing can be traced back to Smithville. My mother doesn't suspect a thing, though she does ask me from the kitchen why I'm whooping at the evening news the night the Langdon story gets picked up by TV.

After that I get really ambitious and try hacking into the national health regulatory commission's database. It's a lot tougher. Every time I make it in, the system's security seals off partitions so I can't follow the tantalizing leads I find. I start each session back at square one. It's a puzzle that keeps resetting itself.

At school, John never meets my eyes. Thankfully, outside of Addison's class, we don't have any classes in common, and I can almost forget he was a part of my life. Which is not quite the killer I thought it would be. I even get invited to junior prom. Frank Lloyd, another computer dweeb, asks me, out by my locker in front of everyone. When I say yes, I hear a far locker slam and turn to see John's back as he walks away.

I might be tempted to fret about the strange ways of boys, but something pretty amazing happens that same afternoon. While I'm on shift I get my toe in the part of the national commission's server that deals with inkatorium adoptions. Far enough in to get excited before I'm shut out. A week passes before I think about anything but how to bypass the security measures I'm measuring myself against.

Then one morning, Frank stops me as I'm about to go into Addison's class.

"Hey," I give him a big smile. Outside of the bad haircut, he's really kind of cute in a young Steve Jobs sort of way.

"I hate to do this, but I'm not going to be able to take you to j-prom after all," he says.

"Why?"

"I got a call from this guy from Rochester Tech who saw my computer animation in the intermediate unit showcase last weekend. He says he thinks I could get a full scholarship there. He's going to arrange an interview but it's the same weekend as the prom."

He fiddles with his binder while people push by us to get into class. "And if I don't get a scholarship I probably won't be able to go anywhere nearly so good."

"Yeah, I know how that is."

We chat a few seconds longer until Addison shoots me a warning look and I hurry into class. As I walk past his desk to get to mine, I notice the smug look on John's face and suddenly remember Rochester Tech is his father's alma mater.

I punch him, hard, on the way through. I don't care a bit when Addison sends me to the principal's office.

*** 

When I get through, I'm prepared.

I take notes. Ingloriously low tech, but completely untraceable. And quick. I'm gone before the system knows I was ever in. Then I sit and fill out the details before time does its number and I forget what my abbreviations mean.

I go out and buy a throwaway phone, then lock myself in my room and call Finn.

"Abbie?" He sounds so surprised he doesn't even sound like himself. "I thought I had programmed your number into my cell."

"Temporary phone. Got a notebook handy?" I ask.

"Sure. But why didn't you just text me, like before?"

"Because I'm not leaving a trail."

I read him the full contact information. I make him read it back to me twice.

"I got it," he says, a little exasperated. "What I don't have is *why* I have it."

"They're the ones who adopted your kid."

Silence.

"Finn?"

When he comes back on his voice is all over the place. I've never heard a grown man cry.

"I can't repay this," he says finally when his voice is almost back to normal. "I'll owe you for the rest of my life."

"Just get him back. And you and Hello Kitty never split up after you get him, you hear?"

I buzz around my room after I hang up, feeling giddy on good.

The next call is a little different. I feel a shiver go through my body even before I key in the number.

"Speak," he says when he picks up.

I give him a tiny taste of the information I've gathered before I finagle free assistance for Finn and Mari, should they need it, for the next six months. Then I'm on for an hour giving Toño what he needs to cut into the adoption racket. He asks questions about things I wouldn't have known to note, but no dealbreakers because he seals the transaction with an honor oath. I have nothing but intuition to base it on but I'm convinced he'll be good to his word.

"Well, damn, America," he says. The teasing familiarity is utterly distinct from the business tone that preceded it, and I feel its electricity pulse through my body. "I'm going to make a shitload of dough. You should have asked for a percentage."

"There *is* one more thing," I say.

"Deal stands as is." All business again.

"Aside from the deal."

I take a breath, then ask.

"Okay," he says, neither businesslike nor familiar this time. Guarded.

"There's something else," I say it before I can think about why I want this to end on my side of the wall he's put up. "I won't be jailbait then."

I hear him inhale. "You're dangerous."

Then he hangs up.

I ditch the phone the next day at school.

***

A lot happens in the next few weeks.

Langdon steps down as head of the Deliman inkatorium. I get a message from Finn that he's gotten a paternity test as the first step in reclaiming his son. My mother gets a job offer to become the head nurse administrator at Community Hospital. She turns it down, but only after she negotiates a raise at the inkatorium with the offer as leverage. My father comes up for my 18th birthday. Frank and I go bowling.

A few days before j-prom, my mom takes me shopping for a dress. We still don't have money to spare but she spends almost half her paycheck on the one I fall in love with. It's the color of toffee; short and made of some material that slides even as it hugs the body. From the front it looks elegant, a tease really because it's backless to the dimple between booty and back. There, in its only nod to glitz, are three brilliant rhinestone buttons.

The afternoon of the prom I let my mother pull my hair back into a high, sleek ponytail and give me a pair of earrings I've never seen before. "Your father gave those to me," she says with a funny look on her face. "They're real diamonds. They're the only thing I wouldn't sell during that bad stretch. They're so tiny they probably wouldn't have fetched much. But they're yours now, honey."

I like the way they sparkle against my skin. My hair looks like a sleek mink pelt, and for the first time, I see my father in the features on my face. Not

132

half bad.

All right, only half good. But that's a lot better than normal.

She hasn't asked about John, but she knows he's not the person who pulls up in the limo with the hawk painted on its door.

He's looking pretty fine, I have to say. He's in a dark suit instead of a tux, but it sits perfectly on his body. He's clean-shaven now, and his hair is even closer cropped than it was when I saw him before. Hot. Edgy. Older. What else can you want for a prom date? Of course, I've paid for this perfection with the information I gave him, but I try not to think too much on that because it makes me feel the worst kind of skeevy.

He gives me a cocky smile when notices me checking him out, but he's perfectly well behaved when he steps up to meet my mother.

He opens the door of the limo for me, then gets in the other side to sit beside me.

"Are you going to mock me all night?" I say. "I know this was a totally stupid request and way beneath your pay grade."

"I'm not mocking, America. Not even close."

I look at him. His dark eyes are amused, and something else.

"What?" I ask, a little taken aback.

"You. Look. Beautiful."

"Shut up."

He laughs.

"How did you get the patch so perfect?" I ask pointing to his wrist. His tattoo's covered seamlessly, but none of the figural ones abutting it – entwined birds and thorned branches – are covered at all.

"Exacto knife," he says, shrugging. "And lots of experience with blades."

It's a reminder. So I don't forget who he really is.

"You don't have a weapon on you, do you?" I ask after a moment.

"It is a matter of sincere regret to me, America, that we live in such different worlds. Yes, of course. Always a weapon. Are there metal detectors at your school?"

"No."

He nods, looks out the window for a bit, then returns his eyes to me. He must read the question in them because he hikes one pant leg up enough for me to see an ankle holster.

When we get to the high school, he gets out, opens the door for me. "Now, steel in your spine. And tell me, who are we trying to make jealous?"

I laugh weakly. "That obvious?"

"You think I'm even a bit of a fool?"

"No. But you *are* hot. And he's already heard me talk about you."

He raises an eyebrow. "Should I take that as encouragement, America?"

I make a rude noise. "Like I'm anything more than a pay stub."

He looks like he's going to say something, then changes his mind.

"What?"

"Give me a visual so I know when to dial it up."

I describe John to him, then turn to the entrance of the school. I must look conflicted, because he seems exasperated when he turns me back to face him.

"You're never going to make him jealous that way, America." He pulls me close to kiss me. It's surprisingly tender.

"Oh," I say when he lets me go.

"What? You thought this jealousy thing would work without kissing?"

"No. It's just … it's not like I imagined."

"You imagined?" He's amused again, but also pleased.

"I thought gang guys would kiss harsh and mean."

"Yeah. Well, I'll keep that in mind," he says.

"My real name's Abbie," I say when we walk through the doors.

"Don't," he warns.

"I'm not scared of you, you know."

His hand is a distraction on my waist as he nudges me toward the table with the beverages. "I'm not one of your boys, America."

"If you were, you wouldn't have poured that for me," I say as he hands me a cup of lime-green punch.

I wait while he takes a sip, then smirk as he sets the cup down straightaway.

"So, why a hawk on the limo?" I ask.

"Fast. Harsh. Mean. But you knew that about my kind already, right?"

His smile is bitter, like nothing I've seen on his face before. And even though I feel a twinge when I see it, his words drive me straight to heated.

"Isn't that what the 'not one of yours' was about? Or the way you talk about guns and knives and us living in different worlds? So I get we're not 'the same kind?'" I glare at him. "And what the hell do you mean by it anyway – that we're different kinds because you're ink or because you're gang? No, don't answer, because either way, it's shit."

He doesn't exactly back down, but he looks away from me momentarily. "Jesus. Are you always this fierce?"

"My dad's wolf clan," I say. "And before you tell me that's too much personal information, I don't care. Got it?"

"My last name means hawk. That's why the limo logo," he says after a moment.

"And I already knew about the wolf thing," he adds.

"R-i-i-i-ght."

He spreads his hands out as if pleading for peace. "Start over?"

"I'm keeping the part where you think I look beautiful. But nothing else."

Except the kiss, I amend mentally, but hell if I'm going to say it.

He doesn't even ask for a dance, just holds out his hand and gives me this sidelong look that takes the bottom right out of my stomach. Then, as the music turns slow and he takes me in his arms, I see John. He looks unbelievably handsome in a white dinner jacket and Rose is beautiful in a long, floaty dress the same color as her name. They're across the dance floor from us, just barely moving, glued to each other and swapping spit.

"Hold it together, America," Toño whispers in my ear. "Half the battle is won with the front you present."

He dances me closer to them.

"She's pretty," he says after a few moments.

"I know."

"But she's not you."

Without any prompting at all I move so close our bodies are breathing in concert. His hand lazily teases the small of my back. The body held against mine is impossible to ignore. Mine sure does funny things in response.

He laughs in my ear when he notices. "You're delicious, America."

"Shut up."

Which makes him laugh harder. "Sorry. I forgot you're a child."

"I am *not*."

His arms tighten around me. They're corded, like steel. His whole body is that way. The eyes that meet mine hold challenge.

"Is this part of the jealously ploy?" I ask.

"If you want," he answers.

"Do you think he's even noticed?"

"He's noticed," Toño says.

"Then why doesn't he make a move?"

"I don't know."

"Would you?"

He steps back for a second and looks at me. I can't hold his gaze and, as my eyes slide away, he pulls me back to him. But not nearly as tight as before. We circle around our space on the dance floor. One song. Two. I almost forget about John. Almost.

"Toño?"

"Don't you ever stay quiet?" His sigh is for effect, exaggerated. "What?"

"What if he doesn't care?"

"Then he doesn't care and you get on with your life, America. Don't give him the advantage by knowing he's hurt you, understand?"

"Is that your trick?"

"Anybody who's ever had to throw down knows it."

"Just pretend you don't care that he's there," he adds after a moment. "You think you can pull that off?"

"Why would I care when I'm in your arms?" I say lightly.

He stops. "Don't you dare treat me as if I'm less than him."

"It's so not like that," I say. I have to pull him back to me.

I rest my head on his shoulder and close my eyes. There's something about the set of his shoulders and the way he holds himself that makes me want to get under his skin and seal up whatever pinpricks I've added to the whole bleeding mess he holds inside.

I slide my hand from his shoulder to his chest and down his shirtfront. I let myself imagine what it might be like to be with him. It's perilous, I know. He carries a trace of scent – cinnamon or ginger, maybe – sweet and biting. It makes me want to taste his mouth again.

I feel a shiver run down my body.

"Cold?" He rubs my back to warm it.

When I look up, what's in his eyes is so complicated I can't begin to decipher it.

"It's not that," I say. "I'm just an idiot. And … confused."

"About what?"

"Me. You."

It's still tender when he kisses me this time, but different. As if he's holding back a volcano. The heat gets through anyway, and I finally get why moths flock to light. I don't care if I burn as long as I don't have to step away.

Which means when John taps me on the shoulder, I come away more than a little disoriented.

"John, Rose, this is Toño," I hear myself introducing them as if I were outside my body. Having stepped away from Toño, I feel lightheaded. Maybe I wobble because he puts his arm around my waist to move me back close. His hand comes to rest lightly on the skin just above the rhinestone buttons, then starts to trace a trail up my back.

For a second I wonder if he knows what effect this has on me, but then I remember I'm paying him for this, and for the way John's jaw tightens when he notices.

"Cut in?" he says. He's not really asking.

Toño moves away immediately and offers his hand to a scowling Rose.

John pulls me to him. "What game are you playing, Abs?"

"No game," I say as we start to move to the music.

"You bring that gangster to the prom," he says, "and then you tongue wrestle with him in front of everyone? I know you're doing it just to mess with me."

"I like him," I say. More than like him. Stupid body. Stupid imagination. Stupid me.

"He's not like us, Abs."

I look into the eyes of the boy I've loved most of my life. "And how's that?"

"For one thing, we're not thugs," he says. "And we don't prey on people's weaknesses or take advantage of them or lie to them."

"Really? Didn't we do all that in order to break certain friends of ours out of the inkatorium?"

"That's different."

"All right, how about telling one girl you love her while secretly doing another? Lying by omission is still a lie."

He hitches his shoulders. "What do you want from me?"

"Nothing," I say, surprised that I mean it.

"If you wanted to show me how much I still want you, you got it. So, what now?"

"I don't know."

He kisses me.

It's so much like it was I'm thrown back in time. John's arms feel like home. When his hands slide down to my butt to move me tighter to him, it would be the easiest thing in the world to follow. But I step back instead.

I look away from him. Both Rose and Toño are watching us. Rose seems like she's on the verge of tears and, before he turns his face back to say something to her, Toño wears the expression my mother does when she talks about the moment she knew she'd never go on to med school.

I want, very badly right then, to reach out and touch the corded arm under its fine, dark fabric cover. But it dances out of reach, deliberately moving away from me.

"I've always loved you, Abbie," John says, drawing my attention back to him.

"But not so much that you'd wait for me," I say.

"Going with Rose was just my way to respect that ridiculous agreement of yours. A way to bide my time until you can be with me," he says, then smiles that smile that he knows melts me. "Isn't that proof of love? Most girls would get that."

"I've never been most girls."

When the song ends, I return him to Rose.

"Let's go," I say to Toño.

"Revenge isn't all that sweet, is it?" he says when he opens the door of the limo for me.

"No."

Once the car gets going, I look out the window at the passing landscape, at once familiar and so unfamiliar I can't make sense of it.

"He's just a boy, America," he says after a while. "Maybe you should cut him a break. We're all idiots at that age."

"I'm his age," I say.

"So maybe you're an idiot too."

I snort, then stay quiet for a long while.

I look over at Toño. He looks back at me.

"How old are you?" I ask.

"Twenty-five."

"Do you remember being 18?"

He grins. "It's only seven years."

"You remember the way your heart tells you crazy things?"

"Sure."

"You remember the way your head isn't clear enough to sort out the mess of thoughts that run through it?"

"Yeah, that too."

"Then why are you here?"

"Because you asked me to be."

"Because I paid you to be, you mean."

"The deal was sealed before you asked me," he says. "You knew you weren't paying and I wasn't buying. I don't buy or sell human beings, America. Not even for a night."

After I turn away, he goes silent for a while.

"Show me your favorite place here."

"Why?"

"Because it's your favorite place." When I look at him his eyes are steady on mine.

"Okay." I lean forward and tap on the dark glass between our seats and the driver's. When it rolls down, I give him directions.

It's weird walking over the crunchy concrete shards in high heels. I have to grab Toño for balance a couple of times then, irritated, I kick the shoes away and take off at a run toward the chute. I don't stop until I'm at the very top, out of breath, with my face tipped up to the stars. A few minutes later he's standing there beside me, also looking up.

"I don't remember the sky having so many stars," he says.

"They're always there, just in some places it's harder to see them because all of the reflected light from houses and streetlights and cars."

"Sad that real light would be eclipsed by imitation," he says.

He glances at me, then back up at the sky. "So why did your boy choose the lesser light? Explain it to me, America."

"I made a vow," I say. "To my mom. That I wouldn't be with anyone until I was at least 19. Older than she was when she married, got pregnant and gave up on her dream of med school. And the thing is, I don't break my promises. Not the real ones anyway. John knows that. He just didn't want to wait."

"Or whatever," I add after a moment. "He ended up getting what he wanted anyway."

"No, he ended up with an imitation of what he wanted. You know it, he knows it. And after tonight, we all know it."

I look at him.

"I feel sorry for the girl," he says.

"Don't. She's as mean as she is pretty."

"She was hurt when she saw you kissing."

I want to ask him how he felt, but I don't dare. After a while I ask, "So, can you guess why this is my favorite place?"

"You can imagine yourself flying right off the chute into tomorrow," he says.

"You are *so* your last name. Not everyone dreams of air and wings, you know."

"Okay, then. You like flirting with danger." I see him smile a little after he says it.

"Yeah, well. But that's not the reason either."

"So, tell me," he says.

"The stars give without any expectation of return. Unconditionally. They shed light on us all the time, no matter what we do or how badly we mess up. Which makes them a whole lot kinder than human beings."

"Nearly everything's kinder than humans."

It just hangs there for a while.

"Toño? Have you ever killed anyone?"

He looks up at the stars again. "Yes."

"I've been arrested, you know. I understand how things don't always end where they start."

"You making excuses for me, America?" When he turns his face back to mine, it's hard and sealed up. "Don't. I'd do it again in an instant. There isn't anything that's going to prevent me from protecting what's mine."

We walk down the chute without talking. He detours to retrieve my shoes while I pick my way to the walkway near the concrete factory building. Funny how when you're going fast you hardly notice what pierces you, but slow down and it becomes intolerable. My feet are throbbing.

He catches up to me, then looks over his shoulder. "Somebody with a flashlight is coming up behind us. At a clip."

"Shit," I say. "Security. If I get caught trespassing here again I'm going to end up in jail."

"You're not," he says as he steers me up the pathway, "going to get caught." When he sees a doorway, he pushes me into its shadow. "Stay out of the light."

"It's too shallow. He's going to see there's someone."

"Someone. But not you," he says.

He thrusts me against the door as his hands find their way behind me to the ponytail he pulls free. "Hide your face with your hair, against my shoulder, so he can't see it," he says. Quiet, almost a whisper.

Then his hands are on the small of my back. I feel the fabric rustling as he hikes my dress up. A hand slides under my thigh to lift my leg to his waist. Then he presses against me.

"Hey! Enough of that now!" I hear Ravenswood – the security guard who busted me before – from somewhere behind Toño's shoulder. "This isn't a bedroom. Take it elsewhere."

I feel Toño shielding me from sight even as he turns to the voice. I press my forehead into the taut trapezoid muscle under his shoulder blade and let my hair swing forward to obscure the sides of my face.

"Cut us a break, man. We weren't hurting anything," I hear him say.

I see the spill of flashlight filtering through my hair. Ravenswood is taking a good look at what he *can* see of me judging from the duration of silence that accompanies the light.

"You can't be here."

"All right. But you know how it is when you've got something this fine at hand." Toño's snicker has one of those sleazy-guy undertones that raises my hackles.

Ravenswood's answering one is even worse. "If you need a place there's an abandoned motel just past the edge of town where most of us go when the girls are underage. No one's going to stop you there."

"Hey, thanks, man. Just let me get it together and we'll be off," he says to Ravenswood.

"Hurry it up."

"A little privacy?"

"Didn't seem to bother you before." But Ravenswood must comply because I hear the crunch of gravel. I keep my face behind the fall of hair as Toño takes his jacket off and drops it around my shoulders. He turns me straight into him so my face is hidden in his chest and his arms around me form a sort of visual barrier. I hear Ravenswood take a couple of steps toward us.

"She seems familiar. Is she from around here?" he asks, leaning in to me. Too close. His breath moves the hair on the back of my neck.

"Maybe you don't have to go." Ravenswood's hand moves under my dress to cup one of my butt cheeks. "There seems to be enough here for both of us."

He starts to slip his fingers between my legs.

I try not to gag.

Toño's body turns to steel as he pulls me out of the security guard's reach. I feel one of his arms leave my body at the same time as his thigh shifts and I know instants later he's got his gun in his hand.

"Back off, man," Toño says, soft and dangerous.

"I've got the cops on rapid dial," Ravenswood counters. "We play nice and share our toys, or I have you busted. She's young enough to earn you statutory."

I'd tell him I'm not, but he'd recognize my voice and then he'd really have a reason to call the cops.

I hear a click as the safety releases. "Try phoning," Toño says.

Ravenswood grunts.

"I thought not. Turn around and go stand by that wall with your back to us. Keep your hands where I can see them. You do all that, I might decide let you live."

Toño hands me his phone while he watches Ravenswood follow his instructions. "Press five. As soon as it rings through, star, twice."

Seconds later the limo pulls up and jumps the curbing to idle right behind us. Its plates are obscured with custom cut magnetic sheeting, as is the logo on its side. All that instruction conveyed by punching three keys.

"Go," Toño gives me a gentle push. "I'll catch up with you."

"No." I grab his hand and start inching toward the limo.

Toño keeps his eyes on Ravenswood. "He and I have unfinished business."

I vaguely register the limo driver getting out of the car and the rear passenger door being opened as I continue to pull Toño toward it.

"America, I'm not going to kill him. Just mess him up a little," he says as he finally turns to look at me. His eyes are hard, but then, not.

"This is who I am. You have to know this."

"I know."

The thing about being small is everyone underestimates how strong you are. I yank him into the back seat of the limo with me, then lean over him to pull the door shut. Seconds later the driver gets inside and we tear off.

"I'm sorry," Toño says after a moment.

He returns his gun to its ankle holster, then leans back in the seat and closes his eyes. "About all of it."

I move close to him and lean my head on his shoulder. After a second, I feel his hand stroking my hair. "You okay?" he asks.

"Fine. You?"

"Pissed off."

"At me?"

He kisses the top of my head. "No. Not at you."

He removes his arm and starts to turn away, but I pull him by his shirt so he has to turn back. When I have his attention, I straddle him and start unbuttoning his shirt.

"America ... don't."

But the longing I see in his eyes blows anything I've seen in John's clear out of the water.

I pull his shirt open over his chest. A deep, pale indent runs in a diagonal from the clavicle near his shoulder to the lower primary feathers of the hawk tattooed on his stomach. I run my finger down the scar. His abdominals tense as I get closer to the waistband of his pants.

"What does the scar mark?"

"The night I wasn't quick enough, or good enough, or strong enough, to save my brother." Then, "The night I figured out the world doesn't care about inks like me."

I lean in to kiss the cut that bisects him. The one that splits his heart.

"I care about inks like you," I say when I straighten up and meet his gaze.

"Yeah?" his voice is husky, as if his control over it has slipped just a bit.

"Yeah."

I lean in and give him a soft little kiss on the chin. He closes his eyes when I move to his forehead, each eyelid and each cheek, working my way to his mouth, Just a tiny, light and darting thing there, like a butterfly landing for a second.

His breathing changes. When he opens his eyes again, he doesn't say anything.

"Take me home with you," I say, soft as the kisses I've been giving him.

"No."

A lump forms in my throat. "Don't you want me?"

His laugh is short, rough. "You already know the answer to that."

"Then?"

His eyes are dark. "I'll wait. For you not to break your promise."

"I don't care about that anymore."

"But I do. I live by the oaths I make, and the ones made to me. It means something, America, and I'm not taking it away from you."

Then he gives me a bitter little smile. "Besides, you're flying on adrenaline right now. You can't trust that what you think you want at the moment is what you really want."

The limo comes to a halt, then idles in front of my house.

The kiss I give him then isn't the kiss of the dithering 18-year-old I've been all night, but something else. Wolfish. Alpha female to the male she's chosen to recognize as alpha also. His arms come around me so tight I wonder if I could break out of them, supposing I ever wanted to.

"Go home," he says, when we finally draw apart.

"Really?"

"Yes, really."

"Why?"

"Because I want you more than I remember wanting anything," he says.

"So?"

"So."

I plant my hand in middle of his chest and push myself to an armlength away.

"You're not even going to text me after you drive away. Are you?" I say.

"No."

"Or call me."

"No."

"Or come to see me."

"Not until."

"Are you planning to go home and fuck some other girl while you think of me?"

"I don't think so," he says.

"Because you won't be with another girl, or because you won't be thinking of me?"

He takes my hand from his chest and pulls me to him, "Are you looking for a promise, America?"

After a moment, I take one of the diamond solitaires out of my ear and push it through the hole I see in his lobe.

He winces as the sharp post pierces closed-over skin, then puts his fingers up to feel the earring. "No one's ever given me anything without expecting me to pay," he says.

"I don't expect anything," I say. "And I don't ask for promises. Because they aren't worth spit if they aren't freely given."

Then I climb off his lap, open the door and start home.

# Abbie: OMGWTF

"America."
I turn back, scowling.
"See you in a year."

"Speak," he says when he picks up.

There are other voices. A babble behind him. Girls among them.

After a few seconds: "Is that you, America?"

When I don't say anything, his voice pitches low. "Is something wrong?"

"No. Yes. No, not really."

"Hang up. But stay there."

I do, and a few seconds later, my phone rings.

"What happened?" He's moved somewhere because there's only silence behind his words now. "You need help?"

I laugh. But it comes out all wrong because I'm also crying.

"Speak to me, America. Who did this to you?" There's steel in his words; a keen edge.

"You did."

I hear him exhale. "Stop. I don't have time for this."

"No, right, what do you care how I'm feeling," I say. "Get back to your party."

"It's not a party. It's a business meeting. An important one that I stepped away from at a crucial moment to call you back. You understand?"

"I don't. But it's okay, go back."

Silence, then, "You're not the only one, you know."

"I kind of suspected that when I heard women's voices in the background."

"What?" The surprise gives way to a laugh. "No, America, your earring's still planted in my ear. I'm not going anywhere."

"That's because you already did."

I hang up.

Weeks later I try again.

"Speak," he says, sleep evident in his voice when he picks up.

"Sorry it's so late, I wanted to make sure I wouldn't interrupt business this time."

"America, nobody bothers me at this hour unless they're bleeding. Real blood. And a lot of it."

There's a long silence.

"Toño?"

"I'm here."

"Am I waiting for something? Or is all just hope and imagination?"

More silence.

"Because if it is, I'd rather know."

"America," he starts, then stops again.

"Forget it," I say, then fumble with the phone.

"Don't. Hang. Up." Each word falls hard, like a bullet.

It takes him a while. "You know how some people have this thing where they get to see bits of the future sometimes?"

"I guess."

"I knew. The first time I saw you in the freetrade zone. That someday I'd get caught on those sharp little wolf teeth of yours."

"Toño ...."

"Go to sleep, America."

Then he hangs up on me.

*\*\**

I've taken to bagging the last two periods of the day since they're both study halls and hoofing it to the Bowlarama with Frank.

"It sucks that you aren't going to be around this summer, Jobs." I say.

My nickname for him. Not only does he look like Steve Jobs did, he loves Macs and all their cocky, quirky crap.

"Told you to apply for the same game design camp, Gates."

I hate that he gets to be named after the cuter tech genius, but I'm pretty sure Gates was the richer, so maybe it all balances out.

"I've still got community service time to do at the inkatorium."

I manage to knock down four pins in my next shot. In time for John, who's just walked over to our lane, to verify that I'm pathetic at this too.

"Get lost, Lloyd. I need to talk to Abbie."

Jobs looks over at me.

I nod.

As soon as he's gone, John sits in the hard plastic chair of the scorekeeper.

"I'm going to spend this summer in England."

I try to swallow my envy. "That's great," I say.

"My parents told me I could invite one of my friends, all expenses paid. Want to come?"

I come closer, study him.

"No," I say after a bit.

"Aren't we ever going to be friends again?"

He looks so miserable, I cave and sit next to him. "Yeah. But it's still a no. I'm almost done with community service but I have to get a paying job after that so I can put some money away for MCC." Mackensie Community College. Not my first choice, but dreams adapt to means.

He looks over to the counter where Jobs is waiting for his slice order, then shakes his head. "Bet he's never offered you what I have. Nor that low-life you brought to the prom."

"Love isn't bought," I say.

"You're an idiot," he says as he walks away.

Two days later, when I skip out of school a period early, a gavilán limo is parked in front of the school. The driver rolls down the passenger side window. "Get in," he says.

I go for the same door as the rolled-down window, but he jerks his head to indicate the back seat.

"You were driving the night of the prom," I say before he slides the glass partition up between back and front.

"I go where he wants me to go. I'm his second."

"What's your name?"

"Ernesto. Neto."

"So, is this a good thing, that he's sent for me?"

"Not to my mind," he says. Then the thunk of the partition closing seals us into separate worlds.

When the limo stops, he rolls down the partition and motions to the cement factory chute. "He's up there."

I hesitate, then realize the whole factory is idle.

Toño's back is to me when I get to the top of the chute. He's looking up at the afternoon sky."If you really look, you can almost see the stars out there now," he says when he hears me come up.

"Told you. Unconditional."

He turns around. "You look good, America."

"What are you doing here?"

He gives me one of his mocking smiles. "Wait, is this the same girl who called me in the middle of the night?"

I dig a couple of small rounds of concrete out of the chute with the toe of my sneaker. "Yeah. Sorry about that."

Now that he's in front of me, I can't look at him. I squint down the chute to the factory building. The sign is in one of those big construction dumpsters and there's scaffolding still up on the blank wall.

"How strange," I say. "The factory must have been sold."

"America," he says softly, "I drove three hours to see you and you're going to stand there talking about the factory?"

Some kisses are just kisses. Others are filled with promises overlaid on regrets, and future overlaid on history. When we stop kissing he docsn't let me go.

"How long can you stay?" I ask.

"Not long. And I can't do this again, America."

I close my eyes, rest my forehead against his chest. "You're killing me, Gavilán."

I can feel his laughter.

"Are you laughing at my pronunciation?" I look up at him.

"Maybe."

"Nice. See if I call you ever again."

"You shouldn't anyway. I'm not ready for anyone to find out about you."

"Because I'm not an ink."

"Because you're up here and I'm in Hastings and I can't protect you."

"But it makes a difference, doesn't it? That I don't have a tat."

"Yes."

# Abbie: OMGWTF

When I pull away from him, he studies me for a moment, then takes a knife out of his pocket. He slices through the patch covering his tattoo. He's so practiced he doesn't even raise a welt on the real skin beneath. When he peels back the pieces of instaskin, the mass of blue lines reveals itself.

"Each line is really a number," he says, then recites them as he glides his finger across the tattoo. As he does, I know I'll remember them always. It's that way with me and code.

"It tracks everything the government cares to know about me. From who I was born to and where, to whether I get the full rights of citizenship or not. Their measure of who I am." His mouth twists a little as he says it.

"Someday it won't be that way," I say.

"They'll still see me as they want to see me," he says. "That's really the mark inks bear that you'll never understand, America."

"Never? Like, not even if we got married and lived together for years and years?"

He grins. "So, we're talking marriage now?"

I feel the heat rise to my cheeks.

I start to mumble something, but his mouth steals whatever my words are going to be. And there's no more time for words in the couple of hours he's stolen for us. Just what passes between us as it always has, fully clothed with desire and aching with promise.

4.

My father starts coming to have dinner with us two or three times a week. There aren't any embarrassing public displays of affection, but I do catch my parents giving each other moony looks that make me want to knock them both about the head and ask them why they couldn't have done this when it mattered to me.

We're on week number three of this strange new routine and a handful of days away from my 19th birthday, when the limo pulls up to the door of the trailer. It's around eight at night and, as it's been since my father's reappearance, my mother is at home instead of the inkatorium.

Neto is out of the limo and is halfway up the porch steps when I meet him.

"I need your help," he says without a hello. "Toño said you're good with computers. He and six other gavilanes were injured on their way to a job, they got hauled off in official-looking vans. I got part of a license plate number from a witness. Can you figure something from that?"

"Wait," I say. I scramble past my parents and into my room. I grab the duffle I've kept intact since Meche put her laptop in it for me in Hastings. I'd discovered the money Meche was going to pay me for Blue Belle tucked in there, along with a stack of wireless/broadband cards, soon after I got back. Now I stuff some clothes in there with them and the laptop, and turn to go. My mother's standing in the doorway.

"Toño's hurt," I say. "I don't know how bad. And he's an ink. You know what that means."

She turns away without a word. I see her go into her bedroom and get on the phone. She's probably calling the cops. I book.

My father wraps his arms around me before I get to the door. I can't break out of them.

"You know, right?" he says. "That love and desire aren't enough? You need luck, too. And we're dogged by its opposite."

"Cut the shit and let go." My mother.

"Just because you can't see it doesn't mean it's not chasing you," he says stubbornly, but he drops his arms.

She's got a plastic kit about the size of what you'd pack to travel. She hands it to me. "There's some stuff that might be useful in it. You'll figure it out. Go."

As soon as I'm in the limo I get on the laptop and the Internet and pray that we don't hit a Smithville dead zone.

"You think we can do anything?" Neto asks as he drives to the interstate. Anywhere we have to go will be more easily reached from there.

"Not with a partial. The DMV's database is too huge. Were they instaskinned?"

"They were supposed to be meeting with the leadership of another gang, so I don't think so. But I'm not sure."

"Okay, given your drive time if they've been taken to an inkatorium, they've probably gotten the GPS chips in them already. Which means as long as they're still instate, Hipco'll have them on track. And thankfully, Hipco's network security is laughable."

"You know, it's kind of pathetic you had to come to me for help," I add as I furiously click keys.

"It was practically the whole top corps that got taken," he says. "It had to have been a set up. An inside thing. A gavilán orchestrating."

My fingers freeze on the keys.

He notices the sudden silence.

"I'm his cousin," he says. "I was with him when Chuy was killed and he nearly got gutted trying to save him. I called the ambulance that never came, and I'm the one who convinced the neighborhood drunk, an ex-Army medic from Puerto Rico, to patch him up. Afterward, when the whole notion of the gavilanes was born, I was there too. There is no way I could ever turn against Toño, you understand?"

I don't say anything, but when he meets my eyes in the rearview mirror I think he gets that I'm sorry.

I concentrate on remembering the exact sequence of numbers coded to Toño's tattoo, then punch them in, and let the slow Hipco system search its way through its database.

"Neto, how're we going to do this if you can't trust any of the other gavilanes?"

"Soon as you get me something to work with I'm going to call a girl I think I can trust. She's mid-level still, so she wasn't in on the job that got them pinched," he says. "And she feels for him what you do."

"Great."

"You'd never want to see him hurt, right?" he says. "There's also a cousin who had his day off today, like me."

"Gang members get days off?"

"Not as you'd understand it, but yes. You getting anything on the computer? We're going to have to choose soon whether to take the northern extension or the southway."

"It's still searching," I say. "So, assuming we're right and they've been taken to an inkatorium, and assuming we manage to somehow break them out, and assuming their injuries aren't so bad we don't kill them in the process, then what? Where do we take them? I'm guessing the gavilanes all know the same safe houses or hideouts or whatever you call them. If there's a turncoat, the injured gavilanes aren't going to be safe anywhere."

"Toño's got some secrets only I know about," he says, meeting my eyes again. "One of them's a place in Hastings."

While I wait for the laptop to cough up some information, I turn the dome light on and open the bag my mother gave me. It is, in essence, everything I'd need to put a GPS tracker in, or take one out. Suture gun, sutures, disposable scalpels, betadine, novocaine, dressings, syringes. Plus some four or five vials of antibiotic.

And a familiar keycard.

"Turn around," I say.

"What?"

"They're in Smithville."

"Is that what that thing says?"

"No. But it will, whenever it gets done searching."

"You sure?"

"Yeah."

He swings the limo around and gets on his phone. He talks rapidly in Spanish, then punches the gas when he hangs up. "Okay, they're on their way to meet us. It'll be a while."

"Where are they meeting us? 'Cause my mom's been great so far but I wouldn't count on her letting us plot this from her trailer."

"Cement factory."

"Hate to tell you, but they've got decent security in place. Live and tech."

"Not anymore."

"What?"

He shakes his head. "He bought it. So you wouldn't run into trouble hanging around the chute staring at the stars."

"Jesus." It's all I can get out without falling apart.

"Yeah, that's what I said too." There's a note of humor in it, the first time I've heard anything like that from Neto.

After a while I get on the phone. He's not the only one with people.

*  *  *

Jobs is waiting by the front door when we pull in. He's sweaty, like he walked the whole way. Maybe even ran. My heart softens with the proof of his devotion.

"Gates?" he looks a bit weirded out when he sees my companion.

"How many nicknames do you have, girl?" Neto says. He grins at me, then goes to the front door of the factory and starts punching a code into the keypad.

"You know what the combination is, right?" I ask.

"I'll get it eventually," he answers without turning around. "I know all the combinations he uses."

"Gates?" Jobs tries again. "You going to explain exactly what we're doing tonight?"

"We're going to rescue the guy I love, and his friends, and it's going to be like that game you designed, only better."

"Oh."

"You still in?"

He nods, but he looks a little green.

150

After Neto figures out the security code, we set up in what looks like a break room with no windows. Neto scrounges around for coffee fixings while I spill the laptop and WiFi cards out of my duffle onto the table.

"Oh my God." Jobs caresses the laptop before he opens it. The capture with Toño's GPS location is still on the desktop. "Tell me you hacked this."

"You'll be hacking far more impressive sites tonight." I outline the plan I've devised for him, and despite a few looks of unadulterated panic, he figures out the processes fast.

"How long until your guys get here?" I ask Neto when I look up.

He punches the question into his cell phone. The text reply is almost instant. "Celia figures they're about 45 minutes away yet."

"Are they in separate limos, or one?"

"Separate. But they're within sight of each other."

I worry this for a bit. "I think they should come into Smithville via different routes. Different roadblocks to get through. Less alarming or suspicious for the locals."

"Tell me and I'll text them."

"Can you write it down for him, Jobs?" I don't even pause to see if he nods. "So, we'll put three of the gavilanes in Celia's limo, three in the other one. What's your cousin's name?"

"Carlos."

"And then Toño alone in yours," I say. "And you take him, only him, to the place no one else knows about."

Neto raises his eyebrows but doesn't say anything.

"You may trust the others," I say, "but I only trust you."

He nods. I notice that Jobs is just sitting there. "Why aren't you writing down instructions for Neto?"

"I don't drive. I don't know any of the routes," he says.

"I do."

I turn to the door of the break room, to the familiar voice.

"I'll write them out for you," John says. "But first I need to talk to Abbie."

"You can talk here, Bro," Neto says. "We're all in this together."

"Alone, Abs," John says. "Chute. Three minutes." Then he's gone.

"What the hell?" Neto asks, frowning.

"He's in love with her," Jobs explains unhelpfully.

Neto shoots me a look. "Is this going to be a problem?"

"Is Celia? Look, he and I have already broken people out of this inkatorium. And I trust him, okay? And Jobs?"

"Yeah?"

"Ever heard of Google Maps?"

When I see John silhouetted against the night sky, I feel my heart clutch. In spite of everything, he didn't hesitate when I called him to help with this craziness.

"I'm going to do this for you, Abs," he says without preamble when he sees me. "All of what you've asked of me, and more if you need me to."

"But there's a price," he adds after a moment.

"What?"

When he doesn't say anything, I turn to leave. "Forget it. I'll do it without you."

"No, you won't." His voice is as dangerous as I've heard Toño's get. "I know too much, and there's no reason not to use it to get him detained in some jail or internment site until he dies of old age. Or to have him deported to wherever his parents or grandparents came from. No reason but you."

"What do you want?"

"You know."

I make sure my voice is as full of contempt as I feel. "Fine. We'll fuck. Are we done here?"

"Not quite. I want a guarantee of sole proprietorship," he says. "Title to you, as it were."

"Jesus, John. I'm not a car."

"You've always been for sale," he says.

It feels like a punch.

He takes out his smartphone, starts keying a number in. "You're out of time. Swear to the deal, or stand aside."

"Deal," I say. "I swear. Now, go home. I'll come to you when I'm done with this."

"I wouldn't want to lose you to a higher bidder while I'm not watching." He puts his arm around my waist. "And you don't want to admit it but you need me."

Neto looks up when we come into the break room. I see him take in John's arm around me. His eyes slide up to mine. I don't know what he sees there, but his voice is expressionless when he speaks.

"All set?"

"Yes," John says pleasantly. "So, Lloyd, show me the routes you've charted out."

He may have become a creep, but he knows his way around Smithville better than anyone. Within seconds he's corrected Jobs' pedestrian routing and come up with something really ingenious.

"When are your people getting here anyway?" he asks Neto.

"Twenty minutes?"

John looks at me. "Time to go."

I nod. "Jobs...."

He looks up from the laptop. For a moment his face is euphoric, then he actually sees me. "What's up with you? You look sick."

"Nerves," I say. "You got it straight, right?"

"Piece of pi. Get it?" Then he cackles.

He actually manages to get me to smile.

We park John's beemer in my mother's tiny private lot and go through the glass door of her office. It's the only one in the whole building that opens with a keycard but doesn't record identity or time. The door actually has an official name: Administrator's Privilege. Every inkatorium has one egress so designated. I had discovered this during my long hours of computer sabotage while I was dying of love for the guy at my side. The one I no longer even want to look at.

I pull two sets of scrubs out of the cupboard where my mother keeps hers. They're not the right color for volunteers but there's no other choice. I drop the travel kit on her desk and start up the computer. Jobs could have gotten this information for us from remote, but why waste talent on the piddling stuff?

"Three of them are at Revere," I say after I've got the day's deliveries on screen. "The others are in the infirmary."

Revere is strictly off limits to any but the most senior staff. It's where they put the inks hopped up on drugs, or on anger, for their first 24 hours at the inkatorium. We'll need to open it with my mom's keycard, and unfortunately the reader there will log all the requisite information. The infirmary, on the other hand, is unlocked and closer to the inkatorium's hub. People are in and out of it all the time. Which means it carries its own brand of risk.

"I'll do the infirmary," John says. "I can charm people out of their questions a lot easier than you can, Abs."

I jam a paper wedge under my mom's office door in case John gets back before me since I'll need the keycard. Then I push it almost shut. You'd have to be right on it to see that it isn't actually latched.

"15 minutes and we're back in the office. With or without them," John says.

We head in opposite directions.

I pass Val at the mothership on my way but she's intent on something that keeps her eyes downcast and doesn't notice me.

I run into Bennett two corridors from my destination.

"They run out of the volunteer scrubs again?" he says, slowing to chat.

I nod. "Somebody must like pink."

He grins at me. "Well, I know it isn't you. You heading for the vending machines?"

There are two around the next corner. Short of where I need to be, but not bad cover. Except I don't have any quarters on me.

"Yeah," I say. "Want me to get you anything?"

"Nah," he says. "They ran out of Snickers bars."

He gives me a little wave as he trots off.

There's no sound coming from Revere and no light leaking beneath the door. I slide the card through the reader and inch the door open. My night vision is pretty good, so it's only seconds before I discern three cots with occupants strapped down on them. Which means they must have gone really crazy at check-in because my mother's protocols limit the use of restraints.

I move silently to the closest. The occupant's asleep, I can tell by the breathing. I grab the shoulder and give it a shake. The breathing changes.

"Are you a gavilán?"

There's no answer. And now the room is absolutely silent. As if all three woke when I shook the one.

"I'm a friend of Toño's," I say. "We're getting you out of here."

"Who's we?" A woman's voice. Raspy.

"Neto. Celia, Carlos and some friends of mine."

There's a low babble of Spanish. They're all women. For a second I'm stunned they're the ones in Revere, in restraints, then remember they've got to be pretty tough to be gavilanes in the first place. I work my way around the room and undo the straps.

While they're rubbing their wrists and ankles, I hook a blanket over the lens of the security camera in the corner. "You might want to shield your eyes because I'm going to turn on the lights."

I go to the cupboard built into the west wall and pull three sets of scrubs. Long-sleeved, dark green ones like the senior CNAs use.

"Heads up," I say, and pitch one set to each. "So, here's the plan. We turn left out of the door, straight through the main nurse's station. While I distract, you take the next right, then count four corridors and take another right. All the way at the end of the hall to the door with 'Administrator' on it. It looks closed, but isn't. And keep the sleeves down over your tattoos."

I pull a bedpan out of the cupboard and hand it to the shortest gavilán, a sweet-looking girl whose round face makes her look about my age. "You hardly look old enough to be a CNA, much less a senior one, so if someone stops you tell them you're a college volunteer but we're out of pink scrubs. Got it?"

"Yes," she says. With a strong Spanish accent.

"Plan B, don't talk." I grab a bottle of betadine from the cupboard, open it and pour a little into the bedpan. Crap brown, with a reddish undercast, like bloody diarrhea. I drop a few half-shredded cotton balls in there to look like floaters. "If anyone gets close to talk to you, just pretend you're losing hold of the bedpan."

"Gross," snickers the tallest. Raspy voice. No accent at all.

"You're allowed to speak," I say.

Her eyebrows shoot up into her forehead. "Who made you boss?"

"Opportunity," I say.

The third – bleached blond and wiry – grabs a couple of sheets out of the cupboard, dips parts of them into the bedpan of betadine, then crumples them up. Close enough to soiled linens to make people keep their distance.

We do a quick run-through of the room, making sure it looks as if it hadn't been occupied in the first place, then I turn off the light and yank the obscuring blanket off the camera. I slip out first and start walking down the corridor. I hear them come out, and the click of the door behind them. At the nurses' station, I hop on the desk, hanging pretty much in front of Val's face.

"Jeez, Abs, you scared me," she starts. "I didn't know you were on tonight."

"Someone called my mom at home to let her know about tonight's no-shows. I owed her, so I'm here."

"I'm glad it wasn't me trying to get last-minute replacements for an overnight shift," Val says. "If I have my way, the no-shows are *so* not getting college credit unless they agree to pull doubles."

"'Us community service types are much more reliable." I grin at her.

"So, anything going on tonight?" I add, trying to sound casual.

"Some nastiness at registration earlier, and Bennett's up to his usual crap, but other than that, no."

"What's up with Bennett?"

"Nothing," she says, but she makes a motion with her hand to indicate drinking. "Just don't tell your mom, okay?"

She studies me a moment, "You're a Chatty Cathy tonight."

"Bored."

She grins. "Get back to work then. Or I won't credit you for your hours either."

None of the girls are there when I swing myself back over the mothership. Good.

I give Val a little wave before I set off.

When I push the door to my mother's office open I can pick out six shadowy silhouettes in the dark.

"Your friend's gone to get the last gavilán from the infirmary," says the raspy-voiced girl.

But I'm not paying attention. I walk over to the figure standing nearest to the administrator's privilege door. He's staring out of the smoked glass and doesn't turn to my approach.

"Your boy tells me you made your first sale tonight," Toño says.

His tone is all business, and though I've heard it before, I haven't been expecting it. It robs me of the words I had been turning over in my head since I left the cement factory.

"It's not my first deal, remember?" I say instead.

"Our deal didn't use people for currency. Tell me he lied to me about that part."

Whatever has held me in one piece threatens to come undone. I sink to the floor, hands over my face.

Toño says something in Spanish. I hear raspy-voice answer, and then footsteps. He drops down by me and grabs my upper arms.

"Go home, America." He says it so quietly I almost miss it. "I'll take care of it."

"No," I say, coming out from behind my hands. My eyes might be full but they haven't spilled over, and the emphasis I give my words is clear. "We do it my way. *No one* gets hurt."

He pulls me up to standing. His laugh is short, wounded. "Too late."

A low sustained whistle sounds clear through the room, and he steps away from me.

John comes through the door with the last gavilán, this one hobbling badly. John looks over and crosses to where I'm standing, but his eyes aren't really on me. And then … nothing prepares me for the way he handles my body in front of everybody, or the way he catches my bottom lip between his teeth with his kiss. I can't help it, I whimper, then taste blood.

"Do we really have time to waste?" says raspy-voice.

John lets go with a laugh. I feel my face burning and I can't look in the direction of any of the gavilanes.

John performs all the incisions to remove the GPS trackers; I swipe with beta and staple the sutures in. My hand shakes all the way through.

"Are we good?" John asks when I'm done. I nod.

"All right. I'm going to ditch the trackers back at the infirmary, I'll be right back." He slips out.

Toño grabs me as soon as John's out the door. "You're bleeding."

"It wasn't intentional."

"Lie to me, lie to him, but don't lie to yourself, America. If he hurt you once he'll hurt you again."

"I made a sale, remember? Only it was me I sold, not you – no matter what you may think. And if the oath costs me more than I imagined, I'm still honor bound."

"This isn't about honor," he says, harsher than he's ever been with me. "I told you before, leave it to me."

"And I told you, no. Not if you ever want to be with me," I say. I know there's no chance at all I'll get to see him again after he drives out of the inkatorium, but he doesn't.

He lets go of me with something like a frustrated growl.

The gavilán limos are parked where they should be, with their logos and plates obscured by magnetic sheeting. They'll drive out of the property following the treeline, and then cut through Harper's pastures and come out behind the abandoned motel Ravenswood had talked about. It's John's route, and a damn good one. The inks will hit no roadblocks at all on their way out. From there, it's on Neto and Celia and Carlos to get the gavilanes through without the benefit of instaskin.

I can't look at Toño as he leaves, but before Neto gets in, I raise my eyes and meet his. He touches his fingers to his forehead and moves them leftward and high, as if trying to convey something by the movement. Or maybe he's just pointing at a star. But if there's anything kind in the night sky, it's not shining down on me.

Less than a minute after I text him the all clear, Jobs sets off the fire alarm. Around us the inkatorium goes noisily into emergency mode, but my mother's office – dark and presumed unpeopled – isn't disturbed.

I can hear the fire engines roaring in the distance as John swings out of the inkatorium's driveway.

"Done," I text Jobs.

"Wait til u see what I did. No traces at all," is the answering text.

"Is that Lloyd you're texting?" John looks over at me.

"Yes."

"Tell him to go home. We're going straight to my house."

"There's stuff I want to pick up at home," I say.

"Tomorrow."

I look out the window while I punch my phone's keypad. "Go hme. U cant imag how i fucked ths."

"Did some1 die?" Jobs texts back.

"Me." I hit send, then turn the phone off.

5.

Nobody can hurt you quite the way someone who has loved you can.

The scars on my body are from that night. Produced with the tip of a knife, honed and precise, so when John's done only my arms, neck and face are clear of the slashes that make me look furred.

The four larger gashes on my face are his too. I think it is intended to look like the mark a wolf would make, so that even my family nickname and my father's clan become reminders of who I really belong to.

There is no sex because, I understand too late, none of it was ever about sex.

When he's done cutting me and entertaining himself with my reaction to the blood, he falls asleep. I dress and walk home.

The lights are on in the trailer. When I open the door, my mother looks up at me from the kitchen table. Her eyes slide from my face to my blouse. I know it is soaked through. I've avoided looking at it so I can keep walking and not faint dead away but I can feel it clinging to the cuts.

I drop in the chair beside her, and after she cleans and dresses the wounds, I close my eyes as she rocks me back and forth and strokes my hair.

I fall asleep I think, for a little while anyway, and when I wake up I don't open my eyes. I'm still being rocked and my hair is still being stroked, though the arms are different. I hear the whimpering of a wolf, and I imagine it must be my father keening as he holds me.

But then I realize it's me. My whimper, my hurt, my keening.

I open my eyes.

They're Toño's arms around me.

"Why are you here?" I ask. Then I remember to duck my head to hide my face from him.

"Because you're here."

He brushes the hair gently off my face and tips it back up to him.

"Your mom gave you a shot of painkiller. Is it wearing off?" His voice is controlled, but I can hear more beneath it.

"Not yet."

"Good. You tell me when it does, I'll go fetch her. She's sleeping at the moment, but she says she has another dose for whenever you need it."

"You should go."

"Soon."

"No, now. If John finds out you're still here he'll follow through with his threats. He'll come up with even more ways to hurt me." Despite my best efforts, a shudder rips through me.

"If he's dead, there's no threat."

I push away from him. "No. Not even after this. Swear it."

When he doesn't say anything, I strike him hard, with the flat of my hand, in the middle of the chest. "Swear it."

158

He grabs my hand, holds it still where I've hit him. "America, I've never lied to you. A man who thinks he can own another human being is a man who deserves to be taken out."

I hate crying, and when I do, it is ugly. I hit him over and over as I howl, but I can't seem to stop even as he pulls me tighter to him.

Then, when I'm down to irregular dry sobs I turn my face up to his. There is no regret in his face, just determination. And pain. I pull away from him.

"I'm sorry. I forgot you were injured too," I say.

"I'm fine, America," he says, a hint of a smile playing on his lips. But the longer he looks at me, the more of the sweetness in that almost-smile leaches away.

"I think I need to go look in a mirror," I say after I put it all together in my head.

"Not yet."

That bad.

"Give it time, America. All wounds need time to heal. Believe me, I know all about this sort of thing."

"How long did yours take?"

"Until you."

At his words something shatters inside me

"Take me home with you," I say. An echo from many months ago, but a broken offer now.

*If you can bear the disfigurement.*

*If you can look at me and see what I was and not what I am.*

*If you can ignore another man's brand.*

I want to say these to him, but I don't.

He tips my head back and gives me a sweet, chaste kiss on the lips, but doesn't say anything. After a while I lean back against him and close my eyes again. He doesn't want to hurt me, I know that, but the silence between us is another knife.

I try to will myself somewhere else. A place with stars.

I hear the faint click of fingers on the keypad of a phone, and a brief, low conversation in Spanish. After five or ten more minutes of silence, I hear the limo pull up outside the door. I steel myself for the goodbye. What's a little more blood on this night?

But he scoops me up and carries me outside in his arms. I open my eyes when he sets me down in the backseat of the limo. He disappears back into the house, and when I see him next it is with my mother – disheveled and still half asleep. He stays outside, speaking with Neto while she gets in the limo beside me.

She reaches out, gingerly touches my injured cheek. "It'll heal up, but it's going to leave a scar. All of the cuts will, I fear."

She sighs, looks away for a moment. When she looks at me again, she gives me a wistful smile. "All those years of pounding it into your head that you should finish your education and not run off with a guy…. God, I hate that he's taking you away from me."

"I asked him to. He feels sorry for me."

"I don't think pity has a thing to do with it."

I shake my head. The pain from the slashes in my face flare with the movement.

"I gave him another shot of painkiller for you, and some antibiotics, and anti-infective ointment to put on the cuts," she says after a moment. "If there's a problem, let me know, I'll call in a prescription to a pharmacy down there."

"Mom … John's going to make trouble for you and Jobs and anyone else he can when he finds out I'm gone."

She pats my uninjured cheek. "You stop thinking about him, okay?" Then, she's gone.

A few minutes later, Toño gets in the limo beside me.

"Ready?" His eyes are on mine long enough that I have to look away.

He must give Neto the sign because the limo starts rolling out of the trailer park.

Later, much later, his hand reaches for mine and he pulls me to him.

***

Toño's secret safe house is Meche's brownstone, and this odd confluence of my past and my future makes me uneasy. The house is huge, and empty of people, and feels different than it did when I was here last. It doesn't help that the first few days the only person I see is Neto.

"Tests of loyalty," Neto says after I ask him where Toño is. "I'm clear, of course, as are a few others. But until everyone's clear they can't know about this place. Or about you. "

"Do I want to know what's involved in the tests?"

"No. Sit," Neto says, placing a plate full of tawny crisp pork pieces, red beans and yellow rice on the kitchen counter in front me.

I eat so quickly he ends up refilling my plate before he sits down himself.

When he does, he pulls a handgun out and lays it on the counter by my plate, "this is for you."

"I can't shoot."

"I'll teach you."

"No, that's not what I mean. My dad taught me how to shoot his Thompson Contender a long time ago. And I'm dead on when I manage to take the shot. But I never could shoot a deer, or even a woodchuck or possum. Just targets. There's no way I could even aim at a person."

"You'd be surprised what you can do if you have to. Keep it on you."

"Where?"

"Waistband's always worked for me."

"Leggings don't really have waistbands."

160

"Underwear then. I don't give a shit. Just have it on you, or I'll pay for your stubbornness." He shoves his plate away from him in disgust.

I thrust the gun into the waist of my leggings, in the hollow of my back. Then I pull my shirt down over it. "Okay?"

He nods. "Keep it under your pillow when you sleep."

He takes the empty plates, then rinses them and puts them in the dishwasher. He starts on the bean pot.

"I'm having a hard time seeing you so domestic," I say. "Doesn't quite fit my image of you."

"The sooner you ditch the image, the better. I'm just like any other guy," he says without turning around

"Only a surer shot."

He turns to look at me. "Yeah."

"You don't much like me being here, do you?"

"I know why he wants you with him. But he needs to focus on rebuilding the gavilanes. Having you around is going to create another problem for him to deal with. He might even lose more gavilanes because of it. Passion is always a weakness, something enemies exploit."

"I'm damaged goods," I say, looking down at my hands. "Really damaged. I won't ever again be who he was waiting for. It's compassion, not passion, that made him bring me here, Neto. And if he didn't have that quality you wouldn't idolize him as you do."

"Idolize is a strong word."

"Respect, then. Or love. Whatever feeds your loyalty."

He gives me a long, inscrutable look, then turns back to his dishwashing.

I wander into the living room and get on one of the computers. Like Mcche's, these are top of the line. Everything's a ghost, routing through remotes and leaving tracks to countless innocent IP addresses. I lose myself in my world.

When I rise I can hardly straighten up. I hobble to the stairs.

I don't remember what I dream about when I fall asleep, but it has me running hard enough for my chest to burn with each breath. I wake once, briefly, and hear a deep, steady rumble and feel something generating heat beside me. But before I can turn to it, I'm asleep again. In the morning there's only an indentation in the memory foam to tell me Toño's spent any time by my side.

I spend the next day on the computer as well, this time with Remi – the tall, raspy-voiced woman from the inkatorium – as my protector. The day after that with Ana – the bleached blond – then Neto again, and like that the three of them alternating for a whole week. I don't know the ways of gangs but I find myself worrying that they're the only three who've passed the loyalty tests. But then maybe they're the only three who can stand being around a non-ink.

At night I change into a shirt of Toño's I've appropriated, climb into bed and fall asleep almost as soon as I stretch out. It's that way now, instant exhaustion. But not restful sleep. And in the morning all that's left is the memory of Toño already gone for the day.

Finally one night when the recurring nightmare chases me awake, I turn to see him stretched out next to me, one arm flung over his eyes. The moonlight is weak and glances off the bare skin of his chest in frail silver glints.

"You're here," I say.

"I'm here." He doesn't move his elbow from over his eyes. A triangular shield to block out the world.

"Are you done with the loyalty tests?"

"I think so."

"Are you okay?"

He laughs. It's not a happy sound.

I stare at the tattoo dead center on his chest. It is an image of a heart struck through by three knives. The oldest, faded and a bit blurred, must represent his brother's death. The other two knives are much newer tattoos; one is so fresh it's still a bit inflamed. I don't know what they signify. There's so much about him I don't know.

He takes his arm from his eyes, then shifts to look at me. I don't remember his eyes being this black or this inconsolably deep.

"What about you, are you doing okay?" he asks.

"I guess."

He reaches over, plays with a strand of my hair. "Are you regretting this?"

"No."

"You deserve better than me," he says after a while.

I yank my hair out of his hand, then turn my back on him. "If you don't want me anymore just say so."

He laughs again, another tortured sound. His arm comes around my waist and pulls me to him. His body against mine is hard. "Who said anything about not wanting?"

Then I'm on my back and my shirt is open and all the scabbed-over cuts form a horrible pelt of possession that can't be ignored.

I flush and turn my face away.

He grasps my chin and turns me back to face him. "America," his eyes bore into mine. "It's me, remember?"

He kisses the marks. Then hikes himself up on an elbow and looks into my face again. "Not tonight, America. Not until you're healed and whole."

"I'll never be that again."

But his mouth on mine insists that I will, and I give up arguing.

*** 

I'd like to say we're together forever.

I'd like to, because every month I spend with him, every day, every hour in which we turn to each other with love and desire and the delight of bodies that

162

fit perfectly together, we become like the stars that blessed us.

One night I open my eyes to the dark and Neto's hand gripping my shoulder.

"Get up. Now."

I blink a couple of times, then my eyes turn sharp. The bed beside me is empty. I look up at Neto, and I know.

I feel a howl start to rip from my throat. He clamps his hand over my mouth. "There'll be time for that later," he says. "Right now, I need to get you out of here."

I grab under my pillow, then pull on jeans, shoes, whatever is at hand. I've never completely unpacked the duffle and for a second I wonder if I always knew it would end this way.

I hear gunshots as we run down the stairs. Before I can pull out my gun and head to where I see Remi and another figure lit by muzzle flashes, Neto pulls me to the steep basement stairs. He moves me through fast and efficient. But I see it anyway.

Toño's splayed on the living room floor. There are ragged gunshot wounds to both shoulder and thigh. But neither of those are killing shots. Death came to him as a knife tore a path that is an eerie echo of his old scar. If it had been possible to heal from this wound he would have borne a perfect X in scar tissue across his torso.

There is so much blood I feel myself sway. The weapons are on the floor, not too far from any of the bodies. Six people to kill just one. The man to Toño's left is indistinguishable after a bullet to the face, and others also sport messy, obliterating wounds. There is a butterfly knife next to one of them. Celia.

As soon as we're downstairs, I stop. "Where were you?" I say.

If it sounds like an accusation that's because it is. The second is chosen because undisputed loyalty puts him there. So he'll jump in front of the bullet, or knife, intended for the first.

"Kitchen. She was one of the ones that sailed through the loyalty test, and in the time since, she's been a model gavilán. I think he was even considering moving her up to top corps. So he didn't hesitate when she asked for a meeting. Christ, he even sent me to make coffee after she arrived," he says.

"She must have found a way to unlock the deckside door so the others could get in. As soon as the commotion started I cracked the pocket doors and started shooting. She dragged him out of the fray, out of my sightline. I thought it was a protective move …."

He falters, then resumes his expressionless narration. "I think she's a late recruit to this, not part of the original ambush. Not that it matters. There's still a driver outside in the gavilán limo they used. He, or she, is Remi's and Ana's business to finish. Got it? Now go."

But even when I'm moving again, I'm not done asking.

"Did Toño kill Celia, or did you?"

"I took her out. Just as I was the one who brought her to the gavilanes in the first place," I hear misery in his voice.

"Was he still alive when you killed her? Did he see it?"

"He knew," he says.

"Good." My voice is so cold it makes his head jerk back.

His limo is parked on the street just behind the privacy fence. I throw my duffle in the back seat then myself in after it. Neto starts the limo as soon as he's inside and we're tearing through the streets of Hastings. I hear him make a call, and then a low and urgent conversation in Spanish, a click, silence.

Hawks are creatures of day, wolves nocturnal. Hawks live from the plummet to earth, wolves from the leap from it. There is no commonality to these predators. But beneath the skin, where Toño's and my souls resided and our hearts beat, we were mated for life. I know whatever my life now brings it'll be nothing to what I've lost.

"What's going to happen to Remi and the others?" I ask.

"If the gavilán in the car gets away, he'll disappear or come after us, rogue or with others. He's probably in league with another gang. I didn't stop to check ink, but Remi and Ana will. As of this moment I only count those two gavilanes as loyal. They'll dispose of the bodies, clean the house of any gavilán traces, that's it," he answers through the open partition. "Then they're out of there. We're broken. The gavilanes are nothing without Toño."

"Do you have instaskin, money, whatever you need to keep going?" I ask.

"Didn't you hear me, America? I have nothing now. I am nothing."

"Don't call me America. Anything else, but never that, understand?"

We ride in silence for a while.

"Where are we going?"

"The place I know he'd want me to take you," he says.

Midway to Smithville I manage to climb through the partition to the front seat. He looks at me as if I've lost my mind.

"You loved him?" I ask once I've settled and buckled myself in.

"Of course I loved him. He was my blood. And my best friend. And the only person in world I could completely trust."

"Not the only one," I say.

I peel one of his hands off the steering wheel and put it on the small round belly only Toño and I knew about.

"Christ," he says as he wrenches his hand away and back onto the steering wheel. He doesn't say anything else. I watch the tears leak out of his eyes and roll down his cheeks unchecked. They catch the glint of the stars.

"He knew?" he asks finally.

"Yes. He was happy."

"It makes it worse," he says after a moment.

"Not for me," I say. I keep my hands on my stomach, a thin veil of skin and muscle the only barrier between me and the tiny heart beating steady beneath it.

After a long time Neto moves his hand off the steering wheel again and places it on my belly. I cover his hand with both of mine.

"Stay in Smithville," I say. "Help me raise him to be a Gavilán. Be his uncle. Or second cousin. Or whatever the actual blood relationship is."

"Family is family," he gives me a bitter smile.

He never does give me an answer about staying, but when we pull into the trailer park and the lights go on in my parents' house, he follows me in the door.

# Del: Sgraffitto

I'm at the Alphabet having a drink with my friend Kurt. It's a rare thing these days. I don't much like coming down off the hill.

He's bartending tonight, and the bar is quiet. None of the Blandon U. kids are back yet, which means my friend has a chance to actually sit for a spell. But he doesn't. He leans against the inside of the bar, keeping an eye on Hoots who looks like he might decide to spew. Any second now. On the other end of the bar, thank God, since I've already spent two hours at the laundromat this week.

Kurt and I don't actually talk much. Never have. Less now that people think I've gone loco. Not that Kurt doesn't think so too, it's just that in his book friendship means hanging through the crazy patches.

Everyone knows your business in Smithville. Hell, two hours after I got the divorce papers to sign I had people stopping me in the streets to express their sympathies. I made the mistake of opening the envelope in the post-office as soon as I had signed for it. Marceline Yeadon, the postmistress for the past centennial or so, must have broken the news to every person who walked through the door. Maybe she left notes for the mail carriers as well.

But it isn't the impending divorce that's put me in my current person-to-be-leary-of status. It wasn't my show at the small Smithville art gallery, either, though that may have given the rumors a nudge. No, it was Ray's funeral that convinced people I'd lost it. My decision to sit with the inks, specifically. Tolerance Smithvillians understood, closeness … not so much.

It was before the inkatorium was built, though talk of a big build had already started circulating. Nearly everyone in town turned out on that sunny Tuesday. First Presbyterian hadn't seen a funeral quite so well attended since the time of the town fathers.

Chato and the crew showed up in suits they had purchased from the thrift shop for the occasion. They were scrubbed and brillantined into shades of soft brown and black patent, and sat in the back two pews of the church. When I arrived the service had already started and all the real Smithvillians had taken care to leave me choice empty pew spots up front. I sat next to Chato. He's pretty stoic but on that day he kept wiping his eyes and it felt good to know he'd be missing Ray with the same quasi-filial ache I was feeling.

Later I drove the inks to the cemetery for the interment – most of them fit themselves in the open back of my pick-up as if we were all going to a carpet job – and they insisted on placing plastic rosaries and prayer cards on the casket. I don't think I've ever seen Pastor Lennox so alarmed.

I inherited everything: business, properties, the whole mini empire. After probate it amounted to a tidy sum. More if I had sold the business then, while we were making money hand over fist. But I kept it going for as long as I could. In truth, Chato and Chema were the only people I could stand being around for any length of time. If I lost them, I'd surely have turned into a hermit like French Louie up in the Adirondacks. The inks were more than coworkers. More than friends. They were the erratics who'd slid into this moraine and found that a brother had been deposited here before them.

"I'm drunker than five men," Hoots says at my shoulder. He's found his way here without my noticing; I've been too enmeshed in thinking about the past to smell the present and run.

"Congratulations," I say.

"Hey, you still have those apartments up on Jackson Road?" Hoots leans way too close to my face when he asks it.

"Sold them soon after I closed the carpeting business," I say, edging away while I glance up at the game playing silently on the bar's TV screen. "Nobody wanted to rent after they found out Ray had housed the temporary inks there."

"People get weird when they hear about diseases," Kurt puts in.

"None of the crew was sick," I say. "But they probably ended up at the inkatorium anyway."

"I don't think so," Hoots says. "I've got a friend up there and she says there aren't any locals."

"You sure she can tell one ink from another?" I say.

There's so much contempt in my words, Kurt gives me a warning look.

"Hey, man, I think it might be time to head home," he says to Hoots.

"Yessh." Hoots drains his glass, then turns around and starts on his way to the door.

Kurt scoots down the bar after Hoots to make sure he gets out the door without incident. When he comes back, he's shaking his head. "You know, one time he fell into a snow bank after leaving here and he was so drunk he couldn't get up out of it. If he hadn't been fished out by a couple of college kids we might have found him frozen there the next morning. Hootsicle."

"What makes a man turn into that?"

Kurt gives me a look. "What you're doing."

I look down at my drink. I've developed a taste for shots of Bacardi 151, nice and neat. "I don't drink that much."

"Naw, man, but you're leaking life. Just like Hoots."

"Since when did you major in philosophy?"

"Since never. But I've got eyes."

"I'm fine."

He takes a pull on his beer. When he's bartending he nurses one glass all night. "So what *did* happen to the inks from your crew?" he asks.

"I don't know."

"Ah yeah." He knows I'm lying, but he's too good a friend to call me on it.

When the inkatorium opened Chato and Chema had come up to my cabin to say goodbye. They saw what it meant before I did. No inks were going to be working and walking the streets of Smithville anymore.

I think we drank a lot that night. I'm pretty sure I was the one who came up with the plan. Then again, maybe I asked the land itself and it said yes in that molten, charismatic tongue I've been given to decipher.

They're living in my woods. In the canvas outfitter tents I've purchased from Cabela's with Roy's pocket change. The homesites are permanent as far as I'm concerned, and by some weird and incomprehensible ink communication system, more of them find their way to us each week. To put down stakes on these hidden 200 acres of Smithville that map the shape of my heart.

Believe it or not, I'm happy. How can I not be? For the first time in years, my heart is full.

***

Harper is a piece of work. A lot of the other farmers criticize the condition of his barnyard. The way his cows' hooves curl up into elf shoes because he neglects to trim them, or the way his heifers' flanks cake with manure soup after rain has made his ponds overflow.

"I think you better get down to my farm," he tells me when we chance upon each other at the grocery store after I leave the Alphabet. Everyone else has moved to a different register because, let's face it, he smells of cow shit.

"Yeah? Why's that?" I ask.

"I need to talk to you about what's straying from your property onto mine," he says, eyes hard and fanatical.

He's my neighbor, but not who I would have chosen to live next to.

"Problem?" I say.

"You might call it that."

It's been a month of problems already. Everyone's on edge from the doings downstate: the mobs, the state of emergency, the fallout from the fires. And up here we've gotten so fed up with the roadblocks – which haven't produced a single ink arrest, only drug and alcohol-related ones – that we've started calling them 'Sweeney's Cash Cows'.

Though they're careful to stay within the confines of our boreal realm unless they're fully instaskinned, I wonder whether my ink enclave has been discovered and the meeting I arrange with Harper is to be a ransoming. He's always hurting for money, maybe we're talking payment for silence.

I arrive at his unkempt barn around sundown. I wait while he hooks his cows to the milking machines and motions at the kid who's helping him to complete the task, then I follow him into the farmhouse.

"Sit," he says, waving at a kitchen chair painted in a chippy, faded yellow.

He sets a water kettle on the stove, then turns to stare at me.

"They say you've got some hidden ink in your background," he says.

"Nope. Skin." It's a term I hate, but no matter. It's what Smithville folk always called my grandmother, even though she had far more French ancestry than Black Seminole.

"I knew your grandma and grandpap, you know."

"I've heard."

"She was a good woman, no matter her blood."

Maybe because of her blood. But I don't say it.

"Pretty, too. In her way. Lots of men envied your grandpap."

"We reminiscing, Harper?"

"No." He takes the kettle off, pours water into a pot with two teabags. He watches it turn dark, I wait.

"I think I got something belongs to you," he says finally.

"Doubtful. I haven't misplaced anything."

"Thing is, even if it isn't yours, I don't think anyone but you would want it."

"What is it?"

He doesn't answer. After pouring me a cup, he ducks out of the kitchen.

I debate whether to follow him.

When he comes back, he's got a folded paper in his hands.

He looks at me. "You got some people living on your land who shouldn't be."

"And if I did?"

"It's nothing to me," he says. "I believe in live and let live."

"Admirable."

He cocks his head and looks as if he's trying to figure whether I'm making fun of him. He must decide not because he hands me the paper. When I unfold it I see the front cover of the exhibition notes from my art show. For a moment my disbelief that he'd go to an art show battles with curiosity about the gallery staff's reaction when they saw him there. Or smelled him.

"I saw your pictures," he says.

"And, what'd you think?"

"Didn't know what to think," he says. "But the thing is, I have a really good memory for faces."

"Yeah?"

"And, see," he says, "I found one of your paintings sleeping between some bales of my heifers' hay this morning."

"What?"

"In my barn. Asleep." He sounds as if he's trying to explain to someone with mental retardation. "One of yours. You know, marked."

He ducks out of the kitchen again. This time he comes back with a person in tow. He's leading her by her wrist. It's blue with lines. In front of her, and behind – as the wake left by a ship cutting through heavy waters – a spray of tiny golden bees.

She doesn't look up through the veil of heavy blond hair.

"What do you want, Harper?" I ask. My voice is strained beyond recognition.

"Nothing," he says.

"Why not?" I edge closer to her. After a few seconds I reach for her hand. I don't remember it being this small. In my memory she lives grander, bigger.

"I'm your neighbor," he says. "You'd do the same if a heifer wandered onto your pasture, wouldn't you?"

"She's not a heifer."

"I know," he says. Maybe it's a trick of my ears, but his voice seems gentler and kinder than it's been.

She doesn't look at me. He doesn't look at me. I look at the sad, painted walls.

"Now what?" I ask. The hand in mine is practically lifeless. I don't want to think how it got that way. I don't want to think how it got here.

"Now you take her home," Harper says.

"That's it?"

"That's it."

"Thank you," I say.

He waves it away.

"Meche," I bend to whisper in her ear.

The honey eyes that turn on me seem to see me for the first time.

"Del?" she says. "I finally found you."

# Del: Sgraffitto

The chatter of the land gets loud when I bring Meche on it. I can feel its hum, its deep-chested rumble, without having to lay my hand on its surface. As I shoot a hand out to steady her when she stumbles, I feel beneath her skin, an answering hum. As if she is harmonizing without words.

I guide her through the woods and down to my cabin without any conversation passing between us. Once she's upstairs in one of the loft bedrooms, she curls on top of the bedclothes and instantly falls asleep. With her coloring and the weight loss that has turned her gangly and big-eyed, she looks like a fawn caught dozing in its hideaway of high grass.

When I go back downstairs, Chato and Chema are there already, sitting at the table with open beers in hand.

"Just make yourselves at home," I grumble. "Are those the last two beers?"

"Yes," says Chato, handing me another, unopened one. They have a standing dinner invitation, these two. Of all the inks they are my *compas*, as they name it. Meaning more than buddies or friends, more like godparents. The child we all share responsibility for is under our feet, around our homes, in our blood. I know they have their own ways of communicating with it; I don't ask how.

"Hey, Boss," says Chato. "I hear we have a guest."

I walk over to the kitchen. I've left a hen of the woods mushroom soaking to loosen the grit that hides in fungal channels. I drain the mushroom, dry it to damp with a dish towel.

"Harper," I say, "found an ink wandering on his property."

"Problem?" Chema asks.

I shrug, start dicing the big mushroom.

"Who?" Chato asks. Wandering onto adjacent property and getting caught with tat in evidence ranks among the gravest on his list of sins.

"Not one of us," I say.

"We're going to have to get another tent," Chema says. "And you might have to buy another composting toilet, what we have is running at capacity already."

"Do we really want to house someone careless enough to get caught in the first place?" Chato asks. A question that holds its own answer.

I hold my hands up to stop him. "I wasn't asking for your permission. She's staying here, no matter what. I was just telling you so you keep an eye out for anything coming from Harper. He was decent enough, but I don't really trust him."

Chema makes a face when he hears what I'm saying, but he doesn't argue. That part always falls to Chato who, though he still calls me boss, doesn't retain a shred of the subservience of an employee.

"So you're not going to listen to us anymore?" he says now. "Is that what you're telling us?"

"No. I'm telling you this ink falls outside of your rules."

"Why?"

For some reason his continued questioning ticks me off. "Because the property's still in my name and I said so?"

But I don't think there's a human alive who can intimidate Chato. Or pull rank on him.

"Swear to God, Boss, if you're going to turn cabrón and not answer our questions, I'm going to beat the crap out of you."

Given a few more minutes he probably would have, because even though I don't stand a chance against him in a fight, I'm not in the habit of backing down either.

"Because I can make instaskin," Meche's voice floats down from above. She must be standing just outside the bedroom door where she can see us but we can't see her.

Chato doesn't seem mollified, but before he can say anything, she adds. "And he knows me from before. And there's a reason I'm here."

When she first starts down the steps, I think she's changed so much they won't recognize her from my paintings. But each step she takes fleshes her out more so that by the time she's standing next to us she's exactly as I remember her. The tiny bees dance in perfect, lazy figure eights around her head.

My *compas* turn to look at me.

"Why didn't you just say so?" Chema says under his breath.

I shrug.

"I guess we'll be off," he says. Loud. So she can hear it.

"No," I say. "Stay for dinner."

The guys look at me as if I've lost my mind.

I introduce them to each other officially then and turn back to making food. The mushroom slices go into the pan sizzling with butter, and as soon as they develop their roasty caramel I throw the venison steaks in with them.

"This place … it's got some special qualities, doesn't it?" I hear Meche ask them.

They don't answer.

"Like, it's big-hearted enough to accommodate all your magicks," she continues.

I turn from my pan a moment. Chato and Chema look pained, as if she's broached the unbroachable. And, really, she has. We don't talk about what we do here – or how – even to each other.

"Which one of you makes the property lines impossible to cross?" she asks, ordinary, as if she were asking who cut the firewood neatly stacked in the woodbox by the stove.

She smiles a little when Chema glances at me, then catches himself and looks down at his beer.

"I tried to get on this property for weeks," she says then. "I kept ending up somewhere else and having to fight to find my way back."

"I set it up so one of the three of us has to bring you onto the land the first time," I say, turning back to the sizzling pan. "Like vouching for you. After that, there's no problem."

I take the pan off the burner and set it aside while I get plates.

"What else?" she asks.

"We've got WiFi and great cell phone reception where we shouldn't," I say. "As if we're in some connectivity bubble. But at the same time, we don't show up on any GPS. I've never asked but I think that's Chato's doing."

"Boss," he says, a bit like a warning.

I hear Meche's delighted laugh as I divvy up the cooked purslane and dress it with a drizzle of malt vinegar.

"Y vos?" she says to Chema. I can't figure how she knows he's Central American and fond of the superinformal form of address.

He doesn't answer.

"Water," I say after a moment. "We shouldn't be able to drink safely from the creek with all the run-off from adjacent pastures, but we can. There's probably a lot more they're both doing, but that's the stuff I know for sure."

There's complete silence as I finish each plate with a scoop of quinoa cooked long enough for the grain to explode and turn fluffy. When I turn around Chato and Chema are glaring at me, Meche looks thoughtful.

"What?" I say as I set the plates in front of them. "She's got magic, too, or hadn't you noticed?"

"Not everyone sees the bees, Del," she says.

Chato grunts, takes a swig of beer, eyes her suspiciously. "I see 'em," he says finally.

Her eyes lock on his. It's weird, like they're taking the measure of each other.

She reaches over and tugs on the thin chain he wears around his neck. The medallion that's usually hidden under his shirt rests in her hand and his seamed, tough face seals right up.

"La Morenita speaks for you," she says. Then she lets the medallion swing back to its place, and pulls out a similar one from under her t-shirt. "La Caridad," she says.

He looks away, but something's changed and I see the tension leave his shoulders.

Chema doesn't wait for her to reach. He yanks a small, square pendant from under his plaid shirt and opens it as he places it in Meche's palm.

"My wife," he says. "She died before I crossed."

She nods as she looks at the photo in its plain locket, then smiles when she hands it back.

"Don't look at me," I say when she turns my way. "I don't wear jewelry."

"And nobody speaks for you." She sounds fond, and just a little bit sad when she says it.

"I hardly speak for me." I grin at her, and after a moment she matches it.

The conversation gets easier as we eat and drink together. Chato and Chema really do finish off all my beers, and by the time they leave it is as if Meche has filled the vacant spaces we didn't even know were between us.

"Will you drink some coffee if I brew another pot?" I say to Meche as she leaves the table and curls her long frame into the Morris chair by the cold woodstove. I hadn't planned it, but now that I'm alone with Meche I'm struck by something a lot like hunger – a craving that calls for mixing a color I can see but can't name, and laying it down so it catches on the tooth of paper just so.

"Sure," she says. "I'll always do coffee."

I tape a sheet of Arches on the backing board as the pot percolates, then start mixing powdered pigments together, guessing at the proportions I'll need to arrive at the color I've envisioned. Meche doesn't move from where she is, but I can tell she's watching my prep. I break to serve the coffee, then wander back to the easel.

"You don't mind, do you?" I ask belatedly as the first, long stroke of color cuts the white paper nearly in half.

I can hear her laugh. It takes three more strokes before I realize there might be more to her answer. I stop, poke my head out from behind the easel to look at her.

"I'd more or less be insulted if you didn't," she says.

"So you *are* a muse."

She shakes her head. The bees fly off for a moment, then return to their usual lemiscate patterns around her. "No. Just Meche."

Completely contrary to my intention, the color of dawn I mix on the palette lays on the paper as a thin wash, not a solid. I'm not sure what I'm painting, but I decide I like the variegated window of rich yellow I've laid on the page and I lose track of time while I consider what to do next. Not a face. And not a realistically rendered landscape either.

"You remember coming to my peña?" she asks after a while.

"Of course."

I shake a couple of grains of red pigment into the shade I've been working, then blindly pick another brush out of the jar. My arm starts to move over the paper without my attention. "There are some things you don't forget."

"Like claiming you had no magic?" she says. "So, tell me, how does it work?"

I don't answer right away. "I ask the land to do for me. It's a conversation for all that I don't always get a straight answer. And it's not my magic, it's the land's. I can't do anything like it anywhere else."

"You've tried?"

"Well, no. But some things you just know."

"And the painting?"

I laugh. "If I had magic for that I'd sell a lot more work than I do."

"But you're pretty particular about your paints."

I look over the messy collection of pots and tubes on the stand with my palette. I wonder that she's noticed.

"I hate acrylics," I say after a moment. "They don't lay on paper or canvas the same way."

"They don't have the same memory," she says.

When I come out from behind the easel to meet her eyes, she adds, "Their pigments aren't ground from components that once knew earth."

Then, "Earth magic, Del. Not particular to this place, much as you love it."

I can feel my jaw lock and set. "Were you asking me about my magic, or telling me?"

She laughs, a little rueful. "Sorry."

I duck back behind the shield of my easel, but don't start painting again. Everything I've asked the land to do since I returned to it runs across my mind as if it were a movie screen. Shale heaving above the creek to form a dry crossing; impassible outcroppings flattening themselves to paths; the stretching and contracting that ultimately exhausts uninvited guests until they turn away from the boundaries of the place.

"You've made it impossible for the rest of the world to touch this land, only abut it, " Meche says quietly. "Your 'conversation' with it has turned it into an in-between place. A spot of safety and kinship. But unfortunately, only for a lucky few."

I look down at the dry pigments I've been using. Suddenly the desire to mix until I stumble upon the color I envisioned is gone. I twist open a tube of prepared paint and squeeze a long snake of color across the palette. It is a deep red with no trace of yellow or orange. I go first for a thinly bristled brush, but then choose a broad fan instead.

"You think I could do more but choose not to," I say, still fiddling, not laying the color over what's gone before.

"Well, what about you?" I say, as I slam the new color on the paper in angry, careless strokes. "As I recall, almost everything about you is morally ambiguous."

"That's what you remember?" she asks quietly. Then, "I'm tied to an element with different gifts and obligations. Mine is the catalyst in a formulation."

As she talks, an uneasy feeling creeps from my gut to my chest.

"I think maybe you scare the shit out of me," I say.

After a while I feel her come to stand behind me.

"Funny how you can still see the yellow and orange through the red," she says when she looks at what I've painted."You wouldn't think it'd be possible."

"It shouldn't be," I say. "It should be opaque. The paint must be old."

"Or behaving badly," I add, a bit like an apology.

"Why bother to paint the other in the first place if you want the red to obscure it?"

I shrug.

"Tell me."

"Sometimes the memory of something is enough."

"Ouch," she says, then gives me a small smile before she heads upstairs.

But I don't believe what I've told her.

I clench the brush, the easel, the stand with tubes and jars of pigment. Anything to keep me from following her exactly as her bees do, blindly chasing infinites.

I don't remember finishing the painting.

But there it is in the morning, still taped to its backing board and ready to be ripped free. It is like nothing I've painted before. The oblong of carmine is underlaid with a visible array of yellow and orange: from lemon to ochre to the rosy, hopeful salmon hues of dawn. Scrawled across the window of paint are evenly spaced lines of words. My handwriting, sloppy but legible.

I lean forward. *Set me as a seal on your heart, as a seal on your arm*, it starts. Then: *for stern as death is love, relentless as the nether world is devotion; its flames are a blazing fire. Deep waters cannot quench love, nor floods sweep it away.*

The painting feels like a breakthrough.

***

I don't count the days.

It might be weeks, or months, or maybe, if I really want to punish myself when I think about it, closer to a year.

As soon as I get back from work every day, I take her with me on my rambles to acquaint her with the farthest reaches of the acreage and everyone making a home on it. Chato and Chema join us every evening for dinner. After, Meche and I talk and mix up batches of skin in infinitely subtle shades until it gets so late we're goofy with exhaustion and coffee. All of our nights end the same way as the first: with me clinging to my strange new paintings so I won't cave to fire and follow her upstairs.

I go searching for her one Saturday morning that I've overslept and she's not in the cabin when I wake up. I walk the expanse of the property, stopping finally at the road that cuts between my land and Harper's.

Some of his sorry-looking cows are in the pasture, but I see the old farmer inside the barn, leaning up against a milking stanchion. Meche's talking to him, brightly gold in the dark of the barn. I call out, and after a few attempts, I catch their attention. They come out of the barn door together, heading toward me as I start across the road to meet them.

Harper is laughing, I remember that and the way he leans in – as if Meche is a lifelong friend – even as I feel my body lift with the impact. I can hear the car stop, the squeal of rubber on asphalt, the babble of four or five voices speaking at once.

Everything seems so normal, except I'm on my back on the road staring up at a perfect Prussian blue sky like the one that greeted me as a kid when I'd passed through the trial of the cave. Meche's face, and behind that Harper's and three other alarmed faces I don't know, swim into view. I wonder at the fact they're so large they block out the sky and manage to turn it black in an instant.

I open my eyes in a dim hospital room, strapped to more monitors than I can count when I turn my head to look. I feel more than see someone get up from the chair in the corner and come to stand by my bed.

"Del?" Cassie's face is creased with lines I haven't seen before.

"I'm here. More or less."

"Shut up, you idiot." I feel her slap me lightly on the arm. "If you knew how worried I've been you wouldn't say anything like that."

"I must have been out quite a while for you to have gotten here from Hastings already."

Her laugh is short, a trace hysterical.

"I've been in Smithville for a week. Mom, too. And Finn came up yesterday."

"Jesus." I try to sit up, but though the rest of me moves, my legs stay put.

Maybe she sees the panic in my eyes. Her hand comes to rest on my cheek, her thumb stroking the skin beneath it with a tenderness I have to work to remember from her.

"It's okay," she says. "I'm going to get you away from this godawful Podunk hospital and take you where someone can actually do something about that."

She stays with me through the nurses' garbled explanations, through the night and into the next morning when the neurologist makes his rounds and tries to explain the weird and woolly ways of the brain. Like how even though my legs are intact, I can't move them and most likely never will again.

I don't say much, just listen, and watch the array of expressions that chase across the faces of family gathered around my bed. Cassie's family, not mine. My family's missing in action, and no matter how much I hope to hear their footsteps in the hall leading to my door, they don't show.

I fade in and out of sleep and the next time I rouse Finn is the one in the room, slumped in the visitor chair in the corner.

"Hey," he says when he notices me awake. "Want me to call Cassie? She's somewhere out there making calls and filing paperwork so you can be transferred down to the medical center in Hastings."

"No," I say. "I have something to ask you."

"Okay, but she and Mom are the ones that have been dealing with the doctors."

"Not about that. I'm reeling with too much information and not enough understanding about all of it anyway. I was just wondering about the people who were with me when I was hit."

Finn shifts in his seat, then leans forward. "Your neighbor's been in a couple of times to check on your progress. And Meche, too. But listen, if you think Cassie's going to let her see you, you're nuts."

"Why not?"

He just gives me a look.

"When are they moving me?"

"Tomorrow."

"I want to see Meche before I go. And Chato and Chema, too."

"Who?"

"Nevermind. Just find a way to get Meche the message, okay?"

He shakes his head, but I know it doesn't mean no even as he leaves.

He comes back after a long absence. "Meche says she knows some instaskinned ink who works graveyard. He'll sneak them in sometime tonight. I don't know when exactly, but keep the lights out and pretend to sleep because I don't think the nurses bother to check on you if they think you're resting comfortably."

"Thanks."

"Don't thank me. It's on you. If Cassie ever hears about it...." He starts to leave again, then stops without turning around.

"Whatever's between you and Meche, you still love my sister, don't you? That's why you haven't signed the divorce papers, right?"

I'm not sure how he knows about the divorce papers, and I don't ask. I don't answer either. I've never been easy with words and to come up with something even remotely close to the truth I'd have to give name to some pretty complicated feelings.

He must sense it because he walks out without waiting for me to respond.

The hours drag on. Around two I wake from a brief nap to a room filled with a buzzing that isn't generated by machines. For a moment I don't say anything. Meche's perfectly visible in the dim room as if she radiates her own light. And in the circle of what she sheds, my *compas*.

They're the ones who move to the side of my bed when they notice I'm awake.

"I'm sorry, guys," I say. "The land will stop barring the way to outsiders as soon as it forgets my voice."

Chema nods. "We're working on it."

"The land's not going to forget you, Boss," Chato interrupts. "You're just going missing for a while."

I close my eyes. "I don't think I'm coming back."

"You don't know that, Boss," he says. "Haga la lucha."

When I open my eyes again only Meche's still in the room.

"You'll stay up on the hill? So there are three elements at work protecting the place?" I ask.

She leans over me and puts her hand to my face in a way eerily reminiscent of Cassie when I first woke, then moves her hand to clasp one of mine.

"Catalysts only work when there's a specific in the formulation already. My specific's not going to be up there on the hill."

# Del: Sgraffitto

"Meche..."

"Of course I'll stay. When have I ever said no to you?" she asks.

"I've been a fool," I say after a long silence. "I squandered all the time we were given."

She grins at me. "Ah, but we made beautiful skin together."

When she hears me laugh, she ducks her head and kisses me.

Time stops for me during those moments when her lips are on mine and our eyes are closed to the same dark. The memory's going to have to last me a lifetime, I know it as she draws away and my eyes stay closed, refusing the goodbye.

I feel her slip something over my head, and its weight comes to rest against my chest. She moves our clasped hands over it, then leaves mine there alone.

"What is it?"

"You, too, have someone to speak for you."

I feel her step away and know, without need of eyes, when she's gone.

A nurse bustles in minutes later to check the monitors and take my blood pressure. With her skin tone and hair color she could easily be an ink, but when she opens her mouth the accent is pure South.

"You're doing good, hon," she says to me. "You'll have no trouble going home tomorrow."

She glances at my chest, then smiles at me. "Pretty," she says. "You be sure to keep that right there where it is 'cause it's just the kind of thing people like to claim for themselves. You know what I mean?" She leaves without waiting for me to answer.

I look down. A long, leather bootlace is around my neck, and strung on it, a beautifully crafted little bee. It's bright and heavy – probably 24-karat gold – and though the delicate wings don't move, when I put my hand to it, I hear it buzz as if it were alive.

I let go of it eventually, but it rests against my heart all night and it never stops resonating.

3.

I spend the next year doing what I imagine the inks have had to do every time a new restriction is placed: adapting to a radically different life.

The worst of the injuries I sustained was to the thalamus, the relay center of the brain. Usually when the motor part is involved in a closed head trauma like mine, people end up with uncontrollable, involuntary movement in the limbs. Dr. Daley likes to say that it's proof of how contrary I really am that my body decided to do the opposite.

The wheelchair is, in some ways, both the toughest part of my new normal and the easiest. My upper body strength has always been pretty decent, so the parts of my routines that rely on maneuvering, hauling myself in and out, or finessing movement don't prove difficult, just exhausting at first.

It's the planning that really gets to me. The city can be a tough place to navigate in a wheelchair: busted up sidewalks, impossible curbs, construction projects that pop up to obstruct even fastidiously charted courses. And then there's the drivers. I'm convinced there is a special circle in Hell reserved for bicyclists. They blithely ignore traffic rules and nearly wing you in the crosswalk as they blow through red lights. No solidarity at all.

Other adjustments have nothing to do with what my body can or can't do.

I paint fulltime because, strangely, the abstract work that continues to pour out of me sells well enough to provide a regular and decent income. Sarai has turned into my unofficial, and unpaid, artist's agent. She finds the gallery that represents me, pushes my work into commission competion and finds ingenious ways to get me the type of publicity that was once the purview of perfoming, not visual, artists. I like to think she does this from belief in what she calls my "modern illuminated manuscript leafs," not because she feels sorry for me.

If I was a prickly cuss before, I've turned more so now, especially about that.

Cassie and I don't fight much except when I suspect a decision she's made hinges on pity or over-protective instinct. I know she loves me – why else would she have stuck the really awful part out? – and I love her too, though it's mostly a quiet type of feeling that rarely achieves incandescence.

Once a month or so, she climbs on top of me and brings us both – skillfully and efficiently – to climax. And when she comes up pregnant, the love changes again.

I hide my continuing obsession with upstate from her. The texts and messages I get aren't from Meche anyway. She's never answered any of my calls or texts or tweets – so as much as I try I can't figure what she meant by saying I'd have someone to speak for me. But Chema is a devoted social media informant and from him I know the community's still there, stable and safely outside of time for all that they've started interacting more closely with one of the ink gangs. The decisions they make aren't the decisions I'd make but, since outside of paying taxes on the land I can do little to help them, I keep my opinions to myself.

I wonder, sometimes, what my life would be if I hadn't stepped in front of that car. But I don't do that often because it's a straight shot from that to despair and I don't want to go there.

Not now.

Not since I looked into my son's eyes.

*** 

Finn meets me at the Lebanon, one of the few truly wheelchair-accessible bars in the city. I've already parked myself at one of the booths when he comes in.

"Good God, you look exhausted," he says as he sits. "Is Satchel still keeping you guys up at night?"

"No," I say. "He's good. Sleeps straight through since he hit six months. And not a minute too soon."

Finn makes eye contact with the barmaid and motions for a duplicate of the drink sitting in front of me on the table. He's going to hate it when he realizes the tawny liquid is añejo rum, not the whiskey he thinks it is, and some perversity keeps me from enlightening him.

"Cassie and Mom locking horns again over you?" he asks when he's returned his eyes to me.

"I guess that's what you'd call it," I say. "Makes me feel a bit like Satchel when they each want to dress him to go out."

He looks a little embarrassed. "It's not that bad ...." His voice peters out.

"Hell, maybe it is," he says ruefully. "I never liked them trying to make my decisions for me. But they can't help themselves."

"Mari rescued you from them," I say.

"Yeah, now she makes my decisions for me." He grins at me. "Face it, women always do that."

His grin fades when he sees my hand go to the lump under my shirt that is the bee pendant.

The barmaid sets the drink down in front of him.

I watch while he takes a sip.

"Funny," he says. "But not." He flags the barmaid again, orders a Jamesons and slides the glass with añejo my way.

"Have you heard anything from Meche?" I ask. It's no use dancing around it, he's already seen me reach for her token.

"Not much and not from her. I understand she's generating most of the eastern seaboard's supply of skin, but I'm not sure from where." He pauses for the barmaid to slide the new drink in front of him. "I should make Del pay for this one," he grouses as he hands her the money. She smiles at him.

"One week I'm convinced she's upstate, the next on the eastern shore, the week after that, somewhere in the western end of the state. I think she's picking up habits from the gangs. You know there's this whole genre of songs that's grown out of the stuff the gangs do up here – a mix of corrido, reggaeton and n'dombolo – and Havana Barbie figures in a couple of them."

The añejo is supposed to go down smooth, but it doesn't. It catches on every jagged shard in my throat.

Finn doesn't give me more than that. He looks around the bar, as if he's looking for anything to change the conversation.

"How's Gus doing?" I ask.

"Wants to come over and spend another painting day with you and Satchel. Never thought I'd be raising a budding artist."

"Every kid's an artist given half a chance."

"Yeah, except his isn't aptitude but hero-worship. I'm trying not to be jealous."

I want to tell him, but Mari doesn't want Finn to know Gus is fully twinned already and mindspeaking anyone with magic enough to hear him. The jealousy comment has a grain of truth in it, and the five-year-old's adoration of me is hard enough for Finn without adding another layer to it.

When Gus comes over for a visit we do make art – with Satchel strapped into the harness I've designed so I can carry him securely while keeping my hands free to paint – but mostly the three of us wander the streets of Hastings together.

Meche was right. My magic isn't restricted to the upstate acreage, though it takes me a while to notice it. The first time it happens I'm stalled, kept from getting to Second Ave Art Supply by the confluence of a streets project, anticipated demolition of a building, and an impromptu street market set up by art students selling their drawings. I'm out of burnt sienna and the piece I'm working on will take nothing else, so I plot possibilities, outlining them in my head. As I work them out mentally the street around me shifts to better accommodate my plan. Mostly its fractional, the ground beneath curbing sinks just enough to make it a passable jog rather than something to hang up my wheels; the chunks of busted up asphalt on the street flatten into traversable, if still choppy and uncomfortable.

But my walks with the boys aren't about making the way easier for me, though that's a pleasant side benefit. We hit every street within an hour of the apartment, and on each block I stop to create an in-between place. Alley, doorway, underpass – it doesn't matter as long as it has at least one component that still remembers the language it spoke when it was part of the earth. And since I can't be there to vouch for those allowed through the boundaries as I was upstate, I ask for tattoos to be the voucher.

When the kids are around, I hear the bee pendant buzz. Satchel's fascinated by it. If I'm not wearing it outside my shirt, he goes looking for it. Often, when we get home from our forays he's asleep against my chest with the small, resonant thing tucked in his mouth.

"Perhaps it'll give him the gift of a golden tongue," Mari teases when she sees it as she picks Gus up.

*You know that's not what it means.* Gus's twin mindspeaks us both, indignant as only the very young can be when they catch their elders softening the truth.

*It doesn't matter what it means,* I project it as gently as I can, so the childlike creature hidden behind my nephew's eyes doesn't hear it as a rebuke. *I'm not taking it away from him.*

But when she gets home from work, Cassie does.

She handles the bee with the revulsion she might if it were a dead thing already in the first stages of decomposition.

"Put that away," she says to me as she disentangles my sleeping son from my arms. "Never let me see it again."

*** 

The night of the meeting, Francine comes to get me. She's bought one of those funky conversion vans just to fit the wheelchair.

"Why do you think I'm bringing you with me?" she asks once I've hauled myself into the front seat and she's tucked the wheelchair in the back.

"Because your group's in dire need of bodies, even disabled ones?"

She shakes her head. The eyes that remind me so much of Finn light on me. They're not looking kind. "You're unappealing when you say such things," she says.

"God forbid I should be unappealing. So tell me."

"I have this feeling we're going to need *exactly* you."

"Wow, that's a first."

She looks away. "My daughter may not want to see it, but I've spent most of my adult life studying recurring motifs in the human story. The existence of magic, and people who can tap into it, is one of the universals. Maybe it's no coincidence that I have a daughter-in-law, a son-in-law and a grandson with some ability."

"Two grandsons."

She looks over at me, sharp-eyed. "What did Satchel do?"

"Nothing yet. But he will. Trust me."

She falls silent for a while.

"Have you been reading Finn's articles?" she asks.

"Sure," I say.

"So you know it's likely they'll finally shutter the inkatoriums."

"That's a good thing, isn't it?"

"If people aren't going to pay attention to myths, the least they could do is read some history," she says, exasperated.

"Why don't you tell me what you think is going to happen," I say to shorten the prologue.

"Even with the disinformation wars going on," she says, "people believe the stories their neighbors tell and what they piece together from witness. They trust what local bloggers and citizen journalists manage to dig up. Which is why the forcible sterilization story still has legs. Now, imagine if all the people who have experienced it were released and around to tell their stories.... The only way to make a story disappear is to erase the ink it's written in."

I wince at her choice of words. "Francine, we're not going to kill off the residents of the inkatoriums just to hide the fact we've sterilized them without consent, or that they never were sick with contagious diseases in the first place, if that's what you're thinking. It's just not going to happen."

"No," she agrees. "As a nation we might be willing to endure the moral hangover from xenophobia, but not genocide."

"Then what are you saying?"

"We'll deport them en masse. Disperse them to the four corners. Not only those who can confirm what happened at the inkatoriums, but all of them. Except the blue tats who haven't been reclassified as non-aliens. Because they're still citizens. Them we'll get to collude with us in our erasure of the rest."

When I don't say anything, she continues. "My group, we're going to find sanctuary and safe houses for as many inks as we can. So no color of tat can be completely disappeared. Or bought. And we're not the only ones. I hear hundreds of churches and synagogues and community centers across the nation have groups like ours."

"Even if there are thousands of other groups like yours, it won't be enough. You know that, right?"

"So, what? Do nothing?"

"I didn't say that. Just … don't get your hopes up, okay?"

We don't say another word until we get to the meeting site.

I recognize the priest when he opens the door; I remember being in a different rectory's kitchen with him. There are only six people in the meeting room, including the priest, all of them Francine's age. The aged face of the Catholic social justice movement.

Because I'm the only representative of my generation in attendance, they look on me with the devotion reserved for a deity. And it freaks me out. Which mythology allows for a god with a disability? I'll have to remember to ask Francine if any does, and if so, whether any good comes of it.

The underground railroad is their originating model, with a trail of planned safe houses leading to both northern and southern borders, they tell me.

"One of the gangs, the gavilanes, has already started on it," Father Tom says. "We're more or less riding their coattails on this. They've got the tech to turn inks into non-inks. And unlimited access to instaskin. But their territory only extends about three-quarters of the way to the northern border."

"The proprietor of a go-kart track upstate says his acreage can be turned into a sanctuary," the priest adds. "I think that makes three landowners we've got lined up so far. We're going to need more, of course. And more safe houses than the gang's secured."

"Well, it has promise at least," I say. "What about the south?"

"Tougher," says Nell, whose SEIU union seal tattoo winks in and out of sight on her floppy upper arm. "The gangs that hold the southways out of Hastings want cash deposits before any agreement can be forged. And they aren't big on installment plans. Plus, there's more distance to plot out."

"Isn't working with gangs beyond the pale for you anyway?" I say to the priest.

"Was," he admits. "But these days when I go to my knees and pray for help, I can't despise the shape it comes in."

When I get home, Cassie's upset at me.

I leave the wheelchair open at the side of the bed, and haul myself in.

"It's a pitifully small effort," I say. "They can use me."

"Whatever."

I reach for her across the gulf of our bed. She's a beautiful woman, at my side every night. I can't help wanting her even when she doesn't want me.

"I'm tired," she says as she turns her back.

I know she's not lying, she is.

Need exhausts, either way it cuts.

# Part Three

"Leave a trail, we'll find your life."
– FedEx Brigade message #1,597

Note in Appendix B, *Tattoo You: A New Methodology for Cataloguing Ephemera from the Ink Incidents,* E. Parkway and C. Riordan (New York, London, Toronto: International Library Association Press), 356.

# Finn: Redaction

1.

It used to make us laugh, the way the letters accusing us of distorting the news to fit our liberal bias came in on the same days as the ones repudiating our conservative agenda. As if there were some morphic resonance about mediabashing that left and right tapped into at exactly the same moment in the vast ocean of time.

Now, of course, nobody bothers to write letters or post comments online.

Because none of what we produce is news.

It looks like news: lots of words in the same column widths and fonts as before; bylines; breakout graphics and pull-quotes. But whether you pick up a tabloid or broadsheet, a newspaper-of-record or the local rag, or haunt multi-platform news sources, you'll notice a remarkable concordance. We're all writing the same stories. Sometimes, we even use the same words.

"Wait," Melinda counsels.

So, in an ironic reversal of what I wanted as a recent college graduate, I settle for writing a kind of fiction while pining for journalism.

Every so often the truth escapes and goes viral.

Here are the records of the sterilized. Here are the memos with the number of participants and e-mails with familiar names and official signatories verifying involvement. Copies and scans appear on dozens of web sites and their mirrors; gifs and pngs and jpegs attached to thousands of tweets; at the top of searches regardless of what's being Googled.

For a few hours they slip under and over and around the Internet restrictions and security measures until they're excised. They're always successfully hunted down and vanished. But days later, they're back anyway.

And then the truth starts popping up where the not-so-wired can also see it. It is written on FedEx labels and stuck on the lampposts, traffic lights and stop signs of Hastings and other cities. As twitter hashtags and accounts are blocked and access goes intermittent, these are the low-tech equivalent tweets: "8th and Callowhill, 2 p.m." on labels that cover the city June 24. And you turn up at that hour to find it raining paper on that street corner, hard copy proof of whatever bit of ugliness is in the process of being excised – or retrofitted to banality – in our collective memories this week.

Like the involuntary sterilizations. The official story these days is that they aren't sterilizations but new and innovative treatments for bipolar disorder, post traumatic stress and a whole host of addictions. There are even videos of the procedures, with nationally renowned talking heads to explain the methodology and aver that, as far as public health initiatives go, this one is efficacious

187

enough to merit continued funding. But then the FedEx Brigade deluges us with copies of the inkatoriums' purchase orders for the chemical agents and pharmaceutical formulations employed and it gets harder and harder to swallow the lies.

Truth apportioned in megabytes and street theater are the only news since the rest of us in the media have turned chickenshit. Still, if Melinda and I are any indication, it doesn't mean journos aren't holding on to a boatload of flash drives stuffed with truth in case we ever regrow balls. Or get tired of living.

Okay. Maybe I'm exaggerating about that last, but here's what I know is spot on: Given enough time every official story ever concocted falls apart. Someday, someone will put together the mathematical or scientific formula that explains why this is always the case. But I don't need proof, I'll settle for certainty of outcome.

## 2

It is as when we first reunited. Every time. Mari and I can hardly keep our hands off each other while we wait for Gussy to fall asleep. But like all little kids, he seems to have a preternatural sense about this and finds ways to postpone his bedtime and keep me absorbed and engaged with him until, from one moment to the next, he simply drops into deep sleep wherever he's at.

As I carry him to his bed I wonder that my heart was ever big enough to fit the love I feel when I look down at his tranquil little face. But later, caught the dark mystery of my wife's eyes, I remember the heart is an infinite place.

Afterward we tell and retell the stories that never make it to the papers. It's a promise we've made to each other, as binding as our wedding vows. We want to hope.

"I happened upon an interesting web site today," I say.

"Yeah?"

"About urban legends."

I know she expects something more substantial when she turns her face to me, eyebrows flying high.

"You're mentioned," I say. "Well, your kind. They call you Primordials, and you supposedly use your magicks to do away with ink-baiting legislators and lily-white nativists. You all sound pretty fearsome, I have to say."

She gets a good, long laugh out of that one. "I wish," she says, wiping the tears from her eyes.

"Don't wish too much. In case you haven't noticed, I'm lily-white."

"Come the revolution, we'll spare you," she says, nestling closer. "I hate sleeping alone."

"Ha. I knew you loved me for my body."

"Your lily-white body," she amends.

I stroke her hair, fall silent.

"Give me something to really feel hopeful about," she says quietly.

It takes me a long time to think of something.

"The FedEx Brigade exists, whoever and whatever they may be. And the people who are bypassing net restrictions to link to the stuff Abbie and the gavilanes sneak onto the web are young," I say. "Hell, Abbie and the gavilanes are pretty young themselves. The world they usher in when we old farts get out of their way is going to be very different than the one we're living in now."

"It's a long time to wait," she says.

"We don't have to wait," I say, gently. "We can leave."

"No."

"Why do you hold on so tenaciously? The Canadians are really much nicer than we are. You'd have to be a ruffian to not lead a decent life there."

"But I'm not Canadian," she says. "Neither are you, and neither is Gus. You just said it, our faith is in the young. If kids Gussy's age leave, there's no hope for the nation we love."

"Mari...."

"Father Tom says Augustine had it right, that the soul takes more pleasure in what it has lost and recovered than what it has had all along. He says, given enough time, even a nation remembers it has a soul."

I pull her to arm's length, look into her face. "I don't care about the nation's soul. I care about us. And I'm tired of the instaskin, the ban on everything that makes you what you are, the worry that someday Gus will be found out and have to wear that goddamned tattoo. I'm tired, and it's time."

*No.*

I hear it clear as a bell.

I think I physically start, because Mari presses back close to me.

*If not now, when?* I try asking.

*Never*, the supernatural being that I am also wedded to says. And though I don't remember ever hearing the jaguar's voice in my head, it is enough like Mari's that I can detect a note of sadness in the word.

It's my sister who's named for a character gifted with prophecy, but when I look into my wife's eyes, I know the future. There'll never be any home but this one for me.

# Finn: Redaction

This is how it happens.

Melinda sends me to cover something completely innocuous.

Now, if your business is news you know the innocuous assignments are always the most onerous of all. The silly features are the ones that generate bad feelings and claims of misrepresentation, or phone calls accusing of bad attitude and worse purpose.

So, I'm telling you, it's just an art show.

Sarai is there, because she's got that gene that makes you believe art's significant. Most of us didn't inherit it. Her parents are there too, after all, they gave her the gene. The only thing that interests me about the whole thing is that Melinda learned about it from a FedEx label in one of the alleyways that gives to the Avenue of the Arts. Sophie, the Gazette's secondary photog now, is here too. Which might give you an idea of how starved the paper is for original content, normally we'd ask for courtesies.

The artist takes her shirt off within the first five minutes of the performance, then stands stock still, as if the sight of her nipples perking in the cool of the performance space is going to be enough to keep us riveted. It's a lazy and far too tame attempt to shock an audience who, let's face it, has seen nipples in a variety of shapes and sizes before.

On the other hand, I've noticed that Mark Nalick, the self-appointed arbiter of Hastings morality who spits while he presents his screeds on YouTube, is here. When I sneak a peek at him, I see his eyes turned fanatical already.

It's one of those performance pieces you either think is genius or reminds you of the way your 5-year-old digresses while he tries to tell a story. The artist patters on about censorship while she divests herself of more and more clothing. Eventually an accomplice seated in the audience hands the artist a cross, which she proceeds to rub suggestively over the exposed areas of her body.

Again, tired.

What hasn't been done already to the cross – that highly charged symbol many of us revere and another good chunk of us think is wielded in direct opposition to its intention? But it's a smart move on the artist's part. Nalick is certain to rail and foam at the mouth about the performance piece now, and that'll fill the gallery with both his supporters and the artist's. It's a win-win for all involved.

And it pisses me off.

Where have the transgressive artists or wild-eyed moralists been as we rewrite ink history? Our history?

But then, just about when I've composed the scathing lede of my story in my head, the hair on the back of my neck stands on end.

The artist pulls the skin off her arms.

The tattoos line up each arm in blue, green and black lines. Of course they aren't the real thing – no ink has multiples of the government tattoo – but they might as well be given the collective in-drawn breath of the audience.

I have a moment to wonder what direction the performance will take before I realize there are people throughout the audience mimicking the artist and pulling instaskin off in sheets.

Were they planted in the audience or did they congregate there thanks to the label tweet? Is their action planned or spontaneous? Is this an art performance or flash mob?

"This is turning to news," I text Melinda. I know she'll send an additional reporter, and I don't care if I have to share a byline so long as we get an honest-to-God news story out of it.

People scramble out of their chairs, knocking them over in their haste to get away.

The inks — or are they non-inks pretending to be inks for a purpose? — scatter.

I grab Sophie's arm. Her mouth's hanging open and she seems to be caught in some slo-mo, syrup moment.

"Start shooting and stay out of reach. And for God's sake, get something on video." I give her a little shove to set her in motion.

I watch cops and pop control agents pour into the space like I once saw maggots showering off a rotting squirrel, they just keep coming like there's no end.

The tasers are out. A man, sixty at least and marked with blue, twitches on the ground dancing to the rhythm of electrodes. A young girl flings an arm up, moving her fingers in what appears to be the sign language of desolation, until she, too, goes down.

A cobblestone crashes through the gallery window. It just misses Sarai's mother. Glass rains down. People start screaming. Another stone smashes through and hits a policewoman whose gun sails out of her hand. And then two more stones follow, flying in without having anything left to smash.

Agents shoot into the crowd.

Outside, people pry more cobbles right out of the street and let them loose.

I can no longer tell those who started inside the gallery from those who've run in. Some people are barehanded, but many have cobbles and guns. The shooting begins in earnest.

I'm trying to move Sarai and her parents toward the closest glassless window, so they can get out, when I mark something dappled skitter by. I rarely see Mari's jaguar, but I sense she's here for some reason, in this jumble of the world's layers all gone chaotic at once. Every way I turn I catch shadowy movement at the edge of my vision.

I head in the direction I think the jaguar's gone.

I see Matthews, newly arrived, on the other side of the gallery. He's standing in a group, gawking at the number of people down, clipped by cobbles or tasers or bullets. I signal him. Interviews. Quotes. Anything.

I chase after the dappled creature, but it darts in and out of other shadows, both solid and spectral, and I almost trip as it stops short. The body laying on the ground in front of it spasms, as if it's been hit while it's down.

Then the creature turns around.

I have a moment to register the dapple of hair, not fur, and the pitted surface of a ruined face. I've never seen the dwarves Mari fears and her twin chases down, but I know that's what stands before me. An etheric projection of the pure evil we human beings are willing to visit on each other. In every age, every country and on every layer of reality.

The creature opens his mouth in a wide smile that shows wicked shards of teeth.

*Kai.*

The harsh whisper insinuates itself into my head and multiplies there, like an neverending echo.

Something slams me from behind and I go down. I struggle to not black out. The dwarf holds my eye with his inhuman one for a few moments, then scurries away.

My hearing fades in and out. I've fallen where I can see others – flesh and shadow – moving through the debris, but I can't move my head. Another heavy blow, this time to my shoulder. My eyes fill with water, and I think I'm going to throw up.

A figure swims into sight. Who? Ink. Gang maybe.... She ducks down to the floor to get a look at me.

"What's going on?" I ask her.

Whatever is affecting my hearing is also affecting my eyes. I almost think I can see the solid and unsolid pandemonium through her. She doesn't answer but lays a hand gently on my forehead. The pain recedes a bit when she does.

"I've been shot, haven't I?" It's getting harder for me to speak, but I have to.

She nods. The wrist that moves back and forth as she smoothes back my hair has a black tattoo on it. A wisp of familiarity. I get the picture of a girl with huge hoop earrings standing on the steps of a church. Nely.

"Mari will be so happy when finds out you're alive," I say.

*Shh, güero.*

Her lips don't move.

"Are you a Primordial then, like Mari and Gussy?"

She smiles. *Like and not like. We serve differently, but the same end.*

That's when I know.

"I'm dying. That's why I can see you."

She looks down at me. What kind eyes she has.

"All the stories I was supposed to write, they won't ever get told now."

*Who says?*

"No one hears the voices of the dead."

*That's what you think.*

Another familiar voice nudges into my head. It is faint, but gaining, as if it's trying to swallow the miles between us. And then another – thinner, younger, less in control – behind it.

Oh my God. My son's fully twinned and I didn't know. And now I'll never recognize the doubled consciousness as I look into his eyes. I'll never meet the being charged with protecting him. I'll never see my son grow into the complex, amazing, magical person he's bound to be.

Pain closes my eyes. This so much worse than the physical suffering.

"They aren't going to get here in time, are they?"

*In time for what, güero? Don't you understand yet what a gift you've been given? Whatever you want to tell them, say it now.*

I don't have time to be eloquent. The thoughts I send to my wife and son through their twins are unpolished and raw. Rough copy. But perhaps love and gratitude doesn't have to be perfectly expressed. Perhaps it just has to be the whole of the story.

Nely's hand comes to rest on my shoulder, and when it does, stillness steals over me. It's not so bad really. Something both warm and cool radiates out from the center of my chest.

Damn.

Matthews is going to get the front page.

# Abbie: Mile marker 324

1.

I'm the one who puts the gavilanes back together again.

From the first I understand the future of the gang is in tech. When I show Neto how easily I retrieve Toño's stranded gavilán fortune – licit and illicit – and rewrite the lives of the people we want to protect, he looks at me as if I'm the miracle he's been waiting for all his life.

Jobs is a gavilán, now, along with about seven of our wiliest cohorts from computer science 303. Remi and Ana, and their lovers and buddies and sisters, are in the reconstituted traditional wing of the gang. Remi is second, I'm co-first.

Lucero is born – Lucy to me, Luz to Neto – and he adores her. She calls Neto Papá from the beginning. It is both sweet and bitter. Neto is just enough like Toño to make me forget, and different enough to make me remember.

Bitterness drives a lot of gang leaders. That, and revenge.

But there's no one left for me to take out on either count. Celia's long dead and none of the others has resurfaced. Not even after the gavilán name was reborn in gang circles. Neto and I think most of the old gavilanes are dead, or if not that, taken secretly into the fold of other gangs. None admits to it, of course, but I don't expect truth from any gang but ours.

Mari has become my closest friend, driven by our twin joy in the children who stand as testimonials to our twin losses. Even though she's in Hastings and I'm in Smithville, we speak to each other regularly. Sometimes we even complain about the way our magicks serve but never suffice. I don't understand her magic, nor she mine, but I can't forget that she was the first to recognize that virtual is every bit as powerful as primordial. The code that comes as naturally as breath to me is the gold strand I add to the skein her animal twin showed me at the inkatorium years ago.

Mari stands as my witness when I marry Neto; I'm with her when she receives Finn's ashes.

His death gets lots of attention from the media – nothing like one of your own dying for you to start taking things seriously – which makes us think perhaps some good will come of the tragedy. Still, in the official obituaries Finn dies a single father. It is a safeguard for Gus, but just another in a line of obliterations and unmakings for Mari.

Then there's the fact that three agents, one cop and 17 inks die alongside Finn that night. The agents and cop get a couple of paragraphs to themselves at the end of the story about Finn, the inks are reduced to a number.

Not even we, who care about such things, know their names.

195

\*\*\*

"Ever wonder who, exactly, the FedEx Brigade are?" Jobs asks me as soon as I walk in the door of the trailer that is the hub of geek gavilandom.

"Duh." I seem to lose whatever maturity the years have bought when I'm around him. It's probably the reason I love working by his side. With him I'm still the Abbie waiting for her life to begin.

"Why? Who's claiming to have pinned down their identity this time?" I ask.

"Nobody. Their latest missives say they're going to out themselves, a week from now, in front of Hastings city hall," he says.

I lean over him and touch the screen to zoom. The fuzzy cell phone photo of a FedEx label gets more pixilated but easier to read. "You've signal boosted this?"

"Of course. I'm seeing photos of Brigades in other places echoing the same call. At least a hundred at my last count. It's all over the web. There's a hashtag trending nationwide, too. #FXax."

"I wish we had a brigade contact," I say. "Depending on what they're planning I'd offer gavilán support."

"Yeah, well, they're resolutely Luddite. I haven't been able to trace any digital footprint."

"Luddite, or better than we are," I say, leaning back on my heels while I study the screen.

"Nobody's better at this than we are. Except maybe Anonymous or LulzSec in their prime."

"How many gavilanes in Hastings this rotation?" I ask.

"Two and one."

Meaning two traditional cells of three, and one digital, seven people total.

"Any top corps?"

"Only Ana. The rest are junior. Virtual gavilán is the ink newbie," he says.

"All right. Keep monitoring and let's figure out what we can do from here. I'll talk to Neto about freeing up some more traditionals to send down to Hastings for the unveiling."

"And I'll go," I add as I start out the door to pick up Lucy from daycare.

"Gates, this could be a whole lot of nothing," he says. "Or worse, a whole lot of head-busting, widow-making stuff."

As if I didn't already know that.

As if I didn't carry that around like a stone in my heart.

\*\*\*

Neto drives.

It's against all rules for both firsts to be on the same job, and in the same limo to boot, but no matter how I argue Neto won't relent. And I won't either. So we leave Lucy and the gavilán hub in Remi's and Jobs' hands.

"What is it?" I say when I notice the expression on Neto's face on the ride down to Hastings. I pitch my voice so it'll stay undetected beneath the babble of Spanish coming from the gavilanes in the back.

"Carlos contacted me," he says.

A ghost. An original gavilán.

"And?" I say, my voice hard.

"He wants to meet," Neto says. "He says he has information about that night. About what went down, and the gang that was in on it. He wants to trade the information for a place in the new gavilanes."

"And you're tempted to hear him out."

He looks at me. "He's my blood, the only family I have left."

"Except Lucy."

"Except her," he says. For a moment I think he's ashamed of his oversight, but it turns out he's resentful instead. "Remi's a fine second, but look at us here, no second for either of us. You know I've got your back, but who's got mine?"

"I do, isn't that how it's supposed to work?" If my voice was hard before it's nothing to what it's become now.

He laughs. It isn't a pleasant sound to hear.

"No virtual gavilán has ever had to raise a gun. You're in this in a different way than I am, Abbie." The tiny diamond solitaire I gave him on our wedding night is in the piercing a quarter-inch beneath his mouth. Its facets flash – cold and hard – as he speaks.

I want to protest, but I stay quiet instead. I know I can be ruthless but it's all just keystrokes and code.

He glances at me. "And when there's no more disinformation to blow apart, when there are no more inks to protect or hide or reinvent or secure safe houses for, then what? Are you still going to be here?"

"Toño wouldn't do it." I keep it low, so none of the gavilanes in back will chance to overhear our argument. "He wouldn't risk what we've built together just to have Carlos at his back. And he certainly wouldn't risk his daughter."

Neto's face closes up.

It's a cheap shot, but I'm not above using cheap or nasty or dirty if I need to.

"Don't ever think you have to remind me that I'm not Toño," he says after a long moment.

His voice is pitched as low as mine but it must carry because the limo goes quiet.

It's the last thing he says for a long time.

\*\*\*

I'm there when it happens.

# Sabrina Vourvoulias - *Ink*

I really shouldn't be given that I'm on digital but the newbie turns out to be a Jobs in miniature, and I leave her at the gavilán safehouse happily fiddling with livestream while I join the traditionals. For once I don't have the distancing of a screen between me and what happens in the world.

They come one by one and form themselves in neat rows in front of the steps that lead up to Hastings City Hall, all with FedEx labels stuck to the front of their shirts. They're inks, of course, because who else cares?

But then more arrive and even though nobody is directing, they automatically fall in place behind the first until the mall is filled. Some have labels, others not. And there are non-inks among them. Actually a lot of non-inks and, at some point, it seems nearly fifty-fifty. They line up together in the street and the park beyond. Thousands of them. Maybe tens of thousands.

Everyone stands in silence until City Hall's clocktower marks 11. Then, as one, the ones with labels lift the posterboards they carry. They hold them above their heads, with each of the photos pasted on the flats facing City Hall. The unlabeled ones, those who carry no posterboards, lift their hands to the sky.

One of the gavilanes tries to catch my hand as I surge forward from the edge of crowd. I walk down each row. Slowly. Taking my time. The faces below are composed to stillness. The faces on the placards, two-dimensional and held up to a bright August sky, belong to the disappeared. Border dumped, in hiding, inkatorium residents. The ones killed in the Art Clash, as it's come to be known. Their names are there. The numeric code of their tattoos are inscribed on the placards, or if the tattoos are falsified, that's written there too. I wonder if it's a trick of my eyes that so many of the two-dimensional faces look familiar.

When I get to the steps of City Hall and turn to look back, it reminds me of the photos I've seen of Arlington Cemetery. The placards and upflung hands aren't crosses, but they, too, are reminders of what we have been willing to lose. And they're endless.

I feel Neto come to stand beside me.

"They don't need us," I say when I turn to him.

He nods, then fits his hand to mine and leads me down the steps of City Hall, and into the crowd. These are my people, I catch myself thinking. I mean both sets, faces above and below, and then I realize it's the first time in my life I've truly felt this way. There is no other, just us.

Real life – what can you say? – every so often it rivals virtual.

## 2.

Neto lays quiet in bed beside me. Since the FedEx foray there's been something like an ice field between us. I reach over and lay my hand on his bicep. At my touch, he turns to look at me.

"You were whimpering in your sleep." There's no emotion in it, just statement of fact.

When people speak of gang members as if they were all of a kind they don't get it. They are distinct, driven by their own motivations and natures even if the circumstance of their gang existence is the same. Though there is a physical resemblance, Neto is very different than Toño. He has never been willing to reveal his vulnerabilities to me in trade for closeness. And he's never asked me to do so either.

"Just a dream," I answer.

His eyes slide to the scars that cover me from collarbone to ankle. Then he leans in to kiss me.

He never hesitates or shies away from my disfigurement. His body has never betrayed anything but desire for me. And yet every time we have sex I experience that one moment when I can't breathe for fear of what might one day break through his eyes.

"I'm sorry," I say as the last few shudders from my body coax the same from his. I lay my head on his chest and close my eyes, relishing the feel of his hands still on me. "It wasn't disrespect, I just have a stupid mouth."

I know I don't have to say more, he understands what I'm talking about.

"Forget it," he says. "It doesn't matter." His hands continue their motion, teasing goosebumps on my skin.

"If you still want to hear Carlos out, I won't stand in your way."

One of his hands strays to my hair and tugs it so my face turns up to his. His eyes lock on mine. There is such a mix of emotion laid out naked for me in that look I have to turn away.

"But you can't meet him here," I say as I bury my face in his chest again. "And not at any other gavilán stronghold either. As co-first I have the right to demand that."

He laughs and pulls me tighter to him.

I never intend that he should do it without a second.

Two days later I'm off duty and putting Lucy down for her afternoon nap. It is always a struggle. And it's not just your regular kid fuss. It is as if every time she surrenders to sleep it confirms a personal failing.

The lids flutter over her eyes. She's got my eye color and Toño's eye shape, but the look she gives me is pure Neto. Hard, stubborn, fiercely striving. It stops my heart for a moment. It really does. I feel the stutter in the center of my chest and in that second before it resumes its regular beat and my daughter finally loses her daily battle, I know.

I take out the phone and hit my app. I've never named it and its icon is inobtrusive enough that no one who borrows my phone is ever tempted to use it. A grid pops up with dots to indicate the exact location of the people I track through their phones. I touch Neto's dot.

It's moving, but not giving me a body temp readout so the phone isn't in his pocket nor close to his body. It's headed south, some ten miles outside of Smithville already. He could be going to Hastings, but I don't think so. I think he's headed for the unstaffed rest stop at mile marker 324, the freezone where I first met Toño and felt the borders of my small world shatter.

Code is like this, and parenting, and my life too: patterns that repeat and repeat and repeat.

I throw open the throttle on of one of the limos, slam it into gear and tear out of the trailer park at a speed only another car with a 12-cylinder Lamborghini engine could hope to match.

I rapid dial Neto. Straight to voice mail. I text him. Wait. Nothing.

I text Jobs next. I know he's on digital rotation at the hub so he can coordinate everything at once, traditional backup and babysitter. If it weren't for the heavy feeling lodged inside me I might laugh at the stunning incongruity of my needs.

The limo is flying on the interstate when I find myself rapid-dialing another number out of the irrational hope that she's really as powerful as I believe her to be.

When I get her voice mail, I hesitate, then pour out the details and my fears jumbled together in one incoherent mess of words. I don't actually know what I expect Mari to do, in all likelihood she won't get the message until it's all over, but I feel stronger afterwards.

Minutes from the destination I hit my app again, hoping I'll be wrong and that Neto's dot will still be moving steadily toward Hastings. But it's static and just where I feared it would be.

I park at the closed truck weigh-in station a quarter mile from the interstate stop because driving the limo into the stop would be a dead giveaway and there's no telling whether there might be another gang involved.

I run until I reach the border of the rest area, then stop to peer through the scraggly trees that shield it from sight. The front parking lot is strangely empty of cars. When I turn my eyes to the entry ramp I see a pair of roadwork stanchions with chain stretched across the roadway to block access.

I work my way through the trees to the back of the stop. The limo is parked where 18-wheelers would normally pull in. That's it. No other car. Which means either this isn't the final meeting place, or Carlos is counting on someone else to drive him out of here when he's done. Not good.

I pull the 9 mm ACP from the back of my waistband and release its safety as I edge around the back, then cross the parking lot fast and in plain sight. There's nobody around the limo, but I find Neto's phone next to the front driver-side wheel.

I ease the back exit of the rest stop open and peer in. The fluorescent lights

200

give the big, open room a bleak look. The only sound in the space is the humming of the lights. There's no one in the main area. No one in the men's or women's bathrooms, either.

The only other enclosed space, behind a grey metal door, is padlocked. I shoot the hasp off. *There*, I think, *I've announced myself and my caliber.* But it turns out to be a supply room full of paper products, five-gallon buckets of industrial cleanser and nothing else.

I go out the front and quickly scour the open, empty lot. Nothing out of ordinary. I hug the wall and double round the corner. Twenty feet to my right, I see a flash of movement out of the corner of my eye. I turn to it.

Some ten or fifteen sourceless shadows teem in the asphalt between me and a commercial dumpster parked far into the weedy, woody stretch where people lawn their dogs. I can't really focus on the shadows and I find I don't want to. Whatever they are, they fill me with an immobilizing dread.

While I stand there a fire springs up from the asphalt. Sparks borne up in the same endlessly repeating patterns hem in what I now see are dwarves. I hear a crescendo of panic emanating from within.

But then a harsh, croaking laugh cuts through the panic. One of the dwarves barrels through the etheric flames. Others follow. In instants, I'm surrounded by identical malignant faces. The first punch doesn't physically hit me, but as it's thrown I feel its impact in my chest. I stagger when my heartbeat threatens to go irregular again.

The air next to my right ear displaces and in front of me, scattering the dwarves temporarily and facing them down, is the magical twin that just jumped over my shoulder.

*Go now.*

The voice that forces itself into my head is a juvenile's and achingly similar to Gus' voice. Gus, who, every time Mari brings him up on her visits, reiterates with absolute certainty he's going to grow up and marry my Lucy.

No matter what layers of world I'm straddling, I'm not letting a child take a hit for me.

I draw a bead on one of the dwarves just as the tiny twin launches itself into the mass of bodies, exactly where I'm aiming. I hear a thin, escalating cat wail as the dwarves' huge fists catch him and knock him around. Fire springs up again, this time separating some of the dwarves from the young cat.

Mari's jaguar jumps over me and into the fray. She knocks the remaining dwarves away from her son, and when one refuses to let go, she opens her mouth and crushes its head between massive, merciless jaws.

A moment later it is Mari's voice that fills my head. *Go, or the time Meche and we are buying for you means nothing.*

I run toward the dumpster, then draw up short. Neto's sprawled on the ground well behind the dumpster, and bleeding from a terrible gunshot wound to his shoulder. Carlos turns to the sound of my steps.

I try not to sway from the sight of my husband's blood. "Move away from him," I say, aiming my gun at Carlos' face.

"You don't really think you're going to make that headshot, do you?" he says. "Not a chance, gabacha. You need to be as close as I am to a target to pull that off."

Then he laughs as he moves his gun so it's aimed at Neto's head. "If you're nice to me I might let him live long enough so you can say goodbye."

"What do you want?"

Another laugh. "What was always mine to claim. The gavilanes."

"There is no gavilanes without Neto."

His eyes narrow. "Funny, I think Neto used to say the same thing about Toño. And now here he is, acting the gavilán first and regularly fucking Toño's girl."

Neto tries to pull himself to sitting but Carlos turns so fast it makes me dizzy and aims a kick that connects with Neto's head.

If I were a real gavilán I would be able to take advantage of this. But I can't. My hand shakes and the gun slips a bit.

I hear a grunt of pain as my husband hits the ground again, then, when Carlos' heavy boot cracks down on his shoulder, he stops moving.

"I knew you couldn't take the shot, gabacha," Carlos says when he turns back to face me. He doesn't even bother to aim his gun at Neto anymore, and what that means is almost enough to make me drop my shaky gun arm. But that stubborn look I see in my daughter's eyes every day isn't learned entirely from Neto.

"You stupid fucker. Even if you've killed Neto, the gavilanes still have a first," I say. I steady my shaky hand by wrapping my other one around the wrist.

He laughs, but I can read what's running through his head as clearly as if it were code. Before he can bring his gun hand up, I put a bullet through his wrist. As his gun drops and he lunges for me, I catch movement out of the corner of my eye and without thinking, turn to it. There's nothing there but another of those dreadful dwarves, already disappearing back where it came from.

The mistake costs me. Carlos grabs me as I'm turned and straps his arms around me. He wrests the gun from me, then crushes my hand as if he intends to fuse the bones together.

I fight going to my knees.

"I don't get off on the scars," he says, "but when I'm first, there'll always be a place in my gavilanes for women who are willing to kneel."

Fury straightens my back.

"You're never going to be first," I say as I shift all my weight to the foot I slam down on his instep.

It does just enough to let me break out of his grip. He catches and twists my hair and I feel it rip out of my head as I jerk away. But the momentum spins me around so I'm facing him again.

Over his shoulder I can see Neto has pulled himself to standing. Blood pumps from the hole in his shoulder as he brings his other arm up to shoot. He blows out the back of Carlos' knee with one shot, then as his cousin starts to fall, blows out the other.

Even on the ground writhing and moaning in his rapidly pooling blood, Carlos reaches for something in his boot. Neto kicks the knife out of his hand without seeming to look, on his way over to me. He pulls me, one-armed, to him and kisses me. It's like no kiss he's given me before and when I come away from it whatever I had thought to say is gone and my mind is blank.

"You did good, America," he says.

A shiver runs down my back, and not only because he's called me America for the first time since Toño's death.

"Now, go," he gives me a gentle shove in the direction of the parking lot. "I don't want you to see what I'm going to do."

"Neto," I say. "Wait. Don't."

But the love I've seen in his eyes retreats behind the hard surface again. "This is who I am," he says, then turns his back to me.

There are still a few shadowy dwarves dancing between the large jaguar and the small as I stumble back and sit hard on the pavement near Neto's limo. Soon I see another gavilán limo pull in and six traditionals pour out of it, guns drawn.

"Where's Neto?" Ana asks when she reaches me.

I nod toward the dumpster. She takes off at a clip, running without notice through the etheric carnage to where I imagine a more earthly one might still be in progress.

I feel a hand drop on my shoulder and look up at Remi.

"You okay?" she asks.

"Define okay," I say.

She sits on the ground next to me. "You were smart to leave your limo where you did. We had to take out most of Southden before turning in. Figures that dishonorable wannabe gang would be involved in something like this."

I meet her eyes. "We're involved in this. Does that mean we're dishonorable too?"

She gives me a wolfish smile, then turns to look to where the four junior traditionals have met up with Ana. She seems to be issuing instructions and soon the juniors tuck their guns into their waistbands and follow her behind the dumpster. When they disappear from sight Remi turns her eyes back to me.

I see empathy in them, but also the iron that got her to the top of the top corps so young.

"Did you think it'd be easy to love him?" she asks after a moment.

"The love showed up by itself. As soon as I saw how he was with Lucy," I say.

"Yeah, but that was then, this is now," she says.

When I don't say anything Remi's eyes go to the etheric cats' final moves against the dwarves on the asphalt.

"You see them," I say.

She nods. "Chato says I have some kind of magic. Or maybe that's just his way of letting me know he wants to hook up."

She tears her gaze from the jaguars to return it to me. "You know today wouldn't have gone down any differently if it were Toño, don't you?"

She waits until I nod, then she gets up, holds a hand out to me and when I take it, pulls me to standing.

"Don't dick around," she says quietly. "What you do next means everything."

"You talk like that to all your firsts?" I try to make a joke of it.

"No," she says. "Only the one who doesn't know whether she's staying or going."

Then she joins the other gavilanes and I'm alone on the tarmac.

# Del: Cold press

1.

When it happens, we're nowhere near prepared.

We get a day's advance notice because Mari's tipped off. The executive order is to be as Francine imagined it, only somehow worse.

Troop transport planes will be deployed for the mass deportation of black and green tats to centralized locations within regions where mutually agreeable compacts have been forged. As citizens, blue tats will not be deported. But neither will they be restored to full citizenship. Instead, the extent of rights accorded will be determined on a state-by-state basis.

What's more, blues who can provide information leading to the successful detention of green or black tats will be moved to the front of the line for near-full rights.

"And it's all predicated on the assumption that the scanners out there are working 100 percent accurately," Francine says. "Which we all know is malarkey."

"Also at the press conference tomorrow, they're making known the existence and proliferation of multiple variants of synthetic skin," Mari says, as if she hasn't heard her mother-in-law. "Civil liberties will temporarily be suspended for non-inks as well as inks, since everyone will be subject to wrist swipes with a solvent to expose concealed tattoos."

"Christ," I say, envisioning what this is going to mean to the inks already sequestered on my land. We each sign off the conference call without other comment.

By the time paratransit drops me at St. Adalbert Church all the old coots from the group are there. And more. Dozens of inks who've been living in the tunnels under the Math buildings swarm the parking lot. I don't know who's told them, or whether the underground ink network is so plugged-in that they've caught wind of the plan even before it's gone public. Grace, Father Tom's parish secretary, refuses to unlock the doors of the church for them.

Father Tom is nowhere to be seen.

I wheel myself into the fracas. In the panic everyone's speaking in Spanish, or other languages that the old coots insist on hearing as Spanish because that's what they expect. I zip from one end of the lot to the other trying to tell people to be patient. That there's a plan in place. At least that's what I think I'm saying. My Spanish is pretty basic.

Fifteen minutes in, three sleek unmarked limos try to pull into the parking lot. Father Tom hops out of the lead car. He ushers the crowd to the lower church meeting room while his secretary shoots worried glares in his wake.

205

When the limos are parked, a man with long, black hair pulled into a neat ponytail, a stud with a diamond chip winking from a piercing under his lip, and the darkest eyes I've ever seen, gets out of the lead vehicle.

"A mess," he says when he catches my eye. "I thought Father Tom said there was already a plan in place."

"He exaggerates a lot," I say.

The guy grins, then his eyes shift to my wheelchair. "It looked like you were trying to get things organized. You need a hand getting down to the meeting room?"

"No. I thought maybe I'd let the worst of the panic cycle through before I venture down." What I don't tell him is that these days I can convince those particular three steps to temporarily turn themselves into a ramp for me.

"Smart." He leans against the limo. A tall woman with dark hair and a shorter one with bleached blond hair get out of the other limos and join him. They're pretty, but with their too-thin eyebrows and dark-rimmed lips, they come off really tough too. The three talk quietly in Spanish much too rapid for me to figure out.

I look around the church's parking lot. People keep arriving, alone, or in small groups. As soon as they try the front doors of the church and see they're still locked they head over to the lower church.

"I wonder how they know to come?" It's just a question I ask myself. But I slip up and let it actually come out my mouth like I do when I'm around Satchel. I don't expect an answer.

The guy comes to stand at the side of my chair. "Everyone underestimates how wired the inks are. Tell one, you tell them all," he says, watching the stragglers.

"Yeah, but who told the one?"

"My wife," he says.

"She routinely monitors certain channels and servers," he adds after a moment. "The government's are, apparently, an invitation to hack so the communications she traced weren't even much of a challenge. Anyway, she told Mari as soon as she had a complete picture, and there you go."

I look up at him. "I thought you were part of a gang."

"I am. The gavilanes are a full service organization." He gives me a mocking smile. "My side works the more traditional avenues. My wife's side, the newer trails. We're a small group, but quite effective. Cutting edge, you might say."

"Who knew Hastings was so far forward?" I say cautiously. However amiable, the guy's gang and probably has a few cutting edges on him as we speak.

"Oh, we're not based in Hastings," he says, then sticks his hand out in introduction. "Neto Gavilán. A sus ordenes."

I know what that means. At your service. Not frigging likely.

"Delevan Ellis," I say while we shake. "Del. I guess I'm part of Mari's network. I'm married to Finn's sister."

He nods. "I know. Gustavo talks about you."

"You know Gussy?"

"Mari brings him up when she comes to visit. He's already decided he's going to marry our Lucero. I tell him he might want to wait; if she takes after her mother she's going to be a handful."

"We should go join Father Tom," Neto adds after a moment. "I'm guessing he'll need some reinforcements just about now."

I nod, then bite my lip when I realize I've blithely assumed he'll be okay with my magic. Because he looks a bit like Chato. It's hard sometimes to keep from falling into one-ink-all-inks kind of thinking even when you can see all around what kind of havoc that wreaks.

He keeps pace with me, even when the steps turn themselves into a ramp, and doesn't say anything, but I see his eyebrows shoot into his forehead and later I catch him giving me an appraising look.

He's right about Father Tom. Francine may be an accomplished scholar but neither she nor any other member of the group of old coots has any idea what to do. Father Tom's swamped by people, everyone talking at once.

Neto pushes his way over to the priest, puts his fingers in his mouth and lets loose a blasting whistle.

The room falls quiet as the last long note dissipates.

"Find a seat," he says in English. "And shut the fuck up already."

They do.

I make my way forward to where Francine slumps onto one of the seats attached to the cafeteria-style tables. "This is a wreck," she says to me."We've so screwed it up. And, have you even seen Mari anywhere?"

I shake my head.

Father Tom's voice pulls us back.

"We only have so much time to get this together," he says. "The news'll likely leak out a couple of hours before the press conference. Once that happens, moving to any hideaway will be near impossible." A wave of sound makes its way through the crowd, growing more alarmed as it flows.

*Step up, Father*, I think at the priest, *or this'll fall apart right quick.*

But it isn't the priest.

"The way the gavilanes see it, the minute the news goes public every underground ink will start trying to find a place to hide out or get away," Neto tells the crowd. "Roads will be clogged, gasoline will run out. And the National Guard will already have been deployed in anticipation of exactly that. So, what's that give us? About 20 hours free and clear of trouble to get to the sanctuaries and safe houses we've lined up on the way to the northern border."

"But I don't want to go north." A plaintive voice from the crowd.

Neto shrugs. "That's the only route my gang holds. You want to go south, Efe is working out of the Costco warehouse on City Ave. and C-30 will be at New Hope Assembly on Bainbridge whenever they get there. You want to go west, there's Shi at the terminal market on Tindall. Reciprocals are in place. For a while anyway. And all bets are off when you hit the point where gangs turn to cartel."

Some twenty people get up.

"Take cash," Neto says. "The fare's running about a grand a piece for instate. The further south you go, the steeper it gets."

"And here?" The woman who asks has four children standing next to her.

"It's not an issue here. But numbers are. The limos each fit ten. With the two clear runs we might get that means 60 people, tops," he says. "I believe the Father's Gang of Five are also driving people free of cost. With four cars and a van, I think that's about 22 per run for them."

Just over 100 slots and there have to be at least 200 people gathered already. And no telling how many more on their way.

"That's not enough." Another voice from the crowd.

"No," Father Tom pipes up. He looks pained. "It isn't. Which means you'll have to pick who to send through today. Tomorrow… well, I don't know what we'll do, but we'll figure something out."

"Or you can stay put," Neto says, something like sympathy in his voice, "and take your chances. At least if you end up on a deportation transport you'll be together with your loved ones."

"You've got about a half hour," Neto adds quietly when he turns to Father Tom. "The limos will need to load up then and your volunteers ought to also."

The priest nods, moves into his ersatz congregation with most of the old coots in tow. It is horrible to witness. The inks tell him the number and ages of their family members, which ones will go, which will stay. In the end, some sort of boarding list will be compiled. Nobody wants to break up families, but that's the only way this is going to work.

But not necessarily for me.

Not that many inks believe in magic, but some do. I wheel myself from family group to family group offering to make their current residences in-between places. Even those who agree to my "house blessing," as they've chosen to call it, don't seem eased. And none of them want to leave for the in-betweening until Father Tom is done with his tally. No matter how I argue that the tally's immaterial if they choose to be in-betweened, they will not be moved.

Mari and Gus finally show up, and as soon as I head back to where they sit with Francine, Gussy launches himself onto my lap to give me a hug.

"Uncle Del," he says. "I'm going on a trip with my mommy. She says I'm not going to come back for a while."

I nod. I'm strangely choked-up when I look in his eyes. What makes him old beyond his years has retreated and all I see is little boy.

"But who's going to keep you painting your stories when I'm gone?" he frets. "Satchel's just a baby and won't know how."

"We'll figure something out," I say.

I meet Mari's eyes over Gus' head.

# Del: Cold press

"You could stay," I say. "You're a blue, things should ease up a bit for you. Isn't that what the latest FedEx Brigade missives counsel anyway? Of course, it probably makes a difference that most of the Brigade members are blues. They don't want to see their numbers drop."

"If you were me, would you want to stay?" she asks.

"No."

She smiles, but like so much these days, there's grief and anger underlaying the fleeting sweetness of it.

"But since I am a blue, Gus and I don't have to go on the first run, or even the second," she tells Francine, "we can wait."

"Gussy doesn't have to go at all. He's not tattooed, he can stay with me." I've never heard Francine plead before. "I *am* officially his guardian."

Mari doesn't even have to say no, the smile she flashes Francine is that feral.

The old woman goes pale and averts her eyes, but when she speaks it is in her usual hard, clipped tones."If we don't take you up on the first or second run, we'll run out of safe houses. And I don't think anyone's going to be willing to risk a third run."

"Neto will, you'll see."

Francine gives her a nod, gets up and walks away. I can tell she's angry from the set of her shoulders.

"You sure?" I say to Mari.

*Who is ever sure? Not even we are given that gift,* says her twin.

Almost a quarter of the adults in the room decide to turn themselves over for deportation. They hang on to the infants and the children too small to survive hardship without them, but really cling to the ones they're letting go. The list Father Tom ends up with is mostly children anyway, the ones just old and young enough to have a chance at a future if they can hide and outwait policy.

Two of the families I've talked to about in-betweening come to me straightaway. They don't live far, but even so, I almost miss the goodbyes at St. Adalbert.

Neto comes over, ruffles Gus' hair. "You coming up to visit Luz?" he says, but he's really asking Mari.

"Third run, if you're game," she says.

"Why not?" He grins. "What's a little added deportation risk among friends? You should see if anyone else is willing to risk it. Might as well have a full limo."

She nods. "I'll ask around."

He turns to me. "Will you still be here when I get back?"

"Sure. I think I can help a bit with those who are staying, and then whatever else they need me to do here."

He gives me a considering look, far too keen for my taste. "Maybe when I finally take Mari and Gus up – let's call it the adrenaline run – you'll come along for a ride."

"It sounds like the gavilanes have everything under control up there," I say.

I wheel myself out to the parking lot to watch the load up. The light falling on the people is like the light that shines through pieces of amber and the people milling around are caught in its resin. There's some last-minute jockeying and pleading from those who haven't been able to get theirs on the boarding list for first or second run, but as soon as the blond gavilán makes a show of taking out her gun and checking the clip, it all dies down.

After the cars drive away I go back inside. Some St. Adalbert parishioners trickle in with me, informed of need by a hidden network that's only a little slower than the one that has brought the inks here. Some of them carry platters of food, others pillows and sleeping bags, and gallons of milk or iced-tea. The meeting room's kitchen area is a center of activity. It'll be a six to eight hour roundtrip for the limos and cars, barring unforeseen problems, and the second round of passengers won't be abandoned for even a minute of the wait.

I make a number of forays out to in-between apartments, though not nearly as many I would have hoped. And who can blame the inks who look at me with a mix of polite indulgence and underlying alarm when I approach them? If I didn't feel the stir in my heart and under my palms, would I believe the inexplicable grace of what pours through me to effect change?

When I have nothing left to do I wheel myself over to the kitchen area to help with the food.

"Hey," a familiar voice pulls me out of the reverie of routine about a half-hour later. Sarai's eyes are trained on me. "Didn't think you'd be here."

"Ditto."

"I'm pretty sure there are already people who'd love to see me and mine corralled in some kind of reprogramming version of the inkatoriums," she says. "Slippery slopes being what they are and all, I figure I better help create some speed bumps. Hey, are Cassie and Satchel around somewhere?"

"No. Francine was. She's the one who got me involved with this group. She'll be back in some hours if you want to wait around."

"God, no. Unlike you, I've never gotten off her shitlist." She looks around. "But I do have to find Father Tom. I'm thinking of using my parents' credit line to rent some school buses to get some more of these folks out of here, and I need his estimate of how many we might need."

"I think I may have just fallen in love with you," I say.

She laughs. "Maybe you better wait and see if I can pull it off before you buy the engagement ring. And don't tell Allison, she's the jealous type." She winks at me as she ambles off to intercept Father Tom.

Allison turns when she hears her name but keeps talking to the group of inks and parishioners clustered around her. "I can't counsel any course of action but compliance," I hear her say. "Lawyers from advocacy organizations across the nation will scramble to file lawsuits, of course. But, I won't lie to you, it'll be a long time before any sort of decision about constitutionality is handed down, especially given the careful alien/non-alien language, and the exclusions in place for citizens."

I'm following her words so closely I hardly notice who sits next to me. When I turn around, it is two sets of madonnas I see – Mari with Gus in arms and Cassie with Satchel.

"Gang's all here," Cassie says as she hands Satchel to me. My little boy plays with the buttons of my shirt, and through the fabric, the bee.

"At one point you would have been literally right," I say.

She looks around the room. "I'm not sure I get why disappearing up there seems any better than just staying put. I mean, if you're going to hide out there's no easier place to do so than a city."

"I don't know," I say."Didn't most of the partisans head to the hills during fascist occupations of World War II?"

Cassie makes a face. "We're not talking fascists and partisans here. And, as a form of resistance, it seems an awful lot like what the government wants anyway. What's the difference between disappearing into the hinterlands or deportation? It ends in the same place, no ink faces next to us on the bus or the street or the elevator."

She's right, and the expression that must be on my face prompts a smile. "You can agree with me and not lose all your cred, you know," she says, amused.

"Anyway, I think there's more courage in the blue tats staying put and working for change from within the system," she says then. It's not directed at me for all that she's looking at me when she says it.

"Because second-class citizens are going to have so much power to effect change, you mean?" Mari says.

"And what change does disappearing and hiding bring about?"

"None. But it makes a difference that I'm the one making the decision of how, and to where, and for how long I disappear." Mari hugs Gussy so hard the little boy squawks.

"All of the alternatives suck," Cassie says after a moment.

"No, really?" Mari says, then quickly turns away. After a time she puts Gussy down, takes his hand and leads him to the upper church.

***

The drivers take just enough time to chow down before getting back on the road for the second run. With the unexpected construction up toward the end of the run the turnaround has taken an additional hour, and everything's going to cut dangerously close to announcement time.

Even with the single school bus Sarai is able to scare up there are still many people left behind. It's excruciating to see them pick up, resigned to the fate of the unchosen. The hall empties out. A couple of parishioners linger, tidying up, along with the handful of inks like Mari who've decided to chance a third run. As the hours wear on, a few of us – Cassie, Father Tom, Grace, Mari and a guy named Ephrem – sit together, watching for the news to officially break.

Around 7:30 a.m., before the drivers are back from the second run, Twitter starts to flood with the rumors. It's a bit scary, actually, how little time it takes. And we're only really tracking the English and Spanish-language tweets. There are hashtags in Urdu, Vietnamese, Korean and a dozen other languages.

Then it all crashes – or is crashed – and we're back to waiting for the traditional media to trot out what's going to happen, and the official version of why.

Looking around the faces left in the hall it dawns on me that on the third run, if the instaskin fails and if the portable scanners are really as unreliable as Francine believes, there won't be a single absolutely undeportable person in Neto's limo.

"Gussy," I call the boy over. "You want me to ride up with you?"

The boy doesn't answer, but the hug he gives me is so tight it hurts.

*Thank you.* Whether it's Mari or twin, the surprise and gratitude comes through the same.

Cassie motions me to come away from the table.

"I don't understand," Cassie says as soon as we're about half a room away from the others.

"Insurance," I say. "For Gus."

She shakes her head, exasperated. "That's Mari's job, not yours. She should just stay put. Or leave Gus with mom."

"But she's not going to, Cassie. And it's little enough to do. If not for her or Gussy, for Finn."

Her face doesn't change, but I know what the mention of her brother does to her. "Cheap shot," she says.

"No," I say. "I mean it."

She sighs, looks away, then back again. "How're you going to get back?"

"As soon as the limo drops people at the sanctuaries, I'll catch a bus. There's one that stops right in front of the hardware store in Smithville, remember?"

Cassie's face turns stony. "Fucking Smithville. That's why you offered."

I feel my stomach drop. "No. Gus and Mari are why I offered. The wheelchair's changed me, Cassie. Satchel's changed me, and you have, too. I'm grounded here now."

"Right."

Satchel picks up on the tension between us and starts wailing. Without thinking, I take the gold bee out from under my shirt. He reaches for it and makes a game of yanking it so my neck bobs up and down. He gives me a gurgling laugh. Then, he opens his palm and bounces the bee. It hangs above his open hand, quietly suspended for a good seven seconds, before it lights on his palm and he clutches it again.

So air's his element. Like Chato.

"Did you see that?" I ask Cassie when I look up.

Her mouth twists. "He's going to get cut on that thing."

"No, I meant what he did. How he kept it floating above his palm. His magic."

She gets up and plucks Satchel from my lap. "Goddamn it, Del, just stop already. Magic is the vain hope of the desperate and powerless, and I hate that you feel so damaged you need to believe in it. But that's you. Not Satchel. Never Satchel, you hear me?"

"Cassie...."

"Give that thing to me," she says.

I take off the pendant and put it in her hand. She wraps her fingers around it.

"Come back when you understand what's real," she says. Then she leaves and takes what I love best with her.

At 9 a.m., when the press conference starts and drivers still aren't back, all our eyes turn to the TV images resolving themselves into what we wanted to believe wouldn't really happen.

Grace gets up, busies herself making coffee for everyone.

"What kind of world is this when you can't tell the good guys from the bad guys?" she asks while she stirs milk and sugar into the cups.

Nobody ventures an answer.

"Breathe," she says roughly as she places a cup in front of me.

It startles me into meeting the eyes looking down at me.

"Sorry?"

"Too late for sorrys," she says.

# Sabrina Vourvoulias - *Ink*

## 2.

I end up in the front seat of Neto's limo. The partition is down, and I can hear Gussy snoring and what passes for conversation between Mari, Ephrem and the others in the back seat.

Lionel, the oldest, is an engineer, and originally from Mexico; Max, a young Dominican who until a week ago sold food from a rolling stand on the streets of Hastings; Elpidia is a college student whose Nicaraguan parents brought her when she was a couple of months old; Ephrem, a Guatemalan working at a bakery; and Gracielle is a Haitian storeowner with ties, she tells me, to the ruler of crossroads.

It is tense in the car, and not only because we're all counting the number of military vehicles on the road. This is a charge into a different type of future than any of us ever imagined. Provided we make it to the sanctuaries, it is a "laying low and peeking under," as my Smithvillians are fond of saying.

Everyone's been fitted with what we believe are acetone-resistant instaskin patches from the Gang of Five's store of the stuff. Except for Gracielle whose patch, she tells us, was purchased off an old Tonton Macoute who runs the sole Haitian gang in Hastings. She hadn't had enough cash on hand to buy transport to one of their safe houses in the south.

So far we haven't hit a barricade. But two-and-a-half hours after the press conference and a half-hour before we should have hit the outskirts of Smithville if we hadn't been driving hellbent for leather, we're going to.

We all watch the minutes tick off on the large digital clock above the remarkably well-appointed National Guard checkpoint while we wait. *It had to have taken them longer than a day to erect*, I think, but Neto shakes his head when I ask him if it was here on his way back from the last full run.

From both left and right drivers aim their cars like wedges to cut in front of us, as if going first will be some advantage in getting through. It's a ludicrous superstition, but we're infected by it also and not letting anyone cut in.

"Motorcycle at 10 o'clock," Mari says. She's preternaturally attuned to the hunt this has become. Every so often I try to make the road buckle a car – or in this case, motorcycle – back to its original spot. But if the land beneath the asphalt is listening to me, it doesn't agree that this jostling for place is important and keeps still.

12:38 p.m. The radio announcers squawk about what's happening in different quadrants of the state. Had we been going south rather than north we wouldn't have hit a checkpoint yet because municipalities down there have been less efficient at mobilizing reserves. Figures. Luck has its favorites, and we aren't among them. On the other hand, at least we aren't on the West Coast where the resistance and counter-resistance has turned dead violent already.

A small Honda sideswipes the limo in an attempt to dislodge the car in front of us. Neto inches forth so there is no space visible between our fender and third-in-line's bumper.

12:45. We're third in line. From here we can see the yellow barricades at the checkpoint that mark the place behind which I – and probably Neto – can hide us for an eternity in the wild pockets of Smithville. There's a contraption just beyond the barricade that a guard cranks as each car stops in place. It brings a line of sharp iron spikes upright during the inspection, then lays it flat again when the car has been cleared to pass.

1:01. "You don't think we're going to make it through, do you?" I say to Neto.

He doesn't answer.

"Did I tell you to call me Ernest?" he says after moment. "Ernest Horn, from the Akwesasne Mohawk Territory."

"How'd you do that? My grandmother actually *had* Seminole blood and she wasn't on the rolls."

"Abbie's father relayed his mother's go-ahead. Most of the folks up at the reservation are quietly interested in seeing just how far we can get with our particular brand of defiance. I hear some of the younger Adamses and Horns might even be considering joining the gavilanes, at least on the digital end, and the upshot of everything is that our stories stand," he says. "For now, anyway."

"Which means?"

"We're getting through, Bro."

Behind us, the crunch of metal and glass. The fifth car in our line plows into the fourth, knocking it clear across one of the feeder lanes. I manage to shift the divider just enough so the car isn't totaled in its spin out.

1:20. We're still second. Nobody in the car currently at the checkpoint has passed the swipe test. Even the smallest, no older than Gussy, is cuffed and marched at gunpoint to a transport bristling with other cuffed inks.

1:35. The car in front of us pulls into the checkpoint. We're first in line, finally.

"What if Gracielle's instaskin patch is one of those that isn't acetone-resistant and dissolves?" Elpidia gives voice to what others have been worrying silently.

"We don't know," I say when nobody else answers. "Maybe the soldiers swipe and reswipe everyone. In which case everyone's instaskin will end up dissolving."

"Maybe they take her and leave us." Lionel. He sounds like he's considering setting Gracielle outside the car preemptively.

"Nobody's getting taken," Neto says. "I'll run the limo through the barricade before that happens. It's as bulletproof as any vehicle can be made to be, and has a badass V12 Lamborghini engine customized to gavilán needs. So stop worrying."

He doesn't mention any countermeasures for the spikes but maybe the people in the back seat can't see them.

"My patch won't dissolve," Gracielle says. "Haven't any of you noticed what they've done by positioning the checkpoint where they have?"

She waits a beat, then continues. "They've made this whole area a crossroads. And Legba holds all points of a crossroads."

I hear Max groan. It sounds like a bunch of others back there join in. I'm in no position to question anyone's faith but I'm not reassured either.

Neto motions for me to feel under my seat. My hand lands on a metal clamp-like device and then, the distinctive stock of a shotgun. Sawed-off, if it fits under there.

"You know how to shoot, I believe?" he says quietly when I look back at him.

I nod. "Deer, anyway."

He gives me a grim smile. "Aim higher."

"Is it going to come to that?"

"Who knows, Bro. I'm not used to anticipating what National Guard or reservists will do. By my measure we're flying way light on weaponry. I've got a piece on me, but that's it.... Either of us flinches, the people in the back seat are going to be toast."

1:55. "This is it," Neto says.

The car currently in the checkpoint moves forward half a foot, then lurches to a stop.

"I've got to pee," Gus says.

Nobody answers, because we're all holding our breath.

2:15. The car in the checkpoint is still there, not moving. All of its occupants are marched away in cuffs. A soldier slides in the driver seat, waits for the spikes to be lowered, then pulls the car over with the others repossessed from their unlucky inks.

2:25. The limo slides into the empty checkpoint almost without noise. Four of the guards crowd the limo and knock on the windows with the muzzles of their semi-automatics. Neto rolls down all the windows at once.

The boy who looks in my window is just that, a boy. In uniform and a little green around the gills. I feel sorry for him.

"Wrist," he says.

When I hold mine out, he pours the acetone on it. A long, steady stream that splashes over his boots, the asphalt, the side of the limo. I hope the other soldiers aren't quite so extravagant with the solvent or we're cooked.

Of course, it doesn't do a thing to my wrist. As soon as the kid steps away from my window, nodding, I sneak a look at Neto. His skin's intact over his tattoo.

He's answering some questions from the oldest-looking of the soldiers, chatting him up. He's a good liar. Convincing and at ease.

I chance a glance through the rolled-down partition. Max is already closing the window on his side. Elpidia and Ephrem's arms are in, and Gracielle's got hers folded in her lap. She winks at me. Only Mari and Lionel still have arms outstretched on the other side of the car.

I decide to breathe.

# Del: Cold press

*Uncle....*

Next to Gus, Mari's face becomes something toothed and snarling.

I bring the shotgun up in one movement and aim high above her foaming wrist.

Does the soldier glance at me then? I don't remember. He loses his grip on Mari the second the shell tears into him. This close the shot doesn't spread, it blows out his shoulder, and in the instant before he drops his eyes meet mine.

Neto punches the gas. I barely have time to project the drop of ground from under the spikes before the limo races over them. There's a tidal wave of sound around me: gunfire, screams, sirens, the sound of a car pushing every last cylinder.

Neto spares me a glance as he guides the limo down back roads at speeds only safe for jets. Then he takes the limo off road without seeming to slow down. The sawed-off is still held loosely in my hand and Mari is covered in blood, not her own. It's all one to me, and insignificant.

How can you tell the good guys from the bad guys?

Look to see whose eyes hold the plea, whose the target.

Then face up to what follows.

### 3.

The eye is a strange organ. Without compassion. Without filter. The true repository of memory.

The administration keeps the images of the inks being loaded onto troop transports for deportation from public view. It's a smart move. Numbers don't mean anything until you see the scale of them, in flesh. When the original timeline proves too optimistic and congressional approval is needed for an extension on the deportation program, no one has an image of the human cost nested in the retina, and the measure passes without fuss.

The inks from the first and second runs up to Smithville end up on Harper's farm and his brother-in-law's go-kart-track-turned-sanctuary. Elpidia and Max join them, preferring the youth-hostel feel of groups bunked in Quonset huts and ramshackle farm buildings to the solitary outfitter tents of those who live on my property.

We've made the land immediately around those structures in-between places, like my land, but some of the residents – mostly older teenagers and their younger siblings or cousins – aren't great at remembering boundary markers. And, let's face it, they're bored to death in their rustic surroundings. So they spend a lot of time at the go-kart track, watching the drivers pitting their skeletal vehicles against one another.

It seems harmless enough to those who are looking out for them – the kids don't really interact with other spectators and all of them speak English as well as any non-ink – but then no Hastings resident really understands how homogenous rural America can be. It takes a surprisingly long time but eventually someone reports the influx of darker-skinned go-kart enthusiasts to Sweeney. About a quarter of the residents of the Quonset hut are nabbed as the best race of the day takes place.

As soon as we hear, Abbie, Mari, Jobs, Meche and I head into town in the hope that between us we have enough – wherewithal, magic, money, smarts – to do something. But if we do or don't soon becomes immaterial, we're too late. By the time we get down there, Sweeney has called the local TV stations and Main Street is choked with news vans. The police chief puts the inks in shackles and marches them down Main as cameras roll and townspeople gather on the sidewalks to gape at the ghastly parade.

Meche and I are together, surrounded by a crowd that doesn't hesitate to grab my wheelchair handles to jostle me out of the way. I'm hung up on the curb in front of Smithville's bike shop, with a clear sightline, when the inks come through three abreast and in tidy lines. The young adults are at the back, deputies shadowing them. But that's not what catches the eye. No, it's the schoolyard worth of 7 and 9 year olds that precede them that does. The shackles around their ankles and wrists are jury-rigged adult ones and they clank and grind as if the metal itself were humiliated by its job.

The children avoid the eyes of those they pass, shame and hurt battling for primacy on the small features. Metal has a good memory of the earth that once surrounded it so I beg those chains and fetters, implore them, to undo themselves right there on the street. An act of supernatural kindness, and a verdict.

But nothing happens.

The metal keeps to its dirge and the children keep to their hopeless march, and Cassie's words about desperation and powerlessness ring in my ears.

I feel Meche's hand wrap itself in mine and when I look up at her, the beautiful, otherwise perfectly composed face is streaked with trails of salt. "Nothing's working," she says without looking at me.

"I know."

She doesn't resist when I pull her down to sit crosswise on my lap, but turns her face into my chest as my arms come around her. "Who does this to kids?" she says after a moment, her voice muffled by the flannel of my shirt.

And because the eye is impartial, because it remembers the young inks' march in exactly the same way it does the young soldier I shot, I have to admit it, at least to myself.

People like me. We do it.

***

Magic is at work even when you think it isn't.

The nation reacts with fiery indignation to the televised images of young people driven, hobbled like cattle. I see the flames literally dance across the layer of existence that acknowledges no boundary and I know that, across the nation, others with Meche's same elemental gift are fanning the indignation too.

The public outcry is such that the footage gets yanked from the airwaves, but Abbie's and Jobs' mobile capture of events sidesteps Internet restrictions and goes viral.

A still from Mari's phone – an ugly shot of an 8-year-old with ankles and wrists bleeding from the rub of the ill-fitting shackles – runs as the full front page of the Hastings Gazette. Finn's old editor gets fired for it, but later the photo earns her – in the name of her resolutely anonymous photographer – a Pulitzer.

Vermont passes the first non-compliance and ink restoration laws a few months after Sweeney's public display. Seven other states have copycat bills in committee, including ours. There are rumblings about a federal bill to be introduced in the next session, and talk of sanctions for top administration officials.

The Ink Incidents, as our undeclared war comes to be called, limps along until its final skirmishes seem no more significant than a particularly hard-fought Super Bowl game. The faces at the top switch, the circumstances morph and the words start seeming less like acid cast on broken skin. But the heart changes more slowly, and it'll be years before we know peace or understand the scope of our losses.

At the end of every day, before opening the door to my cabin, my hand rests for a moment on the plaque of Our Lady of Charity on the doorjamb. I've found a strange sort of faith these days. Faith that when I open the door, it'll be to friends who habitually finish off my beers, to a canvas prepped for the future, and to a woman who puts no borders on real.

# Mari: Fairy tales

1.

*In the days we speak of, snakes twist and twine and braid themselves into one. Their scales slough off in a shower of iridescence, bright as rain on the dusty ground. Like one they will sprout feathers, and winged, take to the sky.*

*In the days we speak of, the jaguars return. The marks on their bodies fade, ghosting under the dark of fur and night. The moon and stars will sing them home.*

*In the days we speak of, a woman finds her way to the edge of the underworld, to a tree that hangs with faces. It is both a beginning and an end.*

\*\*\*

I am their storyteller.

Others try: Francine retelling myths, Abbie turning tweet to story. But the children always come back to me. Satchel only hears my stories once a month, when he comes up to the woods to visit his father, but he's got the kind of mind that holds forever. Even as the years pass and Gus gets tall, Lucero fills out, Satchel turns contemplative, they come for the stories.

I tell them the one about the boy shapeshifter, and the star girl, and the child who bridges worlds. I tell them other tales, too, so they will know that everyone is made of stories.

Each of them at a different time obsesses about my tattoo.

When Gus asks about it I sit with him on the threshold of the little house I built in Del's woods – a structure that wouldn't exist if not for the tattoo – the only home my son remembers.

"This holds not one tale, but many," I say as I trace the blue lines with the tip of a finger. "One of the stories is told in numbers. It is a record of the past, of what you inherit through blood. Another is the story of love it prompted. The third is a chronicle of a battle that is fought again and again. Which would you like to hear?"

Gus, nine and impatient, opts for the version he believes will be the shortest. So I tell the story as he wants to hear it.

Lucero comes to me when she is older, twelve and on the cusp of change. I take her to the part of the woods that flowers first every spring and sit her among the trilliums. The tales the tattoo offers her are complicated: two tattoos, two fathers, two wars fought on different but overlapping fronts.

Her storm-water grey eyes hold mine for a long time after I'm done the telling, but she doesn't say anything. When she gets up to leave she touches her fingers to her forehead and moves them leftward and high. I know it is a gavilán sign that means "don't let the future be written for you," and that it's thrown during a fight when one of yours seems so overwhelmed he or she might be tempted to give up. What I don't know is whether she throws it for me or for herself.

Satchel asks for the tale of the tattoo youngest of all. He is six and so serious I hesitate. But I take him to the huge boulder and sit in its shadow with him. What to tell this child? Both of his parents are privileged; neither of them bore the mark or felt what such a thing leaves beneath the skin. And yet, Satchel's life has been freighted by the tattoo. It is a hard tale to tell a child so young but I do it anyway.

After each telling of the tale of the tattoo, I seal the story with the same words: world without end, amen.

Because telling the truth is always a prayer.

\*\*\*

Ephrem comes to see me one day in my little house in the woods.

He sits where I've imagined Finn sitting, every night since I built this home.

They are dissimilar men. One large and easy, the other small and tied in knots.

"You know my name isn't really Ephrem," he says as I pour him an instant coffee. Anglos never like the stuff, but Latinos are mostly okay with the expedient.

"I changed it when I came here," he says.

"New life, new name. Not so unusual," I say, sitting in a chair across from him.

"I'm from Guatemala," he says. "Like you."

"I was born there, I'm not *from* there," I correct.

He hardly pauses to notice. "The undeclared war there that took your mother and my parents has long been over. The military records of that time have been unearthed and are being catalogued. History has broken open."

"That's good," I say.

He leans back, studies me. "You sound as if it doesn't concern you."

"My undeclared war was a different one," I say.

"They are all our wars," he answers.

I take a sip of hot liquid, feel it sear as it travels down my throat.

"Come with me to Guatemala. Find the full story. Like, what happened to your half-brother? For all you know, he is still alive. For all you know, I'm him."

I lean forward, put my cup down, and reach for his arm.

He lets me hold it and turn it so the tender inner skin of his wrist is exposed.

# Mari: Fairy tales

"You had your tattoo removed," I say.
"I don't want to remember," he says.
"Then what are you offering?" I ask.
He leaves soon after that.

2.

But I do go. By myself.

I have a moment of panic at the airport. I present my wrist to the customs officer and then, when she looks at me quizzically, I remember what she's checking are passports. So many years of wearing my identity on my skin….

I scramble to find the passport, praying I actually packed it. And in some moment of clarity I did. It's pinned on the inside of my handbag, in a plastic baggie along with the one photo I have of my mother and father together. I study that sometimes, and wonder at what it reveals. No matter that my mother is seated on a rock by a rustic footpath, garbed in traditional clothing and hair dressed in a way I'd never think to wear, she is me. And, no matter that my father is much shorter and blonder than Finn as he stands beside my mother for the photo, he loved her despite – and because of – the same set of untranslatables Finn loved in me.

It is a black-and-white testimony of a story that always repeats.

In Guatemala City at the PDH office that oversees investigations into human rights violations – current and historic – I spend time searching through thousands of records until I find my mother's and grandparents' names. No details, just names. I might have gotten as much sitting in the comfort of the gavilán compound if I had managed to secure half a day of Abbie's or Jobs' time.

In the listing of those killed in the village that day I also find the name of the American priest who had hidden me in the tabernacle. The order he was from still keeps a house in the city so I make an appointment to speak to the senior priest. I'm not sure why I do it, perhaps the longing for something familiar in this land I find so utterly foreign.

The priest who opens the door of the Maryknoll house has the bearing of an army man. Father Roger Beckett listens to my story as I stand in the doorway, and when I'm done, studies me at length.

"That village no longer exists," he says. "Even though the structures remain intact no one from the surrounding villages will go near them. They are superstitious and claim the village – in fact, the whole mountaintop – is haunted by the nahuales of the people who died."

"You know this word, nahual?" the priest asks then.

I nod. "The animal twins."

His expression goes sharp, curious. "It wasn't too long after the incident at your mother's village that my order decided to stop ministering in that region altogether. A lot of our priests and catechists got caught in the violence in those days."

"The priest you ask about was buried up in New York State, where the motherhouse for the order is," Father Beckett adds. "Whatever record or personal journal he might have kept, if it exists, is most likely there too. I'm afraid I can't do much for you."

"Would the priest have taken photos, maybe a visual record of the village?"

"It's possible," Father Beckett says. "Our mission in Guatemala started in 1943, so the photos from the timeframe you're interested in might be scattered over a dozen albums. But it's worth a shot. Come with me," he says as he ushers me into the cool, neat library of the house.

Though it is large and full, he finds only one slim photo album labeled as being from the village.

"I'll go make us some coffee," he says, then leaves me to open the musty pages alone.

There are photos of the construction of the village church and of religious processions, each exactly like the last, though the annotations change handwriting and date.

Father Beckett comes back when I'm two yellowed pages from finishing. He sets the cups of steaming liquid in front of us. "Found anything?"

I shake my head. "I've only now gotten to photos from that year. Though, I must say, it's hard to tell them from the ones 30 years older."

He laughs, then comes to look over my shoulder. "It's the huipiles. The unchanging style of the blouse makes the photos look timeless. You have to look at the shoes to note the march of time." He points to one of the photos. "See, plastic sandals instead of handtooled leather ones."

When I turn to the last page, I see his eyes come to rest on my tattoo.

"Did your father explain to you about the huipiles?" he asks.

"Only that each village has its own distinct design and colors," I say. "He could only ever recognize the ones from the villages where he'd installed water systems during his time in the Peace Corps."

"When the Spanish came to Guatemala," the priest's voice takes on a magisterial note, "they couldn't distinguish one indigenous group from the next. So they codified the weavings. That way they could track when someone from the lowlands had inexplicably turned up in the highlands, and vice versa. They created the first truly systematic population control device."

I can feel my mouth twisting into a bitter little grimace when I look at him. "Oh no you didn't. You didn't just imply I 'came by my tattoo honestly,' did you?"

"What I'm saying," he says, "is that you aren't the first to grapple with what that tattoo means."

I turn my eyes back to the photos, but I'm not really looking anymore.

"You could have had it removed," he continues, but gently, the way I've heard Father Tom address the kids he's catechizing. "My understanding is that most people welcomed the new administration's removal program as a way of getting past the misguided policies the tattoo represented, and the bitter history it marked."

"But that's the point, Father," I say, taking care to close the album without damaging the brittle pages. "I know inks weren't the first to endure this sort of thing, nor likely the last. But years from now, when somebody points to my photo in a dusty album in a library like this one, I want him or her to be able to say 'I don't remember the face or the name, but here's the story of the tattoo.'"

"It won't be enough," he says sadly.

"No. But it's a start."

# Mari: Fairy tales

### 3.

I rent a car and brazen my way through narrow roads and hairpin turns to the hotel closest to what remains of the village. The charming, colonial-style edifice has sprung up because there is an interest in native weavings these days, and there are always a few fabric artists and crafters on busman holidays and mini apprenticeships. I hear a smattering of French, German and English, along with Spanish as I register and walk the halls. But Quiché – my mother's first language – only when I'm being served breakfast or when the rooms are made up. I don't understand a word of it, but it tickles some deep recess in my brain.

As does the landscape I see when I hike the five miles from the hotel to the village-that-no-longer-is.

My steps on the footpath are undergirded by *her* purring. After slumbering through the transit and first unsuccessful stabs at harvesting memory, *she* comes fully awake here.

*Is it because you're home?* I ask her.

*That,* she answers. *And because it reminds me of home.*

*What?*

I feel the rumbling I've come to know means *she* is laughing.

*You know, I've never heard any tales of jaguars laughing.* I don't shield her from my irritation

*No? Well, there are jaguars of sweet laughter, and harsh. Jaguars of the moon. And sun. And stars. Jaguars of kings and of sacrifices, too,* she says.

The footpath brings me to an old, tremendously wide but squat tree. It is different than I've imagined it all these years, but I'm certain it's the one.

The one that ran with the blood of the children killed in the village that day.

I stare at it for a long time, but I don't cross the threshold it marks.

\*\*\*

I have dinner at the hotel dining room, then move to the common area that replaces an official bar in establishments this small. All the guests seem to be in the room – friendly and noisy, and drinking. Which is good, because I don't want to have to think about my cowardice on the mountainside. Instead I chime in on conversations about ikat and jaspe and gender-specific weaves, pretending I know more than I do about the warp and weft of my heritage.

I also drink too much, and as the common room crowd starts to thin out, I face an unsteady walk down the corridor to my room. There is a moment after I open the door, when I'm struck by how empty it is. How I am in a strange place, on a strange errand and in a strange mood, without husband or son or friend to mark with me how the light from the full moon flows through the open windows. Or to feel with me the night air like a brush of a moth's wing against the cheek.

But then I remember I'm not alone. Ever.

*Ready?* she asks.

*Not exactly*, I answer. *But it's time anyway, isn't it?*

Though the path is narrow and broken up, I have no problem finding my way. In the silver of the night, the tree is a ghostly sentinel, but when I put my hand to its craggy bark, it is reassuringly solid.

*Which way?* I ask her.

*Around the village, then up to the top of the mountain. To your mother's family compound.*

The central plaza, the church and other village structures don't conform exactly to the version my mind had created when my father first told me the story of my baptism. Still, it feels like memory when I walk through the empty streets.

I feel more than hear when something comes up behind me.

*Don't turn around*, she tells me just as I'm about to do so. *Not yet. Not until it's clear why you are here.*

I pick my way to a steeply inclined footpath. It's a half-mile of hard work on uneven ground. The hair that lays over my neck and midway down my back floats up on the current of whatever is following me.

Something flits at my face, darting away an instant before I flinch.

A cloud races to cover the moon and it is as if someone has turned out the light. The trail turns harder then, sharded with pieces of volcanic glass that cut through the thin-soled flats I'm wearing. *She* jumps, and then I sense her body, a twin, beside mine in the dark.

*Hurry,* she says.

I feel her bound away. The susurrus behind me grows louder when she does.

I have to drop to all fours to make my way in the dark. The scree on the path cuts my palms and my knees. I break through to a clearing just about when the moon decides to show its face again, then straighten up and brush away the grains of stone that have embedded themselves in my hands and legs. My dress, floaty and the color of rich cream – the nicest of the garments I've brought with me to Guatemala – is flecked with blood.

The little houses in the compound look desolate and beaten down by time. *She* leads me on a circuit of them. From each dark and open doorway I see eyeshine.

We stop at a house I don't need to be told was my mother's. The colors on the walls are weathered, but they were once the same shades I've painted my little house in Del's woods.

*Sit*, she tells me. *On the threshold.*

Then she opens her mouth and what comes out is language, but formed by sounds that have nothing human in them.

*Your storyteller is here*, she says, and I understand the translation is for my benefit.

228

# Mari: Fairy tales

As I sit, I see the compound bristle with shapes that flicker between ghostly and solid. All the hundreds of stories I know and have told during my lifetime flee at the sight. She turns her face to me as the panic I'm feeling reaches her.

Her eyes are not something I've looked into at any length. Just that once she jumped, at my request, and showed herself in a way her kind almost never does. Now, the amber eyes shine in the dark and I see bits of my life, moments flashing familiar, in their depths.

*You're not here to tell stories*, she says, *but to listen to them.*

She settles herself on her haunches beside me just as the first nahual comes to stand before me. It wears the shape of an ocelot, and the tale it tells belongs to my mother.

When the creature's last word stops ringing in the quiet night, it steps away and is replaced by another. My grandparents' animal twins, my aunts' and uncles' and cousins' all tell me their stories, and after them others with no blood connection to me. Coatimundis, muskrats, bats, goats, monkeys, turkeys, snakes – any and every kind of nahual – presents itself with the story of its human counterpart long fled to the afterlife.

Then I jerk backward, scrabbling to put space between me and the creature of pitted face and dappled hair that comes to the front. It doesn't have to throw one of its stone hands for my body to remember what it feels like to be caught in its fury.

*The kaibiles also have stories to tell*, my jaguar says.

The tale that comes out of the dwarf's mouth is harsh. The evil to which it is bound hurts. The words – sharp as obsidian – prove their edges on the kaibil and me both.

It is not the only kaibil whose story I hear this night, and as much as I'd like to set those tales aside, I cannot. Every story holds some small fragment of what is true, a trace of the spirit that gives us life.

Hours later I look up and the compound is empty. What was held here is gone. The first tendrils of rosy dawn break through the penumbra.

I turn to the jaguar. *Are we done?*

Her eyes scour the fringe of scrub around the compound. *There is one yet. It has had to travel, for its twin's blood was not spilled here. And yet here is where it has come, year after year, looking to tell its tale.*

It is almost fully morning before I sense its approach. Perhaps it is a little bigger than it was, but it is still a button buck. It picks its way on tiny hooves, straight to me.

And rubs the moist velvet of its face on mine.

# Acknowledgements

I'm convinced there is a special heaven for beta-readers, and for those who, without even knowing they are doing so, provide the encouragement, inspiration, friendship (and coffee) that keeps writers writing. Needless to say, they should not be held accountable for what their coffee and friendship wrought: Angela Arrington, Bo Balder, Raquel Barrios, Hugh Beyer, Michelle Francl-Donnay, Stephen Gerringer, April Grey, Blanca Herrera, Chuck Hinckley, Kay Holt, Lindy Kilby, Jhumpa Lahiri, Bart Leib, Hna. María Lorena, Anna McCarthy, Ellen O'Brien, Bryan Saunders, Morgan Vourvoulias-Saunders, Mons. Hugh Shields, Krys Sipple, Anna Vega, Alberto Vourvoulias and Bill Vourvoulias. You are all my homeland.

And thank you, too, to the Al Día news team: Gabriela Barrantes, David Cruz, Ana Gamboa, Alex Graziano, Hernán Guaracao, Luis López, Arturo Varela and Yesid Vargas, for working to tell our stories, week-in and week-out.

# Author Biography

**Sabrina Vourvoulias** is a Latina newspaper editor, blogger and writer.

An American citizen from birth, she grew up in Guatemala and first moved to the United States when she was 15. She studied writing and filmmaking at Sarah Lawrence College in Bronxville, N.Y.

In addition to numerous articles and editorial columns in several newspapers in Pennsylvania and New York state, her work has been published in *Dappled Things*, *Graham House Review*, La Bloga's *Floricanto*, Poets Responding to SB 1070, *Scheherezade's Bequest* at Cabinet des Fees, *We'Moon*, *Crossed Genres #24*, the anthologies *Fat Girl in a Strange Land* and *Crossed Genres Year Two*, and is slated to appear in upcoming issues of *Bull Spec* and *GUD* magazines.

Her blog Following the Lede (http://followingthelede.blogspot.com) was nominated for a 2011 Latinos in Social Media (LATISM) award. She lives in Pennsylvania with her husband and daughter. Follow her antics on Twitter @followthelede.

77127616R00130

Made in the USA
Middletown, DE
18 June 2018